Praise for
#1 *New York Times* and *USA TODAY* bestselling author

"Roberts' bestselling novels are some of the best
in the romance genre. They are thoughtfully plotted,
well-written stories featuring fascinating characters."
—*USA TODAY*

"With clear-eyed, concise vision and a sure pen,
Roberts nails her characters and settings with awesome precision,
drawing readers into a vividly rendered world of
family-centered war

"A superb author…Ms. F   riter
whose incredible
the ver

"Nora Roberts is among the best."
—*The Washington Post Book World*

"Roberts weaves a story like no one else,
and if possible, she just gets better."
—*Rocky Mountain News*

"[Nora] Roberts' style has a fresh, contemporary snap."
—*Kirkus Reviews*

"There's no mystery about why Roberts
is a bestselling author of romances and mainstream novels:
she delivers the goods with panache and wit."
—*Publishers Weekly*

Dear Reader,

Secrets are all very well and good…until you find someone you want to share them with. In these classic Nora Roberts stories, each of our heroines becomes vulnerable to exposure when love comes calling.

In "Risky Business" cynical Jonas Sharpe has come to Cozumel in search of his brother's killer. But things get complicated when he finds himself drawn to a beguiling beauty who just may be his strongest suspect. Liz Palmer likes the safe little world she's created for herself and isn't sure what to make of the handsome stranger who's barged into her life demanding answers—and stirring her heart!

In "Mind Over Matter" no-nonsense agent Aurora Fields's main priority is the protection of her client's interests—especially when that client is her mother. All her skills are tested when the very persistent, and aggravatingly attractive David Brady enters the scene, demanding the full story. But while she's busy looking out for her mother, it's Aurora herself who may be in danger…of falling for the dashing Mr. Brady.

At the end of the day, it's not our secrets that keep us company… but the warm embrace of the people we choose to share them with. Enjoy!

The Editors

Silhouette Books

NORA ROBERTS

Secrets
& Sunsets

Silhouette® Books

Published by Silhouette Books

America's Publisher of Contemporary Romance

SILHOUETTE BOOKS

SECRETS & SUNSETS

ISBN-13: 978-0-373-28591-4

Copyright © 2010 by Harlequin Books S.A.

The publisher acknowledges the copyright holder of the individual works as follows:

RISKY BUSINESS
Copyright © 1986 by Nora Roberts

MIND OVER MATTER
Copyright © 1987 by Nora Roberts

Visit Silhouette Books at www.eHarlequin.com

Printed in U.S.A.

CONTENTS

Risky Business

For Michael and Darlene,
good friends.

1

"Watch your step, please. Please, watch your step. Thank you." Liz took a ticket from a sunburned man with palm trees on his shirt, then waited patiently for a woman with two bulging straw baskets to dig out another one.

"I hope you haven't lost it, Mabel. I told you to let me hold it."

"I haven't lost it," the woman said testily before she pulled out the little piece of blue cardboard.

"Thank you. Please take your seats." It was several more minutes before everyone was settled and she could take her own. "Welcome aboard the *Fantasy,* ladies and gentlemen."

With her mind on a half dozen other things, Liz began her opening monologue. She gave an absentminded nod to the man on the dock who cast off the ropes before she started the engine. Her voice was pleasant and easy as she took another look at her watch. They were already fifteen minutes behind schedule. She gave one last scan of the beach, skimming by lounge chairs, over bodies already stretched and oiled slick, like offerings to the sun. She couldn't hold the tour any longer.

The boat swayed a bit as she backed it from the dock and took an eastern course. Though her thoughts were scattered, she made the turn from the coast expertly. She could have navigated the boat with her eyes closed. The air that ruffled around her face was soft and already warming, though the hour was early. Harmless and powder-puff white, clouds dotted the horizon. The water, churned by the engine, was as blue as the guidebooks promised. Even after ten years, Liz took none of it for granted—especially her livelihood. Part of that depended on an atmosphere that made muscles relax and problems disappear.

Behind her in the long, bullet-shaped craft were eighteen people seated on padded benches. They were already murmuring about the fish and formations they saw through the glass bottom. She doubted if any of them thought of the worries they'd left behind at home.

"We'll be passing Paraiso Reef North," Liz began in a low, flowing voice. "Diving depths range from thirty to fifty feet. Visibility is excellent, so you'll be able to see star and brain corals, sea fans and sponges, as well as schools of sergeant majors, groupers and parrot fish. The grouper isn't one of your prettier fish, but it's versatile. They're all born female and produce eggs before they change sex and become functioning males."

Liz set her course and kept the speed steady. She went on to describe the elegantly colored angelfish, the shy, silvery small-mouth grunts, and the intriguing and dangerous sea urchin. Her clients would find the information useful when she stopped for two hours of snorkeling at Palancar Reef.

She'd made the run before, too many times to count. It might have become routine, but it was never monotonous. She felt now, as she always did, the freedom of open water, blue sky and the hum of engine with her at the controls. The boat was hers, as were three others, and the little concrete block dive shop close to shore. She'd worked for all of it, sweating through months when the bills were steep and the cash flow slight. She'd made it. Ten years of struggle had been a small price to pay for having something of her own. Turning her back on her country, leaving behind the familiar, had been a small price to pay for peace of mind.

The tiny, rustic island of Cozumel in the Mexican Caribbean promoted peace of mind. It was her home now, the only one that mattered. She was accepted there, respected. No one on the island knew of the humiliation and pain she'd gone through before she'd fled to Mexico. Liz rarely thought of it, though she had a vivid reminder.

Faith. Just the thought of her daughter made her smile. Faith was small and bright and precious, and so far away. Just six weeks, Liz thought, and she'd be home from school for the summer.

Sending her to Houston to her grandparents had been for the best, Liz reminded herself whenever the ache of loneliness became acute. Faith's education was more important than a mother's needs. Liz had worked, gambled, struggled so that Faith could have everything she was entitled to, everything she would have had if her father…

Determined, Liz set her mind on other things. She'd promised herself a decade before that she would cut Faith's father from her mind, just as he had cut her from his life. It had been a mistake, one made in naïveté and passion, one that had changed the course of her life forever. But she'd won something precious from it: Faith.

"Below, you see the wreck of a forty-passenger Convair airliner lying upside down." She slowed the boat so that her passengers could examine the wreck and the divers out for early explorations. Bubbles rose from air tanks like small silver disks. "The wreck's no tragedy," she continued. "It was sunk for a scene in a movie and provides divers with easy entertainment."

Her job was to do the same for her passengers, she reminded herself. It was simple enough when she had a mate on board. Alone, she had to captain the boat, keep up the light, informative banter, deal with snorkel equipment, serve lunch and count heads. It just hadn't been possible to wait any longer for Jerry.

She muttered to herself a bit as she increased speed. It wasn't so much that she minded the extra work, but she felt her paying customers were entitled to the best she could offer. She should have known better than to depend on him. She could have easily arranged for someone else to come along. As it was, she had two men on the dive boat and two more in the shop. Because her second dive boat was due to launch at noon, no one could be spared to mate the glass bottom on a day trip. And Jerry had come through before, she reminded herself. With him on board, the women passengers were so charmed that Liz didn't think they even noticed the watery world the boat passed over.

Who could blame them? she thought with a half smile. If she hadn't been immune to men in general, Jerry might have had her falling over her own feet. Most women had a difficult time resisting dark, cocky looks, a cleft chin and smoky gray eyes. Add to that a lean, muscular build and a glib tongue, and no female was safe.

But that hadn't been why Liz had agreed to rent him a room, or give him a part-time job. She'd needed the extra income, as well as the extra help, and she was shrewd enough to recognize an operator when she saw one. Previous experience had taught her that it made good business sense to have an operator on your side. She told herself he'd better have a good excuse for leaving her without a crew, then forgot him.

The ride, the sun, the breeze relaxed her. Liz continued to speak of the sea life below, twining facts she'd learned while studying marine biology in college with facts she'd learned firsthand in the waters of the Mexican Caribbean. Occasionally one of her passengers would ask a question or call out in excitement over something that skimmed beneath them. She answered, commented and instructed while keeping the flow light. Because three of her passengers were Mexican, she repeated all her information in Spanish. Because there were several children on board, she made certain the facts were fun.

If things had been different, she would have been a teacher. Liz had long since pushed that early dream from her mind, telling herself she was more suited to the business world. Her business world. She glanced over where the clouds floated lazily over the horizon. The sun danced white and sharp on the surface of blue water. Below, coral rose like castles or waved like fans. Yes, she'd chosen her world and had no regrets.

When a woman screamed behind her, Liz let off the throttle. Before she could turn, the scream was joined by another. Her first thought was that perhaps they'd seen one of the sharks that occasionally visited the reefs. Set to calm and soothe, Liz let the boat drift in the current. A woman was weeping in her husband's arms, another held her child's face protectively against her shoulder. The rest were staring down through the clear glass. Liz took off her sunglasses as she walked down the two steps into the cabin.

"Please try to stay calm. I promise you, there's nothing down there that can hurt you in here."

A man with a Nikon around his neck and an orange sun visor over a balding dome gave her a steady look.

"Miss, you'd better radio the police."

Liz looked down through the clear glass, through the crystal blue water. Her heart rose to her throat. She saw now why Jerry had stood her up. He was lying on the white sandy bottom with an anchor chain wrapped around his chest.

★ ★ ★

The moment the plane finished its taxi, Jonas gathered his garment bag and waited impatiently for the door to be opened. When it did, there was a whoosh of hot air and the drone of engines. With a quick nod to the flight attendant he strode down the steep metal stairs. He didn't have the time or the inclination to appreciate the palm trees, the bursts of flowers or the dreamy blue sky. He walked purposefully, eyes straight ahead and narrowed against the sun. In his dark suit and trim tie he could have been a businessman, one who'd come to Cozumel to work, not to play. Whatever grief, whatever anger he felt were carefully masked by a calm, unapproachable expression.

The terminal was small and noisy. Americans on vacation stood in groups laughing or wandered in confusion. Though he knew no Spanish, Jonas passed quickly through customs then into a small, hot alcove where men waited at podiums to rent cars and Jeeps. Fifteen minutes after landing, Jonas was backing a compact out of a parking space and heading toward town with a map stuck in the sun visor. The heat baked right through the windshield.

Twenty-four hours before, Jonas had been sitting in his large, elegantly furnished, air-conditioned office. He'd just won a long, tough case that had taken all his skill and mountains of research. His client was a free man, acquitted of a felony charge that carried a minimum sentence of ten years. He'd accepted his fee, accepted the gratitude and avoided as much publicity as possible.

Jonas had been preparing to take his first vacation in eighteen months. He'd felt satisfied, vaguely tired and optimistic. Two weeks in Paris seemed like the perfect reward for so many months of ten-hour days. Paris, with its ageless sophistication and cool parks, its stunning museums and incomparable food was precisely what suited Jonas Sharpe.

When the call had come through from Mexico, it had taken him several moments to understand. When he'd answered that he did indeed have a brother Jeremiah, Jonas's predominant thought had been that Jerry had gotten himself into trouble again, and he was going to have to bail him out.

By the time he'd hung up the phone, Jonas couldn't think at all. Numb, he'd given his secretary instructions to cancel his Paris arrangements and to make new ones for a flight to Cozumel the next day. Then Jonas had picked up the phone to call his parents and tell them their son was dead.

He'd come to Mexico to identify the body and take his brother home to bury. With a fresh wave of grief, Jonas experienced a sense of inevitability. Jerry had always lived on the edge of disaster. This time he'd stepped over. Since childhood Jerry had courted trouble—charmingly. He'd once joked that Jonas had taken to law so he could find the most efficient way to get his brother out of jams. Perhaps in a sense it had been true.

Jerry had been a dreamer. Jonas was a realist. Jerry had been unapologetically lazy, Jonas a workaholic. They were—had been—two sides of a coin. As Jonas drew up to the police station in San Miguel it was with the knowledge that part of himself had been erased.

The scene at port should have been painted. There were small fishing boats pulled up on the grass. Huge gray ships sat complacently at dock while tourists in flowered shirts or skimpy shorts strolled along the sea wall. Water lapped and scented the air.

Jonas got out of the car and walked to the police station to begin to wade through the morass of paperwork that accompanied a violent death.

Captain Moralas was a brisk, no-nonsense man who had been born on the island and was passionately dedicated to protecting it. He was approaching forty and awaiting the birth of his fifth child. He was proud of his position, his education and his family, though the order often varied. Basically, he was a quiet man who enjoyed classical music and a movie on Saturday nights.

Because San Miguel was a port, and ships brought sailors on leave, tourists on holiday, Moralas was no stranger to trouble or the darker side of human nature. He did, however, pride himself on the low percentage of violent crime on his island. The murder of the American bothered him in the way a pesky fly bothered a man sitting contentedly on his porch swing. A cop didn't have to work in a big city to recognize a professional hit. There was no room for organized crime on Cozumel.

But he was also a family man. He understood love, and he understood grief, just as he understood certain men were compelled to conceal both. In the cool, flat air of the morgue, he waited beside Jonas. The American stood a head taller, rigid and pale.

"This is your brother, Mr. Sharpe?" Though he didn't have to ask.

Jonas looked down at the other side of the coin. "Yes."

In silence, he backed away to give Jonas the time he needed.

It didn't seem possible. Jonas knew he could have stood for hours staring down at his brother's face and it would never seem possible. Jerry had always looked for the easy way, the biggest deal, and he hadn't always been an admirable man. But he'd always been so full of life. Slowly, Jonas laid his hand on his brother's. There was no life there now, and nothing he could do; no amount of maneuvering or pulling of strings would bring it back. Just as slowly he removed his hand. It didn't seem possible, but it was.

Moralas nodded to the attendant. "I'm sorry."

Jonas shook his head. Pain was like a dull-edged knife

through the base of his skull. He coated it with ice. "Who killed my brother, Captain?"

"I don't know. We're investigating."

"You have leads?"

Moralas gestured and started down the corridor. "Your brother had been in Cozumel only three weeks, Mr. Sharpe. At the moment, we are interviewing everyone who had contact with him during that time." He opened a door and stepped out into the air, breathing deeply of the fresh air and the flowers. The man beside him didn't seem to notice the change. "I promise you, we will do everything possible to find your brother's killer."

The rage Jonas had controlled for so many hours bubbled toward the surface. "I don't know you." With a steady hand he drew out a cigarette, watching the captain with narrowed eyes as he lit it. "You didn't know Jerry."

"This is my island." Moralas's gaze remained locked with Jonas's. "If there's a murderer on it, I'll find him."

"A professional." Jonas blew out smoke that hung in the air with no breeze to brush it away. "We both know that, don't we?"

Moralas said nothing for a moment. He was still waiting to receive information on Jeremiah Sharpe. "Your brother was shot, Mr. Sharpe, so we're investigating to find out why, how and who. You could help me by giving me some information."

Jonas stared at the door a moment—the door that led down the stairs, down the corridor and to his brother's body. "I've got to walk," he murmured.

Moralas waited until they'd crossed the grass, then the road. For a moment, they walked near the sea wall in silence. "Why did your brother come to Cozumel?"

"I don't know." Jonas drew deeply on the cigarette until it burned into the filter. "Jerry liked palm trees."

"His business? His work?"

With a half laugh Jonas ground the smoldering filter underfoot. Sunlight danced in diamonds on the water. "Jerry liked to call himself a free-lancer. He was a drifter." And he'd brought complications to Jonas's life as often as he'd brought pleasure. Jonas stared hard at the water, remembering shared lives, diverse opinions. "For Jerry, it was always the next town and the next deal. The last I heard—two weeks ago—he was giving diving lessons to tourists."

"The Black Coral Dive Shop," Moralas confirmed. "Elizabeth Palmer hired him on a part-time basis."

"Palmer." Jonas's attention shifted away from the water. "That's the woman he was living with."

"Miss Palmer rented your brother a room," Moralas corrected, abruptly proper. "She was also among the group to discover your brother's body. She's given my department her complete cooperation."

Jonas's mouth thinned. How had Jerry described this Liz Palmer in their brief phone conversation weeks before? A sexy little number who made great tortillas. She sounded like another one of Jerry's tough ladies on the lookout for a good time and the main chance. "I'll need her address." At the captain's quiet look he only raised a brow. "I assume my brother's things are still there."

"They are. I have some of your brother's personal effects, those that he had on him, in my office. You're welcome to collect them and what remains at Miss Palmer's. We've already been through them."

Jonas felt the rage build again and smothered it. "When can I take my brother home?"

"I'll do my best to complete the paperwork today. I'll need you to make a statement. Of course, there are forms." He looked at Jonas's set profile and felt a new tug of pity. "Again, I'm sorry."

He only nodded. "Let's get it done."

Liz let herself into the house. While the door slammed behind her, she flicked switches, sending two ceiling fans whirling. The sound, for the moment, was company enough. The headache she'd lived with for over twenty-four hours was a dull, nagging thud just under her right temple. Going into the bathroom, she washed down two aspirin before turning on the shower.

She'd taken the glass bottom out again. Though it was off season, she'd had to turn a dozen people away. It wasn't every day a body was found off the coast, and the curious had come in force. Morbid, she thought, then stripped and stepped under the cold spray of the shower. How long would it take, she wondered, before she stopped seeing Jerry on the sand beneath the water?

True, she'd barely known him, but he'd been fun and interesting and good company. He'd slept in her daughter's bed and eaten in her kitchen. Closing her eyes, she let the water sluice over her, willing the headache away. She'd be better, she thought, when the police finished the investigation. It had been hard, very hard, when they'd come to her house and searched through Jerry's things. And the questions.

How much had she known about Jerry Sharpe? He'd been American, an operator, a womanizer. She'd been able to use all three to her benefit when he'd given diving lessons or acted as mate on one of her boats. She'd thought him harmless—sexy, attractive and basically lazy. He'd boasted of making it big, of wheeling a deal that would set him up in style. Liz had considered it so much hot air. As far as she was concerned, nothing set you up in style but years of hard work—or inherited wealth.

But Jerry's eyes had lit up when he'd talked of it, and his grin had been appealing. If she'd been a woman who allowed herself dreams, she would have believed him. But dreams were for the young and foolish. With a little tug of regret, she realized Jerry Sharpe had been both.

Now he was gone, and what he had left was still scattered in her daughter's room. She'd have to box it up, Liz decided as she turned off the taps. It was something, at least. She'd box up Jerry's things and ask that Captain Moralas what to do about them. Certainly his family would want whatever he'd left behind. Jerry had spoken of a brother, whom he'd affectionately referred to as "the stuffed shirt." Jerry Sharpe had been anything but stuffy.

As she walked to the bedroom, Liz wrapped her hair in the towel. She remembered the way Jerry had tried to talk his way between her sheets a few days after he'd moved in. Smooth talk, smooth hands. Though he'd had her backed into the doorway, kissing her before she'd evaded it, Liz had easily brushed him off. He'd taken her refusal good-naturedly, she recalled, and they'd remained on comfortable terms. Liz pulled on an over-sized shirt that skimmed her thighs.

The truth was, Jerry Sharpe had been a good-natured, comfortable man with big dreams. She wondered, not for the first time, if his dreams had had something to do with his death.

She couldn't go on thinking about it. The best thing to do was to pack what had belonged to Jerry back into his suitcase and take it to the police.

It made her feel gruesome. She discovered that after only five minutes. Privacy, for a time, had been all but her only possession. To invade someone else's made her uneasy. Liz folded a faded brown T-shirt that boasted the wearer had hiked the Grand Canyon and tried not to think at all. But she kept seeing him there, joking about sleeping with one of Faith's collection of dolls. He'd fixed the window that had stuck and had cooked paella to celebrate his first paycheck.

Without warning, Liz felt the first tears flow. He'd been so alive, so young, so full of that cocky sense of confidence. She'd hardly had time to consider him a friend, but he'd slept in her daughter's bed and left clothes in her closet.

She wished now she'd listened to him more, been friendlier, more approachable. He'd asked her to have drinks with him and she'd brushed him off because she'd had paperwork to do. It seemed petty now, cold. If she'd given him an hour of her life, she might have learned who he was, where he'd come from, why he'd died.

When the knock at the door sounded, she pressed her hands against her cheeks. Silly to cry, she told herself, when tears never solved anything. Jerry Sharpe was gone, and it had nothing to do with her.

She brushed away the tears as she walked to the door. The headache was easing. Liz decided it would be best if she called Moralas right away and arranged to have the clothes picked up. She was telling herself she really wasn't involved at all when she opened the door.

For a moment she could only stare. The T-shirt she hadn't been aware of still holding slipped from her fingers. She took one stumbling step back as she felt a rushing sound fill her head. Because her vision dimmed, she blinked to clear it. The man in the doorway stared back at her accusingly.

"Jer-Jerry," she managed and nearly screamed when he took a step forward.

"Elizabeth Palmer?"

She shook her head, numb and terrified. She had no superstitions. She believed in action and reaction on a purely practical level. When someone died, they couldn't come back. And yet she stood in her living room with the fans whirling and watched Jerry Sharpe step over her threshold. She heard him speak to her again.

"Are you Liz Palmer?"

"I saw you." She heard her own voice rise with nerves but couldn't take her eyes from his face. The cocky good looks, the cleft chin, the smoky eyes under thick dark brows. It was a face that appealed to a woman's need to risk, or to her dreams of risking. "Who are you?"

"Jonas Sharpe. Jerry was my brother. My twin brother."

When she discovered her knees were shaking, she sat down quickly. No, not Jerry, she told herself as her heartbeat leveled. The hair was just as dark, just as full, but it lacked Jerry's unkempt shagginess. The face was just as attractive, just as ruggedly hewn, but she'd never seen Jerry's eyes so hard, so cold. And this man wore a suit as though he'd been born in one. His stance was one of restrained passion and impatience. It took her a moment, only a moment, before anger struck.

"You did that on purpose." Because her palms were damp she rubbed them against her knees. "It was a hideous thing to do. You knew what I'd think when I opened the door."

"I needed a reaction."

She sat back and took a deep, steadying breath. "You're a bastard, Mr. Sharpe."

For the first time in hours, his mouth curved…only slightly. "May I sit down?"

She gestured to a chair. "What do you want?"

"I came to get Jerry's things. And to talk to you."

As he sat, Jonas took a long look around. His was not the polite, casual glance a stranger indulges himself in when he walks into someone else's home, but a sharp-eyed, intense study of what belonged to Liz Palmer. It was a small living area, hardly bigger than his office. While he preferred muted colors and clean lines, Liz chose bright, contrasting shades and odd knickknacks. Several Mayan masks hung on the walls, and rugs of different sizes and hues were scattered over the floor. The sunlight, fading now, came in slats through red window blinds. There was a big blue pottery vase on a woven mat on the table, but the butter-yellow flowers in it were losing their petals. The table itself didn't gleam with polish, but was covered with a thin layer of dust.

The shock that had had her stomach muscles jumping had eased. She said nothing as he looked around the room because she was looking at him. A mirror image of Jerry, she thought. And weren't mirror images something like negatives? She didn't think he'd be fun to have around. She had a frantic need to order him out, to pitch him out quickly and finally. Ridiculous, she told herself. He was just a man, and nothing to her. And he had lost his brother.

"I'm sorry, Mr. Sharpe. This is a very difficult time for you."

His gaze locked on hers so quickly that she tensed again. She'd barely been aware of his inch-by-inch study of her room, but she couldn't remain unmoved by his study of her.

She wasn't what he'd expected. Her face was all angles—wide cheekbones, a long narrow nose and a chin that came to a suggestion of a point. She wasn't beautiful, but stunning in an almost uncomfortable way. It might have been the eyes, a deep haunted brown, that rose a bit exotically at the outer edge. It might have been the mouth, full and vulnerable. The shirt overwhelmed her body with its yards of material, leaving only long, tanned legs bare. Her hands, resting on the arms of her chair, were small, narrow and ringless. Jonas had thought he knew his brother's taste as well as his own. Liz Palmer didn't suit Jerry's penchant for the loud and flamboyant, or his own for the discreet sophisticate.

Still, Jerry had lived with her. Jonas thought grimly that she was taking the murder of her lover very well. "And a difficult time for you."

His long study had left her shaken. It had gone beyond natural curiosity and made her feel like a specimen, filed and labeled for further research. She tried to remember that grief took different forms in different people. "Jerry was a nice man. It isn't easy to—"

"How did you meet him?"

Words of sympathy cut off, Liz straightened in her chair. She never extended friendliness where it wasn't likely to be accepted. If he wanted facts only, she'd give him facts. "He came by my shop a few weeks ago. He was interested in diving."

Jonas's brow lifted as in polite interest but his eyes remained cold. "In diving."

"I own a dive shop on the beach—rent equipment, boat rides, lessons, day trips. Jerry was looking for work. Since he knew what he was doing, I gave it to him. He crewed on the dive boat, gave some of the tourists lessons, that sort of thing."

Showing tourists how to use a regulator didn't fit with Jonas's last conversation with his brother. Jerry had talked about cooking up a big deal. Big money, big time. "He didn't buy in as your partner?"

Something came into her face—pride, disdain, amusement. Jonas couldn't be sure. "I don't take partners, Mr. Sharpe. Jerry worked for me, that's all."

"All?" The brow came up again. "He was living here."

She caught the meaning, had dealt with it from the police. Liz decided she'd answered all the questions she cared to and that she'd given Jonas Sharpe more than enough of her time. "Jerry's things are in here." Rising, she walked out of the room. Liz waited at the doorway to her daughter's room until Jonas joined her. "I was just beginning to pack his clothes. You'd probably prefer to do that yourself. Take as much time as you need."

When she started to turn away, Jonas took her arm. He wasn't looking at her, but into the room with the shelves of dolls, the pink walls and lacy curtains. And at his brother's clothes tossed negligently over the back of a painted white chair and onto a flowered spread. It hurt, Jonas discovered, all over again.

"Is this all?" It seemed so little.

"I haven't been through the drawers or the closet yet. The police have." Suddenly weary, she pulled the towel from her head. Dark blond hair, still damp, tumbled around her face and shoulders. Somehow her face seemed even more vulnerable. "I don't know anything about Jerry's personal life, his personal belongings. This is my daughter's room." She turned her head until their eyes met. "She's away at school. This is where Jerry slept." She left him alone.

Twenty minutes was all he needed. His brother had traveled light. Leaving the suitcase in the living room, Jonas walked through the house. It wasn't large. The next bedroom was dim in the early evening light, but he could see a splash of orange over a rattan bed and a desk cluttered with files and papers. It smelled lightly of spice and talcum powder. Turning away, he walked toward the back and found the kitchen. And Liz.

It was when he smelled the coffee that Jonas remembered he hadn't eaten since morning. Without turning around, Liz poured a second cup. She didn't need him to speak to know he was there. She doubted he was a man who ever had to announce his presence. "Cream?"

Jonas ran a hand through his hair. He felt as though he were walking through someone else's dream. "No, black."

When Liz turned to offer the cup, he saw the quick jolt. "I'm sorry," she murmured, taking up her own cup. "You look so much like him."

"Does that bother you?"

"It unnerves me."

He sipped the coffee, finding it cleared some of the mists of unreality. "You weren't in love with Jerry."

Liz sent him a look of mild surprise. She realized he'd thought she'd been his brother's lover, but she hadn't thought he'd have taken the next step. "I only knew him a few weeks." Then she laughed, remembering another time, another life. "No, I wasn't in love with him. We had a business relationship, but I liked him. He was cocky and well aware of his own charms. I had a lot of repeat female customers over the past couple of weeks. Jerry was quite an operator," she murmured, then looked up, horrified. "I'm sorry."

"No." Interested, Jonas stepped closer. She was a tall woman, so their eyes stayed level easily. She smelled of the talcum powder and wore no cosmetics. Not Jerry's type, he thought again. But there was something about the eyes. "That's what he was, only most people never caught on."

"I've known others." And her voice was flat. "Not so harmless, not so kind. Your brother was a nice man, Mr. Sharpe. And I hope whoever... I hope they're found."

She watched the gray eyes ice over. The little tremor in her stomach reminded her that cold was often more dangerous than heat. "They will be. I may need to talk with you again."

It seemed a simple enough request, but she backed away from it. She didn't want to talk to him again, she didn't want to be involved in any way. "There's nothing else I can tell you."

"Jerry was living in your house, working for you."

"I don't know anything." Her voice rose as she spun away to

stare out the window. She was tired of the questions, tired of people pointing her out on the beach as the woman who'd found the body. She was tired of having her life turned upside down by the death of a man she had hardly known. And she was nervous, she admitted, because Jonas Sharpe struck her as a man who could keep her life turned upside down as long as it suited him. "I've talked to the police again and again. He worked for me. I saw him a few hours out of the day. I don't know where he went at night, who he saw, what he did. It wasn't my business as long as he paid for the room and showed up to work." When she looked back, her face was set. "I'm sorry for your brother, I'm sorry for you. But it's not my business."

He saw the nerves as her hands unclenched but interpreted them in his own way. "We disagree, Mrs. Palmer."

"Miss Palmer," she said deliberately, and watched his slow, acknowledging nod. "I can't help you."

"You don't know that until we talk."

"All right. I won't help you."

He inclined his head and reached for his wallet. "Did Jerry owe you anything on the room?"

She felt the insult like a slap. Her eyes, usually soft, usually sad, blazed. "He owed me nothing, and neither do you. If you've finished your coffee…"

Jonas set the cup on the table. "I've finished. For now." He gave her a final study. Not Jerry's type, he thought again, or his. But she had to know something. If he had to use her to find out, he would. "Good night."

Liz stayed where she was until the sound of the front door closing echoed back at her. Then she shut her eyes. None of her business, she reminded herself. But she could still see Jerry under her boat. And now, she could see Jonas Sharpe with grief hard in his eyes.

2

Liz considered working in the dive shop the next thing to taking a day off. Taking a day off, actually staying away from the shop and the boats, was a luxury she allowed herself rarely, and only when Faith was home on holiday. Today, she'd indulged herself by sending the boats out without her so that she could manage the shop alone. Be alone. By noon, all the serious divers had already rented their tanks so that business at the shop would be sporadic. It gave Liz a chance to spend a few hours checking equipment and listing inventory.

The shop was a basic cinder-block unit. Now and again, she toyed with the idea of having the outside painted, but could never justify the extra expense. There was a cubbyhole she wryly referred to as an office where she'd crammed an old gray steel desk and one swivel chair. The rest of the room was crowded with equipment that lined the floor, was stacked on shelves or hung from hooks. Her desk had a dent in it the size of a man's foot, but her equipment was top grade and flawless.

Masks, flippers, tanks, snorkels could be rented individually or in any number of combinations. Liz had learned that the wider the choice, the easier it was to move items out and draw the customer back. The equipment was the backbone of her business. Prominent next to the wide square opening that was only closed at night with a heavy wooden shutter was a list, in English and Spanish, of her equipment, her services and the price.

When she'd started eight years before, Liz had stocked enough tanks and gear to outfit twelve divers. It had taken every penny she'd saved—every penny Marcus had given a young, dewy-eyed girl pregnant with his child. The girl had become a woman quickly, and that woman now had a business that could accommodate fifty divers from the skin out, dozens of snorkelers, underwater photographers, tourists who wanted an easy day on the water or gung-ho deep-sea fishermen.

The first boat she'd gambled on, a dive boat, had been christened *Faith,* for her daughter. She'd made a vow when she'd been eighteen, alone and frightened, that the child she carried would have the best. Ten years later, Liz could look around her shop and know she'd kept her promise.

More, the island she'd fled to for escape had become home. She was settled there, respected, depended on. She no longer looked over the expanses of white sand, blue water, longing for Houston or a pretty house with a flowing green lawn. She no longer looked back at the education she'd barely begun, or what she might have been. She'd stopped pining for a man who didn't want her or the child they'd made. She'd never go back. But Faith could. Faith could learn how to speak French, wear silk dresses and discuss wine and music. One day Faith would go back and mingle unknowingly with her cousins on their own level.

That was her dream, Liz thought as she carefully filled tanks. To see her daughter accepted as easily as she herself had been rejected. Not for revenge, Liz mused, but for justice.

"Howdy there, missy."

Crouched near the back wall, Liz turned and squinted against the sun. She saw a portly figure stuffed into a black-and-red wet suit, topped by a chubby face with a fat cigar stuck in the mouth.

"Mr. Ambuckle. I didn't know you were still on the island."

"Scooted over to Cancun for a few days. Diving's better here."

With a smile, she rose to go to her side of the opening. Ambuckle was a steady client who came to Cozumel two or three times a year and always rented plenty of tanks. "I could've told you that. See any of the ruins?"

"Wife dragged me to Tulum." He shrugged and grinned at her with popping blue eyes. "Rather be thirty feet down than climbing over rocks all day. Did get some snorkeling in. But a man doesn't fly all the way from Dallas just to paddle around. Thought I'd do some night diving."

Her smile came easily, adding something soft and approachable to eyes that were usually wary. "Fix you right up. How much longer are you staying?" she asked as she checked an underwater flash.

"Two more weeks. Man's got to get away from his desk."

"Absolutely." Liz had often been grateful so many people from Texas, Louisiana and Florida felt the need to get away.

"Heard you had some excitement while we were on the other side."

Liz supposed she should be used to the comment by now, but a shiver ran up her spine. The smile faded, leaving her face remote. "You mean the American who was murdered?"

"Put the wife in a spin. Almost couldn't talk her into coming back over. Did you know him?"

No, she thought, not as well as she should have. To keep her hands busy, she reached for a rental form and began to fill it out. "As a matter of fact, he worked here a little while."

"You don't say?" Ambuckle's small blue eyes sparkled a bit. But Liz supposed she should be used to that, as well.

"You might remember him. He crewed the dive boat the last time you and your wife went out."

"No kidding?" Ambuckle's brow creased as he chewed on the cigar. "Not that good-looking young man—Johnny, Jerry," he remembered. "Had the wife in stitches."

"Yes, that was him."

"Shame," Ambuckle murmured, but looked rather pleased to have known the victim. "Had a lot of zip."

"Yes, I thought so, too." Liz lugged the tanks through the door and set them on the stoop. "That should take care of it, Mr. Ambuckle."

"Add a camera on, missy. Want to get me a picture of one of those squids. Ugly things."

Amazed, Liz plucked one from the shelf and added it to the list on a printed form. She checked her watch, noted down the time and turned the form for Ambuckle's signature. After signing, he handed her bills for the deposit. She appreciated the fact that Ambuckle always paid in cash, American. "Thanks. Glad to see you back, Mr. Ambuckle."

"Can't keep me away, missy." With a whoosh and a grunt, he hefted the tanks on his shoulders. Liz watched him cross to the walkway before she filed the receipt. Unlocking her cash box, she stored the money.

"Business is good."

She jolted at the voice and looking up again stared at Jonas Sharpe.

She'd never again mistake him for Jerry, though his eyes were almost hidden this time with tinted glasses, and he wore shorts and an open shirt in lieu of a suit. There was a long gold chain around his neck with a small coin dangling. She recalled Jerry had worn one. But something in the way Jonas stood, something in the set of his mouth made him look taller and tougher than the man she'd known.

Because she didn't believe in polite fencing, Liz finished relocking the cash box and began to check the straps and fasteners on a shelf of masks. No faulty equipment went out of her shop. "I didn't expect to see you again."

"You should have." Jonas watched her move down the shelf. She seemed stronger, less vulnerable than she had when he'd seen her a week ago. Her eyes were cool, her voice remote. It made it easier to do what he'd come for. "You have quite a reputation on the island."

She paused long enough to look over her shoulder. "Really?"

"I checked," he said easily. "You've lived here for ten years. Built this place from the first brick and have one of the most successful businesses on the island."

She examined the mask in her hand meticulously. "Are you interested in renting some equipment, Mr. Sharpe? I can recommend the snorkeling right off this reef."

"Maybe. But I think I'd prefer to scuba."

"Fine. I can give you whatever you need." She set the mask down and chose another. "It isn't necessary to be certified to dive in Mexico; however, I'd recommend a few basic lessons before you go down. We offer two different courses—individual or group."

He smiled at her for the first time, a slow, appealing curving of lips that softened the toughness around his mouth. "I might take you up on that. Meantime, when do you close?"

"When I'm ready to." The smile made a difference, she realized, and she couldn't let it. In defense, she shifted her weight on one hip and sent him a look of mild insolence. "This is Cozumel, Mr. Sharpe. We don't run nine to five here. Unless you want to rent some equipment or sign up for a tour, you'll have to excuse me."

He reached in to close his hand over hers. "I didn't come back to tour. Have dinner with me tonight. We can talk."

She didn't attempt to free her hand but stared at him. Running a business had taught her to be scrupulously polite in any circumstances. "No, thank you."

"Drinks, then."

"No."

"Miss Palmer…" Normally, Jonas was known for his deadly, interminable patience. It was a weapon, he'd learned, in the courtroom and out of it. With Liz, he found it difficult to wield it. "I don't have a great deal to go on at this point, and the police haven't made any progress at all. I need your help."

This time Liz did pull away. She wouldn't be sucked in, that she promised herself, not by quiet words or intense eyes. She had her life to lead, a business to run, and most important, a daughter coming home in a matter of weeks. "I won't get involved. I'm sorry, even if I wanted to, there'd be nothing I could do to help."

"Then it won't hurt to talk to me."

"Mr. Sharpe." Liz wasn't known for her patience. "I have very little free time. Running this business isn't a whim or a lark, but a great deal of work. If I have a couple of hours to myself in the evening, I'm not going to spend them being grilled by you. Now—"

She started to brush him off again when a young boy came running up to the window. He was dressed in a bathing suit and slick with suntan lotion. With a twenty-dollar bill crumpled in his hand, he babbled a request for snorkeling equipment for himself and his brother. He spoke in quick, excited Spanish as Liz checked out the equipment, asking if she thought they'd see a shark.

She answered him in all seriousness as she exchanged money for equipment. "Sharks don't live in the reef, but they do visit now and again." She saw the light of adventure in his eyes. "You'll see parrot fish." She held her hands apart to show him how big. "And if you take some bread crumbs or crackers, the sergeant majors will follow you, lots of them, close enough to touch."

"Will they bite?"

She grinned. "Only the bread crumbs. Adios."

He dashed away, kicking up sand.

"You speak Spanish like a native," Jonas observed, and thought it might come in handy. He'd also noticed the pleasure that had come into her eyes when she'd talked with the boy. There'd been nothing remote then, nothing sad or haunted. Strange, he mused, he'd never noticed just how much a barometer of feeling the eyes could be.

"I live here," she said simply. "Now, Mr. Sharpe—"

"How many boats?"

"What?"

"How many do you have?"

She sucked in a deep breath and decided she could humor him for another five minutes. "I have four. The glass bottom, two dive boats and one for deep-sea fishing."

"Deep-sea fishing." That was the one, Jonas decided. A fishing boat would be private and isolated. "I haven't done any in five or six years. Tomorrow." He reached in his wallet. "How much?"

"It's fifty dollars a person a day, but I don't take the boat out for one man, Mr. Sharpe." She gave him an easy smile. "It doesn't make good business sense."

"What's your minimum?"

"Three. And I'm afraid I don't have anyone else lined up. So—"

He set four fifty-dollar bills on the counter. "The extra fifty's to make sure you're driving the boat." Liz looked down at the money. An extra two hundred would help buy the aqua bikes she'd been thinking about. Several of the other dive shops already had them and she kept a constant eye on competition. Aqua biking and wind surfing were becoming increasingly popular, and if she wanted to keep up… She looked back at Jonas Sharpe's dark, determined eyes and decided it wasn't worth it.

"My schedule for tomorrow's already set. I'm afraid I—"

"It doesn't make good business sense to turn down a profit, Miss Palmer." When she only moved her shoulders, he smiled again, but this time it wasn't so pleasant. "I'd hate to mention at the hotel that I couldn't get satisfaction at The Black Coral. It's funny how word of mouth can help or damage a small business."

Liz picked up the money, one bill at a time. "What business are you in, Mr. Sharpe?"

"Law."

She made a sound that might have been a laugh as she pulled out a form. "I should've guessed. I knew someone studying law once." She thought of Marcus with his glib, calculating tongue. "He always got what he wanted, too. Sign here. We leave at eight," she said briskly. "The price includes a lunch on board. If you want beer or liquor, you bring your own. The sun's pretty intense on the water, so you'd better buy some sunscreen." She glanced beyond him. "One of my dive boats is coming back. You'll have to excuse me."

"Miss Palmer…" He wasn't sure what he wanted to say to her, or why he was uncomfortable having completed a successful maneuver. In the end, he pocketed his receipt. "If you change your mind about dinner—"

"I won't."

"I'm at the El Presidente."

"An excellent choice." She walked through the doorway and onto the dock to wait for her crew and clients.

By seven-fifteen, the sun was up and already burning off a low ground mist. What clouds there were, were thin and shaggy and good-natured.

"Damn!" Liz kicked the starter on her motorbike and turned in a little U toward the street. She'd been hoping for rain.

He was going to try to get her involved. Even now, Liz could imagine those dark, patient gray eyes staring into hers, hear the quietly insistent voice. Jonas Sharpe was the kind of man who took no for an answer but was dogged enough to wait however long it took for the yes. Under other circumstances, she'd have admired that. Being stubborn had helped her start and succeed in a business when so many people had shaken their heads and warned her against it. But she couldn't afford to admire Jonas Sharpe. Budgeting her feelings was every bit as important as budgeting her accounts.

She couldn't help him, Liz thought again, as the soft air began to play around her face. Everything she'd known about Jerry had been said at least twice. Of course she was sorry, and had grieved a bit herself for a man she'd hardly known, but murder was a police matter. Jonas Sharpe was out of his element.

She was in hers, Liz thought as her muscles began to relax with the ride. The street was bumpy, patched in a good many places. She knew when to weave and sway. There were houses along the street with deep green grass and trailing vines. Already clothes were waving out on lines. She could hear an early newscast buzzing through someone's open window and the sound of children finishing chores or breakfast before school. She turned a corner and kept her speed steady.

There were a few shops here, closed up tight. At the door

of a market, Señor Pessado fumbled with his keys. Liz tooted her horn and exchanged waves. A cab passed her, speeding down the road to the airport to wait for the early arrivals. In a matter of moments, Liz caught the first scent of the sea. It was always fresh. As she took the last turn, she glanced idly in her rearview mirror. Odd, she thought—hadn't she seen that little blue car yesterday? But when she swung into the hotel's parking lot, it chugged past.

Liz's arrangement with the hotel had been of mutual benefit. Her shop bordered the hotel's beach and encouraged business on both sides. Still, whenever she went inside, as she did today to collect the lunch for the fishing trip, she always remembered the two years she'd spent scrubbing floors and making beds.

"*Buenos días,* Margarita."

The young woman with a bucket and mop started to smile. "*Buenos días, Liz. ¿Cómo está?*"

"*Bien.* How's Ricardo?"

"Growing out of his pants." Margarita pushed the button of the service elevator as they spoke of her son. "Faith comes home soon. He'll be glad."

"So will I." They parted, but Liz remembered the months they'd worked together, changing linen, hauling towels, washing floors. Margarita had been a friend, like so many others she'd met on the island who'd shown kindness to a young woman who'd carried a child but had no wedding ring.

She could have lied. Even at eighteen Liz had been aware she could have bought a ten-dollar gold band and had an easy story of divorce or widowhood. She'd been too stubborn. The baby that had been growing inside her belonged to her. Only to her. She'd feel no shame and tell no lies.

By seven forty-five, she was crossing the beach to her shop, lugging a large cooler packed with two lunches and a smaller one filled with bait. She could already see a few tubes bobbing on the water's surface. The water would be warm and clear and uncrowded. She'd like to have had an hour for snorkeling herself.

"Liz!" The trim, small-statured man who walked toward her was shaking his head. There was a faint, pencil-thin mustache above his lip and a smile in his dark eyes. "You're too skinny to carry that thing."

She caught her breath and studied him up and down. He wore nothing but a skimpy pair of snug trunks. She knew he enjoyed the frank or surreptitious stares of women on the beach. "So're you, Luis. But don't let me stop you."

"So you take the fishing boat today?" He hefted the larger cooler and walked with her toward the shop. "I changed the schedule for you. Thirteen signed up for the glass bottom for the morning. We got both dive boats going out, so I told my cousin Miguel to help fill in today. Okay?"

"Terrific." Luis was young, fickle with women and fond of his tequila, but he could be counted on in a pinch. "I guess I'm going to have to hire someone on, at least part-time."

Luis looked at her, then at the ground. He'd worked closest with Jerry. "Miguel, he's not dependable. Here one day, gone the next. I got a nephew, a good boy. But he can't work until he's out of school."

"I'll keep that in mind," Liz said absently. "Let's just put this right on the boat. I want to check the gear."

On board, Liz went through a routine check on the tackle and line. As she looked over the big reels and massive rods, she wondered, with a little smirk, if the lawyer had ever done any big-game fishing. Probably wouldn't know a tuna if it jumped up and bit his toe, she decided.

The decks were clean, the equipment organized, as she insisted. Luis had been with her the longest, but anyone who worked for Liz understood the hard and fast rule about giving the clients the efficiency they paid for.

The boat was small by serious sport fishing standards, but her clients rarely went away dissatisfied. She knew the waters all along the Yucatan Peninsula and the habits of the game that teemed below the surface. Her boat might not have sonar and fish finders and complicated equipment, but she determined to give Jonas Sharpe the ride of his life. She'd keep him so busy, strapped in a fighting chair, that he wouldn't have time to bother her. By the time they docked again, his arms would ache, his back would hurt and the only thing he'd be interested in would be a hot bath and bed. And if he wasn't a complete fool, she'd see to it that he had a trophy to take back to wherever he'd come from.

Just where was that? she wondered as she checked the gauges on the bridge. She'd never thought to ask Jerry. It hadn't seemed important. Yet now she found herself wondering where Jonas came from, what kind of life he led there. Was he the type who frequented elegant restaurants with an equally elegant woman on his arm? Did he watch foreign films and play bridge? Or did he prefer noisy clubs and hot jazz? She hadn't been able to find his slot as easily as she did with most people she met, so she wondered, perhaps too much. Not my business, she reminded herself and turned to call to Luis.

"I'll take care of everything here. Go ahead and open the shop. The glass bottom should be ready to leave in half an hour."

But he wasn't listening. Standing on the deck, he stared back at the narrow dock. She saw him raise a shaky hand to cross himself. *"Madre de Dios."*

"Luis?" She came down the short flight of stairs to join him. "What—"

Then she saw Jonas, a straw hat covering his head, sunglasses shading his eyes. He hadn't bothered to shave, so that the light growth of beard gave him a lazy, vagrant look accented by a faded T-shirt and brief black trunks. He didn't, she realized, look like a man who'd play bridge. Knowing what was going through Luis's mind, Liz shook his arm and spoke quickly.

"It's his brother, Luis. I told you they were twins."

"Back from the dead," Luis whispered.

"Don't be ridiculous." She shook off the shudder his words brought her. "His name is Jonas and he's nothing like Jerry at all, really. You'll see when you talk to him. You're prompt, Mr. Sharpe," she called out, hoping to jolt Luis out of his shock. "Need help coming aboard?"

"I can manage." Hefting a small cooler, Jonas stepped lightly on deck. "The *Expatriate.*" He referred to the careful lettering on the side of the boat. "Is that what you are?"

"Apparently." It was something she was neither proud nor ashamed of. "This is Luis—he works for me. You gave him a jolt just now."

"Sorry." Jonas glanced at the slim man hovering by Liz's side. There was sweat beading on his lip. "You knew my brother?"

"We worked together," Luis answered in his slow, precise English. "With the divers. Jerry, he liked best to take out the dive boat. I'll cast off." Giving Jonas a wide berth, Luis jumped onto the dock.

"I seem to affect everyone the same way," Jonas observed. "How about you?" He turned dark, direct eyes to her. Though he no longer made her think of Jerry, he unnerved her just the same. "Still want to keep me at arm's length?"

"We pride ourselves in being friendly to all our clients. You've hired the *Expatriate* for the day, Mr. Sharpe. Make yourself comfortable." She gestured toward a deck chair before climbing the steps to the bridge and calling out to Luis. "Tell

Miguel he gets paid only if he finishes out the day." With a final wave to Luis, she started the engine, then cruised sedately toward the open sea.

The wind was calm, barely stirring the water. Liz could see the dark patches that meant reefs and kept the speed easy. Once they were in deeper water, she'd open it up a bit. By midday the sun would be stunningly hot. She wanted Jonas strapped in his chair and fighting two hundred pounds of fish by then.

"You handle a wheel as smoothly as you do a customer."

A shadow of annoyance moved in her eyes, but she kept them straight ahead. "It's my business. You'd be more comfortable on the deck in a chair, Mr. Sharpe."

"Jonas. And I'm perfectly comfortable here." He gave her a casual study as he stood beside her. She wore a fielder's cap over her hair with white lettering promoting her shop. On her T-shirt, the same lettering was faded from the sun and frequent washings. He wondered, idly, what she wore under it. "How long have you had this boat?"

"Almost eight years. She's sound." Liz pushed the throttle forward. "The waters are warm, so you'll find tuna, marlin, swordfish. Once we're out you can start chumming."

"Chumming?"

She sent him a quick look. So she'd been right—he didn't know a line from a pole. "Bait the water," she began. "I'll keep the speed slow and you bait the water, attract the fish."

"Seems like taking unfair advantage. Isn't fishing supposed to be luck and skill?"

"For some people it's a matter of whether they'll eat or not." She turned the wheel a fraction, scanning the water for unwary snorkelers. "For others, it's a matter of another trophy for the wall."

"I'm not interested in trophies."

She shifted to face him. No, he wouldn't be, she decided, not in trophies or in anything else without a purpose. "What are you interested in?"

"At the moment, you." He put his hand over hers and let off the throttle. "I'm in no hurry."

"You paid to fish." She flexed her hand under his.

"I paid for your time," he corrected.

He was close enough that she could see his eyes beyond the tinted lenses. They were steady, always steady, as if he knew he could afford to wait. The hand still over hers wasn't smooth as she'd expected, but hard and worked. No, he wouldn't play bridge, she thought again. Tennis, perhaps, or hand ball, or something else that took sweat and effort. For the first time in years she felt a quick thrill race through her—a thrill she'd been certain she was immune to. The wind tossed the hair back from her face as she studied him.

"Then you wasted your money."

Her hand moved under his again. Strong, he thought, though her looks were fragile. Stubborn. He could judge that by the way the slightly pointed chin stayed up. But there was a look in her eyes that said I've been hurt, I won't be hurt again. That alone was intriguing, but added to it was a quietly simmering sexuality that left him wondering how it was his brother hadn't been her lover. Not, Jonas was sure, for lack of trying.

"If I've wasted my money, it won't be the first time. But somehow I don't think I have."

"There's nothing I can tell you." Her hand jerked and pushed the throttle up again.

"Maybe not. Or maybe there's something you know without realizing it. I've dealt in criminal law for over ten years. You'd be surprised how important small bits of information can be. Talk to me." His hand tightened briefly on hers. "Please."

She thought she'd hardened her heart, but she could feel herself weakening. Why was it she could haggle for hours over the price of scuba gear and could never refuse a softly spoken request? He was going to cause her nothing but trouble. Because she already knew it, she sighed.

"We'll talk." She cut the throttle so the boat would drift. "While you fish." She managed to smile a bit as she stepped away. "No chum."

With easy efficiency, Liz secured the butt of a rod into the socket attached to a chair. "For now, you sit and relax," she told him. "Sometimes a fish is hot enough to take the hook without bait. If you get one, you strap yourself in and work."

Jonas settled himself in the chair and tipped back his hat. "And you?"

"I go back to the wheel and keep the speed steady so we tire him out without losing him." She gathered her hair in one hand and tossed it back. "There're better spots than this, but I'm not wasting my gas when you don't care whether you catch a fish or not."

His lips twitched as he leaned back in the chair. "Sensible. I thought you would be."

"Have to be."

"Why did you come to Cozumel?" Jonas ignored the rod in front of him and took out a cigarette.

"You've been here for a few days," she countered. "You shouldn't have to ask."

"Parts of your own country are beautiful. If you've been here ten years, you'd have been a child when you left the States."

"No, I wasn't a child." Something in the way she said it had him watching her again, looking for the secret she held just beyond her eyes. "I came because it seemed like the right thing to do. It was the right thing. When I was a girl, my parents would come here almost every year. They love to dive."

"You moved here with your parents?"

"No, I came alone." This time her voice was flat. "You didn't pay two hundred dollars to talk about me, Mr. Sharpe."

"It helps to have some background. You said you had a daughter. Where is she?"

"She goes to school in Houston—that's where my parents live."

Toss a child, and the responsibility, onto grandparents and live on a tropical island. It might leave a bad taste in his mouth, but it wasn't something that would surprise him. Jonas took a deep drag as he studied Liz's profile. It just didn't fit. "You miss her."

"Horribly," Liz murmured. "She'll be home in a few weeks, and we'll spend the summer together. September always comes too soon." Her gaze drifted off as she spoke, almost to herself. "It's for the best. My parents take wonderful care of her and she's getting an excellent education—taking piano lessons and ballet. They sent me pictures from a recital, and…" Her eyes filled with tears so quickly that she hadn't any warning. She shifted into the wind and fought them back, but he'd seen them. He sat smoking silently to give her time to recover.

"Ever get back to the States?"

"No." Liz swallowed and called herself a fool. It had been the pictures, she told herself, the pictures that had come in yesterday's mail of her little girl wearing a pink dress.

"Hiding from something?"

She whirled back, tears replaced with fury. Her body was arched like a bow ready to launch. Jonas held up a hand.

"Sorry. I have a habit of poking into secrets."

She forced herself to relax, to strap back passion as she'd taught herself so long ago. "It's a good way to lose your fingers, Mr. Sharpe."

He chuckled. "That's a possibility. I've always considered it worth the risk. They call you Liz, don't they?"

Her brow lifted under the fringe that blew around her brow. "My friends do."

"It suits you, except when you try to be aloof. Then it should be Elizabeth."

She sent him a smoldering look, certain he was trying to annoy her. "No one calls me Elizabeth."

He merely grinned at her. "Why weren't you sleeping with Jerry?"

"I beg your pardon?"

"Yes, definitely Elizabeth. You're a beautiful woman in an odd sort of way." He tossed out the compliment as casually as he tossed the cigarette into the water. "Jerry had a...fondness for beautiful women. I can't figure out why you weren't lovers."

For a moment, only a moment, it occurred to her that no one had called her beautiful in a very long time. She'd needed words like that once. Then she leaned back on the rail, planted her hands and aimed a killing look. She didn't need them now.

"I didn't choose to sleep with him. It might be difficult for you to accept, as you share the same face, but I didn't find Jerry irresistible."

"No?" As relaxed as she was tensed, Jonas reached into the cooler, offering her a beer. When she shook her head, he popped the top on one for himself. "What did you find him?"

"He was a drifter, and he happened to drift into my life. I gave him a job because he had a quick mind and a strong back. The truth was, I never expected him to last over a month. Men like him don't."

Though he hadn't moved a muscle, Jonas had come to attention. "Men like him?"

"Men who look for the quickest way to easy street. He

worked because he liked to eat, but he was always looking for the big strike—one he wouldn't have to sweat for."

"So you did know him," Jonas murmured. "What was he looking for here?"

"I tell you I don't know! For all I know he was looking for a good time and a little sun." Frustration poured out of her as she tossed a hand in the air. "I let him have a room because he seemed harmless and I could use the money. I wasn't intimate with him on any level. The closest he came to talking about what he was up to was bragging about diving for big bucks."

"Diving? Where?"

Fighting for control, she dragged a hand through her hair. "I wish you'd leave me alone."

"You're a realistic woman, aren't you, Elizabeth?"

Her chin was set when she looked back at him. "Yes."

"Then you know I won't. Where was he going to dive?"

"I don't know. I barely listened to him when he got started on how rich he was going to be."

"What did he say?" This time Jonas's voice was quiet, persuading. "Just try to think back and remember what he told you."

"He said something about making a fortune diving, and I joked about sunken treasure. And he said…" She strained to remember the conversation. It had been late in the evening, and she'd been busy, preoccupied. "I was working at home," Liz remembered. "I always seem to handle the books better at night. He'd been out, partying I thought, because he was a little unsteady when he came in. He pulled me out of the chair. I remember I started to swear at him but he looked so damn happy, I let it go. Really, I hardly listened because I was picking up all the papers he'd scattered, but he was saying something about the big time and buying champagne to celebrate. I told him he'd better stick to beer on his salary. That's when he talked about deals coming through and diving for big bucks. Then I made some comment about sunken treasure...."

"And what did he say?"

"Sometimes you make more putting stuff in than taking it out." With a line between her brows, she remembered how he'd laughed when she'd told him to go sleep it off. "He made a pass neither one of us took seriously, and then...I think he made a phone call. I went back to work."

"When was this?"

"A week, maybe one week after I took him on."

"That must have been when he called me." Jonas looked out to sea. And he hadn't paid much attention, either, he reminded himself. Jerry had talked about coming home in style. But then he had always been talking about coming home in style. And the call, as usual, had been collect.

"Did you ever see him with anyone? Talking, arguing?"

"I never saw him argue with anyone. He flirted with the women on the beach, made small talk with the clients and got along just fine with everyone he worked with. I assumed he spent most of his free time in San Miguel. I think he cruised a few bars with Luis and some of the others."

"What bars?"

"You'll have to ask them, though I'm sure the police already have." She took a deep breath. It was bringing it all back again, too close. "Mr. Sharpe, why don't you let the police handle this? You're running after shadows."

"He was my brother." And more, what he couldn't explain, his twin. Part of himself had been murdered. If he were ever to feel whole again, he had to know why. "Haven't you wondered why Jerry was murdered?"

"Of course." She looked down at her hands. They were empty and she felt helpless. "I thought he must've gotten into a fight, or maybe he bragged to the wrong person. He had a bad habit of tossing what money he had around."

"It wasn't robbery or a mugging, Elizabeth. It was professional. It was business."

Her heart began a slow, painful thud. "I don't understand."

"Jerry was murdered by a pro, and I'm going to find out why."

Because her throat was suddenly dry, she swallowed. "If you're right, then that's all the more reason to leave it to the police."

He drew out his cigarettes again, but stared ahead to where the sky met the water. "Police don't want revenge. I do." In his voice, she heard the calm patience and felt a shiver.

Staring, she shook her head. "Even if you found the person who did it, what could you do?"

He took a long pull from his beer. "As a lawyer, I suppose I'd be obliged to see they had their day in court. As a brother…" He trailed off and drank again. "We'll have to see."

"I don't think you're a very nice man, Mr. Sharpe."

"I'm not." He turned his head until his eyes locked on hers. "And I'm not harmless. Remember, if I make a pass, we'll both take it seriously."

She started to speak, then saw his line go taut. "You've got a fish, Mr. Sharpe," she said dryly. "You'd better strap in or he'll pull you overboard."

Turning on her heel, she went back to the bridge, leaving Jonas to fend for himself.

2

It was sundown when Liz parked her bike under the lean-to beside her house. She was still laughing. However much trouble Jonas had caused her, however much he had annoyed her in three brief meetings, she had his two hundred dollars. And he had a thirty-pound marlin—whether he wanted it or not. We deliver, she thought as she jingled her keys.

Oh, it had been worth it, just to see his face when he'd found himself on the other end of the wire from a big, bad-tempered fish. Liz believed he'd have let it go if she hadn't taken the time for one last smirk. Stubborn, she thought again. Yes, any other time she'd have admired it, and him.

Though she'd been wrong about his not being able to handle a rod, he'd looked so utterly perplexed with the fish lying at his feet on the deck that she'd nearly felt sorry for him. But his luck, or the lack of it, had helped her make an easy exit once they'd docked. With all the people crowding around to get a look at his catch and congratulate him, Jonas hadn't been able to detain her.

Now she was ready for an early evening, she thought. And a rainy one if the clouds moving in from the east delivered. Liz let herself into the house, propping the door open to bring in the breeze that already tasted of rain. After the fans were whirling, she turned on the radio automatically. Hurricane season might be a few months off, but the quick tropical storms were unpredictable. She'd been through enough of them not to take them lightly.

In the bedroom she prepared to strip for the shower that would wash the day's sweat and salt from her skin. Because it was twilight, she was already reaching for the light switch when a stray thought stopped her. Hadn't she left the blinds up that morning? Liz stared at them, tugged snugly over the window-sill. Odd, she was sure she'd left them up, and why wasn't the cord wrapped around its little hook? She was fanatical about that kind of detail, she supposed because ropes on a boat were always secured.

She hesitated, even after light spilled into the room. Then she shrugged. She must have been more distracted that morning than she'd realized. Jonas Sharpe, she decided, was taking up too much of her time, and too many of her thoughts. A man like him was bound to do so, even under different circum-stances. But she'd long since passed the point in her life where a man could dominate it. He only worried her because he was interfering in her time, and her time was a precious commodity. Now that he'd had his way, and his talk, there should be no more visits. She remembered, uncomfortably, the way he'd smiled at her. It would be best, she decided, if he went back to where he'd come from and she got on with her own routine.

To satisfy herself, Liz walked over to the first shade and secured the cord. From the other room, the radio announced an evening shower before music kicked in. Humming along with it, she decided to toss together a chicken salad before she logged the day's accounts.

As she straightened, the breath was knocked out of her by

an arm closing tightly around her neck. The dying sun caught a flash of silver. Before she could react, she felt the quick prick of a knife blade at her throat.

"Where is it?"

The voice that hissed in her ear was Spanish. In reflex, she brought her hands to the arm around her neck. As her nails dug in, she felt hard flesh and a thin metal band. She gasped for air, but stopped struggling when the knife poked threateningly at her throat.

"What do you want?" In terror her mind skimmed forward. She had less than fifty dollars cash and no jewelry of value except a single strand of pearls left by her grandmother. "My purse is in on the table. You can take it."

The vicious yank on her hair had her gasping in pain. "Where did he put it?"

"Who? I don't know what you want."

"Sharpe. Deal's off, lady. If you want to live, you tell me where he put the money."

"I don't know." The knife point pricked the vulnerable skin at her throat. She felt something warm trickle down her skin. Hysteria bubbled up behind it. "I never saw any money. You can look—there's nothing here."

"I've already looked." He tightened his hold until her vision grayed from lack of air. "Sharpe died fast. You won't be so lucky. Tell me where it is and nothing happens."

He was going to kill her. The thought ran in her head. She was going to die for something she knew nothing about. Money…he wanted money and she only had fifty dollars. Faith. As she felt herself on the verge of unconsciousness, she thought of her daughter. Who would take care of her? Liz bit down on her lip until the pain cleared her mind. She couldn't die.

"Please…" She let herself go limp in his arms. "I can't tell you anything. I can't breathe."

His hold loosened just slightly. Liz slumped against him and when he shifted, she brought her elbow back with all her strength. She didn't bother to turn around but ran blindly. A rug slid under her feet, but she stumbled ahead, too terrified to look back. She was already calling for help when she hit the front door.

Her closest neighbor was a hundred yards away. She vaulted the little fence that separated the yards and sprinted toward the house. She stumbled up the steps, sobbing. Even as the door opened, she heard the sound of a car squealing tires on the rough gravel road behind her.

"He tried to kill me," she managed, then fainted.

"There is no further information I can give you, Mr. Sharpe." Moralas sat in his neat office facing the waterfront. The file on his desk wasn't as thick as he would have liked. Nothing in his investigation had turned up a reason for Jerry Sharpe's murder. The man who sat across from him stared straight ahead. Moralas had a photo of the victim in the file, and a mirror image a few feet away. "I wonder, Mr. Sharpe, if your brother's death was a result of something that happened before his coming to Cozumel."

"Jerry wasn't running when he came here."

Moralas tidied his papers. "Still, we have asked for the cooperation of the New Orleans authorities. That was your brother's last known address."

"He never had an address," Jonas murmured. Or a conventional job, a steady woman. Jerry had been a comet, always refusing to burn itself out. "I've told you what Miss Palmer said. Jerry was cooking up a deal, and he was cooking it up in Cozumel."

"Yes, having to do with diving." Always patient, Moralas drew out a thin cigar. "Though we've already spoken with Miss Palmer, I appreciate your bringing me the information."

"But you don't know what the hell to do with it."

Moralas flicked on his lighter, smiling at Jonas over the flame. "You're blunt. I'll be blunt as well. If there was a trail to follow to your brother's murder, it's cold. Every day it grows colder. There were no fingerprints, no murder weapon, no witnesses." He picked up the file, gesturing with it. "That doesn't mean I intend to toss this in a drawer and forget about it. If there is a murderer on my island, I intend to find him. At the moment, I believe the murderer is miles away, perhaps in your own country. Procedure now is to backtrack on your brother's activities until we find something. To be frank, Mr. Sharpe, you're not doing yourself or me any good by being here."

"I'm not leaving."

"That is, of course, your privilege—unless you interfere with police procedure." At the sound of the buzzer on his desk, Moralas tipped his ash and picked up the phone.

"Moralas." There was a pause. Jonas saw the captain's thick, dark brows draw together. "Yes, put her on. Miss Palmer, this is Captain Moralas."

Jonas stopped in the act of lighting a cigarette and waited. Liz Palmer was the key, he thought again. He had only to find what lock she fit.

"When? Are you injured? No, please stay where you are, I'll come to you." Moralas was rising as he hung up the phone. "Miss Palmer has been attacked."

Jonas was at the door first. "I'm coming with you."

His muscles ached with tension as the police car raced out of town toward the shore. He asked no questions. In his mind, Jonas could see Liz as she'd been on the bridge hours before—

tanned, slim, a bit defiant. He remembered the self-satisfied smirk she'd given him when he'd found himself in a tug-of-war with a thirty-pound fish. And how neatly she'd skipped out on him the moment they'd docked.

She'd been attacked. Why? Was it because she knew more than she'd been willing to tell him? He wondered if she were a liar, an opportunist or a coward. Then he wondered how badly she'd been hurt.

As they pulled down the narrow drive, Jonas glanced toward Liz's house. The door was open, the shades drawn. She lived there alone, he thought, vulnerable and unprotected. Then he turned his attention to the little stucco building next door. A woman in a cotton dress and apron came onto the porch. She carried a baseball bat.

"You are the police." She nodded, satisfied, when Moralas showed his identification. "I am Señora Alderez. She's inside. I thank the Virgin we were home when she came to us."

"Thank you."

Jonas stepped inside with Moralas and saw her. She was sitting on a patched sofa, huddled forward with a glass of wine in both hands. Jonas saw the liquid shiver back and forth as her hands trembled. She looked up slowly when they came in, her gaze passing over Moralas to lock on Jonas. She stared, with no expression in those deep, dark eyes. Just as slowly, she looked back at her glass.

"Miss Palmer." With his voice very gentle, Moralas sat down beside her. "Can you tell me what happened?"

She took the smallest of drinks, pressed her lips together briefly, then began as though she were reciting. "I came home at sunset. I didn't close the front door or lock it. I went straight into the bedroom. The shades were down, and I thought I'd left them up that morning. The cord wasn't secured, so I went over and fixed it. That's when he grabbed me—from behind. He had his arm around my neck and a knife. He cut me a little." In reflex, she reached up to touch the inch-long scratch her neighbor had already cleaned and fussed over. "I didn't fight because he had the knife at my throat and I thought he would kill me. He was going to kill me." She brought her head up to look directly into Moralas's eyes. "I could hear it in his voice."

"What did he say to you, Miss Palmer?"

"He said, 'Where is it?' I didn't know what he wanted. I told him he could take my purse. He was choking me and he said, 'Where did he put it?' He said Sharpe." This time she looked at Jonas. When she lifted her head, he saw that bruises were already forming on her throat. "He said the deal was off and he wanted the money. If I didn't tell him where it was he'd kill me, and I wouldn't die quickly, the way Jerry had. He didn't believe me when I said I didn't know anything." She spoke directly to Jonas. As she stared at him he felt the guilt rise.

Patient, Moralas touched her arm to bring her attention back to him. "He let you go?"

"No, he was going to kill me." She said it dully, without fear, without passion. "I knew he would whether I told him anything or not, and my daughter—she needs me. I slumped as if I'd fainted, then I hit him. I think I hit him in the throat with my elbow. And I ran."

"Can you identify the man?"

"I never saw him. I never looked."

"His voice."

"He spoke Spanish. I think he was short because his voice was right in my ear. I don't know anything else. I don't know anything about money or Jerry or anything else." She looked back into her glass, abruptly terrified she would cry. "I want to go home."

"As soon as my men make certain it's safe. You'll have police protection, Miss Palmer. Rest here. I'll come back for you and take you home."

She didn't know if it had been minutes or hours since she'd fled through the front door. When Moralas took her back, it was dark with the moon just rising. An officer would remain outside in her driveway and all her doors and windows had been checked. Without a word, she went through the house into the kitchen.

"She was lucky." Moralas gave the living room another quick check. "Whoever attacked her was careless enough to be caught off guard."

"Did the neighbors see anything?" Jonas righted a table that had been overturned in flight. There was a conch shell on the floor that had cracked.

"A few people noticed a blue compact outside the house late this afternoon. Señora Alderez saw it drive off when she opened the door to Miss Palmer, but she couldn't identify the make or the plates. We will, of course, keep Miss Palmer under surveillance while we try to track it down."

"It doesn't appear my brother's killer's left the island."

Moralas met Jonas's gaze blandly. "Apparently whatever deal your brother was working on cost him his life. I don't intend for it to cost Miss Palmer hers. I'll drive you back to town."

"No. I'm staying." Jonas examined the pale pink shell with the crack spreading down its length. He thought of the mark on Liz's throat. "My brother involved her." Carefully, he set the damaged shell down. "I can't leave her alone."

"As you wish." Moralas turned to go when Jonas stopped him.

"Captain, you don't still think the murderer's hundreds of miles away."

Moralas touched the gun that hung at his side. "No, Mr. Sharpe, I don't. *Buenas noches.*"

Jonas locked her door himself, then rechecked the windows before he went back to the kitchen. Liz was pouring her second cup of coffee. "That'll keep you up."

Liz drank half a cup, staring at him. She felt nothing at the moment, no anger, no fear. "I thought you'd gone."

"No." Without invitation, he found a mug and poured coffee for himself.

"Why are you here?"

He took a step closer, to run a fingertip gently down the mark on her throat. "Stupid question," he murmured.

She backed up, fighting to maintain the calm she'd clung to. If she lost control, it wouldn't be in front of him, in front of anyone. "I want to be alone."

He saw her hands tremble before she locked them tighter on the cup. "You can't always have what you want. I'll bunk in your daughter's room."

"No!" After slamming the cup down, she folded her arms across her chest. "I don't want you here."

With studied calm, he set his mug next to hers. When he took her shoulders, his hands were firm, not gentle. When he spoke, his voice was brisk, not soothing. "I'm not leaving you alone. Not now, not until they find Jerry's killer. You're involved whether you like it or not. And so, damn it, am I."

Her breath came quickly, too quickly, though she fought to steady it. "I wasn't involved until you came back and started hounding me."

He'd already wrestled with his conscience over that. Neither one of them could know if it were true. At the moment, he told himself it didn't matter. "However you're involved, you are. Whoever killed Jerry thinks you know something. You'll have an easier time convincing me you don't than you will them. It's time you started thinking about cooperating with me."

"How do I know you didn't send him here to frighten me?"

His eyes stayed on hers, cool and unwavering. "You don't. I could tell you that I don't hire men to kill women, but you wouldn't have to believe it. I could tell you I'm sorry." For the first time, his tone gentled. He lifted a hand to brush the hair back from her face and his thumb slid lightly over her cheekbone. Like the conch shell, she seemed delicate, lovely and damaged. "And that I wish I could walk away, leave you alone, let both of us go back to the way things were a few weeks ago. But I can't. We can't. So we might as well help each other."

"I don't want your help."

"I know. Sit down. I'll fix you something to eat."

She tried to back away. "You can't stay here."

"I am staying here. Tomorrow, I'm moving my things from the hotel."

"I said—"

"I'll rent the room," he interrupted, turning away to rummage through the cupboards. "Your throat's probably raw. This chicken soup should be the best thing."

She snatched the can from his hand. "I can fix my own dinner, and you're not renting a room."

"I appreciate your generosity." He took the can back from her. "But I'd rather keep it on a business level. Twenty dollars a week seems fair. You'd better take it, Liz," he added before she could speak. "Because I'm staying, one way or the other. Sit down," he said again and looked for a pot.

She wanted to be angry. It would help keep everything else bottled up. She wanted to shout at him, to throw him bodily out of her house. Instead she sat because her knees were too weak to hold her any longer.

What had happened to her control? For ten years she'd been running her own life, making every decision by herself, for herself. For ten years, she hadn't asked advice, she hadn't asked for help. Now something had taken control and decisions out of her hands, something she knew nothing about. Her life was part of a game, and she didn't know any of the rules.

She looked down and saw the tear drop on the back of her hand. Quickly, she reached up and brushed others from her cheeks. But she couldn't stop them. One more decision had been taken from her.

"Can you eat some toast?" Jonas asked her as he dumped the contents of the soup in a pan. When she didn't answer, he turned to see her sitting stiff and pale at the table, tears running unheeded down her face. He swore and turned away again. There was nothing he could do for her, he told himself. Nothing he could offer. Then, saying nothing, he came to the table, pulled a chair up beside her and waited.

"I thought he'd kill me." Her voice broke as she pressed a hand to her face. "I felt the knife against my throat and thought I was going to die. I'm so scared. Oh God, I'm so scared."

He drew her against him and let her sob out the fear. He wasn't used to comforting women. Those he knew well were too chic to shed more than a delicate drop or two. But he held her close during a storm of weeping that shook her body and left her gasping.

Her skin was icy, as if to prove the fact that fear made the blood run cold. She couldn't summon the pride to draw herself away, to seek a private spot as she'd always done in a crisis. He didn't speak to tell her everything would be fine; he didn't murmur quiet words of comfort. He was simply there. When she was drained, he still held her. The rain began slowly, patting the glass of the windows and pinging on the roof. He still held her.

When she shifted away, he rose and went back to the stove. Without a word, he turned on the burner. Minutes later he set a bowl in front of her then went back to ladle some for himself. Too tired to be ashamed, Liz began to eat. There was no sound in the kitchen but the slow monotonous plop of rain on wood, tin and glass.

She hadn't realized she could be hungry, but the bowl was empty almost before she realized it. With a little sigh, she pushed it away. He was tipped back in his chair, smoking in silence.

"Thank you."

"Okay." Her eyes were swollen, accentuating the vulnerability that always haunted them. It tugged at him, making him uneasy. Her skin, with its ripe, warm honey glow was pale, making her seem delicate and defenseless. She was a woman, he realized, that a man had to keep an emotional distance from. Get too close and you'd be sucked right in. It wouldn't do to care about her too much when he needed to use her to help both of them. From this point on, he'd have to hold the controls.

"I suppose I was more upset than I realized."

"You're entitled."

She nodded, grateful he was making it easy for her to skim over what she considered an embarrassing display of weakness. "There's no reason for you to stay here."

"I'll stay anyway."

She curled her hand into a fist, then uncurled it slowly. It wasn't possible for her to admit she wanted him to, or that for the first time in years she was frightened of being alone. Since she had to cave in, it was better to think of the arrangement on a practical level.

"All right, the room's twenty a week, first week in advance." He grinned as he reached for his wallet. "All business?"

"I can't afford anything else." After putting the twenty on

the counter, she stacked the bowls. "You'll have to see to your own food. The twenty doesn't include meals."

He watched her take the bowls to the sink and wash them. "I'll manage."

"I'll give you a key in the morning." She took a towel and meticulously dried the bowls. "Do you think he'll be back?" She tried to make her voice casual, and failed.

"I don't know." He crossed to her to lay a hand on her shoulder. "You won't be alone if he does."

When she looked at him, her eyes were steady again. Something inside him unknotted. "Are you protecting me, Jonas, or just looking for your revenge?"

"I do one, maybe I'll get the other." He twined the ends of her hair around his finger, watching the dark gold spread over his skin. "You said yourself I'm not a nice man."

"What are you?" she whispered.

"Just a man." When his gaze lifted to hers, she didn't believe him. He wasn't just a man, but a man with patience, with power and with violence. "I've wondered the same about you. You've got secrets, Elizabeth."

She was breathless. In defense, she lifted her hand to his. "They've got nothing to do with you."

"Maybe they don't. Maybe you do."

It happened very slowly, so slowly she could have stopped it. Yet she seemed unable to move. His arms slipped around her, drawing her close with an arrogant sort of laziness that should have been his undoing. Instead, Liz watched, fascinated, as his mouth lowered to hers.

She'd just thought of him as a violent man, but his lips were soft, easy, persuading. It had been so long since she'd allowed herself to be persuaded. With barely any pressure, with only the slightest hint of power, he sapped the will she'd always relied on. Her mind raced with questions, then clouded over to a fine, smoky mist. She wasn't aware of how sweetly, how hesitantly her mouth answered his.

Whatever impulse had driven him to kiss her was lost in the reality of mouth against mouth. He'd expected her to resist, or to answer with fire and passion. To find her so soft, yielding, unsteady, had his own desire building in a way he'd never experienced. It was as though she'd never been kissed before, never been held close to explore what man and woman have for each other. Yet she had a daughter, he reminded himself. She'd had a child, she was young, beautiful. Other men had held her like this. Yet he felt like the first and had no choice but to treat her with care.

The more she gave, the more he wanted. He'd known needs before. The longer he held her, the longer he wanted to. He understood passions. But a part of himself he couldn't understand held back, demanded restraint. She wanted him—he could feel it. But even as his blood began to swim, his hands, as if under their own power, eased her away.

Needs, so long unstirred, churned in her. As she stared back at him, Liz felt them spring to life, with all their demands and risks. It wouldn't happen to her again. But even as she renewed the vow she felt the soft, fluttering longings waltz through her. It couldn't happen again. But the eyes that were wide and on his reflected confusion and hurt and hope. It was a combination that left Jonas shaken.

"You should get some sleep," he told her, and took care not to touch her again.

So that was all, Liz thought as the flicker of hope died. It was foolish to believe, even for a moment, anything could change. She brought her chin up and straightened her shoulders. Perhaps she'd lost control of many things, but she could still control her heart. "I'll give you a receipt for the rent and the key in the morning. I get up at six." She took the twenty-dollar bill she'd left on the counter and walked out.

4

The jury was staring at him. Twelve still faces with blank eyes were lined behind the rail. Jonas stood before them in a small, harshly lit courtroom that echoed with his own voice. He carried stacks of law books, thick, dusty and heavy enough to make his arms ache. But he knew he couldn't put them down. Sweat rolled down his temples, down his back as he gave an impassioned closing plea for his client's acquittal. It was life and death, and his voice vibrated with both. The jury remained unmoved, disinterested. Though he struggled to hold them, the books began to slip from his grasp. He heard the verdict rebound, bouncing off the courtroom walls.

Guilty. Guilty. Guilty.

Defeated, empty-handed, he turned to the defendant. The man stood, lifting his head so that they stared, eye to eye, twin images. Himself? Jerry. Desperate, Jonas walked to the bench. In black robes, Liz sat above him, aloof with distance. But her eyes were sad as she slowly shook her head. "I can't help you."

Slowly, she began to fade. He reached up to grab her hand, but his fingers passed through hers. All he could see were her dark, sad eyes. Then she was gone, his brother was gone, and he was left facing a jury—twelve cold faces who smiled smugly back at him.

Jonas lay still, breathing quickly. He found himself staring back at the cluster of gaily dressed dolls on the shelf beside the bed. A flamenco dancer raised her castanets. A princess held a glass slipper. A spiffily dressed Barbie relaxed in a pink convertible, one hand raised in a wave.

Letting out a long breath, Jonas ran a hand over his face and sat up. It was like trying to sleep in the middle of a party, he decided. No wonder he'd had odd dreams. On the opposing wall was a collection of stuffed animals ranging from the dependable bear to something that looked like a blue dust rag with eyes.

Coffee, Jonas thought, closing his own. He needed coffee. Trying to ignore the dozens of smiling faces surrounding him, he dressed. He wasn't sure how or where to begin. The coin on his chain dangled before he pulled a shirt over his chest. Outside, birds were sending up a clatter. At home there would have been the sound of traffic as Philadelphia awoke for the day. He could see a bush close to the window where purple flowers seemed to crowd each other for room. There were no sturdy elms, no tidy evergreen hedges or chain-link fences. No law books would help him with what he had to do. There was nothing familiar, no precedents to follow. Each step he took would be taken blindly, but he had to take them. He smelled the coffee the moment he left the room.

Liz was in the kitchen dressed in a T-shirt and what appeared to be the bottoms of a skimpy bikini. Jonas wasn't a man who normally awoke with all batteries charged, but he didn't miss a pair of long, honey-toned legs. Liz finished buttering a piece of toast.

"Coffee's on the stove," she said without turning around.

"There're some eggs in the refrigerator. I don't stock cereal when Faith's away."

"Eggs are fine," he mumbled, but headed for the coffee.

"Use what you want, as long as you replace it." She turned up the radio to listen to the weather forecast. "I leave in a half hour, so if you want a ride to your hotel, you'll have to be ready."

Jonas let the first hot taste of coffee seep into his system. "My car's in San Miguel."

Liz sat down at the table to go over that day's schedule. "I can drop you by the El Presidente or one of the other hotels on the beach. You'll have to take a cab from there."

Jonas took another sip of coffee and focused on her fully. She was still pale, he realized, so that the marks on her neck stood out in dark relief. The smudges under her eyes made him decide she'd slept no better than he had. He tossed off his first cup of coffee and poured another.

"Ever consider taking a day off?"

She looked at him for the first time. "No," she said simply and lowered her gaze to her list again.

So they were back to business, all business, and don't cross the line. "Don't you believe in giving yourself a break, Liz?"

"I've got work to do. You'd better fix those eggs if you want to have time to eat them. The frying pan's in the cupboard next to the stove."

He studied her for another minute, then with a restless movement of his shoulders prepared to cook his breakfast. Liz waited until she was sure his back was to her before she looked up again.

She'd made a fool of herself the night before. She could almost accept the fact that she'd broken down in front of him because he'd taken it so matter-of-factly. But when she added the moments she'd stood in his arms, submissive, willing, hoping, she couldn't forgive herself. Or him.

He'd made her feel something she hadn't felt in a decade. Arousal. He'd made her want what she'd been convinced she didn't want from a man. Affection. She hadn't backed away or brushed him aside as she'd done with any other man who'd approached her. She hadn't even tried. He'd made her feel soft again, then he'd shrugged her away.

So it would be business, she told herself. Straight, impersonal business as long as he determined to stay. She'd put the rent money aside until she could manage the down payment on the aqua bikes. Jonas sat at the table with a plate of eggs that sent steam rising toward the ceiling.

"Your key." Liz slid it over to him. "And your receipt for the first week's rent."

Without looking at it, Jonas tucked the paper in his pocket. "Do you usually take in boarders?"

"No, but I need some new equipment." She rose to pour another cup of coffee and wash her plate. The radio announced the time before she switched it off. She was ten minutes ahead of schedule, but as long as she continued to get up early enough, they wouldn't have to eat together. "Do you usually rent a room in a stranger's house rather than a hotel suite?"

He tasted the eggs and found himself vaguely dissatisfied with his own cooking. "No, but we're not strangers anymore."

Liz watched him over the rim of her cup. He looked a little rough around the edges this morning, she decided. It added a bit too much sexuality to smooth good looks. She debated offering him a razor, then rejected the notion. Too personal. "Yes, we are."

He continued to eat his eggs so that she thought he'd taken her at her word. "I studied law at Notre Dame, apprenticed with Neiram and Barker in Boston, then opened my own practice five years ago in Philadelphia." He added some salt, hoping it would jazz up his cooking. "I specialize in criminal law. I'm not married, and live alone. In an apartment," he added. "On weekends I'm remodeling an old Victorian house I bought in Chadd's Ford."

She wanted to ask him about the house—was it big, did it have those wonderful high ceilings and rich wooden floors? Were the windows tall and mullioned? Was there a garden where roses climbed on trellises? Instead she turned to rinse out her cup. "That doesn't change the fact that we're strangers."

"Whether we know each other or not, we have the same problem."

The cup rattled in the sink as it slipped from her hand. Silently, Liz picked it up again, rinsed it off and set it in the drainer. She'd chipped it, but that was a small matter at the moment. "You've got ten minutes," she said, but he took her arm before she could skirt around him.

"We do have the same problem, Elizabeth." His voice was quiet, steady. She could have hated him for that alone.

"No, we don't. You're trying to avenge your brother's death. I'm just trying to make a living."

"Do you think everything would settle down quietly if I were back in Philadelphia?"

She tugged her arm uselessly. "Yes!" Because she knew she lied, her eyes heated.

"One of the first impressions I had of you was your intelligence. I don't know why you're hiding on your pretty little island, Liz, but you've got a brain, a good one. We both know that what happened to you last night would have happened with or without me."

"All right." She relaxed her arm. "What happened wasn't

because of you, but because of Jerry. That hardly makes any difference to my position, does it?"

He stood up slowly, but didn't release her arm. "As long as someone thinks you knew what Jerry was into, you're the focus. As long as you're the focus, I'm standing right beside you, because directly or indirectly, you're going to lead me to Jerry's killer."

Liz waited a moment until she was sure she could speak calmly. "Is that all people are to you, Jonas? Tools? Means to an end?" She searched his face and found it set and remote. "Men like you never look beyond their own interests."

Angry without knowing why, he cupped her face in his hand. "You've never known a man like me."

"I think I have," she said softly. "You're not unique, Jonas. You were raised with money and expectations, you went to the best schools and associated with the best people. You had your goal set and if you had to step on or over a few people on the way to it, it wasn't personal. That's the worst of it," she said on a long breath. "It's never personal." Lifting her chin, she pushed his hand from her face. "What do you want me to do?"

Never in his life had anyone made him feel so vile. With a few words she'd tried and condemned him. He remembered the dream, and the blank, staring eyes of the jury. He swore at her and turned to pace to the window. He couldn't back away now, no matter how she made him feel because he was right—whether he was here or in Philadelphia, she was still the key.

There was a hammock outside, bright blue and yellow strings stretched between two palms. He wondered if she ever gave herself enough time to use it. He found himself wishing he could take her hand, walk across the yard and lie with her on the hammock with nothing more important to worry about than swatting at flies.

"I need to talk to Luis," he began. "I want to know the places he went with Jerry, the people he may have seen Jerry talk to."

"I'll talk to Luis." When Jonas started to object, Liz shook her head. "You saw his reaction yesterday. He wouldn't be able to talk to you because you make him too nervous. I'll get you a list."

"All right." Jonas fished for his cigarettes and found with some annoyance that he'd left them in the bedroom. "I'll need you to go with me, starting tonight, to the places Luis gives you."

A feeling of stepping into quicksand came strongly. "Why?"

He wasn't sure of the answer. "Because I have to start somewhere."

"Why do you need me?"

And even less sure of this one. "I don't know how long it'll take, and I'm not leaving you alone."

She lifted a brow. "I have police protection."

"Not good enough. In any case, you know the language, the customs. I don't. I need you." He tucked his thumbs in his pockets. "It's as simple as that."

Liz walked over to turn off the coffee and move the pot to a back burner. "Nothing's simple," she corrected. "But I'll get your list, and I'll go along with you under one condition."

"Which is?"

She folded her hands. Jonas was already certain by her stance alone that she wasn't set to bargain but to lay down the rules. "That no matter what happens, what you find out or don't find out, you're out of this house and out of my life when my daughter comes home. I'll give you four weeks, Jonas—that's all."

"It'll have to be enough."

She nodded and started out of the room. "Wash your dishes. I'll meet you out front."

The police car still sat in the driveway when Jonas walked out the front door. A group of children stood on the verge of the road and discussed it in undertones. He heard Liz call one of them by name before she took out a handful of coins. Jonas didn't have to speak Spanish to recognize a business transaction. Moments later, coins in hand, the boy raced back to his friends.

"What was that about?"

Liz smiled after them. Faith would play with those same children throughout the summer. "I told them they were detectives. If they see anyone but you or the police around the house, they're to run right home and call Captain Moralas. It's the best way to keep them out of trouble."

Jonas watched the boy in charge pass out the coins. "How much did you give them?"

"Twenty pesos apiece."

He thought of the current rate of exchange and shook his head. "No kid in Philadelphia would give you the time of day for that."

"This is Cozumel," she said simply and wheeled out her bike.

Jonas looked at it, then at her. The bike would have sent a young teenager into ecstasies. "You drive this thing?"

Something in his tone made her want to smile. Instead, she kept her voice cool. "This thing is an excellent mode of transportation."

"A BMW's an excellent mode of transportation."

She laughed. He hadn't heard her laugh so easily since he'd met her. When she looked back at him, her eyes were warm and friendly. Jonas felt the ground shift dangerously under his feet. "Try to take your BMW on some of the back roads to the coast or into the interior." She swung a leg over the seat. "Hop on, Jonas, unless you want to hike back to the hotel."

Though he had his doubts, Jonas sat behind her. "Where do I put my feet?"

She glanced down and didn't bother to hide the grin. "Well, if I were you, I'd keep them off the ground." With this she started the engine then swung the bike around in the driveway. After adjusting for the added weight, Liz kept the speed steady. Jonas kept his hands lightly at her hips as the bike swayed around ruts and potholes.

"Are there roads worse than this?"

Liz sped over a bump. "What's wrong with this?"

"Just asking."

"If you want sophistication, try Cancun. It's only a few minutes by air."

"Ever get there?"

"Now and again. Last year Faith and I took the *Expatriate* over and spent a couple of days seeing the ruins. We have some shrines here. They're not well restored, but you shouldn't miss them. Still, I wanted her to see the pyramids and walled cities around Cancun."

"I don't know much about archaeology."

"You don't have to. All you need's an imagination."

She tooted the horn. Jonas saw an old, bent man straighten from the door of a shop and wave. "Señor Pessado," she said. "He gives Faith candy they both think I don't know about."

Jonas started to ask her about her daughter, then decided to wait for a better time. As long as she was being expansive, it was best to keep things less personal. "Do you know a lot of people on the island?"

"It's like a small town, I suppose. You don't necessarily have to know someone to recognize their face. I don't know a lot of people in San Miguel or on the east coast. I know a few people from the interior because we worked at the hotel."

"I didn't realize your shop was affiliated with the hotel."

"It's not." She paused at a stop sign. "I used to work in the hotel. As a maid." Liz gunned the engine and zipped across the intersection.

He looked at her hands, lean and delicate on the handlebars. He studied her slender shoulders, thought of the slight hips he was even now holding. It was difficult to imagine her lugging buckets and pails. "I'd have thought you more suited to the front desk or the concierge."

"I was lucky to find work at all, especially during the off season." She slowed the bike a bit as she started down the long drive to El Presidente. She'd indulge herself for a moment by enjoying the tall elegant palms that lined the road and the smell of blooming flowers. She was taking one of the dive boats out today, with five beginners who'd need instruction and constant supervision, but she wondered about the people inside the hotel who came to such a place to relax and to play.

"Is it still gorgeous inside?" she asked before she could stop herself.

Jonas glanced ahead to the large stately building. "Lots of glass," he told her. "Marble. The balcony of my room looks out over the water." She steered the bike to the curb. "Why don't you come in? See for yourself."

She was tempted. Liz had an affection for pretty things, elegant things. It was a weakness she couldn't allow herself. "I have to get to work."

Jonas stepped onto the curb, but put his hand over hers before she could drive away. "I'll meet you at the house. We'll go into town together."

She only nodded before turning the bike back toward the road. Jonas watched her until the sound of the motor died away. Just who was Elizabeth Palmer? he wondered. And why was it becoming more and more important that he find out?

By evening she was tired. Liz was used to working long hours, lugging equipment, diving, surfacing. But after a fairly easy day, she was tired. It should have made her feel secure to have had the young policeman identify himself to her and join her customers on the dive boat. It should have eased her mind that Captain Moralas was keeping his word about protection. It made her feel caged.

All during the drive home, she'd been aware of the police cruiser keeping a discreet distance. She'd wanted to run into her house, lock the door and fall into a dreamless, private sleep. But Jonas was waiting. She found him on the phone in her living room, a legal pad on his lap and a scowl on his face. Obviously a complication at his office had put him in a nasty mood. Ignoring him, Liz went to shower and change.

Because her wardrobe ran for the most part to beachwear, she didn't waste time studying her closet. Without enthusiasm, she pulled out a full cotton skirt in peacock blue and matched it with an oversized red shirt. More to prolong her time alone than for any other reason, she fiddled with her little cache of makeup. She was stalling, brushing out her braided hair, when Jonas knocked on her door. He didn't give her time to answer before he pushed it open.

"Did you get the list?"

Liz picked up a piece of notepaper. She could, of course, snap at him for coming in, but the end result wouldn't change. "I told you I would."

He took the paper from her to study it. He'd shaved, she noticed, and wore a casually chic jacket over bone-colored slacks. But the smoothness and gloss didn't mesh with the toughness around his mouth and in his eyes. "Do you know these places?"

"I've been to a couple of them. I don't really have a lot of time for bar- or club-hopping."

He glanced up and his curt answer slipped away. The shades

behind her were up as she preferred them, but the light coming through the windows was pink with early evening. Though she'd buttoned the shirt high over her throat, her hair was brushed back, away from her face. She'd dawdled over the makeup, but her hand was always conservative. Her lashes were darkened, the lids lightly touched with shadow. She'd brushed some color over her cheeks but not her lips.

"You should be careful what you do to your eyes," Jonas murmured, absently running his thumb along the top curve of her cheek. "They're a problem."

She felt the quick, involuntary tug but stood still. "A problem?"

"My problem." Uneasy, he tucked the paper in his pocket and glanced around the room. "Are you ready?"

"I need my shoes."

He didn't leave her as she'd expected, instead wandering around her room. It was, as was the rest of the house, furnished simply but with jarring color. The spicy scent he'd noticed before came from a wide green bowl filled with potpourri. On the wall were two colored sketches, one of a sunset very much like the quietly brilliant one outside the window, and another of a storm-tossed beach. One was all serenity, the other all violence. He wondered how much of each were inside Elizabeth Palmer. Prominent next to the bed was a framed photograph of a young girl.

She was all smiles in a flowered blouse tucked at the shoulders. Her hair came to a curve at her jawline, black and shiny. A tooth was missing, adding charm to an oval, tanned face. If it hadn't been for the eyes, Jonas would never have connected the child with Liz. They were richly, deeply brown, slightly tilted. Still, they laughed out of the photo, open and trusting, holding none of the secrets of her mother's.

"This is your daughter."

"Yes." Liz slipped on the second shoe before taking the photo out of Jonas's hand and setting it down again.

"How old is she?"

"Ten. Can we get started? I don't want to be out late."

"Ten?" A bit stunned, Jonas stopped her with a look. He'd assumed Faith was half that age, a product of a relationship Liz had fallen into while on the island. "You can't have a ten-year-old child."

Liz glanced down at the picture of her daughter. "I do have a ten-year-old child."

"You'd have been a child yourself."

"No. No, I wasn't." She started to leave again, and again he stopped her.

"Was she born before you came here?"

Liz gave him a long, neutral look. "She was born six months after I moved to Cozumel. If you want my help, Jonas, we go now. Answering questions about Faith isn't part of our arrangement."

But he didn't let go of her hand. As it could become so unexpectedly, his voice was gentle. "He was a bastard, wasn't he?"

She met his eyes without wavering. Her lips curved, but not with humor. "Yes. Oh yes, he was."

Without knowing why he was compelled to, Jonas bent and just brushed her lips with his. "Your daughter's lovely, Elizabeth. She has your eyes."

She felt herself softening again, too much, too quickly. There was understanding in his voice without pity. Nothing could weaken her more. In defense she took a step back. "Thank you. Now we have to go. I have to be up early tomorrow."

The first club they hit was noisy and crowded with a high percentage of American clientele. In a corner booth, a man in a tight white T-shirt spun records on a turntable and announced each selection with a display of colored lights. They ordered a quick meal in addition to drinks while Jonas hoped someone would have a reaction to his face.

"Luis said they came in here a lot because Jerry liked hearing American music." Liz nibbled on hot nachos as she looked around. It wasn't the sort of place she normally chose to spend an evening. Tables were elbow to elbow, and the music was pitched to a scream. Still, the crowd seemed good-natured enough, shouting along with the music or just shouting to each other. At the table beside them a group of people experimented with a bottle of tequila and a bowl of lemon wedges. Since they were a group of young gringos, she assumed they'd be very sick in the morning.

It was definitely Jerry's milieu, Jonas decided. Loud, just this side of wild and crammed to the breaking point. "Did Luis say if he spoke with anyone in particular?"

"Women." Liz smiled a bit as she sampled a tortilla. "Luis was very impressed with Jerry's ability to...interest the ladies."

"Any particular lady?"

"Luis said there was one, but Jerry just called her baby."

"An old trick," Jonas said absently.

"Trick?"

"If you call them all baby, you don't mix up names and complicate the situation."

"I see." She sipped her wine and found it had a delicate taste.

"Could Luis describe her?"

"Only that she was a knockout—a Mexican knockout, if that helps. She had lots of hair and lots of hip. Luis's words," Liz added when Jonas gave her a mild look. "He also said there were a couple of men Jerry talked to a few times, but he always went over to them, so Luis didn't know what they spoke about. One was American, one was Mexican. Since Luis was more interested in the ladies, he didn't pay any attention. But he did say Jerry would cruise the bars until he met up with them, then he'd usually call it a night."

"Did he meet them here?"

"Luis said it never seemed to be in the same place twice."

"Okay, finish up. We'll cruise around ourselves."

By the fourth stop, Liz was fed up. She noticed that Jonas no more than toyed with a drink at each bar, but she was tired of the smell of liquor. Some places were quiet, and on the edge of seamy. Others were raucous and lit with flashing lights. Faces began to blur together. There were young people, not so young people. There were Americans out for exotic night-life, natives celebrating a night on the town. Some courted on dance floors or over tabletops. She saw those who seemed to have nothing but time and money, and others who sat alone nursing a bottle and a black mood.

"This is the last one," Liz told him as Jonas found a table at a club with a crowded dance floor and recorded music.

Jonas glanced at his watch. It was barely eleven. Action rarely heated up before midnight. "All right," he said easily, and decided to distract her. "Let's dance."

Before she could refuse, he was pulling her into the crowd. "There's no room," she began, but his arms came around her.

"We'll make some." He had her close, his hand trailing up her back. "See?"

"I haven't danced in years," she muttered, and he laughed.

"There's no room anyway." Locked together, jostled by the crowd, they did no more than sway.

"What's the purpose in all this?" she demanded.

"I don't know until I find it. Meantime, don't you ever relax?" He rubbed his palm up her back again, finding the muscles taut.

"No."

"Let's try it this way." His gaze skimmed the crowd as he spoke. "What do you do when you're not working?"

"I think about working."

"Liz."

"All right, I read—books on marine life mostly."

"Busman's holiday?"

"It's what interests me."

Her body shifted intimately against his. Jonas forgot to keep his attention on the crowd and looked down at her. "*All* that interests you?"

He was too close. Liz tried to ease away and found his arms very solid. In spite of her determination to remain unmoved, her heart began to thud lightly in her head. "I don't have time for anything else."

She wore no perfume, he noted, but carried the scent of powder and spice. He wondered if her body would look as delicate as it felt against his. "It sounds as though you limit yourself."

"I have a business to run," she murmured. Would it be the same if he kissed her again? Sweet, overpowering. His lips were so close to hers, closer still when he ran his hand through her hair and drew her head back. She could almost taste him.

"Is making money so important?"

"It has to be," she managed, but could barely remember why. "I need to buy some aqua bikes."

Her eyes were soft, drowsy. They made him feel invulnerable. "Aqua bikes?"

"If I don't keep up with the competition…" He pressed a kiss to the corner of her mouth.

"The competition?" he prompted.

"I…the customers will go someplace else. So I…" The kiss teased the other corner.

"So?"

"I have to buy the bikes before the summer season."

"Of course. But that's weeks away. I could make love with you dozens of times before then. Dozens," he repeated as she stared at him. Then he closed his mouth over hers.

He felt her jolt—surprise, resistance, passion—he couldn't be sure. He only knew that holding her had led to wanting her and wanting to needing. By nature, he was a man who preferred his passion in private, quiet spots of his own choosing. Now he forgot the crowded club, loud music and flashing lights. They no longer swayed, but were hemmed into a corner of the dance floor, surrounded, pressed close. Oblivious.

She felt her head go light, heard the music fade. The heat from his body seeped into hers and flavored the kiss. Hot, molten, searing. Though they stood perfectly still, Liz had visions of racing. The breath backed up in her lungs until she released it with a shuddering sigh. Her body, coiled like a spring, went lax on a wave of confused pleasure. She strained closer, reaching up to touch his face. Abruptly the music changed from moody to rowdy. Jonas shifted her away from flailing arms.

"Poor timing," he murmured.

She needed a minute. "Yes." But she meant it in a more general way. It wasn't a matter of time and place, but a matter of impossibility. She started to move away when Jonas's grip tightened on her. "What is it?" she began, but only had to look at his face.

Cautiously, she turned to see what he stared at. A woman in a skimpy red dress stared back at him. Liz recognized the shock in her eyes before the woman turned and fled, leaving her dance partner gaping.

"Come on." Without waiting for her, Jonas sprinted through the crowd. Dodging, weaving and shoving when she had to, Liz dashed after him.

The woman had barely gotten out to the street when Jonas caught up to her. "What are you running away from?" he demanded. His fingers dug into her arms as he held her back against a wall.

"Por favor, no comprendo," she murmured and shook like a leaf.

"Oh yes, I think you do." With his fingers bruising her arms, Jonas towered over her until she nearly squeaked in fear. "What do you know about my brother?"

"Jonas." Appalled, Liz stepped between them. "If this is the way you intend to behave, you'll do without my help." She turned away from him and touched the woman's shoulder. *"Lo siento mucho,"* she began, apologizing for Jonas. "He's lost his brother. His brother, Jerry Sharpe. Did you know him?"

She looked at Liz and whispered. "He has Jerry's face. But he's dead—I saw in the papers."

"This is Jerry's brother, Jonas. We'd like to talk to you."

As Liz had, the woman had already sensed the difference between Jonas and the man she'd known. She'd never have cowered away from Jerry for the simple reason that she'd known herself to be stronger and more clever. The man looming over her now was a different matter.

"I don't know anything."

"Por favor. Just a few minutes."

"Tell her I'll make it worth her while," Jonas added before she could refuse again. Without waiting for Liz to translate, he reached for his wallet and took out a bill. He saw fear change to speculation.

"A few minutes," she agreed, but pointed to an outdoor café. "There."

Jonas ordered two coffees and a glass of wine. "Ask her her name," he told Liz.

"I speak English." The woman took out a long, slim cigarette and tapped it on the tabletop. "I'm Erika. Jerry and I were friends." More relaxed, she smiled at Jonas. "You know, good friends."

"Yes, I know."

"He was very good-looking," she added, then caught her bottom lip between her teeth. "Lots of fun."

"How long did you know him?"

"A couple of weeks. I was sorry when I heard he was dead."

"Murdered," Jonas stated.

Erika took a deep drink of wine. "Do you think it was because of the money?"

Every muscle in his body tensed. Quickly, he shot Liz a warning look before she could speak. "I don't know—it looks that way. How much did he tell you about it?"

"Oh, just enough to intrigue me. You know." She smiled again and held out her cigarette for a light. "Jerry was very charming. And generous." She remembered the little gold bracelet he'd bought for her and the earrings with the pretty blue stones. "I thought he was very rich, but he said he would soon be much richer. I like charming men, but I especially like rich men. Jerry said when he had the money, we could take a trip." She blew out smoke again before giving a philosophical little shrug. "Then he was dead."

Jonas studied her as he drank coffee. She was, as Luis had said, a knockout. And she wasn't stupid. He was also certain her mind was focusing on one point, and one point alone. "Do you know when he was supposed to have the money?"

"Sure, I had to take off work if we were going away. He called me—it was Sunday. He was so excited. 'Erika,' he said, 'I hit the jackpot.' I was a little mad because he hadn't shown up Saturday night. He told me he'd done some quick business in Acapulco and how would I like to spend a few weeks in Monte Carlo?" She gave Jonas a lash-fluttering smile. "I decided to forgive him. I was packed," she added, blowing smoke past Jonas's shoulder. "We were supposed to leave Tuesday afternoon. I saw in the papers Monday night that he was dead. The papers said nothing about the money."

"Do you know who he had business with?"

"No. Sometimes he would talk to another American, a skinny man with pale hair. Other times he would see a Mexican. I didn't like him—he had *mal ojo.*"

"Evil eye," Liz interpreted. "Can you describe him?"

"Not pretty," she said offhandedly. "His face was pitted. His hair was long in the back, over his collar and he was very thin and short." She glanced at Jonas again with a sultry smile that heated the air. "I like tall men."

"Do you know his name?"

"No. But he dressed very nicely. Nice suits, good shoes. And he wore a silver band on his wrist, a thin one that crossed at the ends. It was very pretty. Do you think he knows about the money? Jerry said it was lots of money."

Jonas merely reached for his wallet. "I'd like to find out his name," he told her and set a fifty on the table. His hand closed over hers as she reached for it. "His name, and the name of the American. Don't hold out on me, Erika."

With a toss of her head, she palmed the fifty. "I'll find out the names. When I tell you, it's another fifty."

"When you tell me." He scrawled Liz's number on the back of a business card. "Call this number when you have something."

"Okay." She slipped the fifty into her purse as she stood up. "You know, you don't look as much like Jerry as I thought." With the click of high heels, she crossed the pavement and went back into the club.

"It's a beginning," Jonas murmured as he pushed his coffee aside. When he looked over, he saw Liz studying him. "Problem?"

"I don't like the way you work."

He dropped another bill on the table before he rose. "I don't have time to waste on amenities."

"What would you have done if I hadn't calmed her down? Dragged her off to the nearest alley and beaten it out of her?"

He drew out a cigarette, struggling with temper. "Let's go home, Liz."

"I wonder if you're any different from the men you're looking for." She pushed back from the table. "Just as a matter of interest, the man who broke into my house and attacked me wore a thin band at his wrist. I felt it when he held the knife to my throat."

She watched as his gaze lifted from the flame at the end of the cigarette and came to hers. "I think you two might recognize each other when the time comes."

5

"Always check your gauges," Liz instructed, carefully indicating each one on her own equipment as she spoke. "Each one of these gauges is vital to your safety when you dive. That's true if it's your first dive or your fiftieth. It's very easy to become so fascinated not only by the fish and coral, but the sensation of diving itself, that you can forget you're dependent on your air tank. Always be certain you start your ascent while you have five or ten minutes of air left."

She'd covered everything, she decided, in the hour lesson. If she lectured any more, her students would be too impatient to listen. It was time to give them a taste of what they were paying for.

"We'll dive as a group. Some of you may want to explore on your own, but remember, always swim in pairs. As a final precaution, check the gear of the diver next to you."

Liz strapped on her own weight belt as her group of novices followed instructions. So many of them, she knew, looked on scuba diving as an adventure. That was fine, as long as they remembered safety. Whenever she instructed, she stressed the what ifs just as thoroughly as the how tos. Anyone who went down under her supervision would know what steps to take under any circumstances. Diving accidents were most often the result of carelessness. Liz was never careless with herself or with her students. Most of them were talking excitedly as they strapped on tanks.

"This group." Luis hefted his tank. "Very green."

"Yeah." Liz helped him with the straps. As she did with all her employees, Liz supplied Luis's gear. It was checked just as thoroughly as any paying customer's. "Keep an eye on the honeymoon couple, Luis. They're more interested in each other than their regulators."

"No problem." He assisted Liz with her tank, then stepped back while she cinched the straps. "You look tired, kid."

"No, I'm fine."

When she turned, he glanced at the marks on her neck. The story had already made the rounds. "You sure? You don't look so fine."

She lifted a brow as she hooked on her diving knife. "Sweet of you."

"Well, I mean it. You got me worried about you."

"No need to worry." As Liz pulled on her mask, she glanced over at the roly-poly fatherly type who was struggling with his flippers. He was her bodyguard for the day. "The police have everything under control," she said, and hoped it was true. She wasn't nearly as sure about Jonas.

He hadn't shocked her the night before. She'd sensed that dangerously waiting violence in him from the first. But seeing his face as he'd grabbed Erika, hearing his voice, had left her with a cold, flat feeling in her stomach. She didn't know him well enough to be certain if he would choose to control the violence or let it free. More, how could she know he was capable of leashing it? Revenge, she thought, was never pretty.

And that's what he wanted. Remembering the look in his eyes, Liz was very much afraid he'd get it.

The boat listed, bringing her back to the moment. She couldn't think about Jonas now, she told herself. She had a business to run and customers to satisfy.

"Miss Palmer." A young American with a thin chest and a winning smile maneuvered over to her. "Would you mind giving me a check?"

"Sure." In her brisk, efficient way, Liz began to check gauges and hoses.

"I'm a little nervous," he confessed. "I've never done this sort of thing before."

"It doesn't hurt to be a little nervous. You'll be more careful. Here, pull your mask down. Make sure it's comfortable but snug."

He obeyed, and his eyes looked wide and pale through the glass. "If you don't mind, I think I'll stick close to you down there."

She smiled at him. "That's what I'm here for. The depth here is thirty feet," she told the group in general. "Remember to make your adjustments for pressure and gravity as you descend. Please keep the group in sight at all times." With innate fluidity, she sat on the deck and rolled into the water. With Luis on deck, and Liz treading a few feet away, they waited until each student made his dive. With a final adjustment to her mask, Liz went under.

She'd always loved it. The sensation of weightlessness, the fantasy of being unimpeded, invulnerable. From near the surface, the sea floor was a spread of white. She loitered there a moment, enjoying the cathedral like view. Then, with an easy kick, she moved down with her students.

The newlyweds were holding hands and having the time of their lives. Liz reminded herself to keep them in sight. The policeman assigned to her was plodding along like a sleepy sea turtle. He'd keep her in sight. Most of the others remained in a tight group, fascinated but cautious. The thin American gave her a wide-eyed look that was a combination of pleasure and nerves and stuck close by her side. To help him relax, Liz touched his shoulder and pointed up. In an easy motion, she turned on her back so that she faced the surface. Sunlight streaked thinly through the water. The hull of the dive boat was plainly visible. He nodded and followed her down.

Fish streamed by, some in waves, some on their own. Though the sand was white, the water clear, there was a montage of color. Brain coral rose up in sturdy mounds, the color of saffron. Sea fans, as delicate as lace, waved pink and purple in the current. She signaled to her companion and watched a school of coral sweepers, shivering with metallic tints, turn as a unit and skim through staghorn coral.

It was a world she understood as well as, perhaps better, than the one on the surface. Here, in the silence, Liz often found the peace of mind that eluded her from day to day. The scientific names of the fish and formations they passed were no strangers to her. Once she'd studied them diligently, with dreams of solving mysteries and bringing the beauty of the world of the sea to others. That had been another life. Now she coached tourists and gave them, for hourly rates, something memorable to take home after a vacation. It was enough.

Amused, she watched an angelfish busy itself by swallowing the bubbles rising toward the surface. To entertain her students, she poked at a small damselfish. The pugnacious male clung to his territory and nipped at her. To the right, she saw sand kick up and cloud the water. Signaling for caution, Liz pointed out the platelike ray that skimmed away, annoyed by the intrusion.

The new husband showed off a bit, turning slow somersaults for his wife. As divers gained confidence, they spread out a little farther. Only her bodyguard and the nervous American stayed within an arm span at all times. Throughout the thirty-minute dive, Liz circled the group, watching individual divers. By the time the lesson was over, she was satisfied that her customers had gotten their money's worth. This was verified when they surfaced.

"Great!" A British businessman on his first trip to Mexico clambered back onto the deck. His face was reddened by the sun but he didn't seem to mind. "When can we go down again?"

With a laugh, Liz helped other passengers on board. "You have to balance your down time with your surface time. But we'll go down again."

"What was that feathery-looking stuff?" someone else asked. "It grows like a bush."

"It's a gorgonian, from the Gorgons of mythology." She slipped off her tanks and flexed her muscles. "If you remember, the Gorgons had snakes for hair. The whip gorgonian has a resilient skeletal structure and undulates like a snake with the current."

More questions were tossed out, more answers supplied. Liz noticed the American who'd stayed with her, sitting by himself, smiling a little. Liz moved around gear then dropped down beside him.

"You did very well."

"Yeah?" He looked a little dazed as he shrugged his shoulders. "I liked it, but I gotta admit, I felt better knowing you were right there. You sure know what you're doing."

"I've been at it a long time."

He sat back, unzipping his wet suit to his waist. "I don't mean to be nosy, but I wondered about you. You're American, aren't you?"

It had been asked before. Liz combed her fingers through her wet hair. "That's right."

"From?"

"Houston."

"No kidding." His eyes lit up. "Hell, I went to school in Texas. Texas A and M."

"Really?" The little tug she felt rarely came and went. "So did I, briefly."

"Small world," he said, pleased with himself. "I like Texas. Got a few friends in Houston. I don't suppose you know the Dresscots?"

"No."

"Well, Houston isn't exactly small-town U.S.A." He stretched out long, skinny legs that were shades paler than his arms but starting to tan. "So you went to Texas A and M."

"That's right."

"What'd you study?"

She smiled and looked out to sea. "Marine biology."

"Guess that fits."

"And you?"

"Accounting." He flashed his grin again. "Pretty dry stuff. That's why I always take a long breather after tax time."

"Well, you chose a great place to take it. Ready to go down again?"

He took a long breath as if to steady himself. "Yeah. Hey, listen, how about a drink after we get back in?"

He was attractive in a mild sort of way, pleasant enough. She gave him an apologetic smile as she rose. "It sounds nice, but I'm tied up."

"I'll be around for a couple of weeks. Some other time?"

"Maybe. Let's check your gear."

By the time the dive boat chugged into shore, the afternoon was waning. Her customers, most of them pleased with them-selves, wandered off to change for dinner or spread out on the beach. Only a few loitered near the boat, including her bodyguard and the accountant from America. It occurred to Liz that she might have been a bit brisk with him.

"I hope you enjoyed yourself, Mr...."

"Trydent. But it's Scott, and I did. I might just try it again."

Liz smiled at him as she helped Luis and another of her employees unload the boat. "That's what we're here for."

"You, ah, ever give private lessons?"

Liz caught the look. Perhaps she hadn't been brisk enough. "On occasion."

"Then maybe we could—"

"Hey, there, missy."

Liz shaded her eyes. "Mr. Ambuckle."

He stood on the little walkway, his legs bulging out of the short wet suit. What hair he had was sleeked wetly back. Beside him, his wife stood wearily in a bathing suit designed to slim down wide hips. "Just got back in!" he shouted. "Had a full day of it."

He seemed enormously pleased with himself. His wife looked at Liz and rolled her eyes. "Maybe I should take you out as crew, Mr. Ambuckle."

He laughed, slapping his side. "Guess I'd rather dive than anything." He glanced at his wife and patted her shoulder. "Almost anything. Gotta trade in these tanks, honey, and get me some fresh ones."

"Going out again?"

"Tonight. Can't talk the missus into it."

"I'm crawling into bed with a good book," she told Liz. "The only water I want to see is in the tub."

With a laugh, Liz jumped down to the walkway. "At the moment, I feel the same way. Oh, Mr. and Mrs. Ambuckle, this is Scott Trydent. He just took his first dive."

"Well now." Expansive, Ambuckle slapped him on the back. "How'd you like it?"

"Well, I—"

"Nothing like it, is there? You want try it at night, boy. Whole different ball game at night."

"I'm sure, but—"

"Gotta trade in these tanks." After slapping Scott's back again, Ambuckle hefted his tanks and waddled off toward the shop.

"Obsessed," Mrs. Ambuckle said, casting her eyes to the sky. "Don't let him get started on you, Mr. Trydent. You'll never get any peace."

"No, I won't. Nice meeting you, Mrs. Ambuckle." Obviously bemused, Scott watched her wander back toward the hotel. "Quite a pair."

"That they are." Liz lifted her own tanks. She stored them separately from her rental equipment. "Goodbye, Mr. Trydent."

"Scott," he said again. "About that drink—"

"Thanks anyway," Liz said pleasantly and left him standing on the walkway. "Everything in?" she asked Luis as she stepped into the shop.

"Checking it off now. One of the regulators is acting up."

"Set it aside for Jose to look at." As a matter of habit, she moved into the back to fill her tanks before storage. "All the boats are in, Luis. We shouldn't have too much more business now. You and the rest can go on as soon as everything's checked in. I'll close up."

"I don't mind staying."

"You closed up last night," she reminded him. "What do you want?" She tossed a grin over her shoulder. "Overtime? Go on home, Luis. You can't tell me you don't have a date."

He ran a fingertip over his mustache. "As a matter of fact…"

"A hot date?" Liz lifted a brow as air hissed into her tank.

"Is there any other kind?"

Chuckling, Liz straightened. She noticed Ambuckle

trudging across the sand with his fresh tanks. Her other employees talked among themselves as the last of the gear was stored. "Well, go make yourself beautiful then. The only thing I have a date with is the account books."

"You work too much," Luis mumbled.

Surprised, Liz turned back to him. "Since when?"

"Since always. It gets worse every time you send Faith back to school. Better off if she was here."

That her voice cooled only slightly was a mark of her affection for Luis. "No, she's happy in Houston with my parents. If I thought she wasn't, she wouldn't be there."

"She's happy, sure. What about you?"

Her brows drew together as she picked her keys from a drawer. "Do I look unhappy?"

"No." Tentatively, he touched her shoulder. He'd known Liz for years, and understood there were boundaries she wouldn't let anyone cross. "But you don't look happy either. How come you don't give one of these rich American tourists a spin? That one on the boat—his eyes popped out every time he looked at you."

The exaggeration made her laugh, so she patted his cheek. "So you think a rich American tourist is the road to happiness?"

"Maybe a handsome Mexican."

"I'll think about it—after the summer season. Go home," she ordered.

"I'm going." Luis pulled a T-shirt over his chest. "You look out for that Jonas Sharpe," he added. "He's got a different kind of look in his eyes."

Liz waved him off. *"Hasta luego."*

When the shop was empty, Liz stood, jingling her keys and looking out onto the beach. People traveled in couples, she noted, from the comfortably married duo stretched out on lounge chairs, to the young man and woman curled together on a beach towel. Was it an easy feeling, she wondered, to be half of a set? Or did you automatically lose part of yourself when you joined with another?

She'd always thought of her parents as separate people, yet when she thought of one, the other came quickly to mind. Would it be a comfort to know you could reach out your hand and someone else's would curl around it?

She held out her own and remembered how hard, how strong, Jonas's had been. No, he wouldn't make a relationship a comfortable affair. Being joined with him would be demanding, even frightening. A woman would have to be strong enough to keep herself intact, and soft enough to allow herself to merge. A relationship with a man like Jonas would be a risk that would never ease.

For a moment, she found herself dreaming of it, dreaming of what it had been like to be held close and kissed as though nothing and no one else existed. To be kissed like that always, to be held like that whenever the need moved you—it might be worth taking chances for.

Stupid, she thought quickly, shaking herself out of it. Jonas wasn't looking for a partner, and she wasn't looking for a dream. Circumstances had tossed them together temporarily. Both of them had to deal with their own realities. But she felt a sense of regret and a stirring of wishes.

Because the feeling remained, just beyond her grasp, Liz concentrated hard on the little details that needed attending to before she could close up. The paperwork and the contents of the cash box were transferred to a canvas portfolio. She'd have to swing out of her way to make a night deposit, but she no longer felt safe taking the cash or the checks home. She spent an extra few minutes meticulously filling out a deposit slip.

It wasn't until she'd picked up her keys again that she remembered her tanks. Tucking the portfolio under the counter, she turned to deal with her own gear.

It was perhaps her only luxury. She'd spent more on her personal equipment than she had on all the contents of her closet and dresser. To Liz, the wet suit was more exciting than any French silks. All her gear was kept separate from the shop's inventory. Unlocking the door to the closet, Liz hung up her wet suit, stored her mask, weight belt, regulator. Her knife was sheathed and set on a shelf. After setting her tanks side by side, she shut the door and prepared to lock it again. After she'd taken two steps away she looked down at the keys again. Without knowing precisely why, she moved each one over the ring and identified it.

The shop door, the shop window, her bike, the lock for the chain, the cash box, the front and back doors of her house, her storage room. Eight keys for eight locks. But there was one more on her ring, a small silver key that meant nothing to her at all.

Puzzled, she counted off the keys again, and again found one extra. Why should there be a key on her ring that didn't belong to her? Closing her fingers over it, she tried to think if anyone had given her the key to hold. No, it didn't make sense. Brows drawn together, she studied the key again. Too small for a car or door key, she decided. It looked like the key to a locker, or a box or… Ridiculous, she decided on a long breath. It wasn't her key but it was on her ring. Why?

Because someone put it there, she realized, and opened her hand again. Her keys were often tossed in the drawer at the shop for easy access for Luis or one of the other men. They needed to open the cash box. And Jerry had often worked in the shop alone.

With a feeling of dread, Liz slipped the keys into her pocket. Jonas's words echoed in her head. *"You're involved, whether you want to be or not."*

Liz closed the shop early.

★ ★ ★

Jonas stepped into the dim bar to the scent of garlic and the wail of a squeaky jukebox. In Spanish, someone sang of endless love. He stood for a moment, letting his eyes adjust, then skimmed his gaze over the narrow booths. As agreed, Erika sat all the way in the back, in the corner.

"You're late." She waved an unlit cigarette idly as he joined her.

"I passed it the first time. This place isn't exactly on the tourist route."

She closed her lips over the filter as Jonas lit her cigarette. "I wanted privacy."

Jonas glanced around. There were two men at the bar, each deep in separate bottles. Another couple squeezed themselves together on one side of a booth. The rest of the bar was deserted. "You've got it."

"But I don't have a drink."

Jonas slid out from the booth and bought two drinks at the bar. He set tequila and lime in front of Erika and settled for club soda. "You said you had something for me."

Erica twined a string of colored beads around her finger. "You said you would pay fifty for a name."

In silence, Jonas took out his wallet. He set fifty on the table, but laid his hand over it. "You have the name."

Erika smiled and sipped at her drink. "Maybe. Maybe you want it bad enough to pay another fifty."

Jonas studied her coolly. This was the type his brother had always been attracted to. The kind of woman whose hard edge was just a bit obvious. He could give her another fifty, Jonas mused, but he didn't care to be taken for a sucker. Without a word, he picked up the bill and tucked it into his pocket. He was halfway out of the booth when Erika grabbed his arm.

"Okay, don't get mad. Fifty." She sent him an easy smile as

he settled back again. Erika had been around too long to let an opportunity slip away. "A girl has to make a living, *sí?* The name is Pablo Manchez—he's the one with the face."

"Where can I find him?"

"I don't know. You got the name."

With a nod, Jonas took the bill out and passed it to her. Erika folded it neatly into her purse. "I'll tell you something else, because Jerry was a sweet guy." Her gaze skimmed the bar again as she leaned closer to Jonas. "This Manchez, he's bad. People got nervous when I asked about him. I heard he was mixed up in a couple of murders in Acapulco last year. He's paid, you know, to…" She made a gun out of her hand and pushed down her thumb. "When I hear that, I stop asking questions."

"What about the other one, the American?"

"Nothing. Nobody knows him. But if he hangs out with Manchez, he's not a Boy Scout." Erika tipped back her drink. "Jerry got himself in some bad business."

"Yeah."

"I'm sorry." She touched the bracelet on her wrist. "He gave me this. We had some good times."

The air in the bar was stifling him. Jonas rose and hesitated only a moment before he took out another bill and set it next to her drink. "Thanks."

Erika folded the bill as carefully as the first. *"De nada."*

She'd wanted him to be home. When Liz found the house empty, she made a fist over the keys in her hand and swore in frustration. She couldn't sit still; her nerves had been building all during the drive home. Outside, Moralas's evening shift was taking over.

For how long? she wondered. How long would the police sit patiently outside her house and follow her through her daily routine? In her bedroom, Liz closed the canvas bag of papers and cash in her desk. She regretted not having a lock for it, as well. Sooner or later, she thought, Moralas would back off on the protection. Then where would she be? Liz looked down at the key again. She'd be alone, she told herself bluntly. She had to do something.

On impulse, she started into her daughter's room. Perhaps Jerry had left a case, a box of some kind that the police had overlooked. Systematically she searched Faith's closet. When she found the little teddy bear with the worn ear, she brought it down from the shelf. She'd bought it for Faith before she'd been born. It was a vivid shade of purple, or had been so many years before. Now it was faded a bit, a little loose at the seams. The ear had been worn down to a nub because Faith had always carried him by it. They'd never named it, Liz recalled. Faith had merely called it *mine* and been satisfied.

On a wave of loneliness that rocked her, Liz buried her face against the faded purple pile. "Oh, I miss you, baby," she murmured. "I don't know if I can stand it."

"Liz?"

On a gasp of surprise, Liz stumbled back against the closet door. When she saw Jonas, she put the bear behind her back. "I didn't hear you come in," she said, feeling foolish.

"You were busy." He came toward her to gently pry the bear from her fingers. "He looks well loved."

"He's old." She cleared her throat and took the toy back again. But she found it impossible to stick it back on the top shelf. "I keep meaning to sew up the seams before the stuffing falls out." She set the bear down on Faith's dresser. "You've been out."

"Yes." He'd debated telling her of his meeting with Erika, and had decided to keep what he'd learned to himself, at least for now. "You're home early."

"I found something." Liz reached in her pocket and drew out her keys. "This isn't mine."

Jonas frowned at the key she indicated. "I don't know what you mean."

"I mean this isn't my key, and I don't know how it got on my ring."

"You just found it today?"

"I found it today, but it could have been put on anytime. I don't think I would've noticed." With the vain hope of distancing herself, Liz unhooked it from the others and handed it to Jonas. "I keep these in a drawer at the shop when I'm there. At home, I usually toss them on the kitchen counter. I can't think of any reason for someone to put it with mine unless they wanted to hide it."

Jonas examined the key. "'The Purloined Letter,'" he murmured.

"What?"

"It was one of Jerry's favorite stories when we were kids. I remember when he tested out the theory by putting a book he'd bought for my father for Christmas on the shelf in the library."

"So do you think it was his?"

"I think it would be just his style."

Liz picked up the bear again, finding it comforted her. "It doesn't do much good to have a key when you don't have the lock."

"It shouldn't be hard to find it." He held the key up by the stem. "Do you know what it is?"

"A key." Liz sat on Faith's bed. No, she hadn't distanced herself. The quicksand was bubbling again.

"To a safe-deposit box." Jonas turned it over to read the numbers etched into the metal.

"Do you think Captain Moralas can trace it?"

"Eventually," Jonas murmured. The key was warm in his hand. It was the next step, he thought. It had to be. "But I'm not telling him about it."

"Why?"

"Because he'd want it, and I don't intend to give it to him until I open the lock myself."

She recognized the look easily enough now. It was still revenge. Leaving the bear on her daughter's bed, Liz rose. "What are you going to do, go from bank to bank and ask if you can try the key out? You won't have to call the police, they will."

"I've got some connections—and I've got the serial number." Jonas pocketed the key. "With luck, I'll have the name of the bank by tomorrow afternoon. You may have to take a couple of days off."

"I can't take a couple of days off, and if I could, why should I need to?"

"We're going to Acapulco."

She started to make some caustic comment, then stopped. "Because Jerry told Erika he'd had business there?"

"If Jerry was mixed up in something, and he had something important or valuable, he'd tuck it away. A safe-deposit box in Acapulco makes sense."

"Fine. If that's what you believe, have a nice trip." She started to brush past him. Jonas only had to shift his body to bar the door.

"We go together."

The word "together" brought back her thoughts on couples and comfort. And it made her remember her conclusion about Jonas. "Look, Jonas, I can't drop everything and follow you on some wild-goose chase. Acapulco is very cosmopolitan. You won't need an interpreter."

"The key was on your ring. The knife was at your throat. I want you where I can see you."

"Concerned?" Her face hardened, muscle by muscle. "You're not concerned with me, Jonas. And you're certainly not concerned *about* me. The only thing you care about is your revenge. I don't want any part of it, or you."

He took her by the shoulders until she was backed against the door. "We both know that's not true. We've started something." His gaze skimmed down, lingered on her lips. "And it's not going to stop until we're both finished with it."

"I don't know what you're talking about."

"Yes, you do." He pressed closer so that their bodies met and strained, one against the other. He pressed closer to prove something, perhaps only to himself. "Yes, you do," he repeated. "I came here to do something, and I intend to do it. I don't give a damn if you call it revenge."

Her heart was beating lightly at her throat. She wouldn't call it fear. But his eyes were cold and close. "What else?"

"Justice."

She felt an uncomfortable twinge, remembering her own feelings on justice. "You're not using your law books, Jonas."

"Law doesn't always equal justice. I'm going to find out what happened to my brother and why." He skimmed his hand over her face and tangled his fingers in her hair. He didn't find silk and satin, but a woman of strength. "But there's more now. I look at you and I want you." He reached out, taking her face in his hand so that she had no choice but to look directly at him. "I hold you and I forget what I have to do. Damn it, you're in my way."

At the end of the words, his mouth was crushed hard on hers. He hadn't meant to. He hadn't had a choice. Before he'd been gentle with her because the look in her eyes requested it. Now he was rough, desperate, because the power of his own needs demanded it.

He frightened her. She'd never known fear could be a source of exhilaration. As her heart pounded in her throat, she let him pull her closer, still closer to the edge. He dared her to jump off, to let herself tumble down into the unknown. To risk.

His mouth drew desperately from hers, seeking passion, seeking submission, seeking strength. He wanted it all. He wanted it mindlessly from her. His hands were reaching for her as if they'd always done so. When he found her, she stiffened, resisted, then melted so quickly that it was nearly impossible to tell one mood from the next. She smelled of the sea and tasted of innocence, a combination of mystery and sweetness that drove him mad.

Forgetting everything but her, he drew her toward the bed and fulfillment.

"No." Liz pushed against him, fighting to bring herself back. They were in her daughter's room. "Jonas, this is wrong."

He took her by the shoulders. "Damn it, it may be the only thing that's right."

She shook her head, and though unsteady, backed away. His eyes weren't cold now. A woman might dream of having a man look at her with such fire and need. A woman might toss all caution aside if only to have a man want her with such turbulent desire. She couldn't.

"Not for me. I don't want this, Jonas." She reached up to push back her hair. "I don't want to feel like this."

He took her hand before she could back away. His head was swimming. There had been no other time, no other place, no other woman that had come together to make him ache. "Why?"

"I don't make the same mistake twice."

"This is now, Liz."

"And it's my life." She took a long, cleansing breath and found she could face him squarely. "I'll go with you to

Acapulco because the sooner you have what you want, the sooner you'll go." She gripped her hands together tightly, the only outward sign that she was fighting herself. "You know Moralas will have us followed."

He had his own battles to fight. "I'll deal with that."

Liz nodded because she was sure he would. "Do what you have to do. I'll make arrangements for Luis to take over the shop for a day or two."

When she left him alone, Jonas closed his hands over the key again. It would open a lock, he thought. But there was another lock that mystified and frustrated him. Idly, he picked up the bear Liz had left on the bed. He looked from it to the key in his hand. Somehow he'd have to find a way to bring them together.

6

Acapulco wasn't the Mexico Liz understood and loved. It wasn't the Mexico she'd fled to a decade before, nor where she'd made her home. It was sophisticated and ultra modern with spiraling high-rise hotels crowded together and gleaming in tropical sunlight. It was swimming pools and trendy shops. Perhaps it was the oldest resort in Mexico, and boasted countless restaurants and nightclubs, but Liz preferred the quietly rural atmosphere of her own island.

Still she had to admit there was something awesome about the city, cupped in the mountains and kissed by a magnificent bay. She'd lived all her life in flat land, from Houston to Cozumel. The mountains made everything else seem smaller, and somehow protected. Over the water, colorful parachutes floated, allowing the adventurous a bird's-eye view and a stunning ride. She wondered fleetingly if skimming through the sky would be as liberating as skimming through the water.

The streets were crowded and noisy, exciting in their own way. It occurred to her that she'd seen more people in the hour since they'd landed at the airport than she might in a week on

Cozumel. Liz stepped out of the cab and wondered if she'd have time to check out any of the dive shops.

Jonas had chosen the hotel methodically. It was luxuriously expensive—just Jerry's style. The villas overlooked the Pacific and were built directly into the mountainside. Jonas took a suite, pocketed the key and left the luggage to the bellman.

"We'll go to the bank now." It had taken him two days to match the key with a name. He wasn't going to waste any more time.

Liz followed him out onto the street. True, she hadn't come to enjoy herself, but a look at their rooms and a bite of lunch didn't seem so much to ask. Jonas was already climbing into a cab. "I don't suppose you'd considered making that a request."

He gave her a brief look as she slammed the cab door. "No." After giving the driver their direction, Jonas settled back. He could understand Jerry drifting to Acapulco, with its jet-set flavor, frantic nightlife and touches of luxury. When Jerry landed in a place for more than a day, it was a city that had the atmosphere of New York, London, Chicago. Jerry had never been interested in the rustic, serene atmosphere of a spot like Cozumel. So since he'd gone there, stayed there, he'd had a purpose. In Acapulco, Jonas would find out what it was.

As to the woman beside him, he didn't have a clue. Was she caught up in the circumstances formed before they'd ever met, or was he dragging her in deeper than he had a right to? She sat beside him, silent and a little sulky. Probably thinking about her shop, Jonas decided, and wished he could send her safely back to it. He wished he could turn around, go back to the villa and make love with her until they were both sated.

She shouldn't have appealed to him at all. She wasn't witty, flawlessly polished or classically beautiful. But she did appeal to him, so much so that he was spending his nights awake and restless, and his days on the edge of frustration. He wanted her, wanted to fully explore the tastes of passion she'd given him. He wanted to arouse her until she couldn't think of accounts or customers or schedules. Perhaps it was a matter of wielding power—he could no longer be sure. But mostly, inexplicably, he wanted to erase the memory of how she'd looked when he'd walked into her daughter's room and found her clutching a stuffed bear.

When the cab rolled up in front of the bank, Liz stepped out on the curb without a word. There were shops across the streets, boutiques where she could see bright, wonderful dresses on cleverly posed mannequins. Even with the distance, she caught the gleam and glimmer of jewelry. A limousine rolled by, with smoked glass windows and quiet engine. Liz looked beyond the tall, glossy buildings to the mountains, and space.

"I suppose this is the sort of place that appeals to you."

He'd watched her survey. She didn't have to speak for him to understand that she'd compared Acapulco with her corner of Mexico and found Acapulco lacking. "Under certain circumstances." Taking her arm, Jonas led her inside.

The bank was, as banks should be, quiet and sedate. Clerks wore neat suits and polite smiles. What conversation there was, was carried on in murmurs. Jerry, he thought, had always preferred the ultraconservative in storing his money, just as he'd preferred the wild in spending it. Without hesitation, Jonas strolled over to the most attractive teller. "Good afternoon."

She glanced up. It only took a second for her polite smile to brighten. "Mr. Sharpe, *Buenos días.* It's nice to see you again."

Beside him, Liz stiffened. He's been here before, she thought. Why hadn't he told her? She sent a long, probing look his way. Just what game was he playing?

"It's nice to see you." He leaned against the counter, urbane and, she noted, flirtatious. The little tug of jealousy was as unexpected as it was unwanted. "I wondered if you'd remember me."

The teller blushed before she glanced cautiously toward her supervisor. "Of course. How can I help you today?"

Jonas took the key out of his pocket. "I'd like to get into my box." He simply turned and stopped Liz with a look when she started to speak.

"I'll arrange that for you right away." The teller took a form, dated it and passed it to Jonas. "If you'll just sign here."

Jonas took her pen and casually dashed off a signature. Liz read: *Jeremiah C. Sharpe.* Though she looked up quickly, Jonas was smiling at the teller. Because her supervisor was hovering nearby, the teller stuck to procedure and checked the signature against the card in the files. They matched perfectly.

"This way, Mr. Sharpe."

"Isn't that illegal?" Liz murmured as the teller led them from the main lobby.

"Yes." Jonas gestured for her to precede him through the doorway.

"And does it make me an accessory?"

He smiled at her, waiting while the teller drew the long metal box from its slot. "Yes. If there's any trouble, I'll recommend a good lawyer."

"Great. All I need's another lawyer."

"You can use this booth, Mr. Sharpe. Just ring when you're finished."

"Thanks." Jonas nudged Liz inside, shut, then locked, the door. "How did you know?"

"Know what?" Jonas set the box on a table.

"To go to that clerk? When she first spoke to you, I thought you'd been here before."

"There were three men and two women. The other woman

was into her fifties. As far as Jerry would've been concerned, there would have been only one clerk there."

That line of thinking was clear enough, but his actions weren't. "You signed his name perfectly."

Key in hand, Jonas looked at her. "He was part of me. If we were in the same room, I could have told you what he was thinking. Writing his name is as easy as writing my own."

"And was it the same for him?"

It could still hurt, quickly and unexpectedly. "Yes, it was the same for him."

But Liz remembered Jerry's good-natured description of his brother as a stuffed shirt. The man Liz was beginning to know didn't fit. "I wonder if you understood each other as well as both of you thought." She looked down at the box again. None of her business, she thought, and wished it were as true as she'd once believed. "I guess you'd better open it."

He slipped the key into the lock, then turned it soundlessly. When he drew back the lid, Liz could only stare. She'd never seen so much money in her life. It sat in neat stacks, tidily banded, crisply American. Unable to resist, Liz reached out to touch.

"God, it looks like thousands." She swallowed. "Hundreds of thousands."

His face expressionless, Jonas flipped through the stacks. The booth became as quiet as a tomb. "Roughly three hundred thousand, in twenties and fifties."

"Do you think he stole it?" she murmured, too overwhelmed to notice Jonas's hands tighten on the money. "This must be the money the man who broke into my house wanted."

"I'm sure it is." Jonas set down a stack of bills and picked up a small bag. "But he didn't steal it." He forced his emotions to freeze. "I'm afraid he earned it."

"How?" she demanded. "No one earns this kind of money

in a matter of days, and I'd swear Jerry was nearly broke when I hired him. I know Luis lent him ten thousand pesos before his first paycheck."

"I'm sure he was." He didn't bother to add that he'd wired his brother two hundred before Jerry had left New Orleans. Carefully, Jonas reached under the stack of money and pulled out a small plastic bag, dipped in a finger and tasted. But he'd already known.

"What is that?"

His face expressionless, Jonas sealed the bag. He couldn't allow himself any more grief. "Cocaine."

Horrified, Liz stared at the bag. "I don't understand. He lived in my house. I'd have known if he were using drugs."

Jonas wondered if she realized just how innocent she was of the darker side of humanity. Until that moment, he hadn't fully realized just how intimate he was with it. "Maybe, maybe not. In any case, Jerry wasn't into this sort of thing. At least not for himself."

Liz sat down slowly. "You mean he sold it?"

"Dealt drugs?" Jonas nearly smiled. "No, that wouldn't have been exciting enough." In the corner of the box was a small black address book. Jonas took it out to leaf through it. "But smuggling," he murmured. "Jerry could have justified smuggling. Action, intrigue and fast money."

Her mind was whirling as she tried to focus back on the man she'd known so briefly. Liz had thought she'd understood him, categorized him, but he was more of a stranger now than when he'd been alive. It didn't seem to matter anymore who or what Jerry Sharpe had been. But the man in front of her mattered. "And you?" she asked. "Can you justify it?"

He glanced down at her, over the book in his hands. His eyes were cold, so cold that she could read nothing in them at all. Without answering, Jonas went back to the book.

"He'd listed initials, dates, times and some numbers. It looks as though he made five thousand a drop. Ten drops."

Liz glanced over at the money again. It no longer seemed crisp and neat but ugly and ill used. "That only makes fifty thousand. You said there was three hundred."

"That's right." Plus a bag of uncut cocaine with a hefty street value. Jonas took out his own book and copied down the pages from his brother's.

"What are we going to do with this?"

"Nothing."

"Nothing?" Liz rose again, certain she'd stepped into a dream. "Do you mean just leave it here? Just leave it here in this box and walk away?"

With the last of the numbers copied, Jonas replaced his brother's book. "Exactly."

"Why did we come if we're not going to do anything with it?"

He slipped his own book into his jacket. "To find it."

"Jonas." Before he could close the lid she had her hand on his wrist. "You have to take it to the police. To Captain Moralas."

In a deliberate gesture, he removed her hand, then picked up the bag of coke. She understood rejection and braced herself against it. But it wasn't rejection she saw in his face; it was fury. "You want to take this on the plane, Liz? Any idea on what the penalty is in Mexico for carrying controlled substances?"

"No."

"And you don't want to." He closed the lid, locked it. "For now, just forget you saw anything. I'll handle this in my own way."

"No."

His emotions were raw and tangled, his patience thin. "Don't push me, Liz."

"Push you?" Infuriated, she grabbed his shirtfront and planted her feet. "You've pushed me for days. Pushed me right into the middle of something that's so opposed to the way I've lived I can't even take it all in. Now that I'm over my head in drug smuggling and something like a quarter of a million dollars, you tell me to forget it. What do you expect me to do, go quietly back and rent tanks? Maybe you've finished using me now, Jonas, but I'm not ready to be brushed aside. There's a murderer out there who thinks I know where the money is." She stopped as her skin iced over. "And now I do."

"That's just it," Jonas said quietly. For the second time, he removed her hands, but this time he held on to her wrists. Frightened, he thought. He was sure her pulse beat with fear as well as anger. "Now you do. The best thing for you to do now is stay out of it, let them focus on me."

"Just how am I supposed to do that?"

The anger was bubbling closer, the anger he'd wanted to lock in the box with what had caused it. "Go to Houston, visit your daughter."

"How can I?" she demanded in a whisper that vibrated in the little room. "They might follow me." She looked down at the long, shiny box. "They would follow me. I won't risk my daughter's safety."

She was right, and because he knew it, Jonas wanted to rage. He was boxed in, trapped between love and loyalty and right and wrong. Justice and the law. "We'll talk to Moralas when we get back." He picked up the box again, hating it.

"Where are we going now?"

Jonas unlocked the door. "To get a drink."

★ ★ ★

Rather than going with Jonas to the lounge, Liz took some time for herself. Because she felt he owed her, she went into the hotel's boutique, found a simple one-piece bathing suit and charged it to the room. She hadn't packed anything but a change of clothes and toiletries. If she was stuck in Acapulco for the rest of the evening, she was going to enjoy the private pool each villa boasted.

The first time she walked into the suite, she was dumb-founded. Her parents had been reasonably successful, and she'd been raised in a quietly middle-class atmosphere. Nothing had prepared her for the sumptuousness of the two-bedroom suite overlooking the Pacific. Her feet sank cozily into the carpet. Softly colored paintings were spaced along ivory-papered walls. The sofa, done in grays and greens and blues, was big enough for two to sprawl on for a lazy af-ternoon nap.

She found a phone in the bathroom next to a tub so wide and deep that she was almost tempted to take her dip there. The sink was a seashell done in the palest of pinks.

So this is how the rich play, she mused as she wandered to the bedroom where her overnight bag was set at the end of a bed big enough for three. The drapes of her balcony were open so that she could see the tempestuous surf of the Pacific hurl up and spray. She pulled the glass doors open, wanting the noise.

This was the sort of world Marcus had told her of so many years before. He'd made it seem like a fairy tale with gossamer edges. Liz had never seen his home, had never been permitted to, but he'd described it to her. The white pillars, the white balconies, the staircase that curved up and up. There were servants to bring you tea in the afternoons, a stable where grooms waited to saddle glossy horses. Champagne was drunk from French crystal. It had been a fairy tale, and she hadn't wanted it for herself. She had only wanted him.

A young girl's foolishness, Liz thought now. In her naive way, she'd made a prince out of a man who was weak and selfish and spoiled. But over the years she had thought of the house he'd talked of and pictured her daughter on those wide, curving stairs. That had been her sense of justice.

The image wasn't as clear now, not now that she'd seen wealth in a long metal box and understood where it had come from. Not when she'd seen Jonas's eyes when he'd spoken of his kind of justice. That hadn't been a fairy tale with gossamer edges, but grimly real. She had some thinking to do. But before she could plan for the rest of her life, and for her daughter's, she had to get through the moment.

Jonas. She was bound to him through no choice of her own. And perhaps he was bound to her in the same way. Was that the reason she was drawn to him? Because they were trapped in the same puzzle? If she could only explain it away, maybe she could stop the needs that kept swimming through her. If she could only explain it away, maybe she would be in control again.

But how could she explain the feelings she'd experienced on the silent cab ride back to the hotel? She had had to fight the desire to put her arms around him, to offer comfort when nothing in his manner had indicated he needed or wanted it. There were no easy answers—no answers at all to the fact that she was slowly, inevitably falling in love with him.

It was time to admit that, she decided, because you could never face anything until it was admitted. You could never solve anything until it was faced. She'd lived by that rule years before during the biggest crisis of her life. It still held true.

So she loved him, or very nearly loved him. She was no

longer naive enough to believe that love was the beginning of any answer. He would hurt her. There were no ifs about that. He'd steal from her the one thing she'd managed to hold fast to for ten years. And once he'd taken her heart, what would it mean to him? She shook her head. No more than such things ever mean to those who take them.

Jonas Sharpe was a man on a mission, and she was no more to him than a map. He was ruthless in his own patient way. When he had finished what he'd come to do, he would turn away from her, go back to his life in Philadelphia and never think of her again.

Some women, Liz thought, were doomed to pick the men who could hurt them the most. Making her mind a blank, Liz stripped and changed to her bathing suit. But Jonas, thoughts of Jonas, kept slipping through the barriers.

Maybe if she talked to Faith—if she could touch her greatest link with normality, things would snap back into focus. On impulse, Liz picked up the phone beside her bed and began the process of placing the call. Faith would just be home from school, Liz calculated, growing more excited as she heard the clinks and buzzes on the receiver. When the phone began to ring, she sat on the bed. She was already smiling.

"Hello?"

"Mom?" Liz felt the twin surges of pleasure and guilt as she heard her mother's voice. "It's Liz."

"Liz!" Rose Palmer felt identical surges. "We didn't expect to hear from you. Your last letter just came this morning. Nothing's wrong, is it?"

"No, no, nothing's wrong." Everything's wrong. "I just wanted to talk to Faith."

"Oh, Liz, I'm so sorry. Faith's not here. She has her piano lesson today."

The letdown came, but she braced herself against it. "I forgot." Tears threatened, but she forced them back. "She likes the lessons, doesn't she?"

"She loves them. You should hear her play. Remember when you were taking them?"

"I had ten thumbs." She managed to smile. "I wanted to thank you for sending the pictures. She looks so grown up. Momma, is she…looking forward to coming back?"

Rose heard the need, felt the ache. She wished, not for the first time, that her daughter was close enough to hold. "She's marking off the days on her calendar. She bought you a present."

Liz had to swallow. "She did?"

"It's supposed to be a surprise, so don't tell her I told you."

"I won't." She dashed tears away, grateful she could keep her voice even. It hurt, but was also a comfort to be able to speak to someone who knew and understood Faith as she did. "I miss her. The last few weeks always seem the hardest."

Her voice wasn't as steady as she thought—and a mother hears what others don't. "Liz, why don't you come home? Spend the rest of the month here while she's in school?"

"No, I can't. How's Dad?"

Rose fretted impatiently at the change of subject, then subsided. She'd never known anyone as thoroughly stubborn as her daughter. Unless it was her granddaughter. "He's fine. Looking forward to coming down and doing some diving."

"We'll take one of the boats out—just the four of us. Tell Faith I…tell her I called," she finished lamely.

"Of course I will. Why don't I have her call you back when she gets home? The car pool drops her off at five."

"No. No, I'm not home. I'm in Acapulco—on business." Liz let out a long breath to steady herself. "Just tell her I miss her and I'll be waiting at the airport. You know I appreciate everything you're doing. I just—"

"Liz." Rose interrupted gently. "We love Faith. And we love you."

"I know." Liz pressed her fingers to her eyes. She did know, but was never quite sure what to do about it. "I love you, too. It's just that sometimes things get so mixed up."

"Are you all right?"

She dropped her hand again, and her eyes were dry. "I will be when you get there. Tell Faith I'm marking off the days too."

"I will."

"Bye, Momma."

She hung up and sat until the churning emptiness had run its course. If she'd had more confidence in her parents' support, more trust in their love, would she have fled the States and started a new life on her own? Liz dragged a hand through her hair. She'd never be sure of that, nor could she dwell on it. She'd burned her own bridges. The only thing that was important was Faith, and her happiness.

An hour later, Jonas found her at the pool. She swam laps in long, smooth strokes, her body limber. She seemed tireless, and oddly suited to the private luxury. Her suit was a flashy red, but the cut so simple that it relied strictly on the form it covered for style.

He counted twenty laps before she stopped, and wondered how many she'd completed before he'd come down. It seemed to him as if she swam to drain herself of some tension or sorrow, and that with each lap she'd come closer to succeeding. Waiting, he watched her tip her head back in the water so that her hair slicked back. The marks on her neck had faded. As she stood, water skimmed her thigh.

"I've never seen you relaxed," Jonas commented. But even as he said the words, he could see her muscles tense again. She turned away from her contemplation of the mountains and looked at him.

He was tired, she realized, and wondered if she should have seen it before. There was a weariness around his eyes that hadn't been there that morning. He hadn't changed his clothes, and had his hands tucked into the pockets of bone-colored slacks. She wondered if he'd been up to the suite at all.

"I didn't bring a suit with me." Liz pushed against the side of the pool and hitched herself out. Water rained from her. "I charged this one to the room."

The thighs were cut nearly to the waist. Jonas caught himself wondering just how the skin would feel there. "It's nice."

Liz picked up her towel. "It was expensive."

He only lifted a brow. "I could deduct it from the rent."

Her lips curved a little as she rubbed her hair dry. "No, you can't. But since you're a lawyer, I imagine you can find a way to deduct it from something else. I saved the receipt."

He hadn't thought he could laugh. "I appreciate it. You know, I get the impression you don't think much of lawyers."

Something came and went in her eyes. "I try not to think of them at all."

Taking the towel from her, he gently dried her face. "Faith's father's a lawyer?"

Without moving, she seemed to shift away from him. "Leave it alone, Jonas."

"You don't."

"Actually I do, most of the time. Maybe it's been on my mind the past few weeks, but that's my concern."

He draped the towel around her shoulders and, holding the ends, drew her closer. "I'd like you to tell me about it."

It was his voice, she thought, so calm, so persuasive, that nearly had her opening both mind and heart. She could almost believe as she looked at him that he really wanted to know, to understand. The part of her that was already in love with him needed to believe he might care. "Why?"

"I don't know. Maybe it's that look that comes into your eyes. It makes a man want to stroke it away."

Her chin came up a fraction. "There's no need to feel sorry for me."

"I don't think sympathy's the right word." Abruptly weary, he dropped his forehead to hers. He was tired of fighting demons, of trying to find answers. "Damn."

Uncertain, she stood very still. "Are you all right?"

"No. No, I'm not." He moved away from her to walk to the end of the path where a plot of tiny orange flowers poked up through white gravel. "A lot of things you said today were true. A lot of things you've said all along are true. I can't do anything about them."

"I don't know what you want me to say now."

"Nothing." Hideously tired, he ran both hands over his face. "I'm trying to live with the fact that my brother's dead, and that he was murdered because he decided to make some easy money drug-trafficking. He had a good brain, but he always chose to use it in the wrong way. Every time I look in the mirror, I wonder why."

Liz was beside him before she could cut off her feelings. He hurt. It was the first time she'd seen below the surface to the pain. She knew what it was like to live with pain. "He was different, Jonas. I don't think he was bad, just weak. Mourning him is one thing—blaming yourself for what he did, or for what happened to him, is another."

He hadn't known he needed comfort, but her hand resting

on him had something inside him slowly uncurling. "I was the only one who could reach him, keep him on some kind of level. There came a point where I just got tired of running both our lives."

"Do you really believe you could have prevented him from doing what he did?"

"Maybe. That's something else I have to live with."

"Just a minute." She took his shirtfront in much the same way she had that afternoon. There was no sympathy now, but annoyance on her face. He hadn't known he needed that, as well. "You were brothers, twins, but you were separate people. Jerry wasn't a child to be guided and supervised. He was a grown man who made his decisions."

"That's the trouble. Jerry never grew up."

"And you did," she tossed back. "Are you going to punish yourself for it?"

He'd been doing just that, Jonas realized. He'd gone home, buried his brother, comforted his parents and blamed himself for not preventing something he knew in his heart had been inevitable. "I have to find out who killed him, Liz. I can't set the rest aside until I do."

"We'll find them." On impulse, she pressed her cheek to his. Sometimes the slightest human contact could wash away acres of pain. "Then it'll be over."

He wasn't sure he wanted it to be, not all of it. He ran a hand down her arm, needing the touch of her skin. He found it chilled. "The sun's gone down." He wrapped the towel around her in a gesture that would have been mere politeness with another woman. With Liz, it was for protection. "You'd better get out of that wet suit. We'll have dinner."

"Here?"

"Sure. The restaurant's supposed to be one of the best."

Liz thought of the elegance of their suite and the contents of her overnight bag. "I didn't bring anything to wear."

He laughed and swung an arm around her. It was the first purely frivolous thing he'd heard her say. "Charge something else."

"But—"

"Don't worry, I've got the best crooked accountant in Philadelphia."

7

Because she'd been certain she would never sleep away from home, in a hotel bed, Liz was surprised to wake to full sunlight. Not only had she slept, she realized, she'd slept like a rock for eight hours and was rested and ready to go. True, it was just a little past six, and she had no business to run, but her body was tuned to wake at that hour. A trip to Acapulco didn't change that.

It had changed other things, she reminded herself as she stretched out in the too-big bed. Because of it, she'd become inescapably tangled in murder and smuggling. Putting the words together made her shake her head. In a movie, she might have enjoyed watching the melodrama. In a book, she'd have turned the page to read more. But in her own life, she preferred the more mundane. Liz was too practical to delude herself into believing she could distance herself from any part of the puzzle any longer. For better or worse, she was personally involved in this melodrama. That included Jonas Sharpe. The only question now was which course of action to take.

She couldn't run. That had never been a choice. Liz had already concluded she couldn't hide behind Moralas and his men forever. Sooner or later the man with the knife would come back, or another man more determined or more desperate. She wouldn't escape a second time. The moment she'd looked into the safe-deposit box, she'd become a full-fledged player in the game. Which brought her back full circle to Jonas. She had no choice but to put her trust in him now. If he were to give up on his brother's murder and return to Philadelphia she would be that much more alone. However much she might wish it otherwise, Liz needed him just as much as he needed her.

Other things had changed, she thought. Her feelings for him were even more undefined and confusing than they had started out to be. Seeing him as she had the evening before, hurt and vulnerable, had touched off more than impersonal sympathy or physical attraction. It had made her feel a kinship, and the kinship urged her to help him, not only for her own welfare, but for his. He suffered, for his brother's loss, but also for what his brother had done. She'd loved once, and had suffered, not only because of loss but because of disillusionment.

A lifetime ago? Liz wondered. Did we ever really escape from one lifetime to another? It seemed years could pass, circumstances could change, but we carried our baggage with us through each phase. If anything, with each phase we had to carry a bit more. There was little use in thinking, she told herself as she climbed from the bed. From this point on, she had little choice but to act.

Jonas heard her the moment she got up. He'd been awake since five, restless and prowling. For over an hour he'd been racking his brain and searching his conscience for a way to ease Liz out of a situation his brother, and he himself had locked her into. He'd already thought of several ways to draw attention away from her to himself, but that wouldn't guarantee Liz's safety. She wouldn't go to Houston, and he understood her feelings about endangering her daughter in any way.

As the days passed, he felt he was coming to understand her better and better. She was a loner, but only because she saw it as the safest route. She was a businesswoman, but only because she looked to her daughter's welfare first. Inside, he thought, she was a woman with dreams on hold and love held in bondage. She had steered both toward her child and denied herself. And, Jonas added, she'd convinced herself she was content.

That was something else he understood, because until a few weeks before he had also convinced himself he was content. It was only now, after he'd had the opportunity to look at his life from a distance that he realized he had merely been drifting. Perhaps, when the outward trimmings were stripped away, he hadn't been so different from his brother. For both of them, success had been the main target, they had simply aimed for it differently. Though Jonas had a steady job, a home of his own, there had never been an important woman. He'd put his career first. Jonas wasn't certain he'd be able to do so again. It had taken the loss of his brother to make him realize he needed something more, something solid. Exploring the law was only a job. Winning cases was only a transitory satisfaction. Perhaps he'd known it for some time. After all, he'd bought the old house in Chadd's Ford to give himself something permanent. When had he started thinking about sharing it?

Still, thinking about his own life didn't solve the problem of Liz Palmer and what he was going to do with her. She couldn't go to Houston, he thought again, but there were other places she could go until he could assure her that her life could settle back the way she wanted it. His parents were his first thought, and the quiet country home they'd retired to in Lancaster. If he could find a way to slip her out of Mexico, she would be safe there. It would even be possible to have her daughter join her. Then his conscience would ease. Jonas had no doubt that his parents would accept them both, then dote on them.

Once he'd done what he'd come to do, he could go to Lancaster himself. He'd like to see Liz there, in surroundings he was used to. He wanted time to talk with her about simple things. He wanted to hear her laugh again, as she had only once in all the days he'd known her. Once they were there, away from the ugliness, he might understand his feelings better. Perhaps by then he'd be able to analyze what had happened inside him when she'd pressed her cheek against his and had offered unconditional support.

He'd wanted to hold on to her, to just hold on and the hell with the world. There was something about her that made him think of lazy evenings on cool porches and long Sunday afternoon walks. He couldn't say why. In Philadelphia he rarely took time for such things. Even socializing had become business. And he'd seen for himself that she never gave herself an idle hour. Why should he, a man dedicated to his work, think of lazing days away with a woman obsessed by hers?

She remained a mystery to him, and perhaps that was an answer in itself. If he thought of her too often, too deeply, it was only because while his understanding was growing, he still knew so little. If it sometimes seemed that discovering Liz Palmer was just as important as discovering his brother's killer, it was only because they were tied together. How could he take his mind off one without taking his mind off the other? Yet when he thought of her now, he thought of her stretched out on his mother's porch swing, safe, content and waiting for him.

Annoyed with himself, Jonas checked his watch. It was after nine on the East Coast. He'd call his office, he thought. A few legal problems might clear his mind. He'd no more than picked up the receiver when Liz came out from her bedroom.

"I didn't know you were up," she said, and fiddled nervously with her belt. Odd, she felt entirely different about sharing the plush little villa with him than she did her home. After all, she reasoned, at home he was paying rent.

"I thought you'd sleep longer." He replaced the receiver again. The office could wait.

"I never sleep much past six." Feeling awkward, she wandered to the wide picture window. "Terrific view."

"Yes, it is."

"I haven't stayed in a hotel in…in years," she finished. "When I came to Cozumel, I worked in the same hotel where I'd stayed with my parents. It was an odd feeling. So's this."

"No urge to change the linen or stack the towels?"

When she chuckled, some of the awkwardness slipped away. "No, not even a twinge."

"Liz, when we're finished with all this, when it's behind us, will you talk to me about that part of your life?"

She turned to him, away from the window, but they both felt the distance. "When we're finished with this, there won't be any reason to."

He rose and came to her. In a gesture that took her completely by surprise, he took both of her hands. He lifted one, then the other, to his lips and watched her eyes cloud. "I can't be sure of that," he murmured. "Can you?"

She couldn't be sure of anything when his voice was quiet, his hands gentle. For a moment, she simply absorbed the feeling of being a woman cared for by a man. Then she stepped back, as she knew she had to. "Jonas, you told me once we had the same problem. I didn't want to believe it then, but it was true. It is true. Once that problem is solved, there really isn't anything else between us. Your life and mine are separated by a lot more than miles."

He thought of his house and his sudden need to share it. "They don't have to be."

"There was a time I might have believed that."

"You're living in the past." He took her shoulders, but this time his hands weren't as gentle. "You're fighting ghosts."

"I may have my ghosts, but I don't live in the past. I can't afford to." She put her hands to his wrists, but let them lie there only a moment before she let go. "I can't afford to pretend to myself about you."

He wanted to demand, he wanted to pull her with him to the sofa and prove to her that she was wrong. He resisted. It wasn't the first time he'd used courtroom skill, courtroom tactics, to win on a personal level. "We'll leave it your way for now," he said easily. "But the case isn't closed. Are you hungry?"

Unsure whether she should be uneasy or relieved, Liz nodded. "A little."

"Let's have breakfast. We've got plenty of time before the plane leaves."

She didn't trust him. Though Jonas kept the conversation light and passionless throughout breakfast, Liz kept herself braced for a countermove. He was a clever man, she knew. He was a man, she was certain, who made sure he got his own way no matter how long it took. Liz considered herself a woman strong enough to keep promises made, even when they were to herself. No man, not even Jonas, was going to make her change the course she'd set ten years before. There was only room enough for two loves in her life. Faith and her work.

"I can't get used to eating something at this hour of the morning that's going to singe my stomach lining."

Liz swallowed the mixture of peppers, onions and eggs. "Mine's flame resistant. You should try my chili."

"Does that mean you're offering to cook for me?"

When Liz glanced up she wished he hadn't been smiling at her in just that way. "I suppose I could make enough for two as easily as enough for one. But you don't seem to have any trouble in the kitchen."

"Oh, I can cook. It's just that once I've finished, it never seems worth the bother." He leaned forward to run a finger down her hand from wrist to knuckle. "Tell you what—I'll buy the supplies and even clean up the mess if you handle the chili."

Though she smiled, Liz drew her hand away. "The question is, can you handle the chili? It might burn right through a soft lawyer's stomach."

Appreciating the challenge, he took her hand again. "Why don't we find out? Tonight."

"All right." She flexed her fingers, but he merely linked his with them. "I can't eat if you have my hand."

He glanced down. "You have another one."

He made her laugh when she'd been set to insist. "I'm entitled to two."

"I'll give it back. Later."

"Hey, Jerry!"

The easy smile on Jonas's face froze. Only his eyes changed, locking on to Liz's, warning and demanding. His hand remained on hers, but the grip tightened. The message was very clear—she was to do nothing, say nothing until he'd tallied the odds. He turned, flashing a new smile. Liz's stomach trembled. It was Jerry's smile, she realized. Not Jonas's.

"Why didn't you tell me you were back in town?" A tall, tanned man with sandy blond hair and a trim beard dropped a hand on Jonas's shoulder. Liz caught the glint of a diamond on his finger. He was young, she thought, determined to store everything she could, barely into his thirties, and dressed with slick, trendy casualness.

"Quick trip," Jonas said as, like Liz, he took in every detail. "Little business…" He cast a meaningful glance toward Liz. "Little pleasure."

The man turned and stared appreciatively at Liz. "Is there any other way?"

Thinking fast, Liz offered her hand. "Hello. Since Jerry's too rude to introduce us, we'll have to do it ourselves. I'm Liz Palmer."

"David Merriworth." He took her hand between both of his. They were smooth and uncallused. "Jerry might have trouble with manners, but he's got great taste."

She smiled, hoping she did it properly. "Thank you."

"Pull up a chair, Merriworth." Jonas took out a cigarette. "As long as you keep your hands off my lady." He said it in the good-natured, only-kidding tone Jerry had inevitably used, but his eyes were Jonas's, warning her to tread carefully.

"Wouldn't mind a quick cup of coffee." David pulled over a chair after he checked his watch. "Got a breakfast meeting in a few minutes. So how are things on Cozumel?" He inclined his head ever so slightly. "Getting in plenty of diving?"

Jonas allowed his lips to curve and kept his eyes steady. "Enough."

"Glad to hear it. I was going to check in with you myself, but I've been in the States for a couple weeks. Just got back in last night." He used two sugars after the waiter set a fresh cup of coffee beside him. "Business is good, buddy. Real good."

"What business are you in, Mr. Merriworth?"

He gave Liz a big grin before he winked at Jonas. "Sales, sweetheart. Imports, you might say."

"Really." Because her throat was dry she drank more coffee. "It must be fascinating."

"It has its moments." He turned in his chair so that he could study her face. "So where did Jerry find you?"

"On Cozumel." She sent Jonas a steady look. "We're partners."

David lowered his cup. "That so?"

They were in too deep, Jonas thought, for him to contradict her. "That's so," he agreed.

David picked up his cup again with a shrug. "If it's okay with the boss, it doesn't bother me."

"I do things my way," Jonas drawled. "Or I don't do them."

Amused, and perhaps admiring, David broke into a smile. "That never changes. Look, I've been out of touch for a few weeks. The drops still going smooth?"

With those words, Jonas's last hopes died. What he'd found in the safe-deposit box had been real, and it had been Jerry's. He buttered a roll as though he had all the time in the world. Beneath the table, Liz touched his leg once, hoping he'd take it as comfort. He never looked at her. "Why shouldn't they?"

"It's the classiest operation I've ever come across," David commented, taking a cautious glance around to other tables. "Wouldn't like to see anything screw it up."

"You worry too much."

"You're the one who should worry," David pointed out. "I don't have to deal with Manchez. You weren't around last year when he took care of those two Colombians. I was. You deal with supplies, I stick with sales. I sleep better."

"I just dive," Jonas said, and tapped out his cigarette. "And I sleep fine."

"He's something, isn't he?" David sent Liz another grin. "I knew Jerry here was just the man the boss was looking for. You keep diving, kid." He tipped his cup at Jonas. "It makes me look good."

"Sounds like you two have known each other for a while,"

Liz said with a smile. Under the table, she twisted the napkin in her lap.

"Go way back, don't we, Jer?"

"Yeah. We go back."

"First time we hooked up was six, no, seven years ago. We were working a pigeon drop in L.A. We'd have had that twenty thousand out of that old lady if her daughter hadn't caught on." He took out a slim cigarette case. "Your brother got you out of that one, didn't he? The East Coast lawyer."

"Yeah." Jonas remembered posting the bond and pulling the strings.

"Now I've been working out of here for almost five. A real businessman." He slapped Jonas's arm. "Hell of a lot better than the pigeon drop, huh, Jerry?"

"Pays better."

David let out a roar of laughter. "Why don't I show you two around Acapulco tonight?"

"Gotta get back." Jonas signaled for the check. "Business."

"Yeah, I know what you mean." He nodded toward the restaurant's entrance. "Here's my customer now. Next time you drop down, give a call."

"Sure."

"And give my best to old Clancy." With another laugh, David gave them each a quick salute. They watched him stride across the room and shake hands with a dark-suited man.

"Don't say anything here," Jonas murmured as he signed the breakfast check. "Let's go."

Liz's crumpled napkin slid to the floor as she rose to walk out with him. He didn't speak again until they had the door of the villa closed behind them.

"You had no business telling him we were partners."

Because she'd been ready for the attack, she shrugged it off. "He said more once I did."

"He'd have said just as much if you'd made an excuse and left the table."

She folded her arms. "We have the same problem, remember?"

He didn't care to have his own words tossed back at him. "The least you could have done was to give him another name."

"Why? They know who I am. Sooner or later he's going to talk to whoever's in charge and get the whole story."

She was right. He didn't care for that either. "Are you packed?"

"Yes."

"Then let's check out. We'll go to the airport."

"And then?"

"And then we go straight to Moralas."

"You've been very busy." Moralas held on to his temper as he rocked back in his chair. "Two of my men wasted their valuable time looking for you in Acapulco. You might have told me, Mr. Sharpe, that you planned to take Miss Palmer on a trip."

"I thought a police tail in Acapulco might be inconvenient."

"And now that you have finished your own investigation, you bring me this." He held up the key and examined it. "This which Miss Palmer discovered several days ago. As a lawyer, you must understand the phrase 'withholding evidence.'"

"Of course." Jonas nodded coolly. "But neither Miss Palmer nor myself could know the key was evidence. We speculated, naturally, that it might have belonged to my brother. Withholding a speculation is hardly a crime."

"Perhaps not, but it is poor judgment. Poor judgment often translates into an offense."

Jonas leaned back in his chair. If Moralas wanted to argue law, they'd argue law. "If the key belonged to my brother, as executor of his estate, it became mine. In any case, once it was proved to me that the key did indeed belong to Jerry, and that the contents of the safe-deposit box were evidence, I brought both the key and a description of the contents to you."

"Indeed. And do you also speculate as to how your brother came to possess those particular items?"

"Yes."

Moralas waited a beat, then turned to Liz. "And you, Miss Palmer—you also have your speculations?"

She had her hands gripped tightly in her lap, but her voice was matter-of-fact and reasonable. "I know that whoever attacked me wanted money, obviously a great deal of money. We found a great deal."

"And a bag of what Mr. Sharpe…speculates is cocaine." Moralas folded his hands on the desk with the key under them. "Miss Palmer, did you at any time see Mr. Jeremiah Sharpe in possession of cocaine?"

"No."

"Did he at any time speak to you of cocaine or drug-trafficking?"

"No, of course not. I would have told you."

"As you told me about the key?" When Jonas started to protest, Moralas waved him off. "I will need a list of your customers for the past six weeks, Miss Palmer. Names and, wherever possible, addresses."

"My customers? Why?"

"It's more than possible that Mr. Sharpe used your shop for his contacts."

"My shop." Outraged, she stood up. "My boats? Do you think he could have passed drugs under my nose without me being aware?"

Moralas took out a cigar and studied it. "I very much hope

you were unaware, Miss Palmer. You will bring me the list of clients by the end of the week." He glanced at Jonas. "Of course, you are within your rights to demand a warrant. It will simply slow down the process. And I, of course, am within my rights to hold Miss Palmer as a material witness."

Jonas watched the pale blue smoke circle toward the ceiling. It was tempting to call Moralas's bluff simply as an exercise in testing two ends of the law. And in doing so, he and the captain could play tug-of-war with Liz for hours. "There are times, Captain, when it's wiser not to employ certain rights. I think I'm safe in saying that the three of us in this room want basically the same thing." He rose and flicked his lighter at the end of Moralas's cigar. "You'll have your list, Captain. And more."

Moralas lifted his gaze and waited.

"Pablo Manchez," Jonas said, and was gratified to see Moralas's eyes narrow.

"What of Manchez?"

"He's on Cozumel. Or was," Jonas stated. "My brother met with him several times in local bars and clubs. You may also be interested in David Merriworth, an American working out of Acapulco. Apparently he's the one who put my brother onto his contacts in Cozumel. If you contact the authorities in the States, you'll find that Merriworth has an impressive rap sheet."

In his precise handwriting, Moralas noted down the names, though he wasn't likely to forget them. "I appreciate the information. However, in the future, Mr. Sharpe, I would appreciate it more if you stayed out of my way. *Buenas tardes,* Miss Palmer."

Moments later, Liz strode out to the street. "I don't like being threatened. That's what he was doing, wasn't it?" she demanded. "He was threatening to put me in jail."

Very calm, even a bit amused, Jonas lit a cigarette. "He was pointing out his options, and ours."

"He didn't threaten to put you in jail," Liz muttered.

"He doesn't worry as much about me as he does about you."

"Worry?" She stopped with her hand gripping the handle of Jonas's rented car.

"He's a good cop. You're one of his people."

She looked back toward the police station with a scowl. "He has a funny way of showing it." A scruffy little boy scooted up to the car and gallantly opened the door for her. Even as he prepared to hold out a hand, Liz was digging for a coin.

"Gracias."

He checked the coin, grinned at the amount and nodded approval. *"Buenas tardes, señorita."* Just as gallantly he closed the door for her while the coin disappeared into a pocket.

"It's a good thing you don't come into town often," Jonas commented.

"Why?"

"You'd be broke in a week."

Liz found a clip in her purse and pulled back her hair. "Because I gave a little boy twenty-five pesos?"

"How much did you give the other kid before we went in to Moralas?"

"I bought something from him."

"Yeah." Jonas swung away from the curb. "You look like a woman who can't go a day without a box of Chiclets."

"You're changing the subject."

"That's right. Now tell me where I can find the best place for buying ingredients for chili."

"You want me to cook for you tonight?"

"It'll keep your mind off the rest. We've done everything we can do for the moment," he added. "Tonight we're going to relax."

She would have liked to believe he was right. Between

nerves and anger, she was wound tight. "Cooking's supposed to relax me?"

"Eating is going to relax you. It's just an unavoidable circumstance that you have to cook it first."

It sounded so absurd that she subsided. "Turn left at the next corner. I tell you what to buy, you buy it, then you stay out of my way."

"Agreed."

"And you clean up."

"Absolutely."

"Pull over here," she directed. "And remember, you asked for it."

Liz never skimped when she cooked, even taking into account that authentic Mexican spices had more zing than the sort sold in the average American supermarket. She'd developed a taste for Mexican food and Yucatán specialties when she'd been a child, exploring the peninsula with her parents. She wasn't an elaborate cook, and when alone would often make do with a sandwich, but when her heart was in it, she could make a meal that would more than satisfy.

Perhaps, in a way, she wanted to impress him. Liz found she was able to admit it while she prepared a Mayan salad for chilling. It was probably very natural and harmless to want to impress someone with your cooking. After peeling and slicing an avocado, she found, oddly enough, she was relaxing.

So much of what she'd done in the past few days had been difficult or strange. It was a relief to make a decision no more vital than the proper way to slice her fruits and vegetables. In the end, she fussed with the arrangement a bit more, pleased with the contrasting colors of greens and oranges and cherry tomatoes. It was, she recalled, the only salad she could get Faith to eat because it was the only one Faith considered pretty enough. Liz didn't realize she was smiling as she began to sauté onions and peppers. She added a healthy dose of garlic and let it all simmer.

"It already smells good," Jonas commented as he strode through the doorway.

She only glanced over her shoulder. "You're supposed to stay out of my way."

"You cook, I take care of the table."

Liz only shrugged and turned back to the stove. She measured, stirred and spiced until the kitchen was filled with a riot of scent. The sauce, chunky with meat and vegetables, simmered and thickened on low heat. Pleased with herself, she wiped her hands on a cloth and turned around. Jonas was sitting comfortably at the table watching her.

"You look good," he told her. "Very good."

It seemed so natural, their being together in the kitchen with a pot simmering and a breeze easing its way through the screen. It made her remember how hard it was not to want such simple things in your life. Liz set the cloth down and found she didn't know what to do with her hands. "Some men think a woman looks best in front of a stove."

"I don't know. It's a toss-up with the way you looked at the wheel of a boat. How long does that have to cook?"

"About a half hour."

"Good." He rose and went to the counter where he'd left two bottles. "We have time for some wine."

A little warning signal jangled in her brain. Liz decided she needed a lid for the chili. "I don't have the right glasses."

"I already thought of that." From a bag beside the bottle, he pulled out two thin-stemmed wineglasses.

"You've been busy," she murmured.

"You didn't like me hovering over you in the market. I had to do something." He drew out the cork, then let the wine breathe.

"These candles aren't mine."

He turned to see Liz fiddling with the fringe of one of the woven mats he'd set on the table. In the center were two deep blue tapers that picked up the color in the border of her dishes.

"They're ours," Jonas told her.

She twisted the fringe around one finger, let it go, then twisted it again. The last time she'd burned candles had been during a power failure. These didn't look sturdy, but slender and frivolous. "There wasn't any need to go to all this trouble. I don't—"

"Do candles and wine make you uneasy?"

Dropping the fringe, she let her hands fall to her sides. "No, of course not."

"Good." He poured rich red wine into both glasses. Walking to her, he offered one. "Because I find them relaxing. We did agree to relax."

She sipped, and though she wanted to back away, held her ground. "I'm afraid you may be looking for more than I can give."

"No." He touched his glass to hers. "I'm looking for exactly what you can give."

Recognizing when she was out of her depth, Liz turned toward the refrigerator. "We can start on the salad."

He lit the candles and dimmed the lights. She told herself it didn't matter. Atmosphere was nothing more than a pleasant addition to a meal.

"Very pretty," Jonas told her when she'd mixed the dressing and arranged avocado slices. "What's it called?"

"It's a Mayan salad." Liz took the first nibble and was satisfied. "I learned the recipe when I worked at the hotel. Actually, that's where most of my cooking comes from."

"Wonderful," Jonas decided after the first bite. "It makes me wish I'd talked you into cooking before."

"A one time only." She relaxed enough to smile. "Meals aren't—"

"Included in the rent," Jonas finished. "We might negotiate."

This time she laughed at him and chose a section of grape-fruit. "I don't think so. How do you manage in Philadelphia?"

"I have a housekeeper who'll toss together a casserole on Wednesdays." He took another bite, enjoying the contrast of crisp greens and spicy dressing. "And I eat out a lot."

"And parties? I suppose you go to a lot of parties."

"Some business, some pleasure." He'd almost forgotten what it was like to sit in a kitchen and enjoy a simple meal. "To be honest, it wears a bit. The cruising."

"Cruising?"

"When Jerry and I were teenagers, we might hop in the car on a Friday night and cruise. The idea was to see what teenage girls had hopped in their cars to cruise. The party circuit's just adult cruising."

She frowned a bit because it didn't seem as glamorous as she'd imagined. "It seems rather aimless."

"Doesn't seem. Is."

"You don't appear to be a man who does anything without a purpose."

"I've had my share of aimless nights," he murmured. "You come to a point where you realize you don't want too many more." That was just it, he realized. It wasn't the work, the hours spent closeted with law books or in a courtroom. It was the nights without meaning that left him wanting more. He lifted the wine to top off her glass, but his eyes stayed on hers. "I came to that realization very recently."

Her blood began to stir. Deliberately, Liz pushed her wine

aside and rose to go to the stove. "We all make decisions at certain points in our lives, realign our priorities."

"I have the feeling you did that a long time ago."

"I did. I've never regretted it."

That much was true, he thought. She wasn't a woman for regrets. "You wouldn't change it, would you?"

Liz continued to spoon chili into bowls. "Change what?"

"If you could go back eleven years and take a different path, you wouldn't do it."

She stopped. From across the room he could see the flicker of candlelight in her eyes as she turned to him. More, he could see the strength that softness and shadows couldn't disguise. "That would mean I'd have to give up Faith. No, I wouldn't do it."

When she set the bowls on the table, Jonas took her hand. "I admire you."

Flustered, she stared down at him. "What for?"

"For being exactly what you are."

$\mathcal{8}$

No smooth phrases, no romantic words could have affected her more deeply. She wasn't used to flattery, but flattery, Liz was sure, could be brushed easily aside by a woman who understood herself. Sincere and simple approval was a different matter. Perhaps it was the candlelight, the wine, the intimacy of the small kitchen in the empty house, but she felt close to him, comfortable with him. Without being aware of it happening, Liz dropped her guard.

"I couldn't be anything else."

"Yes, you could. I'm glad you're not."

"What are you?" she wondered as she sat beside him.

"A thirty-five-year-old lawyer who's just realizing he's wasted some time." He lifted his glass and touched it to hers. "To making the best of whatever there is."

Though she wasn't certain she understood him, Liz drank, then waited for him to eat.

"You could fuel an engine with this stuff." Jonas dipped his spoon into the chili again and tasted. Hot spice danced on his tongue. "It's great."

"Not too hot for your Yankee stomach?"

"My Yankee stomach can handle it. You know, I'm surprised you haven't opened a restaurant, since you can cook like this."

She wouldn't have been human if the compliment hadn't pleased her. "I like the water more than I like the kitchen."

"I can't argue with that. So you picked this up in the kitchen when you worked at the hotel?"

"That's right. We'd take a meal there. The cook would show me how much of this and how much of that. He was very kind," Liz remembered. "A lot of people were kind."

He wanted to know everything—the small details, the feelings, the memories. Because he did, he knew he had to probe with care. "How long did you work there?"

"Two years. I lost count of how many beds I made."

"Then you started your own business?"

"Then I started the dive shop." She took a thin cracker and broke it in two. "It was a gamble, but it was the right one."

"How did you handle it?" He waited until she looked over at him. "With your daughter?"

She withdrew. He could hear it in her voice. "I don't know what you mean."

"I wonder about you." He kept the tone light, knowing she'd never respond to pressure. "Not many women could have managed all you've managed. You were alone, pregnant, making a living."

"Does that seem so unusual?" It made her smile to think of it. "There are only so many choices, aren't there?"

"A great many people would have made a different one."

With a nod, she accepted. "A different one wouldn't have been right for me." She sipped her wine as she let her mind drift back. "I was frightened. Quite a bit at first, but less and less as time when on. People were very good to me. It might have been different if I hadn't been lucky. I went into labor when I was cleaning room 328." Her eyes warmed as if she'd just seen something lovely. "I remember holding this stack of towels in my hand and thinking, 'Oh God, this is it, and I've only done half my rooms.'" She laughed and went back to her meal. Jonas's bowl sat cooling.

"You worked the day your baby was born?"

"Of course. I was healthy."

"I know men who take the day off if they need a tooth filled."

She laughed again and passed him the crackers. "Maybe women take things more in stride."

Only some women, he thought. Only a few exceptional women. "And afterward?"

"Afterward I was lucky again. A woman I worked with knew Señora Alderez. When Faith was born, her youngest had just turned five. She took care of Faith during the day, so I was able to go right back to work."

The cracker crumbled in his hand. "It must have been difficult for you."

"The only hard part was leaving my baby every morning, but the señora was wonderful to Faith and to me. That's how I found this house. Anyway, one thing led to another. I started the dive shop."

He wondered if she realized that the more simply she described it, the more poignant it sounded. "You said the dive shop was a gamble."

"Everything's a gamble. If I'd stayed at the hotel, I never would have been able to give Faith what I wanted to give her. And I suppose I'd have felt cheated myself. Would you like some more?"

"No." He rose to take the bowls himself while he thought out how to approach her. If he said the wrong thing, she'd pull away again. The more she told him, the more he found he needed to know. "Where did you learn to dive?"

"Right here in Cozumel, when I was just a little older than

Faith." As a matter of habit she began to store the leftovers while Jonas ran water in the sink. "My parents brought me. I took to it right away. It was like, I don't know, learning to fly I suppose."

"Is that why you came back?"

"I came back because I'd always felt peaceful here. I needed to feel peaceful."

"But you must have still been in school in the States."

"I was in college." Crouching, Liz shifted things in the refrigerator to make room. "My first year. I was going to be a marine biologist, a teacher who'd enlighten class after class on the mysteries of the sea. A scientist who'd find all the answers. It was such a big dream. It overwhelmed everything else to the point where I studied constantly and rarely went out. Then I—" She caught herself. Straightening slowly, she closed the refrigerator. "You'll want the lights on to do those dishes."

"Then what?" Jonas demanded, taking her shoulder as she hit the switch.

She stared at him. Light poured over them without the shifting shadows of candles. "Then I met Faith's father, and that was the end of dreams."

The need to know eclipsed judgment. He forgot to be careful. "Did you love him?"

"Yes. If I hadn't, there'd have been no Faith."

It wasn't the answer he'd wanted. "Then why are you raising her alone?"

"That's obvious, isn't it?" Anger surged as she shoved his hand aside. "He didn't want me."

"Whether he did or didn't, he was responsible to you and the child."

"Don't talk to me about responsibility. Faith's my responsibility."

"The law sees things otherwise."

"Keep your law," she snapped. "He could quote it chapter and verse, and it didn't mean a thing. We weren't wanted."

"So you let pride cut you off from your rights?" Impatient with her, he stuck his hands in his pockets and strode back to the sink. "Why didn't you fight for what you were entitled to?"

"You want the details, Jonas?" Memory brought its own particular pain, its own particular shame. Liz concentrated on the anger. Going back to the table, she picked up her glass of wine and drank deeply.

"I wasn't quite eighteen. I was going to college to study exactly what I wanted to study so I could do exactly what I wanted to do. I considered myself a great deal more mature than some of my classmates who flitted around from class to class more concerned about where the action would be that night. I spent most of my evenings in the library. That's where I met him. He was in his last year and knew if he didn't pass the bar there'd be hell to pay at home. His family had been in law or politics since the Revolution. You'd understand about family honor, wouldn't you?"

The arrow hit the mark, but he only nodded.

"Then you should understand the rest. We saw each other every night in the library, so it was natural that we began to talk, then have a cup of coffee. He was smart, attractive, wonderfully mannered and funny." Almost violently, she blew out the candles. The scent carried over and hung in the room. "I fell hard. He brought me flowers and took me for long quiet drives on Saturday nights. When he told me he loved me, I believed him. I thought I had the world in the palm of my hand."

She set the wine down again, impatient to be finished. Jonas said nothing. "He told me we'd be married as soon as he established himself. We'd sit in his car and look at the stars and he'd tell me about his home in Dallas and the wonderful rooms.

The parties and the servants and the chandeliers. It was like a story, a lovely happily-ever-after story. Then one day his mother came." Liz laughed, but gripped the back of her chair until her knuckles were white. She could still feel the humiliation.

"Actually, she sent her driver up to the dorm to fetch me. Marcus hadn't said a thing about her visiting, but I was thrilled that I was going to meet her. At the curb was this fabulous white Rolls, the kind you only see in movies. When the driver opened the door for me, I was floating. Then I got in and she gave me the facts of life. Her son had a certain position to maintain, a certain image to project. She was sure I was a very nice girl, but hardly suitable for a Jensann of Dallas."

Jonas's eyes narrowed at the name, but he said nothing. Restless, Liz went to the stove and began to scrub the surface. "She told me she'd already spoken with her son and he understood the relationship had to end. Then she offered me a check as compensation. I was humiliated, and worse, I was pregnant. I hadn't told anyone yet, because I'd just found out that morning. I didn't take her money. I got out of the Rolls and went straight to Marcus. I was sure he loved me enough to toss it all aside for me, and for our baby. I was wrong."

Her eyes were so dry that they hurt. Liz pressed her fingers to them a moment. "When I went to see him, he was very logical. It had been nice; now it was over. His parents held the purse strings and it was important to keep them happy. But he wanted me to know we could still see each other now and again, as long as it was on the side. When I told him about the baby, he was furious. How could I have done such a thing? *I*."

Liz tossed the dishrag into the sink so that hot, soapy water heaved up. "It was as though I'd conceived the baby completely on my own. He wouldn't have it, he wouldn't have some silly girl who'd gotten herself pregnant messing up his life. He told me I had to get rid of it. It—as though Faith were a thing to be erased and forgotten. I was hysterical. He lost his temper. There were threats. He said he'd spread word that I was sleeping around and his friends would back him up. I'd never be able to prove the baby was his. He said my parents would be embarrassed, perhaps sued if I tried to press it. He tossed around a lot of legal phrases that I couldn't understand, but I understood he was finished with me. His family had a lot of pull at the college, and he said he'd see that I was dismissed. Because I was foolish enough to believe everything he said, I was terrified. He gave me a check and told me to go out of state—better, out of the country—to take care of things. That way no one would have to know.

"For a week I did nothing. I went through my classes in a daze, thinking I'd wake up and find out it had all been a bad dream. Then I faced it. I wrote my parents, telling them what I could. I sold the car they'd given me when I graduated from high school, took the check from Marcus and came to Cozumel to have my baby."

He'd wanted to know, even demanded, but now his insides were raw. "You could have gone to your parents."

"Yes, but at the time Marcus had convinced me they'd be ashamed. He told me they'd hate me and consider the baby a burden."

"Why didn't you go to his family? You were entitled to be taken care of."

"Go to them?" He'd never heard venom in her voice before. "Be taken care of by them? I'd have gone to hell first."

He waited a moment, until he was sure he could speak calmly. "They don't even know, do they?"

"No. And they never will. Faith is mine."

"And what does Faith know?"

"Only what she has to know. I'd never lie to her."

"And do you know that Marcus Jensann has his sights set on the senate, and maybe higher?"

Her color drained quickly and completely. "You know him?"

"By reputation."

Panic came and went, then returned in double force. "He doesn't know Faith exists. None of them do. They can't."

Watching her steadily, he took a step closer. "What are you afraid of?"

"Power. Faith is mine, she's going to stay mine. None of them will ever touch her."

"Is that why you stay here? Are you hiding from them?"

"I'll do whatever's necessary to protect my child."

"He's still got you running scared." Furious for her, Jonas took her arms. "He's got a frightened teenager strapped inside of you who's never had the chance to stretch and feel alive. Don't you know a man like that wouldn't even remember who you are? You're still running away from a man who wouldn't recognize you on the street."

She slapped him hard enough to make his head snap back. Breathing fast, she backed away from him, appalled by a show of violence she hadn't been aware of possessing. "Don't tell me what I'm running from," she whispered. "Don't tell me what I feel." She turned and fled. Before she'd reached the front door he had her again, whirling her around, gripping her hard. He no longer knew why his anger was so fierce, only that he was past the point of controlling it.

"How much have you given up because of him?" Jonas demanded. "How much have you cut out of your life?"

"It's my life!" she shouted at him.

"And you won't share it with anyone but your daughter. What the hell are you going to do when she's grown? What the hell are you going to do in twenty years when you have nothing but your memories?"

"Don't." Tears filled her eyes too quickly to be blinked away.

He grabbed her close again, twisting until she had to look at him. "We all need someone. Even you. It's about time someone proved it to you."

"No."

She tried to turn her head but he was quick. With his mouth crushed on hers she struggled, but her arms were trapped between their bodies and his were ironlike around her. Emotions already mixed with fear and anger became more confused with passion. Liz fought not to give in to any of them as his mouth demanded both submission and response.

"You're not fighting me," he told her. His eyes were close, searing into hers. "You're fighting yourself. You've been fighting yourself since the first time we met."

"I want you to let me go." She wanted her voice to be strong, but it trembled.

"Yes. You want me to let you go just as much as you want me not to. You've been making your own decisions for a long time, Liz. This time I'm making one for you."

Her furious protest was lost against his mouth as he pressed her down to the sofa. Trapped under him, her body began to heat, her blood began to stir. Yes, she was fighting herself. She had to fight herself before she could fight him. But she was losing.

She heard her own moan as his lips trailed down her throat, and it was a moan of pleasure. She felt the hard line of his body against hers as she arched under him, but it wasn't a movement of protest. Want me, she seemed to say. Want me for what I am.

Her pulse began to thud in parts of her body that had been quiet for so many years. Life burst through her like a torrid wind through thin glass until every line of defense was shattered. With a desperate groan, she took his face in her hands and dragged his mouth back to hers.

She could taste the passion, the life, the promises. She wanted them all. Recklessness, so long chained within, tore free and ruled. A sound bubbled in her throat she wasn't even aware was a laugh as she wrapped herself around him. She wanted. He wanted. The hell with the rest.

He wasn't sure what had driven him—anger, need, pain. All he knew now was that he had to have her, body, soul and mind. She was wild beneath him, but no longer in resistance. Every movement was a demand that he take more, give more, and nothing seemed fast enough. She was a storm set to rage, a fire desperate to consume. Whatever he'd released inside of her had whipped out and taken him prisoner.

He pulled the shirt over her head and tossed it aside. His heartbeat thundered. She was so small, so delicate. But he had a beast inside him that had been caged too long. He took her breast in his mouth and sent them both spinning. She tasted so fresh: a cool, clear glass of water. She smelled of woman at her most unpampered and most seductive. He felt her body arch against his, taut as a bowstring, hot as a comet. The innocence that remained so integral a part of her trembled just beneath wanton passion. No man alive could have resisted it; any man alive might have wished for it. His mouth was buried at her throat when he felt the shirt rip away from his back.

She hardly knew what she was doing. Touching him sent demands to her brain that she couldn't deny. She wanted to feel him against her, flesh to flesh, to experience an intimacy she'd so long refused to allow herself. There'd been no one else. As Liz felt her skin fused to his she understood why. There was only one Jonas. She pulled his mouth back to hers to taste him again.

He drew off her slacks so that she was naked, but she didn't feel vulnerable. She felt invulnerable. Hardly able to breathe, she struggled with his. Then she gave him no choice. Desperate for that final release, she wrapped her legs around him and drew him into her until she was filled. At the shock of that first ragged peak, her eyes flew open. Inches away, he watched her face. Her mouth trembled open, but before she could catch her breath, he was driving her higher, faster. She couldn't tell how long they balanced on the edge, trapped between pleasure and fulfillment. Then his arms came around her, hers around his. Together, they broke free.

She didn't speak. Her system leveled slowly, and she was helpless to hurry it. He didn't move. He'd shifted his weight, but his arms had come around her and stayed there. She needed him to speak, to say something that would put what had happened in perspective. She'd only had one other lover and had learned not to expect.

Jonas rested his forehead against her shoulder a moment. He was wrestling with his own demons. "I'm sorry, Liz."

He could have said nothing worse. She closed her eyes and forced her emotions to drain. She nearly succeeded. Steadier, she reached for the tangle of clothes on the floor. "I don't need an apology." With her clothes in a ball in her arm, she walked quickly to the bedroom.

On a long breath, Jonas sat up. He couldn't seem to find the right buttons on Liz Palmer. Every move he made seemed to be a move in reverse. It still stunned him that he'd been so rough with her, left her so little choice in the final outcome. He'd be better off hiring her a private bodyguard and moving himself back to the hotel. It was true he didn't want to see her hurt and felt a certain responsibility for her welfare, but he didn't seem to be able to act on it properly. When she'd stood in the kitchen telling him what she'd been through, something had begun to boil in him. That it had taken the form of passion in the end wasn't something easily explained or justified. His apology had been inadequate, but he had little else.

Drawing on his pants, Jonas started for his room. It snouldn't have surprised him to find himself veering toward Liz's. She was just pulling on a robe. "It's late, Jonas."

"Did I hurt you?"

She sent him a look that made guilt turn over in his stomach. "Yes. Now I want to take a shower before I go to bed."

"Liz, there's no excuse for being so rough, and there's no making it up to you, but—"

"Your apology hurt me," she interrupted. "Now if you've said all you have to say, I'd like to be alone."

He stared at her a moment, then dragged a hand through his hair. How could he have convinced himself he understood her when she was now and always had been an enigma? "Damn it, Liz, I wasn't apologizing for making love to you, but for the lack of finesse. I practically tossed you on the ground and ripped your clothes off."

She folded her hands and tried to keep calm. "I ripped yours."

His lips twitched, then curved. "Yeah, you did."

Humor didn't come into her eyes. "And do you want an apology?"

He came to her then and rested his hands on her shoulders. Her robe was cotton and thin and whirling with bright color. "No. I guess what I'd like is for you to say you wanted me as much as I wanted you."

Her courage weakened, so she looked beyond him. "I'd have thought that was obvious."

"Liz." His hand was gentle as he turned her face back to his.

"All right. I wanted you. Now—"

"Now," he interrupted. "Will you listen?"

"There's no need to say anything."

"Yes, there is." He walked with her to the bed and drew her down to sit. Moonlight played over their hands as he took hers. "I came to Cozumel for one reason. My feelings on that haven't changed but other things have. When I first met you I thought you knew something, were hiding something. I linked everything about you to Jerry. It didn't take long for me to see there was something else. I wanted to know about you, for myself."

"Why?"

"I don't know. It's impossible not to care about you." At her look of surprise, he smiled. "You project this image of pure self-sufficiency and still manage to look like a waif. Tonight, I purposely maneuvered you into talking about Faith and what had brought you here. When you told me I couldn't handle it."

She drew her hand from his. "That's understandable. Most people have trouble handling unwed mothers."

Anger bubbled as he grabbed her hand again. "Stop putting words in my mouth. You stood in the kitchen talking and I could see you, young, eager and trusting, being betrayed and hurt. I could see what it had done to you, how it had closed you off from things you wanted to do."

"I told you I don't have any regrets."

"I know." He lifted her hand and kissed it. "I guess for a moment I needed to have them for you."

"Jonas, do you think anyone's life turns out the way they plan it as children?"

He laughed a little as he slipped an arm around her and drew her against him. Liz sat still a moment, unsure how to react to the casual show of affection. Then she leaned her head against his shoulder and closed her eyes. "Jerry and I were going to be partners."

"In what?"

"In anything."

She touched the coin on the end of his chain. "He had one of these."

"Our grandparents gave them to us when we were kids. They're identical five-dollar gold pieces. Funny, I always wore mine heads up. Jerry wore his heads down." He closed his fingers over the coin. "He stole his first car when we were sixteen."

Her fingers crept up to his. "I'm sorry."

"The thing was he didn't need to—we had access to any car in the garage. He told me he just wanted to see if he could get away with it."

"He didn't make life easy for you."

"No, he didn't make life easy. Especially for himself. But he never did anything out of meanness. There were times I hated him, but I never stopped loving him."

Liz drew closer. "Love hurts more than hate."

He kissed the top of her head. "Liz, I don't suppose you've ever talked to a lawyer about Faith."

"Why should I?"

"Marcus has a responsibility, a financial responsibility at the least, to you and Faith."

"I took money from Marcus once. Not again."

"Child support payments could be set up very quietly. You could stop working seven days a week."

Liz took a deep breath and pulled away until she could see his face. "Faith is my child, has been my child only since the moment Marcus handed me a check. I could have had the abortion and gone back to my life as I'd planned it. I chose not to. I chose to have the baby, to raise the baby, to support the baby. She's never given me anything but pleasure from the moment she was born, and I have no intention of sharing her."

"One day she's going to ask you for his name."

Liz moistened her lips, but nodded. "Then one day I'll tell her. She'll have her own choice to make."

He wouldn't press her now, but there was no reason he couldn't have his law clerk begin to investigate child support laws and paternity cases. "Are you going to let me meet her? I know the deal is for me to be out of the house and out of your life when she gets back. I will, but I'd like the chance to meet her."

"If you're still in Mexico."

"One more question."

The smile came more easily. "One more."

"There haven't been any other men, have there?"

The smile faded. "No."

He felt twin surges of gratitude and guilt. "Then let me show you how it should be."

"There's no need—"

Gently, he brushed the hair back from her face. "Yes, there is. For both of us." He kissed her eyes closed. "I've wanted you from the first." His mouth on hers was as sweet as spring rain and just as gentle. Slowly, he slipped the robe from her shoulders, following the trail with warm lips. "Your skin's like gold," he murmured, then traced a finger over her breasts where the tone changed. "And so pale. I want to see all of you."

"Jonas—"

"All of you," he repeated, looking into her eyes until the heat kindled again. "I want to make love with all of you."

She didn't resist. Never in her life had anyone ever touched her with such reverence, looked at her with such need. When he urged her back, Liz lay on the bed, naked and waiting.

"Lovely," Jonas murmured. Her body was milk and honey

in the moonlight. And her eyes were dark—dark and open and uncertain. "I want you to trust me." He began a slow journey of exploration at her ankles. "I want to know when I look at you that you're not afraid of me."

"I'm not afraid of you."

"You have been. Maybe I've even wanted you to be. No more." His tongue slid over her skin and teased the back of her knees. The jolt of power had her rising up and gasping. "Jonas."

"Relax." He ran a hand lightly up her hip. "I want to feel your bones melt. Lie back, Liz. Let me show you how much you can have."

She obeyed, only because she hadn't the strength to resist. He murmured to her, stroking, nibbling, until she was too steeped in what he gave to give in return. But he wanted her that way, wanted to take her as though she hadn't been touched before. Not by him, not by anyone. Slowly, thoroughly and with great, great patience he seduced and pleasured. He thought as his mouth skimmed up her thigh that he could hear her skin hum.

She'd never known anything could be like this—so deep, so dark. There was a freedom here, she discovered, that she'd once only associated with diving down through silent fathoms. Her body could float, her limbs could be weightless, but she could feel every touch, every movement. Dreamlike, sensations drifted over her, so soft, so misty, each blended into the next. How long could it go on? Perhaps, after all, there were forevers.

She was lean, with muscles firm in her legs. Like a dancer's he thought, disciplined and trained. The scent from the bowl on her dresser spiced the air, but it was her fragrance, cool as a waterfall, that swam in his head. His mind emptied of everything but the need to delight her. Love, when unselfish, has incredible power.

His tongue plunged into the heat and his hands gripped hers as she arched, stunned at being flung from a floating world to a churning one. He drew from her, both patient and relentless, until she shuddered to climax and over. When her hands went limp in his, he brought them back to his body and pleasured himself.

She hadn't known passion could stretch so far or a body endure such a barrage of sensations. His hands, rough at the palm, showed her secrets she'd never had the chance to imagine. His lips, warmed from her own skin, opened mysteries and whispered the answers. He gentled her, he enticed her, he stroked with tenderness and he devoured. Gasping for air, she had no choice but to allow him whatever he wanted, and to strain for him to show her more.

When he was inside of her she thought it was all, and more, than she could ever want. If this was love, she'd never tasted it. If this was passion, she'd only skimmed its surface. Now it was time to risk the depths. Willing, eager, she held on to him.

It was trust he felt from her, and trust that moved him unbearably. He thought he'd needed before, desired before, but never so completely. Though he knew what it was to be part of another person, he'd never expected to feel the merger again. Strong, complex, unavoidable, the emotion swamped him. He belonged to her as fully as he'd wanted her to belong to him.

He took her slowly, so that the thrill that coursed through her seemed endless. His skin was moist when she pressed her lips to his throat. The pulse there was as quick as her own. A giddy sense of triumph moved through her, only to be whipped away with passion before it could spread.

Then he drew her up to him, and her body, liquid and limber with emotion, rose like a wave to press against his. Wrapped close, mouths fused, they moved together. Her hair fell like rain down her back. She could feel his heartbeat fast against her breast.

Still joined, they lowered again. The rhythm quickened. Desperation rose. She heard him breathe her name before the gates burst open and she was lost in the flood.

9

She woke slowly, with a long, lazy stretch. Keeping her eyes closed, Liz waited for the alarm to ring. It wasn't often she felt so relaxed, even when waking, so she pampered herself and absorbed the luxury of doing nothing. In an hour, she mused, she'd be at the dive shop shifting through the day's schedule. The glass bottom, she thought, frowning a little. Was she supposed to take it out? Odd that she couldn't remember. Then with a start, it occurred to her that she didn't remember because she didn't know. She hadn't handled the schedule in two days. And last night…

She opened her eyes and looked into Jonas's.

"I could watch your mind wake up." He bent over and kissed her. "Fascinating."

Liz closed her fingers over the sheet and tugged it a little higher. What was she supposed to say? She'd never spent the night with a man, never awoken with one. She cleared her throat and wondered if every man awoke as sexily disheveled as Jonas Sharpe. "How did you sleep?" she managed, and felt ridiculous.

"Fine." He smiled as he brushed her hair from her cheek with a fingertip. "And you?"

"Fine." Her fingers moved restlessly on the sheet until he closed his hands over them. His eyes were warm and heavy and made her heart pound.

"It's a little late to be nervous around me, Elizabeth."

"I'm not nervous." But color rose to her cheeks when he pressed his lips to her naked shoulder.

"Still, it's rather flattering. If you're nervous…" He turned his head so the tip of his tongue could toy with her ear. "Then you're not unmoved. I wouldn't like to think you felt casually about being with me—yet."

Was it possible to want so much this morning what she'd sated herself with the night before? She didn't think it should be, and yet her body told her differently. She would, as she always did, listen to her intellect first. "It must be almost time to get up." One hand firmly on the sheets, she rose on her elbows to look at the clock. "That's not right." She blinked and focused again. "It can't be eight-fifteen."

"Why not?" He slipped a hand beneath the sheet and stroked her thigh.

"Because." His touch had her pulses speeding. "I always set it for six-fifteen."

Finding her a challenge, Jonas brushed light kisses over her shoulder, down her arm. "You didn't set it last night."

"I always—" She cut herself off. It was hard enough to try to think when he was touching her, but when she remembered the night before, it was nearly impossible to understand why she had to think. Her mind hadn't been on alarms and schedules and customers when her body had curled into Jonas's to sleep. Her mind, as it was now, had been filled with him.

"Always what?"

She wished he wouldn't distract her with fingertips sliding

gently over her skin. She wished he could touch her everywhere at once. "I always wake up at six, whether I set it or not."

"You didn't this time." He laughed as he eased her back down. "I suppose I should be flattered again."

"Maybe I flatter you too much," she murmured and started to shift away. He simply rolled her back to him. "I have to get up."

"No, you don't."

"Jonas, I'm already late. I have to get to work."

Sunlight dappled over her face. He wanted to see it over the rest of her. "The only thing you have to do is make love with me." He kissed her fingers, then slowly drew them from the sheet. "I'll never get through the day without you."

"The boats—"

"Are already out, I'm sure." He cupped her breast, rubbing his thumb back and forth over the nipple. "Luis seems competent."

"He is. I haven't been in for two days."

"One more won't hurt."

Her body vibrated with need that slowly wound itself into her mind. Her arms came up to him, around him. "No, I guess it won't."

She hadn't stayed in bed until ten o'clock since she'd been a child. Liz felt as irresponsible as one as she started the coffee. True, Luis could handle the shop and the boats as well as she, but it wasn't his job. It was hers. Here she was, brewing coffee at ten o'clock, with her body still warm from loving. Nothing had been the same since Jonas Sharpe had arrived on her doorstep.

"It's useless to give yourself a hard time for taking a morning off," Jonas said from behind her.

Liz popped bread into the toaster. "I suppose not, since I don't even know today's schedule."

"Liz." Jonas took her by the arms and firmly turned her around. He studied her, gauging her mood before he spoke. "You know, back in Philadelphia I'm considered a workaholic. I've had friends express concern over the workload I take on and the hours I put in. Compared to you, I'm retired."

Her brows drew together as they did when she was concentrating. Or annoyed. "We each do what we have to do."

"True enough. It appears what I have to do is harass you until you relax."

She had to smile. He said it so reasonably and his eyes were laughing. "I'm sure you have a reputation for being an expert on harassment."

"I majored in it at college."

"Good for you. But I'm an expert at budgeting my own time. And there's my toast." He let her pluck it out, waited until she'd buttered it, then took a piece for himself.

"You mentioned diving lessons."

She was still frowning at him when she heard the coffee begin to simmer. She reached for one cup, then relented and took two. "What about them?"

"I'll take one. Today."

"Today?" She handed him his coffee, drinking her own standing by the stove. "I'll have to see what's scheduled. The way things have been going, both dive boats should already be out."

"Not a group lesson, a private one. You can take me out on the *Expatriate*."

"Luis usually takes care of the private lessons."

He smiled at her. "I prefer dealing with the management."

Liz dusted crumbs from her fingers. "All right then. It'll cost you."

He lifted his cup in salute. "I never doubted it."

★ ★ ★

Liz was laughing when Jonas pulled into a narrow parking space at the hotel. "If he'd picked your pocket, why did you defend him?"

"Everyone's entitled to representation," Jonas reminded her. "Besides, I figured if I took him on as a client, he'd leave my wallet alone."

"And did he?"

"Yeah." Jonas took her hand as they crossed the sidewalk to the sand. "He stole my watch instead."

She giggled, a foolish, girlish sound he'd never heard from her. "And did you get him off?"

"Two years probation. There, it looks like business is good."

Liz shielded her eyes from the sun and looked toward the shop. Luis was busily fitting two couples with snorkel gear. A glance to the left showed her only the *Expatriate* remained in dock. "Cozumel's becoming very popular," she murmured.

"Isn't that the idea?"

"For business?" She moved her shoulders. "I'd be a fool to complain."

"But?"

"But sometimes I think it would be nice if I could block out the changes. I don't want to see the water choked with suntan oil. *Hola,* Luis."

"Liz!" His gaze passed over Jonas briefly before he grinned at her. "We thought maybe you deserted us. How did you like Acapulco?"

"It was…different," she decided, and was already scooting behind the counter to find the daily schedule. "Any problems?"

"Jose took care of a couple repairs. I brought Miguel back to fill in, but I keep an eye on him. Got this—what do you call it—brochure on the aqua bikes." He pulled out a colorful pamphlet, but Liz only nodded.

"The Brinkman party's out diving. Did we take them to Palancar?"

"Two days in a row. Miguel likes them. They tip good."

"Hmm. You're handling the shop alone."

"No problem. Hey, there was a guy." He screwed up his face as he tried to remember the name. "Skinny guy, American. You know the one you took out on the beginners' trip?"

She flipped through the receipts and was satisfied. "Trydent?"

"*Sí,* that was it. He came by a coupla times."

"Rent anything?"

"No." Luis wiggled his eyebrows at her. "He was looking for you."

Liz shrugged it off. If he hadn't rented anything, he didn't interest her. "If everything's under control here, I'm going to take Mr. Sharpe out for a diving lesson."

Luis looked quickly at Jonas, then away. The man made him uneasy, but Liz looked happier than she had in weeks. "Want me to get the gear?"

"No, I'll take care of it." She looked up and smiled at Jonas. "Write Mr. Sharpe up a rental form and give him a receipt for the gear, the lesson and the boat trip. Since it's…" She trailed off as she checked her watch. "Nearly eleven, give him the half-day rate."

"You're all heart," Jonas murmured as she went to the shelves to choose his equipment.

"You got the best teacher," Luis told him, but couldn't manage more than another quick look at Jonas.

"I'm sure you're right." Idly, Jonas swiveled the newspaper Luis had tossed on the counter around to face him. He missed being able to sit down with the morning paper over coffee. The

Spanish headlines told him nothing. "Anything going on I should know about?" Jonas asked, indicating the paper.

Luis relaxed a bit as he wrote. Jonas's voice wasn't so much like Jerry's when you weren't looking at him. "Haven't had a chance to look at it yet. Busy morning."

Going with habit, Jonas turned the paper over. There, in a faded black-and-white picture, was Erika. Jonas's fingers tightened. He glanced back and saw that Liz was busy, her back to him. Without a word, he slid the paper over the receipt Luis was writing.

"Hey, that's the—"

"I know," Jonas said in an undertone. "What does it say?"

Luis bent over the paper to read. He straightened again very slowly, and his face was ashen. "Dead," he whispered. "She's dead."

"How?"

Luis's fingers opened and closed on the pen he held. "Stabbed."

Jonas thought of the knife held at Liz's throat. "When?"

"Last night." Luis had to swallow twice. "They found her last night."

"Jonas," Liz called from the back, "how much do you weigh?"

Keeping his eyes on Luis, Jonas turned the paper over again. "One seventy. She doesn't need to hear this now," he added under his breath. He pulled bills from his wallet and laid them on the counter. "Finish writing the receipt."

After a struggle, Luis mastered his own fear and straightened. "I don't want anything to happen to Liz."

Jonas met the look with a challenge that held for several humming seconds before he relaxed. The smaller man was terrified, but he was thinking of Liz. "Neither do I. I'm going to see nothing does."

"You brought trouble."

"I know." His gaze shifted beyond Luis to Liz. "But if I leave, the trouble doesn't."

For the first time, Luis forced himself to study Jonas's face. After a moment, he blew out a long breath. "I liked your brother, but I think it was him who brought trouble."

"It doesn't matter anymore who brought it. I'm going to look out for her."

"Then you look good," Luis warned softly. "You look real good."

"First lesson," Liz said as she unlocked her storage closet. "Each diver carries and is responsible for his own gear." She jerked her head back to where Jonas's was stacked. With a last look at Luis, he walked through the doorway to gather it up.

"Preparing for a dive is twice as much work as diving itself," she began as she hefted her tanks. "It's a good thing it's worth it. We'll be back before sundown, Luis. *Hasta luego.*"

"Liz." She stopped, turning back to where Luis hovered in the doorway. His gaze passed over Jonas, then returned to her. *"Hasta luego,"* he managed, and closed his fingers over the medal he wore around his neck.

The moment she was on board, Liz restacked her gear. As a matter of routine, she checked all the *Expatriate*'s gauges. "Can you cast off?" she asked Jonas.

He ran a hand down her hair, surprising her. She looked so competent, so in charge. He wondered if by staying close he was protecting or endangering. It was becoming vital to believe the first. "I can handle it."

She felt her stomach flutter as he continued to stare at her. "Then you'd better stop looking at me and do it."

"I like looking at you." He drew her close, just to hold her. "I could spend years looking at you."

Her arms came up, hesitated, then dropped back to her

sides. It would be so easy to believe. To trust again, give again, be hurt again. She wanted to tell him of the love growing inside her, spreading and strengthening with each moment. But if she told him she'd no longer have even the illusion of control. Without control, she was defenseless.

"I clocked you on at eleven," she said, but couldn't resist breathing deeply of his scent and committing it to memory.

Because she made him smile again, he drew her back. "I'm paying the bill, I'll worry about the time."

"Diving lesson," she reminded him. "And you can't dive until you cast off."

"Aye, aye, sir." But he gave her a hard, breath-stealing kiss before he jumped back on the dock.

Liz drew air into her lungs and let it out slowly before she turned on the engines. All she could hope was that she looked more in control than she felt. He was winning a battle, she mused, that he didn't even know he was fighting. She waited for Jonas to join her again before she eased the throttle forward.

"There are plenty of places to dive where we don't need the boat, but I thought you'd enjoy something away from the beaches. Palancar is one of the most stunning reefs in the Caribbean. It's probably the best place to start because the north end is shallow and the wall slopes rather than having a sheer vertical drop-off. There are a lot of caves and passageways, so it makes for an interesting dive."

"I'm sure, but I had something else in mind."

"Something else?"

Jonas took a small book out of his pocket and flipped through it. "What do these numbers look like to you?"

Liz recognized the book. It was the same one he'd used in Acapulco to copy down the numbers from his brother's book in the safe-deposit box. He still had his priorities, she reminded herself, then drew back on the throttle to let the boat idle.

The numbers were in precise, neat lines. Any child who'd paid attention in geography class would recognize them. "Longitude and latitude."

He nodded. "Do you have a chart?"

He'd planned this since he'd first seen the numbers, she realized. Their being lovers changed nothing else. "Of course, but I don't need it for this. I know these waters. That's just off the coast of Isla Mujeres." Liz adjusted her course and picked up speed. Perhaps, she thought, the course had already been set for both of them long before this. They had no choice but to see it through. "It's a long trip. You might as well relax."

He put his hands on her shoulders to knead. "We won't find anything, but I have to go."

"I understand."

"Would you rather I go alone?"

She shook her head violently, but said nothing.

"Liz, this had to be his drop point. By tomorrow, Moralas will have the numbers and send his own divers down. I have to see for myself."

"You're chasing shadows, Jonas. Jerry's gone. Nothing you can do is going to change that."

"I'll find out why. I'll find out who. That'll be enough."

"Will it?" With her hand gripping the wheel hard, she looked over her shoulder. His eyes were close, but they held that cool, set look again. "I don't think so—not for you." Liz turned her face back to the sea. She would take him where he wanted to go.

Isla Mujeres, Island of Women, was a small gem in the water. Surrounded by reefs and studded with untouched lagoons, it was one of the perfect retreats of the Caribbean. Party boats from the continental coast or one of the other islands cruised there daily to offer their customers snorkeling or diving at its best. It had once been known by pirates and blessed by a goddess. Liz anchored the boat off the southwest coast. Once again, she became the teacher.

"It's important to know and understand both the name and the use of every piece of equipment. It's not just a matter of stuffing in a mouthpiece and strapping on a tank. No smoking," she added as Jonas took out a cigarette. "It's ridiculous to clog up your lungs in the first place, and absurd to do it before a dive."

Jonas set the pack on the bench beside him. "How long are we going down?"

"We'll keep it under an hour. The depth here ranges to eighty feet. That means the nitrogen in your air supply will be over three times denser than what your system's accustomed to. In some people at some depths, this can cause temporary imbalances. If you begin to feel light-headed, signal to me right away. We'll descend in stages to give your body time to get used to the changes in pressure. We ascend the same way in order to give the nitrogen time to expel. If you come up too quickly, you risk decompression sickness. It can be fatal." As she spoke, she spread out the gear with the intention of explaining each piece. "Nothing is to be taken for granted in the water. It is not your milieu. You're dependent on your equipment and your own good sense. It's beautiful and it's exciting, but it's not an amusement park."

"Is this the same lecture you give on the dive boat?"

"Basically."

"You're very good."

"Thank you." She picked up a gauge. "Now—"

"Can we get started?" he asked and reached for his wet suit.

"We are getting started. You can't dive without a working knowledge of your equipment."

"That's a depth gauge." He nodded toward her hand as he stripped down to black briefs. "A very sophisticated one. I wouldn't think most dive shops would find it necessary to stock that quality."

"This is mine," she murmured. "But I keep a handful for rentals."

"I don't think I mentioned that you have the best-tended equipment I've ever seen. It isn't in the same league with your personal gear, but it's quality. Give me a hand, will you?"

Liz rose to help him into the tough, stretchy suit. "You've gone down before."

"I've been diving since I was fifteen." Jonas pulled up the zipper before bending over to check the tanks himself.

"Since you were fifteen." Liz yanked off her shirt and tossed it aside. Fuming, she pulled off her shorts until she wore nothing but a string bikini and a scowl. "Then why did you let me go on that way?"

"I liked hearing you." Jonas glanced up and felt his blood surge. "Almost as much as I like looking at you."

She wasn't in the mood to be flattered, less in the mood to be charmed. Without asking for assistance, she tugged herself into her wet suit. "You're still paying for the lesson."

Jonas grinned as he examined his flippers. "I never doubted it."

She strapped on the rest of her gear in silence. It was difficult even for her to say if she were really angry. All she knew was the day, and dive, weren't as simple as they had started out to be. Lifting the top of a bench, she reached into a compartment and took out two short metal sticks shaped like bats.

"What's this for?" Jonas asked as she handed him one.

"Insurance." She adjusted her mask. "We're going down to the caves where the sharks sleep."

"Sharks don't sleep."

"The oxygen content in the water in the cave keeps them quiescent. But don't think you can trust them."

Without another word, she swung over the side and down the ladder.

The water was as clear as glass, so she could see for more than a hundred feet. As she heard Jonas plunge in beside her, Liz turned to assure herself he did indeed know what he was doing. Catching her skeptical look, Jonas merely circled his thumb and forefinger, then pointed down.

He was tense. Liz could feel it from him, though she understood it had nothing to do with his skill underwater. His brother had dived here once—she was as certain of it as Jonas. And the reason for his dives had been the reason for his death. She no longer had to think whether she was angry. In a gesture as personal as a kiss, she reached out a hand and took his.

Grateful, Jonas curled his fingers around hers. He didn't know what he was looking for, or even why he continued to look when already he'd found more than he'd wanted to. His brother had played games with the rules and had lost. Some would say there was justice in that. But they'd shared birth. He had to go on looking, and go on hoping.

Liz saw the first of the devilfish and tugged on Jonas's hand. Such things never failed to touch her spirit. The giant manta rays cruised together, feeding on plankton and unconcerned with the human intruders. Liz kicked forward, delighted to swim among them. Their huge mouths could crush and devour crustaceans. Their wingspan of twenty feet and more was awesome. Without fear, Liz reached out to touch. Pleasure came easily, as it always did to her in the sea. Her eyes were laughing as she reached out again for Jonas.

They descended farther, and some of his tension began to dissolve. There was something different about her here, a lightness, an ease that dissolved the sadness that always seemed to linger in her eyes. She looked free, and more, as happy as he'd ever seen her. If it were possible to fall in love in a matter of moments, Jonas fell in love in those, forty feet below the surface with a mermaid who'd forgotten how to dream.

Everything she saw, everything she could touch fascinated her. He could see it in the way she moved, the way she looked at everything as though it were her first dive. If he could have found a way, he would have stayed with her there, surrounded by love and protected by fathoms.

They swam deeper, but leisurely. If something evil had been begun, or been ended there, it had left no trace. The sea was calm and silent and full of life too lovely to exist in the air.

When the shadow passed over, Liz looked up. In all her dives, she'd never seen anything so spectacular. Thousands upon thousands of silvery grunts moved together in a wave so dense that they might have been one creature. Eyes wide with the wonder of it, Liz lifted her arms and took her body up. The wave swayed as a unit, avoiding intrusion. Delighted, she signaled for Jonas to join her. The need to share the magic was natural. This was the pull of the sea that had driven her to study, urged to explore and invited her once to dream. With her fingers linked with Jonas's, she propelled them closer. The school of fish split in half so that it became two unified forms swirling on either side of them. The sea teemed with them, thick clouds of silver so tightly grouped that they seemed fused together.

For a moment she was as close to her own fantasies as she had ever been, floating free, surrounded by magic, with her lover's hand in hers. Impulsively, she wrapped her arms around Jonas and held on. The clouds of fish swarmed around them, linked into one, then swirled away.

He could feel her pulse thud when he reached for her wrist. He could see the fascinated delight in her eyes. Hampered by his human frailty in the water, he could only touch his hand to her cheek. When she lifted her own to press it closer, it was enough. Side by side they swam toward the seafloor.

The limestone caves were eerie and compelling. Once Jonas saw the head of a moray eel slide out and curve, either in curiosity or warning. An old turtle with barnacles crusting his back rose from his resting place beneath a rock and swam between them. Then at the entrance to a cave, Liz pointed and shared another mystery.

The shark moved across the sand, as a dog might on a hearth rug. His small, black eyes stared back at them as his gills slowly drew in water. While they huddled just inside the entrance, their bubbles rising up through the porous limestone and toward the surface, the shark shifted restlessly. Jonas reached for Liz's hand to draw her back, but she moved a bit closer, anxious to see.

In a quick move, the shark shot toward the entrance. Jonas was grabbing for Liz and his knife, when she merely poked at the head with her wooden bat. Without pausing, the shark swam toward the open sea and vanished.

He wanted to strangle her. He wanted to tell her how fascinating she was to watch. Since he could do neither, Jonas merely closed a hand over her throat and gave her a mock shake. Her laughter had bubbles dancing.

They swam on together, parting from time to time to explore separate interests. He decided she'd forgotten his purpose in coming, but thought it was just as well. If she could take this hour for personal freedom, he was glad of it. For him, there were demands.

The water and the life in it were undeniably beautiful, but Jonas noticed other things. They hadn't seen another diver and their down time was nearly up. The caves where the sharks slept were also a perfect place to conceal a cache of drugs. Only the very brave or the very foolish would swim in their territory at night. He thought of his brother and knew Jerry would have considered it the best kind of adventure. A man with a reason could swim into one of the caves while the sharks were out feeding, and leave or take whatever he liked.

Liz hadn't forgotten why Jonas had come. Because she thought she could understand a part of what he was feeling, she gave him room. Here, eighty feet below the surface, he was searching for something, anything, to help him accept his brother's death. And his brother's life.

It would come to an end soon, Liz reflected. The police had the name of the go-between in Acapulco. And the other name that Jonas had given them, she remembered suddenly. Where had he gotten that one? She looked toward him and realized there were things he wasn't telling her. That, too, would end soon, she promised herself. Then she found herself abruptly out of air.

She didn't panic. Liz was too well trained to panic. Immediately, she checked her gauge and saw that she had ten full minutes left. Reaching back, she ran a hand down her hose and found it unencumbered. But she couldn't draw air.

Whatever the gauge said, her life was on the line. If she swam toward the surface, her lungs would be crushed by the pressure. Forcing herself to stay calm, she swam in a diagonal toward Jonas. When she caught his ankle, she tugged sharply. The smile he turned with faded the moment he saw her eyes. Recognizing her signal, he immediately removed his regulator and passed it to her. Liz drew in air. Nodding, she handed it back to him. Their bodies brushing, her hand firm on his shoulder, they began their slow ascent.

Buddy-breathing, they rose closer to the surface, restraining themselves from rushing. What took only a matter of minutes seemed to drag on endlessly. The moment Liz's head broke water, she pushed back her mask and gulped in fresh air.

"What happened?" Jonas demanded, but when he felt her begin to shake, he only swore and pulled her with him to the ladder. "Take it easy." His hand was firm at her back as she climbed up.

"I'm all right." But she collapsed on a bench, without the energy to draw off her tanks. Her body shuddered once with relief as Jonas took the weight from her. With her head between her knees, she waited for the mists to clear. "I've never had anything like that happen," she managed. "Not at eighty feet."

He was rubbing her hands to warm them. "What did happen?"

"I ran out of air."

Enraged, he took her by the shoulders and dragged her back to a sitting position. "Ran out of air? That's unforgivably careless. How can you give lessons when you haven't the sense to watch your own gauges?"

"I watched my gauge." She drew air in and let it out slowly. "I should have had another ten minutes."

"You rent diving equipment, for God's sake! How can you be negligent with your own? You might've died."

The insult to her competence went a long way toward smothering the fear. "I'm never careless," she snapped at him. "Not with rental equipment or my own." She dragged the mask from her head and tossed it on the bench. "Look at my gauge. I should have had ten minutes left."

He looked, but it didn't relieve his anger. "Your equipment should be checked. If you go down with a faulty gauge you're inviting an accident."

"My equipment has been checked. I check it myself after

every dive, and it was fine before I stored it. I filled those tanks myself." The alternative came to her even as she finished speaking. Her face, already pale, went white. "God, Jonas, I filled them myself. I checked every piece of equipment the last time I went down."

He closed a hand over hers hard enough to make her wince. "You keep it in the shop, in that closet."

"I lock it up."

"How many keys?"

"Mine—and an extra set in the drawer. They're rarely used because I always leave mine there when I go out on the boats."

"But the extra set would have been used when we were away?"

The shaking was starting again. This time it wasn't as simple to control it. "Yes."

"And someone used the key to the closet to get in and tamper with your equipment."

She moistened her lips. "Yes."

The rage ripped inside him until he was nearly blind with it. Hadn't he just promised to watch out for her, to keep her safe? With intensely controlled movements, he pulled off his flippers and discarded his mask. "You're going back. You're going to pack, then I'm putting you on a plane. You can stay with my family until this is over."

"No."

"You're going to do exactly what I say."

"No," she said again and managed to draw the strength to stand. "I'm not going anywhere. This is the second time someone's threatened my life."

"And they're not going to have a chance to do it again."

"I'm not leaving my home."

"Don't be a fool." He rose. Knowing he couldn't touch her,

he unzipped his wet suit and began to strip it off. "Your business isn't going to fall apart. You can come back when it's safe."

"I'm not leaving." She took a step toward him. "You came here looking for revenge. When you have it, you can leave and be satisfied. Now I'm looking for answers. I can't leave because they're here."

Struggling to keep his hands gentle, he took her face between them. "I'll find them for you."

"You know better than that, don't you, Jonas? Answers don't mean anything unless you find them yourself. I want my daughter to be able to come home. Until I find those answers, until it's safe, she can't." She lifted her hands to his face so that they stood as a unit. "We both have reasons to look now."

He sat, took his pack of cigarettes and spoke flatly. "Erika's dead."

The anger that had given her the strength to stand wavered. "What?"

"Murdered." His voice was cold again, hard again. "A few days ago I met her, paid her for a name."

Liz braced herself against the rail. "The name you gave to the captain."

Jonas lit his cigarette, telling himself he was justified to put fear back into her eyes. "That's right. She asked some questions, got some answers. She told me this Pablo Manchez was bad, a professional killer. Jerry was killed by a pro. So, it appears, was Erika."

"She was shot?"

"Stabbed," Jonas corrected and watched Liz's hand reach involuntarily for her own neck. "That's right." He drew violently on the cigarette then hurled it overboard before he rose. "You're going back to the States until this is all over."

She turned her back on him a moment, needing to be

certain she could be strong. "I'm not leaving, Jonas. We have the same problem."

"Liz—"

"No." When she turned back her chin was up and her eyes were clear. "You see, I've run from problems before, and it doesn't work."

"This isn't a matter of running, it's a matter of being sensible."

"You're staying."

"I don't have a choice."

"Then neither do I."

"Liz, I don't want you hurt."

She tilted her head as she studied him. She could believe that, she realized, and take comfort in it. "Will you go?"

"I can't. You know I can't."

"Neither can I." She wrapped her arms around him, pressed her cheek to his shoulder in a first spontaneous show of need or affection. "Let's go home," she murmured. "Let's just go home."

10

Every morning when Liz awoke she was certain Captain Moralas would call to tell her it was all over. Every night when she closed her eyes, she was certain it was only a matter of one more day. Time went on.

Every morning when Liz awoke she was certain Jonas would tell her he had to leave. Every night when she slept in his arms, she was certain it was the last time. He stayed.

For over ten years her life had had a certain purpose. Success. She'd started the struggle toward it in order to survive and to provide for her child. Somewhere along the way she'd learned the satisfaction of being on her own and making it work. In over ten years, Liz had gone steadily forward without detours. A detour could mean failure and the loss of independence. It had been barely a month since Jonas had walked into her house and her life. Since that time the straight road she had followed had forked. Ignoring the changes hadn't helped, fighting them hadn't worked. Now it no longer seemed she had the choice of which path to follow.

Because she had to hold on to something, she worked every day, keeping stubbornly to her old routine. It was the only aspect of her life that she could be certain she could control.

Though it brought some semblance of order to her life, it didn't keep Liz's mind at rest. She found herself studying her customers with suspicion. Business thrived as the summer season drew closer. It didn't seem as important as it had even weeks before, but she kept the shop open seven days a week.

Jonas had taken the fabric of her life, plucked at a few threads and changed everything. Liz had come to the point that she could admit nothing would ever be quite the same again, but she had yet to come to the point that she knew what to do about it. When he left, as she knew he would, she would have to learn all over again how to suppress longings and black out dreams.

They would find Jerry Sharpe's killer. They would find the man with the knife. If she hadn't believed that, Liz would never have gone on day after day. But after the danger was over, after all questions were answered, her life would never be as it had been. Jonas had woven himself into it. When he went away, he'd leave a hole behind that would take all her will to mend.

Her life had been torn before. Liz could comfort herself that she had put it together again. The shape had been different, the texture had changed, but she had put it together. She could do so again. She would have to.

There were times when she lay in bed in the dark, in the early hours of the morning, restless, afraid she would have to begin those repairs before she was strong enough.

Jonas could feel her shift beside him. He'd come to understand she rarely slept peacefully. Or she no longer slept peacefully. He wished she would lean on him, but knew she never would. Her independence was too vital, and opposingly, her insecurity was too deep to allow her to admit a need for another. Even the sharing of a burden was difficult for her. He wanted to soothe. Through his adult life, Jonas had carefully chosen companions who had no problems, required no advice, no comfort, no support. A woman who required such things required an emotional attachment he had never been willing to make. He wasn't a selfish man, simply a cautious one. Throughout his youth, and through most of his adult life, he'd picked up the pieces his brother had scattered. Consciously or unconsciously, Jonas had promised himself he'd never be put in the position of having to do so for anyone else.

Now he was drawing closer and closer to a woman who elicited pure emotion, then tried to deflect it. He was falling in love with a woman who needed him but refused to admit it. She was strong and had both the intelligence and the will to take care of herself. And she had eyes so soft, so haunted, that a man would risk anything to protect her from any more pain.

She had completely changed his life. She had altered the simple, tidy pattern he'd been weaving for himself. He *needed* to soothe, to protect, to share. There was nothing he could do to change that. Whenever he touched her, he came closer to admitting there was nothing he would do.

The bed was warm and the room smelled of the flowers that grew wild outside the open window. Their scent mixed with the bowl of potpourri on Liz's dresser. Now and then the breeze ruffled through palm fronds so that the sound whispered but didn't disturb. Beside him was a woman whose body was slim and restless. Her hair spread over her pillow and onto his, carrying no more fragrance than wind over water. The moonlight trickled in, dipping into corners, filtering over the bed so he could trace her silhouette. As she tossed in sleep, he drew her closer. Her muscles were tense, as though she were prepared to reject the gift of comfort even before it was offered. Slowly, as her breath whispered at his throat, he began to massage her shoulders. Strong shoulders, soft skin. He found the combination irresistible. She murmured, shifting toward him, but he didn't know if it was acceptance or request. It didn't matter.

She felt so good there; she felt right there. All questions, all doubts could wait for the sunrise. Before dawn they would share the need that was in both of them. In the moonlight, in the quiet hours, each would have what the other could offer. He touched his mouth lightly, ever so lightly, to hers.

She sighed, but it was only a whisper of a sound—a sigh in sleep as her body relaxed against his. If she dreamed now, she dreamed of easy things, calm water, soft grass. He trailed a hand down her back, exploring the shape of her. Long, lean, slender and strong. He felt his own body warm and pulse. Passion, still sleepy, began to stir.

She seemed to wake in stages. First her skin, then her blood, then muscle by muscle. Her body was alert and throbbing before her mind raced to join it. She found herself wrapped around Jonas, already aroused, already hungry. When his mouth came to hers again, she answered him.

There was no hesitation in her this time, no moment of doubt before desire overwhelmed reason. She wanted to give herself to him as fully as it was possible to give. It wouldn't be wise to speak her feelings out loud. It couldn't be safe to tell him with words that her heart was stripped of defenses and open for him. But she could show him, and by doing so give them both the pleasure of love without restrictions.

Her arms tightened around him as her mouth roamed madly over his. She drew his bottom lip inside the heat, inside the moistness of her mouth and nibbled, sucked until his breath came fast and erratic. She felt the abrupt tension as his body pressed against hers and realized he, too, could be seduced. He, too, could be aroused beyond reason. And she realized with a heady sort of wonder that she could be the seducer, she could arouse.

She shifted her body under his, tentatively, but with a slow rhythm that had him murmuring her name and grasping for control. Instinctively she sought out vulnerabilities, finding them one by one, learning from them, taking from them. Her tongue flicked over his throat, seeking then enjoying the subtle, distinct taste of man. His pulse was wild there, as wild as hers. She shifted again until she lay across him and his body was hers for the taking.

Her hands were inexperienced so that her stroking was soft and hesitant. It drove him mad. No one had ever been so sweetly determined to bring him pleasure. She pressed kisses over his chest, slowly, experimentally, then rubbed her cheek over his skin so that the touch both soothed and excited.

His body was on fire, yet it seemed to float free so that he could feel the passage of air breathe cool over his flesh. She touched, and the heat spread like brushfire. She tasted and the moistness from her lips was like the whisper of a night breeze, cooling, calming.

"Tell me what you want." She looked up and her eyes were luminous in the moonlight, dark and beautiful. "Tell me what to do."

It was almost more than he could bear, the purity of the request, the willingness to give. He reached up so that his hands were lost in her hair. He could have kept her there forever, arched above him with her skin glowing gold in the thin light, her hair falling pale over her shoulders, her eyes shimmering with need. He drew her down until their lips met again. Hunger exploded between them. She didn't need to be told, she didn't need to be taught. Her body took over so that her own desire drove them both.

Jonas let reason go, let control be damned. Gripping her hips, he drew her up, then brought her to him, brought himself into her with a force that had her gasping in astonished pleasure. As she shuddered again, then again, he reached for her hands. Their fingers linked as she arched back and let her need set the pace. Frantic. Desperate. Uncontrollable. Pleasure, pain, delight, terror all whipped through her, driving her on, thrusting her higher.

He couldn't think, but he could feel. Until that moment, he wouldn't have believed it possible to feel so much so intensely. Sensations racked him, building and building and threatening to explode until the only sound he could hear was the roar of his own heart inside his head. With his eyes half open he could see her above him, naked and glorious in the moonlight. And when she plunged him beyond sensation, beyond sight and reason, he could still see her. He always would.

It didn't seem possible. It didn't, Liz thought, seem reasonable that she could be managing the shop, dealing with customers, stacking equipment when her system was still soaking up every delicious sensation she'd experienced just before dawn. Yet she was there, filling out forms, giving advice, quoting prices and making change. Still it was all mechanical. She'd been wise to delegate the diving tours and remain on shore.

She greeted her customers, some old and some new, and tried not to think too deeply about the list she'd been forced to give Moralas. How many of them would come to the Black Coral for equipment or lessons if they knew that by doing only that they were under police investigation? Jerry Sharpe's murder, and her involvement in it, could endanger her business far more than a slow season or a rogue hurricane.

Over and above her compassion, her sympathy and her hopes that Jonas could put his mind and heart at rest was a desperate need to protect her own, to guard what she'd built from nothing for her daughter. No matter how she tried to bury it, she couldn't completely block out the resentment she felt for being pulled into a situation that had been none of her making.

Yet there was a tug-of-war waging inside of her. Resentment for the disruption of her life battled against the longing to have Jonas remain in it. Without the disruption, he never would have come to her. No matter how much she tried, she could never regret the weeks they'd had together. She promised herself that she never would. It was time to admit that she had a great scope of love that had been trapped inside her. Rejected once, it had refused to risk again. But Jonas had released it, or perhaps she'd released it herself. Whatever happened, however it ended, she'd been able to love again.

"You're a hard lady to pin down."

Startled out of her own thoughts, Liz looked up. It took her a moment to remember the face, and a moment still to link a name with it. "Mr. Trydent." She rose from her desk to go to the counter. "I didn't realize you were still on the island."

"I only take one vacation a year, so I like to make the most of it." He set a tall paper cup that bounced with ice on the counter. "I figured this was the only way to get you to have a drink with me."

Liz glanced at the cup and wondered if she'd been business-like or rude. At the moment she would have liked nothing better than to be alone with her own thoughts, but a customer was a customer. "That's nice of you. I've been pretty tied up."

"No kidding." He gave her a quick smile that showed straight teeth and easy charm. "You're either out of town or out on a boat. So I thought about the mountain and Mohammed." He glanced around. "Things are pretty quiet now."

"Lunchtime," Liz told him. "Everyone who's going out is already out. Everyone else is grabbing some food or a siesta before they decide how to spend the afternoon."

"Island living."

She smiled back. "Exactly. Tried any more diving?"

He made a face. "I let myself get talked into a night dive with Mr. Ambuckle before he headed back to Texas. I'm planning on sticking to the pool for the rest of my vacation."

"Diving's not for everyone."

"You can say that again." He drank from the second cup he'd brought, then leaned on the counter. "How about dinner? Dinner's for everyone."

She lifted a brow, a little surprised, a little flattered that he seemed bent on a pursuit. "I rarely eat out."

"I like home cooking."

"Mr. Trydent—"

"Scott," he corrected.

"Scott, I appreciate the offer, but I'm…" How did she put it? Liz wondered. "I'm seeing someone."

He laid a hand on hers. "Serious?"

Not sure whether she was embarrassed or amused, Liz drew her hand away. "I'm a serious sort of person."

"Well." Scott lifted his cup, watching her over the rim as he drank. "I guess we'd better stick to business then. How about explaining the snorkeling equipment to me?"

With a shrug, Liz glanced over her shoulder. "If you can swim, you can snorkel."

"Let's just say I'm cautious. Mind if I come in and take a look?"

She'd been ungracious enough for one day, Liz decided. She sent him a smile. "Sure, look all you want." When he'd skirted around the counter and through the door, she walked with him to the back shelves. "The snorkel's just a hollow tube with a mouthpiece," she began as she took one down to offer it. "You put this lip between your teeth and breathe normally through your mouth. With the tube attached to a face mask, you can paddle around on the surface indefinitely."

"Okay. How about all the times I see these little tubes disappear under the water?"

"When you want to go down, you hold your breath and let out a bit of air to help you descend. The trick is to blow out and clear the tube of water when you surface. Once you get the knack, you can go down and up dozens of times without ever taking your face out of the water."

Scott turned the snorkel over in his hand. "There's a lot to see down there."

"A whole world."

He was no longer looking at the snorkel, but at her. "I guess you know a lot about the water and the reefs in this area. Know much about Isla Mujeres?"

"Excellent snorkeling and diving." Absently, Liz took down a mask to show him how to attach the snorkel. "We offer full- and half-day trips. If you're adventurous enough, there are caves to explore."

"And some are fairly remote," he said idly.

"For snorkeling you'd want to stay closer to the reefs, but an experienced diver could spend days around the caves."

"And nights." Scott passed the snorkel through his fingers as he watched her. "I imagine a diver could go down there at night and be completely undisturbed."

She wasn't certain why she felt a trickle of alarm. Automatically, she glanced over his shoulder to where her police guard half dozed in the sun. Silly, she told herself with a little shrug. She'd never been one to jump at shadows. "It's a dangerous area for night diving."

"Some people prefer danger, especially when it's profitable."

Her mouth was dry, so she swallowed as she replaced the mask on the shelf. "Perhaps. I don't."

This time his smile wasn't so charming or his eyes so friendly. "Don't you?"

"I don't know what you mean."

"I think you do." His hand closed over her arm. "I think you know exactly what I mean. What Jerry Sharpe skimmed off the top and dumped in that safe-deposit box in Acapulco was petty cash, Liz." He leaned closer as his voice lowered. "There's a lot more to be made. Didn't he tell you?"

She had a sudden, fierce memory of a knife probing against her throat. "He didn't tell me anything. I don't know anything." Before she could evade, he had her backed into a corner. "If I scream," she managed in a steady voice, "there'll be a crowd of people here before you can take a breath."

"No need to scream." He held up both hands as if to show her he meant no harm. "This is a business discussion. All I want to know is how much Jerry told you before he made the mistake of offending the wrong people."

When she discovered she was trembling, Liz forced herself to stop. He wouldn't intimidate her. What weapon could he hide in a pair of bathing trunks and an open shirt? She straightened her shoulders and looked him directly in the eye. "Jerry didn't tell me anything. I said the same thing to your friend when he had the knife at my throat. It didn't satisfy him, so he put a damaged gauge on my tanks."

"My partner doesn't understand much about finesse," Scott said easily. "I don't carry knives, and I don't know enough about your diving equipment to mess with the gauges. What I know about is you, and I know plenty. You work too hard, Liz, getting up at dawn and hustling until sundown. I'm just trying to give you some options. Business, Liz. We're just going to talk business."

It was his calm, reasonable attitude that had her temper whipping out. He could be calm, he could be reasonable, and people were dead. "I'm not Jerry and I'm not Erika, so keep that in mind. I don't know anything about the filthy business you're into, but the police do, and they'll know more. If you think you can frighten me by threatening me with a knife or damaging my equipment, you're right. But that doesn't stop me from wishing every one of you to hell. Now get out of my shop and leave me alone."

He studied her face for a long ten seconds, then backed an inch or two away. "You've got me wrong, Liz. I said this was a business discussion. With Jerry gone, an experienced diver would come in handy, especially one who knows the waters around here. I'm authorized to offer you five thousand dollars. Five thousand American dollars for doing what you do best. Diving. You go down, drop off one package and pick up another. No names, no faces. Bring the package back to me unopened and I hand you five thousand in cash. Once or twice a week, and you can build up a nice little nest egg. I'd say a woman raising a kid alone could use some extra money."

Fear had passed into fury; she clenched her hands together. "I told you to get out," she repeated. "I don't want your money."

He smiled and touched a finger to her cheek. "Give it some thought. I'll be around if you change your mind."

Liz waited for her breathing to level as she watched him walk away. With deliberate movements, she locked the shop, then walked directly to her police guard. "I'm going home," she told him as he sprang to attention. "Tell Captain Moralas to meet me there in half an hour." Without waiting for a reply, she strode across the sand.

★ ★ ★

Fifteen minutes later, Liz slammed into her house. The ride home hadn't calmed her. At every turn she'd been violated. At every turn, her privacy and peace had been disrupted. This last incident was the last she'd accept. She might have been able to handle another threat, another demand. But he'd offered her a job. Offered to pay her to smuggle cocaine, to take over the position of a man who'd been murdered. Jonas's brother.

A nightmare, Liz thought as she paced from window to window. She wished she could believe it was a nightmare. The cycle was drawing to a close, and she felt herself being trapped in the center. What Jerry Sharpe had started, she and Jonas would be forced to finish, no matter how painful. No matter how deadly. Finish it she would, Liz promised herself. The cycle would be broken, no matter what she had to do. She would be finished with it so her daughter could come home safely. Whatever she had to do, she would see to that.

At the sound of a car approaching, Liz went to the front window. Jonas, she thought, and felt her heart sink. Did she tell him now that she'd met face-to-face with the man who might have killed his brother? If he had the name, if he knew the man, would he race off in a rage for the revenge he'd come so far to find? And if he found his revenge, could the cycle ever be broken? Instead, she was afraid it would revolve and revolve around them, smothering everything else. She saw Jonas, a man of the law, a man of patience and compassion, shackled forever within the results of his own violence. How could she save him from that and still save herself?

Her hand was cold as she reached for the door and opened it to meet him. He knew there was something wrong before he touched her. "What are you doing home? I went by the shop and it was closed."

"Jonas." She did the only thing she knew how. She drew him against her and held on. "Moralas is on his way here."

"What happened?" A little skip of panic ran through him before he could stop it. He held her away, searching her face. "Did something happen to you? Were you hurt?"

"No, I'm not hurt. Come in and sit down."

"Liz, I want to know what happened."

She heard the sound of a second engine and looked down the street to see the unmarked car. "Moralas is here," she murmured. "Come inside, Jonas. I'd rather go through this only once."

There was really no decision to be made, Liz told herself as she moved away from the door to wait. She would give Moralas and Jonas the name of the man who had approached her. She would tell them exactly what he'd said. By doing so she would take herself one step further away from the investigation. They would have a name, a face, a location. They would have motive. It was what the police wanted, it was what she wanted. She glanced at Jonas as Moralas came up the front walk. It was what Jonas wanted. What he needed. And by giving it to him, she would take herself one step further way from him.

"Miss Palmer." Moralas took off his hat as he entered, glanced briefly at Jonas and waited.

"Captain." She stood by a chair but didn't sit. "I have some information for you. There's an American, a man named Scott Trydent. Less than an hour ago he offered me five thousand dollars to smuggle cocaine off the reef of Isla Mujeres."

Moralas's expression remained impassive. He tucked his hat under his arm. "And have you had previous dealings with this man?"

"He joined one of my diving classes. He was friendly. Today he came by the shop to talk to me. Apparently he believed that

I…" She trailed off to look at Jonas. He stood very still and very quiet just inside the door. "He thought that Jerry had told me about the operation. He'd found out about the safe-deposit box. I don't know how. It was as though he knew every move I've made for weeks." As her nerves began to fray, she dragged a hand through her hair. "He told me that I could take over Jerry's position, make the exchange in the caves near Isla Mujeres and be rich. He knows…" She had to swallow to keep her voice from trembling. "He knows about my daughter."

"You would identify him?"

"Yes. I don't know if he killed Jerry Sharpe." Her gaze shifted to Jonas again and pleaded. "I don't know, but I could identify him."

Moralas watched the exchange before crossing the room. "Please sit down, Miss Palmer."

"You'll arrest him?" She wanted Jonas to say something, anything, but he continued to stand in silence. "He's part of the cocaine ring. He knows about Jerry's Sharpe's murder. You have to arrest him."

"Miss Palmer." Moralas urged her down on the sofa, then sat beside her. "We have names. We have faces. The smuggling ring currently operating in the Yucatan Peninsula is under investigation by both the Mexican and the American governments. The names you and Mr. Sharpe have given me are not unfamiliar. But there is one we don't have. The person who organizes, the person who undoubtedly ordered the murder of Jerry Sharpe. This is the name we need. Without it, the arrest of couriers, of salesmen, is nothing. We need this name, Miss Palmer. And we need proof."

"I don't understand. You mean you're just going to let Trydent go? He'll just find someone else to make the drops."

"It won't be necessary for him to look elsewhere if you agree."

"No." Before Liz could take in Moralas's words, Jonas was

breaking in. He said it quietly, so quietly that chills began to race up and down her spine. He took out a cigarette. His hands were rock steady. Taking his time, he flicked his lighter and drew until the tip glowed red. He blew out a stream of smoke and locked his gaze on Moralas. "You can go to hell."

"Miss Palmer has the privilege to tell me so herself."

"You're not using her. If you want someone on the inside, someone closer to the names and proof, I'll make the drop."

Moralas studied him, saw the steady nerves and untiring patience along with simmering temper. If he'd had a choice, he'd have preferred it. "It isn't you who has been asked."

"Liz isn't going down."

"Just a minute." Liz pressed both hands to her temples. "Are you saying you want me to see Trydent again, to tell him I'll take the job? That's crazy. What purpose could there be?"

"You would be a decoy." Moralas glanced down at her hands. Delicate, yes, but strong. There was nothing about Elizabeth Palmer he didn't know. "The investigation is closing in. We don't want the ring to change locations at this point. If the operation appears to go smoothly, there should be no move at this time. You've been the stumbling block, Miss Palmer, for the ring, and the investigation."

"How?" Furious, she started to stand. Moralas merely put a hand on her arm.

"Jerry Sharpe lived with you, worked for you. He had a weakness for women. Neither the police nor the smugglers have been sure exactly what part you played. Jerry Sharpe's brother is now living in your home. The key to the safe-deposit box was found by you."

"Guilty by association, Captain?" Her voice took on that ice-sharp edge Jonas had heard only once or twice before. "Have I had police protection, or have I been under surveillance?"

Moralas's tone never altered. "One serves the same purpose as the other."

"If I'm under suspicion, haven't you considered that I might simply take the money and run?"

"That's precisely what we want you to do."

"Very clever." Jonas wasn't certain how much longer he could hold on to his temper. It would have given him great satisfaction to have picked Moralas up bodily and thrown him out of the house. Out of Liz's life. "Liz double-crosses them, annoying the head of the operation. It's then necessary to eliminate her the way my brother was eliminated."

"Except that Miss Palmer will be under police protection at all times. If this one drop goes as we plan, the investigation will end, and the smugglers, along with your brother's killer, will be caught and punished. This is what you want?"

"Not if it means risking Liz. Plant your own pigeon, Moralas."

"There isn't time. With your cooperation, Miss Palmer, we can end this. Without it, it could take months."

Months? she thought. Another day would be a lifetime. "I'll do it."

Jonas was beside her in a heartbeat, pulling her off the couch. "Liz—"

"My daughter comes home in two weeks." She put her hands on his arms. "She won't come back to anything like this."

"Take her someplace else." Jonas gripped her shoulders until his fingers dug into flesh. "We'll go someplace else."

"Where?" she demanded. "Every day I tell myself I'm pulling away from this thing and every day it's a lie. I've been in it since Jerry walked in the door. We can't change that. Until it's over, really over, nothing's going to be right."

He knew she was right, had known it from the first moment. But too much had changed. There was a desperation in him now that he'd never expected to feel. It was all for her. "Come back to the States with me. It will be over."

"Will it? Will you forget your brother was murdered? Will you forget the man who killed him?" His fingers tightened, his eyes darkened, but he said nothing. Her breath came out in a sigh of acceptance. "No, it won't be over until we finish it. I've run before, Jonas. I promised myself I'd never run again."

"You could be killed."

"I've done nothing and they've nearly killed me twice." She dropped her head on his chest. "Please help me."

He couldn't force her to bend his way. Two of the things he most admired in her were her capacity to give and her will to stand firm. He could plead with her, he could argue, but he could never lie. If she ran, if they ran, they'd never be free of it. His arm came around her. Her hair smelled of summer and sea air. And before the summer ended, he promised himself, she'd be free. They'd both be free.

"I go with her." He met Moralas's eyes over her head.

"That may not be possible."

"I'll make it possible."

11

She'd never been more frightened in her life. Every day she worked in the shop, waiting for Scott Trydent to approach. Every evening she locked up, went home and waited for the phone to ring. Jonas said little. She no longer knew what he did with the hours they were apart, but she was aware that he was planning his own move, in his own time. It only frightened her more.

Two days passed until her nerves were stretched thinner and tighter than she would have believed possible. On the beach, people slept or read novels, lovers walked by arm in arm. Children chattered and ran. Snorkelers splashed around the reef. She wondered why nothing seemed normal, or if it ever would again. At sundown she emptied her cash box, stacked gear and began to lock up.

"How about that drink?"

Though she'd thought she'd braced herself for the moment when it would begin, Liz jolted. Her head began to throb in a slow, steady rhythm she knew would last for hours. In the pit of her stomach she felt the twist come and go from panicked excitement. From this point on, she reminded herself, she had no room to panic. She turned and looked at Scott. "I was wondering if you'd come back."

"Told you I'd be around. I always figure people need a couple of days to mull things over."

She had a part to play, Liz reminded herself. She had to do it well. Carefully, she finished locking up, then turned back to him. She didn't smile. It was to be a business discussion, cut-and-dried. "We can get a drink over there." She pointed to the open-air thatched-roof restaurant overhanging the reef. "It's public."

"Suits me." Though he offered his hand, she ignored it and began to walk.

"You used to be friendlier."

"You used to be a customer." She sent him a sideways look. "Not a business partner."

"So…" She saw him glance right, then left. "You've mulled."

"You need a diver, I need money." Liz walked up the two wooden stairs and chose a chair that had her back to the water. Seconds after she sat, a man settled himself into a corner table. One of Moralas's, she thought, and ordered herself to be calm. She'd been briefed and rebriefed. She knew what to say, how to say it, and that the waiter who would serve them carried a badge and a gun. "Jerry didn't tell me a great deal," she began, and ordered an American soft drink. "Just that he made the drop and collected the money."

"He was a good diver."

Liz swallowed the little bubble of fear. "I'm better."

Scott grinned at her. "So I'm told."

A movement beside her had her glancing over, then freezing. A dark man with a pitted face took the chair beside her. Liz knew he wore a thin silver band on his wrist before she looked for it.

"Pablo Manchez, Liz Palmer. Though I think you two have met."

"Señorita." Manchez's thin mouth curved as he took her hand.

"Tell your friend to keep his hands to himself." Calmly, Jonas pulled a chair up to the table. "Why don't you introduce me, Liz?" When she could do no more than stare at him, he settled back. "I'm Jonas Sharpe. Liz and I are partners." He leveled his gaze to Manchez. This was the man, he thought, whom he'd come thousands of miles to see. This was the man he'd kill. Jonas felt the hatred and the fury rise. But he knew how to strap the emotions and wait. "I believe you knew my brother."

Manchez's hand dropped from Liz's and went to his side. "Your brother was greedy and stupid."

Liz held her breath as Jonas reached in his pocket. Slowly, he pulled out his cigarettes. "I'm greedy," he said easily as he lit one. "But I'm not stupid. I've been looking for you." He leaned across the table. With a slow smile, he offered Manchez the cigarettes.

Manchez took one and broke off the filter. His hands were beautiful, with long spidery fingers and narrow palms. Liz fought back a shudder as she looked at them. "So you found me."

Jonas was still smiling as he ordered a beer. "You need a diver."

Scott sent Manchez a warning look. "We have a diver."

"What you have is a team. Liz and I work together." Jonas blew out a stream of smoke. "Isn't that right, Liz?"

He wanted them. He wasn't going to back off until he had them. And she had no choice. "That's right."

"We don't need no team." Manchez started to rise.

"You need us." Jonas took his beer as it was served. "We already know a good bit about your operation. Jerry wasn't good at keeping secrets." Jonas took a swig from the bottle. "Liz and I are more discreet. Five thousand a drop?"

Scott waited a beat, then held a hand up, signaling Manchez. "Five. If you want to work as a team, it's your business how you split it."

"Fifty-fifty." Liz spread her fingers around Jonas's beer. "One of us goes down, one stays in the dive boat."

"Tomorrow night. Eleven o'clock. You come to the shop. Go inside. You'll find a waterproof case. It'll be locked."

"So will the shop," Liz put in. "How does the case get inside?"

Manchez blew smoke between his teeth. "I got no problem getting in."

"Just take the case," Scott interrupted. "The coordinates will be attached to the handle. Take the boat out, take the case down, leave it. Then come back up and wait exactly an hour. That's when you dive again. All you have to do is take the case that's waiting for you back to the shop and leave it."

"Sounds smooth," Jonas decided. "When do we get paid?"

"After you do the job."

"Half up front." Liz took a long swallow of beer and hoped her heart would settle. "Leave twenty-five hundred with the case or I don't dive."

Scott smiled. "Not as trusting as Jerry."

She gave him a cold, bitter look. "And I intend to stay alive."

"Just follow the rules."

"Who makes them?" Jonas took the beer back from Liz. Her hand slipped down to his leg and stayed steady.

"You don't want to worry about that," Manchez advised. The cigarette was clamped between his teeth as he smiled. "He knows who you are."

"Just follow the coordinates and keep an eye on your watch." Scott dropped bills on the table as he rose. "The rest is gravy."

"Stay smart, Jerry's brother." Manchez gave them both a slow smile. *"Adios, señorita."*

Jonas calmly finished his beer as the two men walked away.

"You weren't supposed to interfere during the meeting," Liz began in a furious undertone. "Moralas said—"

"The hell with Moralas." He crushed out his cigarette, watching as the smoke plumed up. "Is that the man who put the bruises on your neck?"

Her hand moved up before she could stop it. Halfway to her throat, Liz curled her fingers into a ball and set her hand on the table. "I told you I didn't see him."

Jonas turned his head. His eyes, as they had before, reminded her of frozen smoke. "Was it the man?"

He didn't need to be told. Liz leaned closer and spoke softly. "I want it over, Jonas. And I don't need revenge. You were supposed to let me meet with Scott and set things up by myself."

In an idle move, he tilted the candle on the table toward him and lit it. "I changed my mind."

"Damn you, you could've messed everything up. I don't want to be involved but I am. The only way to get uninvolved is to finish it. How do we know they won't just back off now that you've come into it?"

"Because you're right in the middle, and you always have been." Before she could speak, he took her arm. His face was close, his voice cool and steady. "I was going to use you. From the minute I walked into your house, I was going to use you to get to Jerry's killer. If I had to walk all over you, if I had to knock you out of the way or drag you along with me, I was going to use you. Just the way Moralas is going to use you. Just the way the others are going to use you." The heat of the candle flickered between them as he drew her closer. "The way Jerry used you."

She swallowed the tremor and fought against the pain. "And now?"

He didn't speak. They were so close that he could see himself reflected in her eyes. In them, surrounding his own reflection, he saw the doubts and the defiance. His hand came to the back of her neck, held there until he could feel the rhythm of her pulse. With a simmering violence, he pulled her against him and covered her mouth with his. A flare that was passion, a glimmer that was hope—he didn't know which to reach for. So he let her go.

"No one's going to hurt you again," he murmured. "Especially not me."

It was the longest day of her life. Liz worked and waited as the hours crawled by. Moralas's men mixed with the vacationers on the beach. So obviously, it seemed to Liz, that she wondered everyone else didn't notice them as though they wore badges around their necks. Her boats went out, returned and went out again. Tanks and equipment were checked and rented. She filled out invoices and accepted credit cards as if there were some importance to daily routine. She wished for the day to end. She hoped the night would never come.

A thousand times she thought of telling Moralas she couldn't go through with it. A thousand times she called herself a coward. But as the sun went down and the beach began to clear, she realized courage wasn't something that could be willed into place. She would run, if she had the choice. But as long as she was in danger, Faith was in danger. When the sun went down, she locked the shop as if it were the end of any ordinary day. Before she'd pocketed her keys, Jonas was beside her.

"There's still time to change your mind."

"And do what? Hide?" She looked out at the beach, at the sea, at the island that was her home. And her prison. Why had she never seen it as a prison until Jonas had come to it? "You've already told me how good I am at hiding."

"Liz—"

She shook her head to stop him. "I can't talk about it. I just have to do it."

They drove home in silence. In her mind, Liz went over her instructions, every point, every word Moralas had pushed at her. She was to follow the routine, make the exchange, then turn the case with the money over to the police who'd be waiting near the dock. She'd wait for the next move. And while she waited, she'd never be more than ten feet away from a cop. It sounded foolproof. It made her stomach churn.

There was a man walking a dog along the street in front of her house. One of Moralas's men. The man whittling on her neighbor's porch had a gun under his denim vest. Liz tried to look at neither of them.

"You're going to have a drink, some food and a nap," Jonas ordered as he steered her inside.

"Just the nap."

"The nap first then." After securing the lock, Jonas followed her into the bedroom. He lowered the shades. "Do you want anything?"

It was still so hard to ask. "Would you lie down with me?"

He came to her. She was already curled on her side, so he drew her back against him and wrapped her close. "Will you sleep?"

"I think so." In sleep she could find escape, if only temporarily. But she didn't close her eyes. "Jonas?"

"Hmm?"

"After tonight—after we've finished, will you hold me like this again?"

He pressed his lips to her hair. He didn't think he could love her any more. He was nearly certain if he told her she'd pull away. "As long as you want. Just sleep."

Liz let her eyes close and her mind empty.

The case was small, the size of an executive briefcase. It seemed too inconspicuous to be the catalyst for so much danger.

Beside it, on the counter of Liz's shop, was an envelope. Inside was a slip of paper with longitude and latitude printed. With the slip of paper were twenty-five one-hundred-dollar bills.

"They kept their part of the bargain," Jonas commented.

Liz merely shoved the envelope into a drawer. "I'll get my equipment."

Jonas watched her. She'd rather do this on her own, he reflected. She'd rather not think she had someone to lean on, to turn to. He took her tanks before she could heft them. She was going to learn, he reminded himself, that she had a great deal more than that. "The coordinates?"

"The same that were in Jerry's book." She found herself amazingly calm as she waited to lock the door behind him. They were being watched. She was aware that Moralas had staked men in the hotel. She was just as certain Manchez was somewhere close. She and Jonas didn't speak again until they were on the dive boat and had cast off. "This could end it." She glanced at him as she set her course.

"This could end it."

She was silent for a moment. All during the evening hours she'd thought about what she would say to him, how she would say it. "Jonas, what will you do?"

The flame of his lighter hissed, flared, then was quiet. "What I have to do."

The fear tasted like copper in her mouth, but it had nothing to do with herself and everything to do with Jonas. "If we make the exchange tonight, turn the second case over to Moralas. They'll have to come out in the open. Manchez, and the man who gives the orders."

"What are you getting at, Liz?"

"Manchez killed your brother."

Jonas looked beyond her. The sea was black. The sky was

black. Only the hum of the motor broke the silence. "He was the trigger."

"Are you going to kill him?"

Slowly, he turned back to her. The question had been quiet, but her eyes weren't. They sent messages, posed argument, issued pleas. "It doesn't involve you."

That hurt deeply, sharply. With a nod, she followed the shimmer of light on the water. "Maybe not. But if you let hate rule what you do, how you think, you'll never be free of it. Manchez will be dead, Jerry will still be dead and you…" She turned to look at him again. "You'll never really be alive again."

"I didn't come all this way, spend all this time, to let Manchez walk away. He kills for money and because he enjoys it. He enjoys it," Jonas repeated viciously. "You can see it in his eyes."

And she had. But she didn't give a damn about Manchez. "Do you remember telling me once that everyone was entitled to representation?"

He remembered. He remembered everything he'd once believed in. He remembered how Jerry had looked in the cold white light of the morgue. "It didn't have anything to do with this."

"I suppose you change the rules when it's personal."

"He was my brother."

"And he's dead." With a sigh she lifted her face so that the wind could cool her skin. "I'm sorry, Jonas. Jerry's dead and if you go through with what you've planned, you're going to kill something in yourself." And, though she couldn't tell him, something in her. "Don't you trust the law?"

He tossed his cigarette into the water, then leaned on the rail. "I've been playing with it for years. It's the last thing I'd trust."

She wanted to go to him but didn't know how. Still, no

matter what he did, she was beside him. "Then you'll have to trust yourself. And so will I."

Slowly, he crossed to her. Taking her face in his hands, he tried to understand what she was telling him, what she was still holding back. "Will you?"

"Yes."

He leaned to press a kiss to her forehead. Inside there was a need, a fierce desire to tell her to head the boat out to sea and keep going. But that would never work, not for either of them. They stood on the boat together, and stood at the crossroads. "Then start now." He kissed her again before he turned and lifted one of the compartment seats. Liz frowned as she saw the wet suit.

"What are you doing?"

"I arranged to have Luis leave this here for me."

"Why? We can't both go down."

Jonas stripped down to his trunks. "That's right. I'm diving, you're staying with the boat."

Liz stood very straight. It wouldn't do any good to lose her temper. "The arrangements were made on all sides, Jonas. I'm diving."

"I'm changing the arrangements." He tugged the wet suit up to his waist before he looked at her. "I'm not taking any more chances with you."

"You're not taking chances with me. I am. Jonas, you don't know these waters. I do. You've never gone down here at night. I have."

"I'm about to."

"The last thing we need right now is for you to start behaving like an overprotective man."

He nearly laughed as he snapped the suit over his shoulders. "That's too bad, then, because that's just what we've got."

"I told Manchez and Trydent I was going down."

"I guess your reputation's shot when you lie to murderers and drug smugglers."

"Jonas, I'm not in the mood for jokes."

He strapped on his diver's knife, adjusted his weight belt, then reached for his mask. "Maybe not. And maybe you're not in the mood to hear this. I care about you. Too damn much." He reached out, gripping her chin. "My brother dragged you into this because he never wasted two thoughts about anyone else in his life. I pulled you in deeper because all I was thinking about was payback. Now I'm thinking about you, about us. You're not going down. If I have to tie you to the wheel, you're not going down."

"I don't want you to go." She balled her fists against his chest. "If I was down, all I'd think about was what I was doing. If I stay up here, I won't be able to stop thinking about what could happen to you."

"Time me." He lifted the tanks and held them out to her. "Help me get them on."

Hadn't she told herself weeks before that he wasn't a man who'd lose an argument? Her hands trembled a bit as she slipped the straps over his shoulders. "I don't know how to handle being protected."

He hooked the tanks as he turned back to her. "Practice."

She closed her eyes. It was too late for talk, too late for arguments. "Bear northeast as you dive. The cave's at eighty feet." She hesitated only a moment, then picked up a spear gun. "Watch out for sharks."

When he was over the side, she lowered the case to him. In seconds, he was gone and the sea was black and still. In her mind, Liz followed him fathom by fathom. The water would be dark so that he would be dependent on his gauges and the thin beam of light. Night creatures would be feeding. Squid, the moray, barracuda. Sharks. Liz closed her mind to it.

She should have forced him to let her go. How? Pacing the deck, she pushed the hair back from her face. He'd gone to protect her. He'd gone because he cared about her. Shivering, she sat down to rub her arms warm again. Was this what it was like to be cared for by a man? Did it mean you had to sit and wait? She was up again and pacing. She'd lived too much of her life doing to suddenly become passive. And yet… To hear him say he cared. Liz sat again and waited.

She'd checked her watch four times before she heard him at the ladder. On a shudder of relief, she dashed over to the side to help him. "I'm going down the next time," she began.

Jonas pulled off his light, then his tanks. "Forget it." Before she could protest, he dragged her against him. "We've got an hour," he murmured against her ear. "You want to spend it arguing?"

He was wet and cold. Liz wrapped herself around him. "I don't like being bossed around."

"Next time you can boss me around." He dropped onto a bench and pulled her with him. "I'd forgotten what it was like down there at night. Fabulous." And it was nearly over, he told himself. The first step had been taken, the second one had to follow. "I saw a giant squid. Scared the hell out of him with the light. I swear he was thirty feet long."

"They get bigger." She rested her head on his shoulder and tried to relax. They had an hour. "I was diving with my father once. We saw one that was nearly sixty."

"Made you nervous?"

"No. I was fascinated. I remember I swam close enough to touch the tentacles. My father gave me a twenty-minute lecture when we surfaced."

"I imagine you'd do the same thing with Faith."

"I'd be proud of her," Liz began, then laughed. "Then I'd give her a twenty-minute lecture."

For the first time that night he noticed the stars. The sky was alive with them. It made him think of his mother's porch swing and long summer nights. "Tell me about her."

"You don't want to get me started."

"Yes, I do." He slipped an arm around her shoulder. "Tell me about her."

With a half smile, Liz closed her eyes. It was good to think of Faith, to talk of Faith. A picture began to emerge for Jonas of a young girl who liked school because there was plenty to do and lots of people. He heard the love and the pride, and the wistfulness. He saw the dark, sunny-faced girl in the photo and learned she spoke two languages, liked basketball and hated vegetables.

"She's always been sweet," Liz reflected. "But she's no angel. She's very stubborn, and when she's crossed, her temper isn't pretty. Faith wants to do things herself. When she was two she'd get very annoyed if I wanted to help her down the stairs."

"Independence seems to run in the family."

Liz moved her shoulders. "We've needed it."

"Ever thought about sharing?"

Her nerves began to hum. Though she shifted only a bit, it was away from him. "When you share, you have to give something up. I've never been able to afford to give up anything."

It was an answer he'd expected. It was an answer he intended to change. "It's time to go back down."

Liz helped him back on with his tanks. "Take the spear gun. Jonas…" He was already at the rail before she ran to him. "Hurry back," she murmured. "I want to go home. I want to make love with you."

"Hell of a time to bring that up." He sent her a grin, curled and fell back into the water.

Within five minutes Liz was pacing again. Why hadn't she thought to bring any coffee? She'd concentrate on that. In little more than an hour they could be huddled in her kitchen with a pot brewing. It wouldn't matter that there would be police surrounding the house. She and Jonas would be inside. Together. Perhaps she was wrong about sharing. Perhaps… When she heard the splash at the side of the boat, she was at the rail like a shot.

"Jonas, did something happen? Why—" She found herself looking down the barrel of a .22.

"*Señorita.*" Manchez tossed his mask and snorkel onto a bench as he climbed over the side. *"Buenas noches."*

"What are you doing here?" She struggled to sound indignant as the blood rushed from her face. No, she wasn't brave, she realized. She wasn't brave at all. "We had a deal."

"You're an amateur," he told her. "Like Sharpe was an amateur. You think we'd just forget about the money?"

"I don't know anything about the money Jerry took." She gripped the rail. "I've told you that all along."

"The boss decided you were a loose end, pretty lady. You do us a favor and make this delivery. We do you a favor. We kill you quickly."

She didn't look at the gun again. She didn't dare. "If you keep killing your divers, you're going to be out of business."

"We're finished in Cozumel. When your friend brings up the case, I take it and go to Merida. I live in style. You don't live at all."

She wanted to sit because her knees were shaking. She stood because she thought she might never be able to again. "If you're finished in Cozumel, why did you set up this drop?"

"Clancy likes things tidy."

"Clancy?" The name David Merriworth had mentioned, Liz remembered, and strained to hear any sound from the water.

"There's a few thousand in cocaine down there, that's all. A few thousand dollars in the case coming up. The boss figures it's worth the investment to make it look like you were doing the dealing with Sharpe. Then you two have an argument and shoot each other. Case closed."

"You killed Erika too, didn't you?"

"She asked too many questions." He lowered the gun. "You ask too many questions."

Light flooded the boat and the water so quickly that Liz's first instinct was to freeze. Before the next reaction had fully registered, she was tumbling into the water and diving blind.

How could she warn Jonas? Liz groped frantically in the water as lights played on the surface above her. She had no tanks, no mask, no protection. Any moment he'd be surfacing, unaware of any danger. He had no protection but her.

Without equipment, she'd be helpless in a matter of moments. She fought to stay down, keeping as close to the ladder as she dared. Her lungs were ready to burst when she felt the movement in the water. Liz turned toward the beam of light.

When he saw her, his heart nearly stopped. She looked like a ghost clinging to the hull of the boat. Her hair was pale and floating out in the current, her face was nearly as white as his light. Before his mind could begin to question, he was pushing his mouthpiece between her lips and giving her air. There could be no communication but emotion. He felt the fear. Jonas steadied the spear gun in his arm and surfaced.

"Mr. Sharpe." Moralas caught him in the beam of a spotlight. Liz rose up beside him. "We have everything under control." On the deck of her boat, Liz saw Manchez handcuffed and flanked by two divers. "Perhaps you will give my men and their prisoner a ride back to Cozumel."

She felt Jonas tense. The spear gun was set and aimed. Even through the mask, she could see his eyes burning, burning as only ice can. "Jonas, please." But he was already starting up the ladder. She hauled herself over the rail and tumbled onto the deck, cold and dripping. "Jonas, you can't. Jonas, it's over."

He barely heard her. All his emotion, all his concentration was on the man who stood only feet away. Their eyes were locked. It gave him no satisfaction to watch the blood drain from Manchez's face, or the knowledge leap frantically into his eyes. It was what he'd come for, what he'd promised himself. The medallion on the edge of his chain dangled and reminded him of his brother. His brother was dead. No satisfaction. Jonas lowered the gun.

Manchez tossed back his head. "I'll get out," he said quietly. The smile started to spread. "I'll get out."

The spear shot out and plowed into the deck between Manchez's feet. Liz saw the smile freeze on his face an instant before one formed on Jonas's. "I'll be waiting."

Could it really be over? It was all Liz could think when she awoke, warm and dry, in her own bed. She was safe, Jonas was safe, and the smuggling ring on Cozumel was broken. Of course, Jonas had been furious. Manchez had been watched, they had been watched, but the police had made their presence known only after Liz had been held at gunpoint.

But he'd gotten what he'd come for, she thought. His brother's killer was behind bars. He'd face a trial and justice. She hoped it was enough for Jonas.

The morning was enough for her. The normality of it. Happy, she rolled over and pressed her body against Jonas's. He only drew her closer.

"Let's stay right here until noon."

She laughed and nuzzled against his throat. "I have—"

"A business to run," he finished.

"Exactly. And for the first time in weeks I can run it without having this urge to look over my shoulder. I'm happy." She looked at him, then tossed her arms around his neck and squeezed. "I'm so happy."

"Happy enough to marry me?"

She went still as a stone, then slowly, very slowly drew away. "What?"

"Marry me. Come home with me. Start a life with me."

She wanted to say yes. It shocked her that her heart burned to say yes. Pulling away from him was the hardest thing she'd ever done. "I can't."

He stopped her before she could scramble out of bed. It hurt, he realized, more than he could possibly have anticipated. "Why?"

"Jonas, we're two different people with two totally separate lives."

"We stopped having separate lives weeks ago." He took her hands. "They're not ever going to be separate again."

"But they will." She drew her hands away. "After you're back in Philadelphia for a few weeks, you'll barely remember what I look like."

He had her wrists handcuffed in his hands. The fury that surfaced so seldom in him seemed always on simmer when he was around her. "Why do you do that?" he demanded. "Why can't you ever take what you're given?" He swung her around until she was beneath him on the bed. "I love you."

"Don't." She closed her eyes as the wish nearly eclipsed the reason. "Don't say that to me."

Shut out. She was shutting him out. Jonas felt the panic come first, then the anger. Then the determination. "I will say it. If I say it enough, sooner or later you'll start to believe it. Do you think all these nights have been a game? Haven't you felt it? Don't you feel anything?"

"I thought I felt something once before."

"You were a child." When she started to shake her head, he gripped her tighter. "Yes, you were. In some ways you still are, but I know what goes through you when you're with me. I know. I'm not a ghost, I'm not a memory. I'm real and I want you."

"I'm afraid of you," she whispered. "I'm afraid because you make me want what I can't have. I won't marry you, Jonas, because I'm through taking chances with my life and I won't take chances with my child's life. Please let me go."

He released her, but when she stood, his arms went around her. "It isn't over for us."

She dropped her head against his chest, pressed her cheek close. "Let me have the few days we have left. Please let me have them."

He lifted her chin. Everything he needed to know was in her eyes. A man who knew and who planned to win could afford to wait. "You haven't dealt with anyone as stubborn as you are before this. And you haven't nearly finished dealing with me." Then his hand gentled as he stroked her hair. "Get dressed. I'll take you to work."

Because he acted as though nothing had been said, Liz relaxed. It was impossible, and she knew it. They'd known each other only weeks, and under circumstances that were bound to intensify any feelings. He cared. She believed that he cared, but love—the kind of love needed to build a marriage—was too much to risk.

She loved. She loved so much that she pushed him away when she wanted to pull him closer. He needed to go back to his life, back to his world. After time had passed, if he thought of her he'd think with gratitude that she had closed a door he'd opened on impulse. She would think of him. Always.

By the time Liz was walking toward the shop, she'd settled her mind. "What are you going to do today?"

"Me?" Jonas, too, had settled his mind. "I'm going to sit in the sun and do nothing."

"Nothing?" Incredulous, Liz stared at him. "All day?"

"It's known as relaxing, or taking a day off. If you do it several days running, it's called a vacation. I was supposed to have one in Paris."

Paris, she thought. It would suit him. She wondered briefly how the air smelled in Paris. "If you get bored, I'm sure one of the boats could use the extra crew."

"I've had enough diving for a few days, thanks." Jonas plopped down on a chaise in front of the shop. It was the best place to keep an eye on her.

"Miguel." Liz automatically looked around for Luis. "You're here early."

"I came with Luis. He's checking out the dive boat—got an early tour."

"Yes, I know." But she wouldn't trust Miguel to run the shop alone for long. "Why don't you help him? I'll take care of the counter."

"*Bueno.* Oh, there were a couple of guys looking at the fishing boat. Maybe they want to rent."

"I'll take a look. You go ahead." Walking back, she crouched beside Jonas. "Keep an eye on the shop for me, will you? I've got a couple of customers over by the *Expatriate.*"

Jonas adjusted his sunglasses. "What do you pay per hour?"

Liz narrowed her eyes. "I might cook dinner tonight."

With a smile, he got up to go behind the counter. "Take all the time you need."

He made her laugh. Liz strolled down the walkway and to the pier, drinking up the morning. She could use a good fishing cruise. The aqua bikes had been ordered, but they still had to be paid for. Besides, she'd like the ride herself. It made her think of Jonas and his unwanted catch a few weeks before. Liz laughed again as she approached the men beside her boat.

"Buenos días," she began. "Mr. Ambuckle." Beaming a smile, Liz held out a hand. "I didn't know you were back. Is this one of your quick weekend trips?"

"That's right." His almost bald head gleamed in the sun as he patted her hand. "When the mood strikes me I just gotta move."

"Thinking about some big-game fishing this time around?"

"Funny you should mention it. I was just saying to my associate here that I only go for the big game."

"Only the big game." Scott Trydent turned around and pushed back his straw hat. "That's right, Clancy."

"Now don't turn around, honey." Ambuckle's fingers clamped over hers before she could move. "You're going to get on the boat, nice and quiet. We have some talking to do, then we might just take a little ride."

"How long have you been using my dive shop to smuggle?" Liz saw the gun under Scott's jacket. She couldn't signal to Jonas, didn't dare.

"For the past couple of years I've found your shop's location unbeatable. You know, they ship that stuff up from Colombia and dump in Miami. The way the heat's been on the past few years, you take a big chance using the regular routes. It takes longer this way, but I lose less merchandise."

"And you're the organizer," she murmured. "You're the man the police want."

"I'm a businessman," he said with a smile. "Let's get on board, little lady."

"The police are watching," Liz told him as she climbed on deck.

"The police have Manchez. If he hadn't tried to pull a double cross, the last shipment would have gone down smooth."

"A double cross?"

"That's right," Scott put in as he flanked her. "Pablo decided he could make more free-lancing than by being a company man."

"And by reporting on his fellow employee, Mr. Trydent moves up in rank. I work my organization on the incentive program."

Scott grinned at Ambuckle. "Can't beat the system."

"You had Jerry Sharpe killed." Struggling to believe what was happening, Liz stared at the round little man who'd chatted with her and rented her tanks. "You had him shot."

"He stole a great deal of money from me." Ambuckle's face puckered as he thought of it. "A great deal. I had Manchez dispose of him. The truth is, I'd considered you as a liaison for some time. It seemed simpler, however, just to use your shop. My wife's very fond of you."

"Your wife." Liz thought of the neat, matronly woman in skirted bathing suits. "She knows you smuggle drugs, and she knows you kill people?"

"She thinks we have a great stockbroker." Ambuckle grinned. "I've been moving snow for ten years, and my wife wouldn't know coke from powdered sugar. I like to keep business and family separate. The little woman's going to be sick when she finds out you had an accident. Now we're going to take a little ride. And we're going to talk about the three hundred thousand our friend Jerry slipped out from under my nose. Cast off, Scott."

"No!" Thinking only of survival, Liz made a lunge toward the dock. Ambuckle had her on the deck with one shove. He shook his head, dusted his hands and turned to her. "I'd wanted to keep this from getting messy. You know, I switched gauges on your tanks, figuring you'd back off. Always had a soft spot for you, little lady. But business is business." With a wheezy sigh, he turned to Scott. "Since you've taken over Pablo's position, I assume you know how to deal with this."

"I certainly do." He took out a revolver. His eyes locked on Liz's. When she caught her breath, he turned the barrel toward Ambuckle. "You're under arrest." With his other hand, he pulled out a badge. "You have the right to remain silent…" It was the last thing Liz heard before she buried her face in her hands and wept.

12

"I want to know what the hell's been going on." They were in Moralas's office, but Jonas wouldn't sit. He stood behind Liz's chair, his fingers curled tight over the back rung. If anyone had approached her, he would have struck first and asked questions later. He'd already flattened the unfortunate detective who'd tried to hold him back when he'd seen Liz on the deck of the *Expatriate* with Scott.

With his hands folded on his desk, Moralas gave Jonas a long, quiet look. "Perhaps the explanation should come from your countryman."

"Special Agent Donald Scott." The man Liz had known as Scott Trydent sat on the corner of Moralas's desk. "Sorry for the deception, Liz." Though his voice was calm and matter-of-fact, it couldn't mask the excitement that bubbled from him. As he sipped his coffee, he glanced up at Jonas. Explanations wouldn't go over easily with this one, he thought. But he'd always believed the ends justified the means. "I've been after that son of a bitch for three years." He drank again, savoring triumph. "It took us two before we could infiltrate the ring, and even then I couldn't make contact with the head man. To get to him I had to go through more channels than you do with the Company. He's been careful. For the past eight months I've been working with Manchez as Scott Trydent. He was the closest I could get to Ambuckle until two days ago."

"You used her." Jonas's hand went to Liz's shoulder. "You put her right in the middle."

"Yeah. The problem was, for a long time we weren't sure just how involved she was. We knew about your shop, Liz. We knew you were an experienced diver. In fact, there isn't anything about you my organization didn't know. For some time, you were our number-one suspect."

"Suspect?" She had her hands folded neatly in her lap, but the anger was boiling. "You suspected me."

"You left the U.S. over ten years ago. You've never been back. You have both the contacts and the means to have run the ring. You keep your daughter off the island for most of the year and in one of the best schools in Houston."

"That's my business."

"Details like that become our business. When you took Jerry Sharpe in and gave him a job, we leaned even further toward you. He thought differently, but then we weren't using him for his opinions."

She felt Jonas's fingers tighten and reached up to them as she spoke. "Using him?"

"I contacted Jerry Sharpe in New Orleans. He was someone else we knew everything about. He was a con, an operator, but he had style." He took another swig of coffee as he studied Jonas. "We made him a deal. If he could get on the inside, feed us information, we'd forget about a few…indiscretions. I liked your brother," Scott said to Jonas. "Really liked him. If he'd been able to settle a bit, he'd have made a hell of a cop. 'Conning the bad guys,' he called it."

"Are you saying Jerry was working for you?" Jonas felt his

emotions race toward the surface. The portrait he'd barely been able to force himself to accept was changing.

"That's right." Scott took out a cigarette and watched the match flare as he struck it. "I liked him—I mean that. He had a way of looking at things that made you forget they were so lousy."

That was Jerry, Jonas thought. To give himself a moment, he walked to the window. He could see the water lapping calmly against the hulls of boats. He could see the sun dancing down on it and children walking along the sea wall. The scene had been almost the same the day he'd arrived on Cozumel. Some things remained the same; others altered constantly. "What happened?"

"He had a hard time following orders. He wanted to push them too fast too far. He told me once he had something to prove, to himself and to the other part of him. The better part of him."

Jonas turned slowly. The pain came again, an ache. Liz saw it in his eyes and went to stand with him. "Go on."

"He got the idea into his head to rip off the money from a shipment. I didn't know about it until he called me from Acapulco. He figured he'd put the head man in a position where he'd have to deal personally. I told him to stay put, that we were scrubbing him. He'd have been taken back to the States and put somewhere safe until the job was over." He tossed the match he'd been holding into an ashtray on Moralas's desk. "He didn't listen. He came back to Cozumel and tried to deal with Manchez himself. It was over before I knew. Even if I'd have known, I can't be sure I could've stopped it. We don't like to lose civilians, Mr. Sharpe. I don't like to lose friends."

The anger drained from him degree by degree. It would have been so like Jerry, Jonas thought. An adventure, the excitement, the impulsiveness. "Go on."

"Orders came down to put the pressure on Liz." Scott gave

a half laugh that had nothing to do with humor. "Orders from both sides. It wasn't until after your trip to Acapulco that we were sure you weren't involved in the smuggling. You stopped being a suspect and became the decoy."

"I came to the police." She looked at Moralas. "I came to you. You didn't tell me."

"I wasn't aware of Agent Scott's identity until yesterday. I knew only that we had a man on the inside and that it was necessary to use you."

"You were protected," Scott put in. "There wasn't a day you weren't guarded by Moralas's men and by mine. Your being here complicated things," he said to Jonas. "You were pushing too close to the bone. I guess you and Jerry had more in common than looks."

Jonas felt the weight on the chain around his neck. "Maybe we did."

"Well, we'd come to the point where we had to settle for Manchez and a few others or go for broke. We went for broke."

"The drop we made. It was a setup."

"Manchez had orders to do whatever he had to to get back the money Jerry had taken. They didn't know about the safe-deposit box." He blew out a stream of smoke. "I had to play it pretty fast and loose to keep that under wraps. But then we didn't know about it either, until you led us to it. As far as Ambuckle was concerned, you had the money, and he was going to get it back. He wanted it to look as though you'd been running the smuggling operation together. When you were found dead, the heat would be off of him. He planned to lie low a while, then pick up business elsewhere. I had that from Manchez. You were set up," he agreed. "So was he. I got to Merriworth, made enough noise about how Manchez was about to double-cross to set him off. When Manchez was snorkeling to your boat, I was on the phone with the man I knew as Clancy. I got a promotion, and Clancy came back to deal with you himself."

Liz tried to see it as he did, as a chess game, as any game with pawns. She couldn't. "You knew who he was yesterday morning and you still had me get on that boat."

"There were a dozen sharpshooters in position. I had a gun, Ambuckle didn't. We wanted him to order Liz's murder, and we wanted him to tell her as much as possible. When this goes to court, we want it tidy. We want him put away for a long time. You're a lawyer, Sharpe. You know how these things can go. We can make a clean collar, have a stack of evidence and lose. I've watched too many of these bastards walk." He blew out smoke between set teeth. "This one's not walking anywhere but into federal prison."

"There is still the question of whether these men will be tried in your country or mine." Moralas spoke softly, and didn't move when Scott whirled on him.

"Look, Moralas—"

"This will be discussed later. You have my thanks and my apologies," he said to Jonas and Liz. "I regret we saw no other way."

"So do I," Liz murmured, then turned to Scott. "Was it worth it?"

"Ambuckle brought thousands of pounds of cocaine into the States. He's responsible for more than fifteen murders in the U.S. and Mexico. Yeah, it was worth it."

She nodded. "I hope you understand that I never want to see you again." After closing her hand around Jonas's she managed a smile. "You were a lousy student."

"Sorry we never had that drink." He looked back at Jonas. "Sorry about a lot of things."

"I appreciate what you told me about my brother. It makes a difference."

"I'm recommending him for a citation. They'll send it to your parents."

"It'll mean a great deal to them." He offered his hand and meant it. "You were doing your job—I understand that. We all do what we have to do."

"That doesn't mean I don't regret it."

Jonas nodded. Something inside him was free, completely free. "As to putting Liz through hell for the past few weeks…" Very calmly, Jonas curled his hand into a fist and planted it solidly on Scott's jaw. The thin man snapped a chair in half as he crashed into it on his way to the floor.

"Jonas!" Stunned, Liz could do no more than stare. Then, incredibly, she felt the urge to giggle. With one hand over her mouth, she leaned into Jonas and let the laughter come. Moralas remained contentedly at his desk, sipping coffee.

Scott rubbed his jaw gingerly. "We all do what we have to do," he murmured.

Jonas only turned his back. "Goodbye, Captain."

Moralas stayed where he was. "Goodbye, Mr. Sharpe." He rose and, in a rare show of feeling, took Liz's hand and kissed it. *"Vaya con dios."*

He waited until the door had shut behind them before he looked down at Scott again. "Your government will, of course, pay for the chair."

He was gone. She'd sent him away. After nearly two weeks, Liz awoke every morning with the same thoughts. Jonas was gone. It was for the best. After nearly two weeks she awoke every morning struggling to convince herself. If she'd followed her heart, she would have said yes the moment he'd asked her to marry him. She would have left everything she'd built behind and gone with him. And ruined his life, perhaps her own.

He was already back in his own world, poring through law books, facing juries, going to elegant dinner parties. By now, she was sure his time in Cozumel was becoming vague. After all, he hadn't written. He hadn't called. He'd left the day after Ambuckle had been taken into custody without another word about love. He'd conquered his ghosts when he'd faced Manchez and had walked away whole.

He was gone, and she was once more standing on her own. As she was meant to, Liz thought. She'd have no regrets. That she'd promised herself. What she'd given to Jonas had been given without conditions or expectations. What he'd given to her she'd never lose.

The sun was high and bright, she thought. The air was as mellow as quiet music. Her lover was gone, but she, too, was whole. A month of memories could be stretched to last a lifetime. And Faith was coming home.

Liz pulled her bike into a parking space and listened to the thunder of a plane taking off. Even now Faith and her parents were crossing the Gulf. Liz left her bike and walked toward the terminal. It was ridiculous to feel nervous, she told herself, but she couldn't prevent it. It was ridiculous to arrive at the airport nearly an hour early, but she'd have gone mad at home. She skirted around a bed of marigolds and geraniums. She'd buy flowers, she decided. Her mother loved flowers.

Inside the terminal, the air was cool and full of noise. Tourists came and went but rarely passed the shops without a last-minute purchase. Liz started in the first store and worked her way down, buying consistently and strictly on impulse. By the time she arrived at the gate, she carried two shopping bags and an armful of dyed carnations.

Any minute, she thought. She'd be here any minute. Liz shifted both bags to one hand and nervously brushed at her hair. Passengers waited for their flights by napping in the black plastic chairs or reading guidebooks. She watched a woman check her lipstick in a compact mirror and wondered if she had time to run into the ladies room to examine her own face. Gnawing on her lip, she decided she couldn't leave, even for a moment. Neither could she sit, so she paced back and forth in front of the wide windows and watched the planes come and go. It was late. Planes were always late when you were waiting for them. The sky was clear and blue. She knew it was equally clear in Houston because she'd been checking the weather for days. But the plane was late. Impatient, she walked back to security to ask about the status. She should have known better.

Liz got a shrug and the Mexican equivalent of It'll be here when it comes. In another ten minutes, she was ready to scream. Then she saw it. She didn't have to hear the flight announcement to know. With her heart thudding dully, she waited by the door.

Faith wore blue striped pants and a white blouse. Her hair's grown, Liz thought as she watched her daughter come down the steps. She's grown—though she knew it would never do to tell Faith so. She'd just wrinkle her nose and roll her eyes. Her palms were wet. Don't cry, don't cry, Liz ordered herself. But the tears were already welling. Then Faith looked up and saw her. With a grin and a wave she was racing forward. Liz dropped her bags and reached out for her daughter.

"Mom, I got to sit by the window, but I couldn't see our house." As she babbled, Faith held her mother's neck in a stranglehold. "I brought you a present."

With her face buried against Faith's throat, Liz drew in the scents—powder, soap and chocolate from the streak on the front of the white blouse. "Let me look at you." Drawing her back, Liz soaked up the sight of her. She's beautiful, Liz realized with a jolt. Not just cute or sweet or pretty any longer. Her daughter was beautiful.

I can't let her go again. It hit her like a wall. I'll never be able to let her go again. "You've lost a tooth," Liz managed as she brushed back her daughter's hair.

"Two." Faith grinned to show the twin spaces. "Grandma said I could put them under my pillow, but I brought them with me so I can put them under my real pillow. Will I get pesos?"

"Yes." Liz kissed one cheek, then the other. "Welcome home."

With her hand firmly in Faith's, Liz rose to greet her parents. For a moment she just looked at them, trying to see them as a stranger would. Her father was tall and still slim, though his hairline was creeping back. He was grinning at her the way he had whenever she'd done something particularly pleasing to him. Her mother stood beside him, lovely in her tidy way. She looked now, as she'd always looked to Liz, like a woman who'd never had to handle a crisis more stressful than a burned roast. Yet she'd been as solid and as sturdy as a rock. There were tears in her eyes. Liz wondered abruptly if the beginning of the summer left her mother as empty as the end of the summer left her.

"Momma." Liz reached out and was surrounded. "Oh, I've missed you. I've missed you all so much." *I want to go home.* The thought surged up inside her and nearly poured out. She needed to go home.

"Mom." Faith tugged on the pocket of her jeans. "Mom."

Giddy, Liz turned and scooped her up. "Yes." She covered her face with kisses until Faith giggled. "Yes, yes, yes!"

Faith snuggled in. "You have to say hello to Jonas."

"What?"

"He came with us. You have to say hi."

"I don't—" Then she saw him, leaning against the window, watching—waiting patiently. The blood rushed out of her head to her heart until she was certain something would burst. Holding onto Faith, Liz stood where she was. Jonas walked to her, took her face in both hands and kissed her hard.

"Nice to see you," he murmured, then bent down to pick up the bags Liz had dropped. "I imagine these are for you," he said as he handed Liz's mother the flowers.

"Yes." Liz tried to gather the thoughts stumbling through her mind. "I forgot."

"They're lovely." She sent her daughter a smile. "Jonas is going to drive us to the hotel. I invited him to dinner tonight. I hope you don't mind. You always make enough."

"No, I… Of course."

"We'll see you then." She gave Liz another brief kiss. "I know you want to get Faith home and have some time together. We'll see you tonight."

"But I—"

"Our bags are here. We're going to deal with customs."

Before Liz could say another word, she was alone with her daughter.

"Can we stop by and see Señor Pessado?"

"Yes," Liz said absently.

"Can I have some candy?"

Liz glanced down to the chocolate stain on Faith's blouse. "You've already had some."

Faith just smiled. She knew she could depend on Señor Pessado. "Let's go home now."

Liz waited until Faith was unpacked, until the crystal bird Faith had bought her was hanging in the window and her daughter had consumed two tacos and a pint of milk.

"Faith…" She wanted her voice to be casual. "When did you meet Mr. Sharpe?"

"Jonas? He came to Grandma's house." Faith turned the doll Liz had brought her this way and that for inspection.

"To Grandma's? When?"

"I don't know." She decided to call the doll Cassandra because it was pretty and had long hair. "Can I have my ice cream now?"

"Oh—yes." Liz walked over to get it out of the freezer. "Faith, do you know why he went to Grandma's?"

"He wanted to talk to her, I guess. To Grandpa, too. He stayed for dinner. I knew Grandma liked him because she made cherry pies. I liked him, too. He can play the piano really good." Faith eyed the ice cream and was satisfied when her mother added another scoop. "He took me to the zoo."

"What?" The bowl nearly slipped out of Liz's hand as she set it down. "Jonas took you to the zoo?"

"Last Saturday. We fed popcorn to the monkeys, but mostly we ate it." She giggled as she shoveled in ice cream. "He tells funny stories. I scraped my knee." Remembering suddenly, Faith pulled up her slacks to show off her wound.

"Oh, baby." It was small and already scabbed over, but Liz brushed a kiss over it anyway. "How'd you do this?"

"At the zoo. I was running. I can run really fast in my new sneakers, but I fell down. I didn't cry."

Liz rolled the slacks down. "I'm sure you didn't."

"Jonas didn't get mad or anything. He cleaned it all up with his handkerchief. It was pretty messy. I bled a lot." She smiled at that, pleased with herself. "He said I have pretty eyes just like you."

A little thrill of panic raced through her, but she couldn't stop herself. "Did he? What else did he say?"

"Oh, we talked about Mexico and about Houston. He wondered which I liked best."

Liz rested her hands on her daughter's knees. This is what matters, she realized. This was all that really mattered. "What did you tell him?"

"I like it best where you are." She scraped the bottom of the bowl. "He said he liked it best there, too. Is he going to be your boyfriend?"

"My—" Liz managed, just barely, to suppress the laugh. "No."

"Charlene's mother has a boyfriend, but he isn't as tall as Jonas and I don't think he ever took Charlene to the zoo. Jonas said sometime maybe we could go see the Liberty Bell. Do you think we can?"

Liz picked up the ice cream dish and began to wash it. "We'll see," she muttered.

"Listen, someone's coming." Faith was up like a shot and dashing for the front door. "It's Jonas!" With a whoop, she was out of the door and running full steam.

"Faith!" Liz hurried from the kitchen and reached the porch in time to see Faith hurl herself at Jonas. With a laugh, he caught her, tossed her in the air then set her down again in a move so natural that it seemed he'd been doing so all his life. Liz knotted the dishcloth in her hands.

"You came early." Pleased, Faith hung on to his hand. "We were talking about you."

"Were you?" He tousled Faith's hair but looked up at Liz. "That's funny, because I was thinking about you."

"We're going to make paella because that's what Grandpa likes best. You can help."

"Faith—"

"Love to," Jonas interrupted. "After I talk to your mother." At the foot of the stairs he crouched down to Faith's level. "I'd really like to talk to your mom alone."

Faith's mouth screwed up. "Why?"

"I have to convince her to marry me."

He ignored Liz's gasp and watched for Faith's reaction. Her eyes narrowed and her mouth pursed. "She said you weren't her boyfriend. I asked."

He grinned and leaned closer. "I just have to talk her into it."

"Grandma says nobody can ever talk my mom into anything. She has a hard head."

"So do I, and I make a living talking people into things. But maybe you could put in a few good words for me later."

As Faith considered, her eyes brightened. "Okay. Mom, can I see if Roberto's home? You said he had new puppies."

Liz stretched out the cloth then balled it again. "Go ahead, but just for a little while."

Jonas straightened as he watched Faith race toward the house across the street. "You've done an excellent job with your daughter, Elizabeth."

"She's done a great deal of it herself."

He turned and saw the nerves on her face. It didn't displease him. But he remembered the way she'd looked when she had opened her arms to Faith at the airport. He wanted, he would, see her look that way again. "Do you want to talk inside?" he began as he walked up the steps. "Or right here?"

"Jonas, I don't know why you've come back, but—"

"Of course you know why I've come back. You're not stupid."

"We don't have anything to talk about."

"Fine." He closed the distance quickly. She didn't resist, though she told herself she would. When he dragged her against him, she went without hesitation. Her mouth locked hungrily to his, and for a moment, just for a moment, the world was right again. "If you don't want to talk, we'll go inside and make love until you see things a little more clearly."

"I see things clearly." Liz put her hands on his arms and started to draw away.

"I love you."

He felt the shudder, saw the flash of joy in her eyes before she looked away. "Jonas, this isn't possible."

"Wrong. It's entirely possible—in fact, it's already done. The point is, Liz, you need me."

Her eyes narrowed to slits. "What I need I take care of."

"That's why I love you," he said simply and took the wind out of her sails.

"Jonas—"

"Are you going to tell me you haven't missed me?" She opened her mouth, then shut it again. "Okay, so you take the Fifth on that one." He stepped back from her. "Are you going to deny that you've spent some sleepless nights in the past couple of weeks, that you've thought about what happened between us? Are you going to stand here and look at me now and tell me you're not in love with me?"

She'd never been able to lie well. Liz turned and meticulously spread the dishcloth over the porch rail. "Jonas, I can't run my life on my feelings."

"From now on you can. Did you like the present Faith brought you?"

"What?" Confused, she turned back. "Yes, of course I did."

"Good. I brought you one too." He took a box out of his pocket. Liz saw the flash of diamond and nearly had her hand behind her back before he caught it in his. Firmly, he slipped the ring on. "It's official."

She wouldn't even look at it. She couldn't stop herself. The diamond was shaped in a teardrop and as white and glossy as a wish. "You're being ridiculous," she told him, but couldn't make herself take it off.

"You're going to marry me." He took her shoulders and leaned her back against a post. "That's not negotiable. After that, we have several options. I can give up my practice and live in Cozumel. You can support me."

She let out a quick breath that might have been a laugh. "Now you're really being ridiculous."

"You don't like that one. Good, I didn't care for it either. You can come back to Philadelphia with me. I'll support you."

Her chin went up. "I don't need to be supported."

"Excellent. We agree on the first two options." He ran his hands through her hair and discovered he wasn't feeling as patient as he'd thought he would. "Now, you can come back to the States. We'll take a map and you can close your eyes and pick a spot. That's where we'll live."

"We can't run our lives this way." She pushed him aside to walk down the length of the porch and back. But part of her was beginning to believe they could. "Don't you see how impossible it is?" she demanded as much of herself as of him. "You have your career. I have my business. I'd never be a proper wife for someone like you."

"You're the only wife for someone like me." He grabbed her shoulders again. No, he wasn't feeling patient at all. "Damn it, Liz, you're the only one. If the business is important to you, keep it. Have Luis run it. We can come back a half a dozen times a year if you want. Start another business. We'll go to Florida, to California, anywhere you want where they need a good dive shop. Or..." He waited until he was sure he had her full attention. "You could go back to school."

He saw it in her eyes—the surprise, the dream, then the denial. "That's over."

"The hell it is. Look at you—it's what you want. Keep the shop, build another, build ten others, but give yourself something for yourself."

"It's been more than ten years."

He lifted a brow. "You said once you wouldn't change anything."

"And I meant it, but to go back now, after all this time."

"Afraid?"

Her eyes narrowed; her spine stiffened. "Yes."

He laughed, delighted with her. "Woman, in the past few weeks, you've been through hell and out again. And you're afraid of a few college courses?"

With a sigh, she turned away. "I might not be able to make it."

"So what?" He whirled her back again. "So you fall flat on your face. I'll be right there falling down with you. It's time for risking, Liz. For both of us."

"Oh, I want to believe you." She lifted a hand to rest it on his face. "I want to. I do love you, Jonas. So much."

She was locked against him again, lost in him. "I need you, Liz. I'm not going back without you."

She clung to him a moment, almost ready to believe. "But it's not just me. You have to understand I can't do whatever I'd like."

"Faith?" He drew her back again. "I've spent the past weeks getting to know her. My main objective when I started was to ingratiate myself. I figured the only way to get to you was through her."

So she'd already surmised. "Afternoons at the zoo?"

"That's right. Thing was, I didn't know she was as easy to fall for as her mother. I want her."

The hand Liz had lifted to her hair froze. "I don't understand."

"I want her to be mine—legally, emotionally. I want you to agree to let me adopt her."

"Adopt..." Whatever she might have expected from him, it hadn't been this. "But she's—"

"Yours?" he interrupted. "No, she's going to be ours. You're going to have to share her. And if you're set on her going to school in Houston, we'll live in Houston. Within the year I expect she should have a brother or sister because she needs family as much as we do."

He was offering her everything, everything she'd ever wanted and had refused to believe in. She had only to hold out her hand. The idea terrified her. "She's another man's child. How will you be able to forget that?"

"She's your child," he reminded her. "You told me yourself she was your child only. Now she's going to be mine." Taking her hands, he kissed them. "So are you."

"Jonas, do you know what you're doing? You're asking for a wife who'll have to start from scratch and a half-grown daughter. You're complicating your life."

"Yeah, and maybe I'm saving it."

And hers. Her blood was pumping again, her skin was tingling. For the first time in years she could look at her life and see no shadows. She closed her eyes and breathed deeply before she turned. "Be sure," she whispered. "Be absolutely sure. If I let myself go, if I say yes and you change your mind, I'll hate you for the rest of my life."

He took her by the shirtfront. "In one week, we're going to my parents' farm in Lancaster, calling the local minister, justice of the peace or witch doctor and we're getting married. Adoption papers are being drawn up. When we settle in as a family, we're all having the same name. You and Faith and I."

With a sigh, Liz leaned back again against the post and studied his face. It was beautiful, she decided. Strong, passionate, patient. Her life was going to be bound up with that face. It was as real as flesh and blood and as precious as dreams. Her lover was back, her child was with her and nothing was impossible.

"When I first met you, I thought you were the kind of man who always got what he wanted."

"And you were right." He took her hands again and held them. "Now what are we going to tell Faith?" he demanded.

Her lips curved slowly. "I guess we'd better tell her you talked me into it."

★ ★ ★ ★ ★

Mind Over Matter

1

He'd expected a crystal ball, pentagrams and a few tea leaves. Burning candles and incense wouldn't have surprised him. Though he wouldn't admit it to anyone, he'd actually looked forward to it. As a producer of documentaries for public television, David Brady dealt in hard facts and meticulous research. Anything and everything that went into one of his productions was checked and rechecked, most often personally. The truth was, he'd thought an afternoon with a fortune teller would bring him a refreshing, even comic, relief from the daily pressure of scripts, storyboards and budgets. She didn't even wear a turban.

The woman who opened the door of the comfortable suburban home in Newport Beach looked as though she would more likely be found at a bridge table than a séance. She smelled of lilacs and dusting powder, not musk and mystery. David's impression that she was housekeeper or companion to the renowned psychic was immediately disabused.

"Hello." She offered a small, attractive hand and a smile. "I'm Clarissa DeBasse. Please come in, Mr. Brady. You're right on time."

"Miss DeBasse." David adjusted his thinking and accepted her hand. He'd done enough research so far to be prepared for the normalcy of people involved in the paranormal. "I appreciate your seeing me. Should I wonder how you know who I am?"

As their hands linked, she let impressions of him come and go, to be sorted out later. Intuitively she felt he was a man she could trust and rely on. It was enough for the moment. "I could claim precognition, but I'm afraid it's simple logic. You were expected at one-thirty." Her agent had called to remind her, or Clarissa would still be knee-deep in her vegetable garden. "I suppose it's possible you're carrying brushes and samples in that briefcase, but I have the feeling it's papers and contracts. Now I'm sure you'd like some coffee after your drive down from L.A."

"Right again." He stepped into a cozy living room with pretty blue curtains and a wide couch that sagged noticeably in the middle.

"Sit down, Mr. Brady. I just brought the tray out, so the coffee's hot."

Deciding the couch was unreliable, David chose a chair and waited while Clarissa sat across from him and poured coffee into two mismatched cups and saucers. It took him only a moment to study and analyze. He was a man who leaned heavily on first impressions. She looked, as she offered cream and sugar, like anyone's favorite aunt—rounded without being really plump, neat without being stiff. Her face was soft and pretty and had lined little in fifty-odd years. Her pale blond hair was cut stylishly and showed no gray, which David attributed to her hairdresser. She was entitled to her vanity, he thought. When she offered the cup, he noted the symphony of rings on her hands. That, at least, was in keeping with the image he had projected.

"Thank you. Miss DeBasse, I have to tell you, you're not at all what I expected."

Comfortable with herself, she settled back. "You were expecting me to greet you at the door with a crystal ball in my hands and a raven on my shoulder."

The amusement in her eyes would have had some men shifting in their chairs. David only lifted a brow. "Something like that." He sipped his coffee. The fact that it was hot was the only thing going for it. "I've read quite a bit about you in the past few weeks. I also saw a tape of your appearance on *The Barrow Show*." He probed gently for the right phrasing. "You have a different image on camera."

"That's showbiz," she said so casually he wondered if she was being sarcastic. Her eyes remained clear and friendly. "I don't generally discuss business, particularly at home, but since it seemed important that you see me, I thought we'd be more comfortable this way." She smiled again, showing the faintest of dimples in her cheeks. "I've disappointed you."

"No." And he meant it. "No, you haven't." Because his manners went only so far, he put the coffee down. "Miss DeBasse—"

"Clarissa." She beamed such a bright smile at him he had no trouble returning it.

"Clarissa, I want to be honest with you."

"Oh, that's always best." Her voice was soft and sincere as she folded her hands on her lap.

"Yeah." The childlike trust in her eyes threw him for a moment. If she was a hard-edged, money-oriented con, she was doing a good job disguising it. "I'm a very practical man. Psychic phenomena, clairvoyance, telepathy and that sort of thing, don't fit into my day-to-day life."

She only smiled at him, understanding. Whatever thoughts came into her head remained there. This time David did shift in his chair.

"I decided to do this series on parapsychology mainly for its entertainment value."

"You don't have to apologize." She lifted her hand just as a large black cat leaped into her lap. Without looking at it, Clarissa stroked it from head to tail. "You see, David, someone in my position understands perfectly the doubts and the fascination people have for…such things. I'm not a radical." As the cat curled up in her lap, she continued to pet it, looking calm and content. "I'm simply a person who's been given a gift, and a certain responsibility."

"A responsibility?" He started to reach in his pocket for his cigarettes, then noticed there were no ashtrays.

"Oh, yes." As she spoke, Clarissa opened the drawer of the coffee table and took out a small blue dish. "You can use this," she said in passing, then settled back again. "A young boy might receive a toolbox for his birthday. It's a gift. He has choices to make. He can use his new tools to learn, to build, to repair. He can also use them to saw the legs off tables. He could also put the toolbox in his closet and forget about it. A great many of us do the last, because the tools are too complicated or simply too overwhelming. Have you ever had a psychic experience, David?"

He lit a cigarette. "No."

"No?" There weren't many people who would give such a definitive no. "Never a sense of déjà vu, perhaps?"

He paused a moment, interested. "I suppose everyone's had a sense of doing something before, being somewhere before. A feeling of mixed signals."

"Perhaps. Intuition, then."

"You consider intuition a psychic gift?"

"Oh, yes." Enthusiasm lit her face and made her eyes young. "Of course it depends entirely on how it's developed, how it's channeled, how it's used. Most of us use only a fraction of what we have because our minds are so crowded with other things."

"Was it impulse that led you to Matthew Van Camp?"

A shutter seemed to come down over her eyes. "No."

Again he found her puzzling. The Van Camp case was the one that had brought her prominently into the public eye. He would have thought she would have been anxious to speak of it, elaborate, yet she seemed to close down at the mention of the name. David blew out smoke and noticed that the cat was watching him with bored but steady eyes. "Clarissa, the Van Camp case is ten years old, but it's still one of the most celebrated and controversial of your successes."

"That's true. Matthew is twenty now. A very handsome young man."

"There are some who believe he'd be dead if Mrs. Van Camp hadn't fought both her husband and the police to have you brought in on the kidnapping."

"And there are some who believe the entire thing was staged for publicity," she said so calmly as she sipped from her cup. "Alice Van Camp's next movie was quite a box-office success. Did you see the film? It was wonderful."

He wasn't a man to be eased off-track when he'd already decided on a destination. "Clarissa, if you agree to be part of this documentary, I'd like you to talk about the Van Camp case."

She frowned a bit, pouted almost, as she petted her cat. "I don't know if I can help you there, David. It was a very traumatic experience for the Van Camps, very traumatic. Bringing it all up again could be painful for them."

He hadn't reached his level of success without knowing how and when to negotiate. "If the Van Camps agreed?"

"Oh, then that's entirely different." While she considered, the cat stirred in her lap, then began to purr loudly. "Yes, entirely different. You know, David, I admire your work. I saw your documentary on child abuse. It was gripping and very upsetting."

"It was meant to be."

"Yes, exactly." She could have told him a great deal of the world was upsetting, but didn't think he was ready to understand how she knew, and how she dealt with it. "What is it you're looking for with this?"

"A good show." When she smiled he was sure he'd been right not to try to con her. "One that'll make people think and question."

"Will you?"

He tapped out his cigarette. "I produce. How much I question I suppose depends on you."

It seemed like not only the proper answer, but the truest one. "I like you, David. I think I'd like to help you."

"I'm glad to hear that. You'll want to look over the contract and—"

"No." She cut him off as he reached for his briefcase. "Details." She explained them away with a gesture of her hand. "I let my agent bother with those things."

"Fine." He'd feel more comfortable discussing terms with an agent. "I'll send them over if you give me a name."

"The Fields Agency in Los Angeles."

She'd surprised him again. The comfortable auntlike lady had one of the most influential and prestigious agencies on the Coast. "I'll have them sent over this afternoon. I'd enjoy working with you, Clarissa."

"May I see your palm?"

Every time he thought he had her cataloged, she shifted on him. Still, humoring her was easy. David offered his hand. "Am I going to take an ocean voyage?"

She was neither amused nor offended. Though she took his

hand, palm up, she barely glanced at it. Instead she studied him with eyes that seemed abruptly cool. She saw a man in his early thirties, attractive in a dark, almost brooding way despite the well-styled black hair and casually elegant clothes. The bones in his face were strong, angular enough to warrant a second glance. His brows were thick, as black as his hair, and dominated surprisingly quiet eyes. Or their cool, pale green appeared quiet at first glance. She saw a mouth that was firm, full enough to gain a woman's attention. The hand in hers was wide, long fingered, artistic. It vied with a rangy, athletic build. But she saw beyond that.

"You're a very strong man, physically, emotionally, intellectually."

"Thank you."

"Oh, I don't flatter, David." It was a gentle, almost maternal reproof. "You haven't yet learned how to temper this strength with tenderness in your relationships. I suppose that's why you've never married."

She had his attention now, reluctantly. But he wasn't wearing a ring, he reminded himself. And anyone who cared to find out about his marital status had only to make a few inquiries. "The standard response is I've never met the right woman."

"In this case it's perfectly true. You need to find someone every bit as strong as you are. You will, sooner than you think. It won't be easy, of course, and it will only work between you if you both remember the tenderness I just spoke of."

"So I'm going to meet the right woman, marry and live happily ever after?"

"I don't tell the future, ever." Her expression changed again, becoming placid. "And I only read palms of people who interest me. Shall I tell you what my intuition tells me, David?"

"Please."

"That you and I are going to have an interesting and long-term relationship." She patted his hand before she released it. "I'm going to enjoy that."

"So am I." He rose. "I'll see you again, Clarissa."

"Yes. Yes, of course." She rose and nudged the cat onto the floor. "Run along now, Mordred."

"Mordred?" David repeated as the cat jumped up to settle himself on the sagging sofa cushion.

"Such a sad figure in folklore," Clarissa explained. "I always felt he got a bad deal. After all, we can't escape our destiny, can we?"

For the second time David felt her cool, oddly intimate gaze on him. "I suppose not," he murmured, and let her lead him to the door.

"I've so enjoyed our chat, David. Please come back again."

David stepped out into the warm spring air and wondered why he felt certain he would.

"Of course he's an excellent producer, Abe. I'm just not sure he's right for Clarissa."

A. J. Fields paced around her office in the long, fluid gait that always masked an overflow of nervous energy. She stopped to straighten a picture that was slightly tilted before she turned back to her associate. Abe Ebbitt was sitting with his hands folded on his round belly, as was his habit. He didn't bother to push back the glasses that had fallen down his nose. He watched A.J. patiently before he reached up to scratch one of the two clumps of hair on either side of his head.

"A.J., the offer is very generous."

"She doesn't need the money."

His agent's blood shivered at the phrase, but he continued to speak calmly. "The exposure."

"Is it the right kind of exposure?"

"You're too protective of Clarissa, A.J."

"That's what I'm here for," she countered. Abruptly she stopped, and sat on the corner of her desk. When Abe saw her brows draw together, he fell silent. He might speak to her when she was in this mood, but she wouldn't answer. He respected and admired her. Those were the reasons he, a veteran Hollywood agent, was working for the Fields Agency, instead of carving up the town on his own. He was old enough to be her father, and realized that a decade before their roles would have been reversed. The fact that he worked for her didn't bother him in the least. The best, he was fond of saying, never minded answering to the best. A minute passed, then two.

"She's made up her mind to do it," A.J. muttered, but again Abe remained silent. "I just—" Have a feeling, she thought. She hated to use that phrase. "I just hope it isn't a mistake. The wrong director, the wrong format, and she could be made to look like a fool. I won't have that, Abe."

"You're not giving Clarissa enough credit. You know better than to let your emotions color a business deal, A.J."

"Yeah, I know better." That's why she was the best. A.J. folded her arms and reminded herself of it. She'd learned at a very young age how to channel emotion. It had been more than necessary; it had been vital. When you grew up in a house where your widowed mother often forgot little details like the mortgage payment, you learned how to deal with business in a businesslike way or you went under. She was an agent because she enjoyed the wheeling and dealing. And because she was damn good at it. Her Century City office with its lofty view of Los Angeles was proof of just how good. Still, she hadn't gotten there by making deals blindly.

"I'll decide after I meet with Brady this afternoon."

Abe grinned at her, recognizing the look. "How much more are you going to ask for?"

"I think another ten percent." She picked up a pencil and tapped it against her palm. "But first I intend to find out exactly what's going into this documentary and what angles he's going for."

"Word is Brady's tough."

She sent him a deceptively sweet smile that had fire around the edges. "Word is so am I."

"He hasn't got a prayer." He rose, tugging at his belt. "I've got a meeting. Let me know how it goes."

"Sure." She was already frowning at the wall when he closed the door.

David Brady. The fact that she personally admired his work would naturally influence her decision. Still, at the right time and for the right fee, she would sign a client to play a tea bag in a thirty-second local commercial. Clarissa was a different matter. Clarissa DeBasse had been her first client. Her only client, A.J. remembered, during those first lean years. If she was protective of her, as Abe had said, A.J. felt she had a right to be. David Brady might be a successful producer of quality documentaries for public television, but he had to prove himself to A. J. Fields before Clarissa signed on the dotted line.

There'd been a time when A.J. had had to prove herself. She hadn't started out with a staff of fifteen in an exclusive suite of offices. Ten years before, she'd been scrambling for clients and hustling deals from an office that had consisted of a phone booth outside a corner deli. She'd lied about her age. Not too many people had been willing to trust their careers to an eighteen-year-old. Clarissa had.

A.J. gave a little sigh as she worked out a kink in her shoulder. Clarissa didn't really consider what she did, or what she had, a career as much as a calling. It was up to A.J. to haggle over the details.

She was used to it. Her mother had always been such a warm, generous woman. But details had never been her strong point. As a child, it had been up to A.J. to remember when the bills were due. She'd balanced the checkbook, discouraged door-to-door salesmen and juggled her schoolwork with the household budget. Not that her mother was a fool, or neglectful of her daughter. There had always been love, conversation and interest. But their roles had so often been reversed. It was the mother who would claim the stray puppy had followed her home and the daughter who had worried how to feed it.

Still, if her mother had been different, wouldn't A.J. herself be different? That was a question that surfaced often. Destiny was something that couldn't be outmaneuvered. With a laugh, A.J. rose. Clarissa would love that one, she mused.

Walking around her desk, she let herself sink into the deep, wide-armed chair her mother had given her. The chair, unlike the heavy, clean-lined desk, was extravagant and impractical. Who else would have had a chair made in cornflower-blue leather because it matched her daughter's eyes?

A.J. realigned her thoughts and picked up the DeBasse contract. It was in the center of a desk that was meticulously in order. There were no photographs, no flowers, no cute paperweights. Everything on or in her desk had a purpose, and the purpose was business.

She had time to give the contract one more thorough going-over before her appointment with David Brady. Before she met with him, she would understand every phrase, every clause and every alternative. She was just making a note on the final clause, when her buzzer rang. Still writing, A.J. cradled the phone at her ear.

"Yes, Diane."

"Mr. Brady's here, A.J."

"Okay. Any fresh coffee?"

"We have sludge at the moment. I can make some."

"Only if I buzz you. Bring him back, Diane."

She turned her notepad back to the first page, then rose as the door opened. "Mr. Brady." A.J. extended her hand, but stayed behind her desk. It was, she'd learned, important to establish certain positions of power right from the start. Besides, the time it took him to cross the office gave her an opportunity to study and judge. He looked more like someone she might have for a client than a producer. Yes, she was certain she could have sold that hard, masculine look and rangy walk. The laconic, hard-boiled detective on a weekly series; the solitary, nomadic cowboy in a feature film. Pity.

David had his own chance for study. He hadn't expected her to be so young. She was attractive in that streamlined, no-nonsense sort of way he could respect professionally and ignore personally. Her body seemed almost too slim in the sharply tailored suit that was rescued from dullness by a fire-engine-red blouse. Her pale blond hair was cut in a deceptively casual style that shagged around the ears, then angled back to sweep her collar. It suited the honey-toned skin that had been kissed by the sun—or a sunlamp. Her face was oval, her mouth just short of being too wide. Her eyes were a rich blue, accentuated by clever smudges of shadow and framed now with oversize glasses. Their hands met, held and released as hands in business do dozens of times every day.

"Please sit down, Mr. Brady. Would you like some coffee?"

"No, thank you." He took a chair and waited until she settled behind the desk. He noticed that she folded her hands over the contract. No rings, no bracelets, he mused. Just a slender, black-banded watch. "It seems we have a number of mutual acquaint-ances, Ms. Fields. Odd that we haven't met before."

"Yes, isn't it?" She gave him a small, noncommittal smile. "But, then, as an agent, I prefer staying in the background. You met Clarissa DeBasse."

"Yes, I did." So they'd play stroll around the bush for a while, he decided, and settled back. "She's charming. I have to admit, I'd expected someone, let's say, more eccentric."

This time A.J.'s smile was both spontaneous and generous. If David had been thinking about her on a personal level, his opinion would have changed. "Clarissa is never quite what one expects. Your project sounds interesting, Mr. Brady, but the details I have are sketchy. I'd like you to tell me just what it is you plan to produce."

"A documentary on psychic phenomena, or psi, as I'm told it's called in studies, touching on clairvoyance, parapsychology, ESP, palmistry, telepathy and spiritualism."

"Séances and haunted houses, Mr. Brady?"

He caught the faint disapproval in her tone and wondered about it. "For someone with a psychic for a client, you sound remarkably cynical."

"My client doesn't talk to departed souls or read tea leaves." A.J. sat back in the chair in a way she knew registered confi-dence and position. "Miss DeBasse has proved herself many times over to be an extraordinarily sensitive woman. She's never claimed to have supernatural powers."

"Supernormal."

She drew in a quiet breath. "You've done your homework. Yes, 'supernormal' is the correct term. Clarissa doesn't believe in overstatements."

"Which is one of the reasons I want Clarissa DeBasse for my program."

A.J. noted the easy use of the possessive pronoun. Not the program, but *my* program. David Brady obviously took his work personally. So much the better, she decided. Then he wouldn't care to look like a fool. "Go on."

"I've talked to mediums, palmists, entertainers, scientists, parapsychologists and carnival gypsies. You'd be amazed at the range of personalities."

A.J. stuck her tongue in her cheek. "I'm sure I would."

Though he noticed her amusement, he let it pass. "They run from the obviously fake to the absolutely sincere. I've spoken with heads of parapsychology departments in several well-known institutions. Every one of them mentioned Clarissa's name."

"Clarissa's been generous with herself." Again he thought he detected slight disapproval. "Particularly in the areas of research and testing."

And there would be no ten percent there. He decided that explained her attitude. "I intend to show possibilities, ask questions. The audience will come up with its own answers. In the five one-hour segments I have, I'll have room to touch on everything from cold spots to tarot cards."

In a gesture she'd thought she'd conquered long ago, she drummed her fingers on the desk. "And where does Miss DeBasse fit in?"

She was his ace in the hole. But he wasn't ready to play her yet. "Clarissa is a recognizable name. A woman who's 'proved herself,' to use your phrase, to be extraordinarily sensitive. Then there's the Van Camp case."

Frowning, A.J. picked up a pencil and began to run it through her fingers. "That was ten years ago."

"The child of a Hollywood star is kidnapped, snatched from his devoted nanny as he plays in the park. The ransom call demands a half a million. The mother's frantic—the police are baffled. Thirty-six hours pass without a clue as the boy's parents desperately try to get the cash together. Over the father's objection, the mother calls a friend, a woman who did her astrological chart and occasionally reads palms. The woman comes, of course, and sits for an hour holding some of the boy's things—his baseball glove, a stuffed toy, the pajama top he'd worn to bed the night before. At the end of that hour, the woman gives the police a description of the boy's kidnappers and the exact location of the house where he's being held. She even describes the room where he's being held, down to the chipped paint on the ceiling. The boy sleeps in his own bed that night."

David pulled out a cigarette, lit it and blew out smoke, while A.J. remained silent. "Ten years doesn't take away that kind of impact, Ms. Fields. The audience will be just as fascinated today as they were then."

It shouldn't have made her angry. It was sheer foolishness to respond that way. A.J. continued to sit silently as she worked back the surge of temper. "A great many people call the Van Camp case a fraud. Dredging that up after ten years will only dredge up more criticism."

"A woman in Clarissa's position must have to deal with criticism continually." He saw the flare come into her eyes— fierce and fast.

"That may be, but I have no intention of allowing her to sign a contract that guarantees it. I have no intention of seeing my client on a televised trial."

"Hold it." He had a temper of his own and could respect hers—if he understood it. "Clarissa goes on trial every time she's in the public eye. If her abilities can't stand up to cameras and questions, she shouldn't be doing what she does. As her agent, I'd think you'd have a stronger belief in her competence."

"My beliefs aren't your concern." Intending to toss him and his contract out, A.J. started to rise, when the phone interrupted her. With an indistinguishable oath, she lifted the receiver. "No calls, Diane. No—oh." A.J. set her teeth and composed herself. "Yes, put her on."

"Oh, I'm so sorry to bother you at work, dear."

"That's all right. I'm in a meeting, so—"

"Oh, yes, I know." Clarissa's calm, apologetic voice came quietly in her ear. "With that nice David Brady."

"That's a matter of opinion."

"I had a feeling you wouldn't hit it off the first time." Clarissa sighed and stroked her cat. "I've been giving that contract business a great deal of thought." She didn't mention the dream, knowing her agent wouldn't want to hear it. "I've decided I want to sign it right away. Now, now, I know what you're going to say," she continued before A.J. could say a word. "You're the agent—you handle the business. You do whatever you think best about clauses and such, but I want to do this program."

A.J. recognized the tone. Clarissa had a feeling. There was never any arguing with Clarissa's feelings. "We need to talk about this."

"Of course, dear, all you like. You and David iron out the details. You're so good at that. I'll leave all the terms up to you, but I will sign the contract."

With David sitting across from her, A.J. couldn't take the satisfaction of accepting defeat by kicking her desk. "All right. But I think you should know I have feelings of my own."

"Of course you do. Come to dinner tonight."

She nearly smiled. Clarissa loved to feed you to smooth things over. Pity she was such a dreadful cook. "I can't. I have a dinner appointment."

"Tomorrow."

"All right. I'll see you then."

After hanging up, A.J. took a deep breath and faced David again. "I'm sorry for the interruption."

"No problem."

"As there's nothing specific in the contract regarding the Van Camp case, including that in the program would be strictly up to Miss DeBasse."

"Of course. I've already spoken to her about it."

A.J. very calmly, very deliberately bit her tongue. "I see. There's also nothing specific about Miss DeBasse's position in the documentary. That will have to be altered."

"I'm sure we can work that out." So she was going to sign, David mused, and listened to a few other minor changes A.J. requested. Before the phone rang, she'd been ready to pitch him out. He'd seen it in her eyes. He held back a smile as they negotiated another minor point. He was no clairvoyant, but he would bet his grant that Clarissa DeBasse had been on the other end of that phone. A.J. Fields had been caught right in the middle. Best place for agents, he thought, and settled back.

"We'll redraft the contract and have it to you tomorrow."

Everybody's in a hurry, she thought, and settled back herself. "Then I'm sure we can do business, Mr. Brady, if we can settle one more point."

"Which is?"

"Miss DeBasse's fee." A.J. flipped back the contract and adjusted the oversize glasses she wore for reading. "I'm afraid this is much less than Miss DeBasse is accustomed to accepting. We'll need another twenty percent."

David lifted a brow. He'd been expecting something along these lines, but he'd expected it sooner. Obviously A.J. Fields hadn't become one of the top in her profession by doing the expected. "You understand we're working in public television.

Our budget can't compete with network. As producer, I can offer another five percent, but twenty is out of reach."

"And five is inadequate." A.J. slipped off her glasses and dangled them by an earpiece. Her eyes seemed larger, richer, without them. "I understand public television, Mr. Brady, and I understand your grant." She gave him a charming smile. "Fifteen percent."

Typical agent, he thought, not so much annoyed as fatalistic. She wanted ten, and ten was precisely what his budget would allow. Still, there was a game to be played. "Miss DeBasse is already being paid more than anyone else on contract."

"You're willing to do that because she'll be your biggest draw. I also understand ratings."

"Seven."

"Twelve."

"Ten."

"Done." A.J. rose. Normally the deal would have left her fully satisfied. Because her temper wasn't completely under control it was difficult to appreciate the fact that she'd gotten exactly what she'd intended to get. "I'll look for the revised contracts."

"I'll send them by messenger tomorrow afternoon. That phone call…" He paused as he rose. "You wouldn't be dealing with me without it, would you?"

She studied him a moment and cursed him for being sharp, intelligent and intuitive. All the things she needed for her client. "No, I wouldn't."

"Be sure to thank Clarissa for me." With a smile smug enough to bring her temper back to boil he offered his hand.

"Goodbye, Mr.…." When their hands met this time, her voice died. Feelings ran into her with the impact of a slap, leaving her weak and breathless. Apprehension, desire, fury and delight rolled through her at the touch of flesh to flesh. She had only a moment to berate herself for allowing temper to open the door.

"Ms. Fields?" She was staring at him, through him, as though he were an apparition just risen from the floorboards. In his, her hand was limp and icy. Automatically David took her arm. If he'd ever seen a woman about to faint, he was seeing one now. "You'd better sit down."

"What?" Though shaken, A.J. willed herself back. "No, no, I'm fine. I'm sorry, I must have been thinking of something else." But as she spoke, she broke all contact with him and stepped back. "Too much coffee, too little sleep." And stay away from me, she said desperately to herself as she leaned back on the desk. Just stay away. "I'm glad we could do business, Mr. Brady. I'll pass everything along to my client."

Her color was back, her eyes were clear. Still David hesitated. A moment before she'd looked fragile enough to crumble in his hands. "Sit down."

"I beg your—"

"Damn it, sit." He took her by the elbow and nudged her into a chair. "Your hands are shaking." Before she could do anything about it, he was kneeling in front of her. "I'd advise canceling that dinner appointment and getting a good night's sleep."

She curled her hands together on her lap to keep him from touching her again. "There's no reason for you to be concerned."

"I generally take a personal interest when a woman all but faints at my feet."

The sarcastic tone settled the flutters in her stomach. "Oh, I'm sure you do." But then he took her face in his hand and had her jerking. "Stop that."

Her skin was as soft as it looked, but he would keep that thought for later. "Purely a clinical touch, Ms. Fields. You're not my type."

Her eyes chilled. "Where do I give thanks?"

He wondered why the cool outrage in her eyes made him want to laugh. To laugh, and to taste her. "Very good," he murmured, and straightened. "Lay off the coffee," he advised, and left her alone before he did something ridiculous.

And alone, A.J. brought her knees up to her chest and pressed her face to them. What was she going to do now? she demanded as she tried to squeeze herself into a ball. What in God's name was she going to do?

2

A.J. seriously considered stopping for a hamburger before going on to dinner at Clarissa's. She didn't have the heart for it. Besides, if she was hungry enough she would be able to make a decent showing out of actually eating whatever Clarissa prepared.

With the sunroof open, she sat back and tried to enjoy the forty-minute drive from her office to the suburbs. Beside her was a slim leather portfolio that held the contracts David Brady's office had delivered, as promised. Since the changes she'd requested had been made, she couldn't grumble. There was absolutely no substantial reason for her to object to the deal, or to her client working with Brady. All she had was a feeling. She'd been working on that since the previous afternoon.

It had been overwork, she told herself. She hadn't felt anything but a quick, momentary dizziness because she'd stood so fast. She hadn't felt anything for or about David Brady.

But she had.

A.J. cursed herself for the next ten miles before she brought herself under control.

She couldn't afford to be the least bit upset when she arrived in Newport Beach. There was no hiding such things from a woman like Clarissa DeBasse. She would have to be able to discuss not only the contract terms, but David Brady himself with complete objectivity or Clarissa would home in like radar.

For the next ten miles she considered stopping at a phone booth and begging off. She didn't have the heart for that, either.

Relax, A.J. ordered herself, and tried to imagine she was home in her apartment, doing long, soothing yoga exercises. It helped, and as the tension in her muscles eased, she turned up the radio. She kept it high until she turned the engine off in front of the tidy suburban home she'd helped pick out.

A.J. always felt a sense of self-satisfaction as she strolled up the walk. The house suited Clarissa, with its neat green lawn and pretty white shutters. It was true that with the success of her books and public appearances Clarissa could afford a house twice as big in Beverly Hills. But nothing would fit her as comfortably as this tidy brick ranch.

Shifting the brown bag that held wine under her arm, A.J. pushed open the door she knew was rarely locked. "Hello! I'm a six-foot-two, three-hundred-and-twenty-pound burglar come to steal all your jewelry. Care to give me a hand?"

"Oh, did I forget to lock it again?" Clarissa came bustling out of the kitchen, wiping her hands on an already smeared and splattered apron. Her cheeks were flushed from the heat of the stove, her lips already curved in greeting.

"Yes, you forgot to lock it again." Even with an armload of wine, A.J. managed to hug her. Then she kissed both cheeks as she tried to unobtrusively sniff out what was going on in the kitchen.

"It's meat loaf," Clarissa told her. "I got a new recipe."

"Oh." A.J. might have managed the smile if she hadn't remembered the last meat loaf so clearly. Instead she concentrated on the woman. "You look wonderful. I'd swear you were running into L.A. and sneaking into Elizabeth Arden's once a week."

"Oh, I can't be bothered with all that. It's too much worrying that causes lines and sags, anyway. You should remember that."

"So I look like a hag, do I?" A.J. dropped her portfolio on the table and stepped out of her shoes.

"You know I didn't mean that, but I can tell you're worried about something."

"Dinner," A.J. told her, evading. "I only had time for a half a sandwich at lunch."

"There, I've told you a dozen times you don't eat properly. Come into the kitchen. I'm sure everything's about ready."

Satisfied that she'd distracted Clarissa, A.J. started to follow.

"Then you can tell me what's really bothering you."

"Doesn't miss a trick," A.J. muttered as the doorbell rang.

"Get that for me, will you?" Clarissa cast an anxious glance at the kitchen. "I really should check the brussels sprouts."

"Brussels sprouts?" A.J. could only grimace as Clarissa disappeared into the kitchen. "Bad enough I have to eat the meat loaf, but brussels sprouts. I should have had the hamburger." When she opened the door her brows were already lowered.

"You look thrilled to see me."

One hand still on the knob, she stared at David. "What are you doing here?"

"Having dinner." Without waiting for an invitation, David stepped forward and stood with her in the open doorway. "You're tall. Even without your shoes."

A.J. closed the door with a quiet snap. "Clarissa didn't explain this was a business dinner."

"I think she considers it purely social." He hadn't yet figured out why he hadn't gotten the very professional Ms. Fields out of his mind. Maybe he'd get some answers before the evening was up. "Why don't we think of it that way—A.J.?"

Manners had been ingrained in her by a quietly determined mother. Trapped, A.J. nodded. "All right, David. I hope you enjoy living dangerously."

"I beg your pardon?"

She couldn't resist the smile. "We're having meat loaf." She took the bottle of champagne he held and examined the label. "This should help. Did you happen to have a big lunch?"

There was a light in her eyes he'd never noticed before. It was a laugh, a joke, and very appealing. "What are you getting at?"

She patted his shoulder. "Sometimes it's best to go into these things unprepared. Sit down and I'll fix you a drink."

"Aurora."

"Yes?" A.J. answered automatically before she bit her tongue.

"Aurora?" David repeated, experimenting with the way it sounded in his voice. "That's what the *A* stands for?"

When A.J. turned to him her eyes were narrowed. "If just one person in the business calls me that, I'll know exactly where they got it from. You'll pay."

He ran a finger down the side of his nose, but didn't quite hide the smile. "I never heard a thing."

"Aurora, was that—" Clarissa stopped in the kitchen doorway and beamed. "Yes, it was David. How lovely." She studied both of them, standing shoulder to shoulder just inside her front door. For the instant she concentrated, the aura around them was very clear and very bright. "Yes, how lovely," she repeated. "I'm so glad you came."

"I appreciate your asking me." Finding Clarissa as charming as he had the first time, David crossed to her. He took her hand, but this time brought it to his lips. Pleasure flushed her cheeks.

"Champagne, how nice. We'll open it after I sign the contracts." She glanced over his shoulder to see A.J. frowning. "Why don't you fix yourself and David a drink, dear? I won't be much longer."

A.J. thought of the contracts in her portfolio, and of her own doubts. Then she gave in. Clarissa would do precisely what Clarissa wanted to do. In order to protect her, she had to stop fighting it and accept. "I can guarantee the vodka—I bought it myself."

"Fine—on the rocks." David waited while she went to a cabinet and took out a decanter and glasses.

"She remembered the ice," A.J. said, surprised when she opened the brass bucket and found it full.

"You seem to know Clarissa very well."

"I do." A.J. poured two glasses, then turned. "She's much more than simply a client to me, David. That's why I'm concerned about this program."

He walked to her to take the glass. Strange, he thought, you only noticed her scent when you stood close, very close. He wondered if she used such a light touch to draw men to her or to block their way. "Why the concern?"

If they were going to deal with each other, honesty might help. A.J. glanced toward the kitchen and kept her voice low. "Clarissa has a tendency to be very open with certain people. Too open. She can expose too much of herself, and leave herself vulnerable to all manner of complications."

"Are you protecting her from me?"

A.J. sipped from her drink. "I'm trying to decide if I should."

"I like her." He reached out to twine a lock of A.J.'s hair around his finger, before either of them realized his intention. He dropped his hand again so quickly she didn't have the chance to demand it. "She's a very likable woman," David continued as he turned to wander around the room. He wasn't a man to touch a business associate, especially one he barely knew, in so casual a manner. To give himself distance, he walked to the window to watch birds flutter around a feeder in the side yard. The cat was out there, he noticed, sublimely disinterested as it sunned itself in a last patch of sunlight.

A.J. waited until she was certain her voice would be properly calm and professional. "I appreciate that, but your project comes first, I imagine. You want a good show, and you'll do whatever it takes to produce one."

"That's right." The problem was, he decided, that she wasn't as tailored and streamlined as she'd been the day before. Her blouse was soft and silky, the color of poppies. If she'd had a jacket to match the snug white skirt, she'd left it in her car. She was shoeless and her hair had been tossed by the wind. He took another drink. She still wasn't his type. "But I don't believe I have a reputation for exploiting people in order to get it. I do my job, A.J., and expect the same from anyone who works with me."

"Fair enough." She finished the unwanted drink. "My job is to protect Clarissa in every way."

"I don't see that we have a problem."

"There now, everything's ready." Clarissa came out to see her guests not shoulder to shoulder, but with the entire room between them. Sensitive to mood, she felt the tension, confusion and distrust. Quite normal, she decided, for two stubborn, self-willed people on opposing ends. She wondered how long it would take them to admit attraction, let alone accept it. "I hope you're both hungry."

A.J. set down her empty glass with an easy smile. "David tells me he's starved. You'll have to give him an extra portion."

"Wonderful." Delighted, she led the way into the dining area. "I love to eat by candlelight, don't you?" She had a pair of candles burning on the table, and another half-dozen tapers on the sideboard. A.J. decided the romantic light definitely helped the looks of the meat loaf. "Aurora brought the wine, so I'm sure it's lovely. You pour, David, and I'll serve."

"It looks wonderful," he told her, and wondered why A.J. muffled a chuckle.

"Thank you. Are you from California originally, David?" Clarissa asked as she handed A.J. a platter.

"No, Washington State." He tipped Beaujolais into Clarissa's glass.

"Beautiful country." She handed Aurora a heaping bowl of mashed potatoes. "But so cold."

He could remember the long, windy winters with some nostalgia. "I didn't have any trouble acclimating to L.A."

"I grew up in the East and came out here with my husband nearly thirty years ago. In the fall I'm still the tiniest bit homesick for Vermont. You haven't taken any vegetables, Aurora. You know how I worry that you don't eat properly."

A.J. added brussels sprouts to her plate and hoped she'd be able to ignore them. "You should take a trip back this year," A.J. told Clarissa. One bite of the meat loaf was enough. She reached for the wine.

"I think about it. Do you have any family, David?"

He'd just had his first experience with Clarissa's cooking and hadn't recovered. He wondered what recipe she'd come across that called for leather. "Excuse me?"

"Any family?"

"Yes." He glanced at A.J. and saw the knowing smirk. "Two brothers and a sister scattered around Washington and Oregon."

"I came from a big family myself. I thoroughly enjoyed my childhood." Reaching out, she patted A.J.'s hand. "Aurora was an only child."

With a laugh A.J. gave Clarissa's hand a quick squeeze. "And

I thoroughly enjoyed my childhood." Because she saw David politely making his way through a hill of lumpy potatoes, she felt a little tug on her conscience. A.J. waited until it passed. "What made you choose documentaries, David?"

"I'd always been fascinated by little films." Picking up the salt, he used it liberally. "With a documentary, the plot's already there, but it's up to you to come up with the angles, to find a way to present it to an audience and make them care while they're being entertained."

"Isn't it more of a learning experience?"

"I'm not a teacher." Bravely he dipped back into the meat loaf. "You can entertain with truth and speculation just as satisfyingly as you can entertain with fiction."

Somehow watching him struggle with the meal made it more palatable for her. "No urge to produce the big film?"

"I like television," he said easily, and reached for the wine. They were all going to need it. "I happen to think there's too much pap and not enough substance."

A.J.'s brow lifted, to disappear under a thin fringe of bangs. "Pap?"

"Unfortunately network television's rife with it. Shows like *Empire,* for instance, or *It Takes Two.*"

"Really." A.J. leaned forward. "*Empire* has been a top-rated show for four years." She didn't add that it was a personal favorite.

"My point exactly. If a show like that retains consistently high ratings—a show that relies on steam, glitter and contrivance—it proves that the audience is being fed a steady stream of garbage."

"Not everyone feels a show has to be educational or 'good' for it to be quality. The problem with public television is that it has its nose up in the air so often the average American ignores it. After working eight hours, fighting traffic, coping with children and dealing with car repair bills, a person's entitled to relax."

"Absolutely." Amazing, he thought, how lovely she became when you lit a little fire under her. Maybe she was a woman who needed conflict in her life. "But that same person doesn't have to shut off his or her intelligence to be entertained. That's called escapism."

"I'm afraid I don't watch enough television to see the difference," Clarissa commented, pleased to see her guests clearing their plates. "But don't you represent that lovely woman who plays on *Empire?*"

"Audrey Cummings." A.J. slipped her fingers under the cup of her wineglass and swirled it lightly. "A very accomplished actress, who's also played Shakespeare. We've just made a deal to have her take the role of Maggie in a remake of *Cat on a Hot Tin Roof.*" The success of that deal was still sweet. Sipping her wine, she tilted her head at David. "For a play that deals in a lot of steam and sweat, it's amazing what longevity it's had. We can't claim it's a Verdi opera, can we?"

"There's more to public television than Verdi." He'd touched a nerve, he realized. But, then, so had she. "I don't suppose you caught the profile on Taylor Brooks? I thought it was one of the most detailed and informative on a rock star I'd ever seen." He picked up his wine in a half toast. "You don't represent him, too, do you?"

"No." She decided to play it to the hilt. "We dated casually a couple of years ago. I have a rule about keeping business and personal relationships separated."

"Wise." He lifted his wine and sipped. "Very wise."

"Unlike you, I have no prejudices when it comes to television. If I did, you'd hardly be signing one of my top clients."

"More meat loaf?" Clarissa asked.

"I couldn't eat another bite." A.J. smiled at David. "Perhaps David would like more."

"As much as I appreciate the home cooking, I can't." He tried not to register too much relief as he stood. "Let me help you clear up."

"Oh, no." Rising, Clarissa brushed his offer aside. "It relaxes me. Aurora, I think David was just a bit disappointed with me the first time we met. Why don't you show him my collection?"

"All right." Picking up her wineglass, A.J. gestured to him to follow. "You've scored points," she commented. "Clarissa doesn't show her collection to everyone."

"I'm flattered." But he took her by the elbow to stop her as they started down a narrow hallway. "You'd prefer it if I kept things strictly business with Clarissa."

A.J. lifted the glass to her lips and watched him over the rim. She'd prefer, for reasons she couldn't name, that he stayed fifty miles from Clarissa. And double that from her. "Clarissa chooses her own friends."

"And you make damn sure they don't take advantage of her."

"Exactly. This way." Turning, she walked to a door on the left and pushed it open. "It'd be more effective by candlelight, even more with a full moon, but we'll have to make do." A.J. flicked on the light and stepped out of his view.

It was an average-size room, suitable to a modern ranch house. Here, the windows were heavily draped to block the view of the yard—or to block the view inside. It wasn't difficult to see why Clarissa would use the veil to discourage the curious. The room belonged in a tower—or a dungeon.

Here was the crystal ball he'd expected. Unable to resist, David crossed to a tall, round-topped stand to examine it. The glass was smooth and perfect, reflecting only the faintest hint of the deep blue cloth beneath it. Tarot cards, obviously old and well used, were displayed in a locked case. At a closer look he saw they'd been hand painted. A bookshelf held everything from voodoo to telekinesis. On the shelf with them was a candle in the shape of a tall, slender woman with arms lifted to the sky.

A Ouija board was set out on a table carved with pentagrams. One wall was lined with masks of pottery, ceramic, wood, even papier-mâché. There were dowsing rods and pendulums. A glass cabinet held pyramids of varying sizes. There was more— an Indian rattle, worn and fragile with age, Oriental worry beads in jet, others in amethyst.

"More what you expected?" A.J. asked after a moment.

"No." He picked up another crystal, this one small enough to rest in the palm of his hand. "I stopped expecting this after the first five minutes."

It was the right thing for him to say. A.J. sipped her wine again and tried not to be too pleased. "It's just a hobby with Clarissa, collecting the obvious trappings of the trade."

"She doesn't use them?"

"A hobby only. Actually, it started a long time ago. A friend found those tarot cards in a little shop in England and gave them to her. After that, things snowballed."

The crystal was cool and smooth in his hand as he studied her. "You don't approve?"

A.J. merely shrugged her shoulders. "I wouldn't if she took it seriously."

"Have you ever tried this?" He indicated the Ouija board.

"No."

It was a lie. He wasn't sure why she told it, or why he was certain of it. "So you don't believe in any of this."

"I believe in Clarissa. The rest of this is just showmanship."

Still, he was intrigued with it, intrigued with the fascination it held for people through the ages. "You've never been tempted to ask her to look in the crystal for you?"

"Clarissa doesn't need the crystal, and she doesn't tell the future."

He glanced into the clear glass in his hand. "Odd, you'd think if she can do the other things she's reported to be able to do, she could do that."

"I didn't say she couldn't—I said she doesn't."

David looked up from the crystal again. "Explain."

"Clarissa feels very strongly about destiny, and the tampering with it. She's refused, even for outrageous fees, to predict."

"But you're saying she could."

"I'm saying she chooses not to. Clarissa considers her gift a responsibility. Rather than misuse it in any way, she'd push it out of her life."

"Push it out." He set the crystal down. "Do you mean she— a psychic—could just refuse to be one. Just block out the…let's say power, for lack of a better term. Just turn it off?"

Her fingers had dampened on the glass. A.J. casually switched it to her other hand. "To a large extent, yes. You have to be open to it. You're a receptacle, a transmitter—the extent to which you receive or transmit depends on you."

"You seem to know a great deal about it."

He was sharp, she remembered abruptly. Very sharp. A.J. smiled deliberately and moved her shoulders again. "I know a great deal about Clarissa. If you spend any amount of time with her over the next couple of months, you'll know quite a bit yourself."

David walked to her. He watched her carefully as he took the wineglass from her and sipped himself. It was warm now and seemed more potent. "Why do I get the impression that you're uncomfortable in this room. Or is it that you're uncomfortable with me?"

"Your intuition's missing the mark. If you'd like, Clarissa can give you a few exercises to sharpen it."

"Your palms are damp." He took her hand, then ran his fingers down to the wrist. "Your pulse is fast. I don't need intuition to know that."

It was important—vital—that she keep calm. She met his eyes levelly and hoped she managed to look amused. "That probably has more to do with the meat loaf."

"The first time we met you had a very strong, very strange reaction to me."

She hadn't forgotten. It had given her a very restless night. "I explained—"

"I didn't buy it," he interrupted. "I still don't. That might be because I found myself doing a lot of thinking about you."

She'd taught herself to hold her ground. She'd had to. A.J. made one last attempt to do so now, though his eyes seemed much too quiet and intrusive, his voice too firm. She took her wineglass back from him and drained it. She learned it was a mistake, because she could taste him as well as the wine. "David, try to remember I'm not your type." Her voice was cool and faintly cutting. If she'd thought about it a few seconds longer, she would have realized it was the wrong tactic.

"No, you're not." His hand cupped her nape, then slid up into her hair. "But what the hell."

When he leaned closer, A.J. saw two clear-cut choices. She could struggle away and run for cover, or she could meet him with absolute indifference. Because the second choice seemed the stronger, she went with it. It was her next mistake.

He knew how to tempt a woman. How to coax. When his

lips lowered to hers they barely touched, while his hand continued to stroke her neck and hair. A.J.'s grip on the wineglass tightened, but she didn't move, not forward, not away. His lips skimmed hers again, with just the hint of his tongue. The breath she'd been holding shuddered out.

As her eyes began to close, as her bones began to soften, he moved away from her mouth to trace his lips over her jaw. Neither of them noticed when the wineglass slipped out of her hand to land on the carpet.

He'd been right about how close you had to get to be tempted by her scent. It was strong and dark and private, as though it came through her pores to hover on her skin. As he brought his lips back to hers, he realized it wasn't something he'd forget. Nor was she.

This time her lips were parted, ready, willing. Still he moved slowly, more for his own sake now. This wasn't the cool man-crusher he'd expected, but a warm, soft woman who could draw you in with vulnerability alone. He needed time to adjust, time to think. When he backed away he still hadn't touched her, and had given her only the merest hint of a kiss. They were both shaken.

"Maybe the reaction wasn't so strange after all, Aurora," he murmured. "Not for either of us."

Her body was on fire; it was icy; it was weak. She couldn't allow her mind to follow suit. Drawing all her reserves of strength, A.J. straightened. "If we're going to be doing business—"

"And we are."

She let out a long, patient breath at the interruption. "Then you'd better understand the ground rules. I don't sleep around, not with clients, not with associates."

It pleased him. He wasn't willing to ask himself why. "Narrows the field, doesn't it?"

"That's my business," she shot back. "My personal life is entirely separate from my profession."

"Hard to do in this town, but admirable. However…" He couldn't resist reaching up to play with a stray strand of hair at her ear. "I didn't ask you to sleep with me."

She caught his hand by the wrist to push it away. It both surprised and pleased her to discover his pulse wasn't any steadier than hers. "Forewarned, you won't embarrass yourself by doing so and being rejected."

"Do you think I would?" He brought his hand back up to stroke a finger down her cheek. "Embarrass myself."

"Stop it."

He shook his head and studied her face again. Attractive, yes. Not beautiful, hardly glamorous. Too cool, too stubborn. So why was he already imagining her naked and wrapped around him? "What is it between us?"

"Animosity."

He grinned, abruptly and completely charming her. She could have murdered him for it. "Maybe part, but even that's too strong for such a short association. A minute ago I was wondering what it would be like to make love with you. Believe it or not, I don't do that with every woman I meet."

Her palms were damp again. "Am I supposed to be flattered?"

"No. I just figure we'll deal better together if we understand each other."

The need to turn and run was desperate. Too desperate. A.J. held her ground. "Understand this. I represent Clarissa DeBasse. I'll look out for her interests, her welfare. If you try to do anything detrimental to her professionally or personally, I'll cut you off at the knees. Other than that, we really don't have anything to worry about."

"Time will tell."

For the first time she took a step away from him. A.J. didn't consider it a retreat as she walked over and put her hand on the light switch. "I have a breakfast meeting in the morning. Let's get the contracts signed, Brady, so we can both do our jobs."

3

Preproduction meetings generally left his staff frazzled and out of sorts. David thrived on them. Lists of figures that insisted on being balanced appealed to the practical side of him. Translating those figures into lights, sets and props challenged his creativity. If he hadn't enjoyed finding ways to merge the two, he never would have chosen to be a producer.

He was a man who had a reputation for knowing his own mind and altering circumstances to suit it. The reputation permeated his professional life and filtered through to the personal. As a producer he was tough and, according to many directors, not always fair. As a man he was generous and, according to many women, not always warm.

David would give a director creative freedom, but only to a point. When the creative freedom tempted the director to veer from David's overall view of a project, he stopped him dead. He would discuss, listen and at times compromise. An astute director would realize that the compromise hadn't affected the producer's wishes in the least.

In a relationship he would give a woman an easy, attentive companion. If a woman preferred roses, there would be roses. If she enjoyed rides in the country, there would be rides in the country. But if she attempted to get beneath the skin, he stopped her dead. He would discuss, listen and at times compromise. An astute woman would realize the compromise hadn't affected the man in the least.

Directors would call him tough, but would grudgingly admit they would work with him again. Women would call him cool, but would smile when they heard his voice over the phone.

Neither of these things came to him through carefully thought-out strategy, but simply because he was a man who was careful with his private thoughts—and private needs.

By the time the preproduction meetings were over, the location set and the format gelled, David was anxious for results. He'd picked his team individually, down to the last technician. Because he'd developed a personal interest in Clarissa DeBasse, he decided to begin with her. His choice, he was certain, had nothing to do with her agent.

His initial desire to have her interviewed in her own home was cut off quickly by a brief memo from A. J. Fields. Miss DeBasse was entitled to her privacy. Period. Unwilling to be hampered by a technicality, David arranged for the studio to be decorated in precisely the same homey, suburban atmosphere. He'd have her interviewed there by veteran journalist Alex Marshall. David wanted to thread credibility through speculation. A man of Marshall's reputation could do it for him.

David kept in the background and let his crew take over. He'd had problems with this director before, but both projects they'd collaborated on had won awards. The end product, to David, was the bottom line.

"Put a filter on that light," the director ordered. "We may have to look like we're sitting in the furniture department in the mall, but I want atmosphere. Alex, if you'd run through your intro, I'd like to get a fix on the angle."

"Fine." Reluctantly Alex tapped out his two-dollar cigar and went to work. David checked his watch. Clarissa was late, but not late enough to cause alarm yet. In another ten minutes he'd have an assistant give her a call. He watched Alex run through the intro flawlessly, then wait while the director fussed with the lights. Deciding he wasn't needed at the moment, David opted to make the call himself. Only he'd make it to A.J.'s office. No harm in giving her a hard time, he thought as he pushed through the studio doors. She seemed to be the better for it.

"Oh, David, I do apologize."

He stopped as Clarissa hurried down the hallway. She wasn't anyone's aunt today, he thought, as she reached out to take his hands. Her hair was swept dramatically back, making her look both flamboyant and years younger. There was a necklace of silver links around her neck that held an amethyst the size of his thumb. Her makeup was artfully applied to accent clear blue eyes, just as her dress, deep and rich, accented them. This wasn't the woman who'd fed him meat loaf.

"Clarissa, you look wonderful."

"Thank you. I'm afraid I didn't have much time to prepare. I got the days mixed, you see, and was right in the middle of weeding my petunias when Aurora came to pick me up."

He caught himself looking over her shoulder and down the hall. "She's here?"

"She's parking the car." Clarissa glanced back over her shoulder with a sigh. "I know I'm a trial to her, always have been."

"She doesn't seem to feel that way."

"No, she doesn't. Aurora's so generous."

He'd reserve judgment on that one. "Are you ready, or would you like some coffee or tea first?"

"No, no, I don't like any stimulants when I'm working. They

tend to cloud things." Their hands were still linked when her gaze fastened on his. "You're a bit restless, David."

She said it the moment he'd looked back, and seen A.J. coming down the hall. "I'm always edgy on a shoot," he said absently. Why was it he hadn't noticed how she walked before? Fast and fluid.

"That's not it," Clarissa commented, and patted his hand. "But I won't invade your privacy. Ah, here's Aurora. Should we start?"

"We already have," he murmured, still watching A.J.

"Good morning, David. I hope we haven't thrown you off schedule."

She was as sleek and professional as she'd been the first time he'd seen her. Why was it now that he noticed small details? The collar of her blouse rose high on what he knew was a long, slender neck. Her mouth was unpainted. He wanted to take a step closer to see if she wore the same scent. Instead he took Clarissa's arm. "Not at all. I take it you want to watch."

"Of course."

"Just inside here, Clarissa." He pushed open the door. "I'd like to introduce you to your director, Sam Cauldwell. Sam." It didn't appear to bother David that he was interrupting his director. A.J. noticed that he stood where he was and waited for Cauldwell to come to him. She could hardly censure him for it when she'd have used the same technique herself. "This is Clarissa DeBasse."

Cauldwell stemmed obvious impatience to take her hand. "A pleasure, Miss DeBasse. I read both your books to give myself a feel for your segment of the program."

"That's very kind of you. I hope you enjoyed them."

"I don't know if 'enjoyed' is the right word." He gave a quick shake of his head. "They certainly gave me something to think about."

"Miss DeBasse is ready to start whenever you're set."

"Great. Would you mind taking a seat over here. We'll take a voice test and recheck the lighting."

As Cauldwell led her away, David saw A.J. watching him like a hawk. "You make a habit of hovering over your clients, A.J.?"

Satisfied that Clarissa was all right for the moment, A.J. turned to him. "Yes. Just the way I imagine you hover over your directors."

"All in a day's work, right? You can get a better view from over here."

"Thanks." She moved with him to the left of the studio, watching as Clarissa was introduced to Alex Marshall. The veteran newscaster was tall, lean and distinguished. Twenty-five years in the game had etched a few lines on his face, but the gray threading through his hair contrasted nicely with his deep tan. "A wise choice for your narrator," she commented.

"The face America trusts."

"There's that, of course. Also, I can't imagine him putting up with any nonsense. Bring in a palm reader from Sunset Boulevard and he'll make her look like a fool regardless of the script."

"That's right."

A.J. sent him an even look. "He won't make a fool out of Clarissa."

He gave her a slow, acknowledging nod. "That's what I'm counting on. I called your office last week."

"Yes, I know." A.J. saw Clarissa laugh at something Alex said. "Didn't my assistant get back to you?"

"I didn't want to talk to your assistant."

"I've been tied up. You've very nearly recreated Clarissa's living room, haven't you?"

"That's the idea. You're trying to avoid me, A.J." He shifted just enough to block her view, so that she was forced to look at him. Because he'd annoyed her, she made the look thorough, starting at his shoes, worn canvas high-tops, up the casual pleated slacks to the open collar of his shirt before she settled on his face.

"I'd hoped you catch on."

"And you might succeed at it." He ran his finger down her lapel, over a pin of a half-moon. "But she's going to get in the way." He glanced over his shoulder at Clarissa.

She schooled herself for this, lectured herself and rehearsed the right responses. Somehow it wasn't as easy as she'd imagined. "David, you don't seem to be one of those men who are attracted to rejection."

"No." His thumb continued to move over the pin as he looked back at her. "You don't seem to be one of those women who pretend disinterest to attract."

"I don't pretend anything." She looked directly into his eyes, determined not a flicker of her own unease would show. "I am disinterested. And you're standing in my way."

"That's something that might get to be a habit." But he moved aside.

It took nearly another forty-five minutes of discussion, changes and technical fine-tuning before they were ready to shoot. Because she was relieved David was busy elsewhere, A.J. waited patiently. Which meant she only checked her watch half a dozen times. Clarissa sat easily on the sofa and sipped water. But whenever she glanced up and looked in her direction, A.J. was glad she'd decided to come.

The shoot began well enough. Clarissa sat with Alex on the sofa. He asked questions; she answered. They touched on clairvoyance, precognition, Clarissa's interest in astrology. Clarissa had a knack for taking long, confusing phrases and making them simple, understandable. One of the reasons she was often in demand on the lecture circuit was her ability to take the mysteries of psi and relate them to the average person. It was one area A.J. could be certain Clarissa DeBasse would handle herself. Relaxing, she took a piece of hard candy out of her briefcase in lieu of lunch.

They shot, reshot, altered angles and repeated themselves for the camera. Hours passed, but A.J. was content. Quality was the order of day. She wanted nothing less for Clarissa.

Then they brought out the cards.

She'd nearly taken a step forward, when the slightest signal from Clarissa had her fuming and staying where she was. She hated this, and always had.

"Problem?"

She hadn't realized he'd come up beside her. A.J. sent David a killing look before she riveted her attention on the set again. "We didn't discuss anything like this."

"The cards?" Surprised by her response, David, too, watched the set. "We cleared it with Clarissa."

A.J. set her teeth. "Next time, Brady, clear it with me."

David decided that whatever nasty retort he could make would wait when Alex's broadcaster's voice rose rich and clear in the studio. "Miss DeBasse, using cards to test ESP is a rather standard device, isn't it?"

"A rather limited test, yes. They're also an aid in testing telepathy."

"You've been involved in testing of this sort before, at Stanford, UCLA, Columbia, Duke, as well as institutions in England."

"Yes, I have."

"Would you mind explaining the process?"

"Of course. The cards used in laboratory tests are generally two colors, with perhaps five different shapes. Squares, circles, wavy lines, that sort of thing. Using these, it's possible to determine chance and what goes beyond chance. That is, with two colors, it's naturally a fifty-fifty proposition. If a subject hits the colors fifty percent of the time, it's accepted as chance. If a subject hits sixty percent, then it's ten percent over chance."

"It sounds relatively simple."

"With colors alone, yes. The shapes alter that. With, say, twenty-five cards in a run, the tester is able to determine by the number of hits, or correct answers, how much over chance the subject guessed. If the subject hits fifteen times out of twenty-five, it can be assumed the subject's ESP abilities are highly tuned."

"She's very good," David murmured.

"Damned right she is." A.J. folded her arms and tried not to be annoyed. This was Clarissa's business, and no one knew it better.

"Could you explain how it works—for you, that is?" Alex idly shuffled the pack of cards as he spoke to her. "Do you get a feeling when a card is held up?"

"A picture," Clarissa corrected. "One gets a picture."

"Are you saying you get an actual picture of the card?"

"An actual picture can be held in your hand." She smiled at him patiently. "I'm sure you read a great deal, Mr. Marshall."

"Yes, I do."

"When you read, the words, the phrasings make pictures in your head. This is very similar to that."

"I see." His doubt was obvious, and to David, the perfect reaction. "That's imagination."

"ESP requires a control of the imagination and a sharpening of concentration."

"Can anyone do this?"

"That's something that's still being researched. There are some who feel ESP can be learned. Others believe psychics are born. My own opinion falls in between."

"Can you explain?"

"I think every one of us has certain talents or abilities, and the degree to which they're developed and used depends on the individual. It's possible to block these abilities. It's more usual, I think, to simply ignore them so that they never come into question."

"Your abilities have been documented. We'd like to give an impromptu demonstration here, with your cooperation."

"Of course."

"This is an ordinary deck of playing cards. One of the crew purchased them this morning, and you haven't handled them. Is that right?"

"No, I haven't. I'm not very clever with games." She smiled, half apologetic, half amused, and delighted the director.

"Now if I pick a card and hold it like this." Alex pulled one from the middle of the deck and held its back to her. "Can you tell me what it is?"

"No." Her smile never faded as the director started to signal to stop the tape. "You'll have to look at the card, Mr. Marshall, think of it, actually try to picture it in your mind." As the tape continued to roll, Alex nodded and obliged her. "I'm afraid you're not concentrating very hard, but it's a red card. That's better." She beamed at him. "Nine of diamonds."

The camera caught the surprise on his face before he turned the card over. Nine of diamonds. He pulled a second card and repeated the process. When they reached the third, Clarissa stopped, frowning.

"You're trying to confuse me by thinking of a card other than the one in your hand. It blurs things a bit, but the ten of clubs comes through stronger."

"Fascinating," Alex murmured as he turned over the ten of clubs. "Really fascinating."

"I'm afraid this sort of thing is often no more than a parlor game," Clarissa corrected. "A clever mentalist can do nearly the same thing—in a different way, of course."

"You're saying it's a trick."

"I'm saying it can be. I'm not good at tricks myself, so I don't try them, but I can appreciate a good show."

"You started your career by reading palms." Alex set down the cards, not entirely sure of himself.

"A long time ago. Technically anyone can read a palm, interpret the lines." She held hers out to him. "Lines that represent finance, emotion, length of life. A good book out of the library will tell you exactly what to look for and how to find it. A sensitive doesn't actually read a palm so much as absorb feelings."

Charmed, but far from sold, Alex held out his. "I don't quite see how you could absorb feelings by looking at the palm of my hand."

"You transmit them," she told him. "Just as you transmit everything else, your hopes, your sorrows, your joys. I can take your palm and at a glance tell you that you communicate well and have a solid financial base, but that would hardly be earth-shattering news. But..." She held her own out to him. "If you don't mind," she began, and cupped his hand in hers. "I can look again and say that—" She stopped, blinked and stared at him. "Oh."

A.J. made a move forward, only to be blocked by David. "Let her be," he muttered. "This is a documentary, remember. We can't have it staged and tidy. If she's uncomfortable with this part of the tape we can cut it."

"If she's uncomfortable you will cut it."

Clarissa's hand was smooth and firm under Alex's, but her eyes were wide and stunned. "Should I be nervous?" he asked, only half joking.

"Oh, no." With a little laugh, she cleared her throat. "No, not at all. You have very strong vibrations, Mr. Marshall."

"Thank you. I think."

"You're a widower, fifteen, sixteen years now. You were a very good husband." She smiled at him, relaxed again. "You can be proud of that. And a good father."

"I appreciate that, Miss DeBasse, but again, it's hardly news."

She continued as if he hadn't spoken. "Both your children are settled now, which eases your mind, as it does any parent's. They never gave you a great deal of worry, though there was a period with your son, during his early twenties, when you had some rough spots. But some people take longer to find their niche, don't they?"

He wasn't smiling anymore, but staring at her as intensely as she stared at him. "I suppose."

"You're a perfectionist, in your work and in your private life. That made it a little difficult for your son. He couldn't quite live up to your expectations. You shouldn't have worried so much, but of course all parents do. Now that he's going to be a father himself, you're closer. The idea of grandchildren pleases you. At the same time it makes you think more about the future—your own mortality. But I wonder if you're wise to be thinking of retiring. You're in the prime of your life and too used to deadlines and rushing to be content with that fishing boat for very long. Now if you'd—" She stopped herself with a little shake of the head. "I'm sorry. I tend to ramble on when someone interests me. I'm always afraid of getting too personal."

"Not at all." He closed his hand into a loose fist. "Miss DeBasse, you're quite amazing."

"Cut!" Cauldwell could have gotten down on his knees and kissed Clarissa's feet. Alex Marshall considering retirement. There hadn't been so much as a murmur of it on the grapevine. "I want to see the playback in thirty minutes. Alex, thank you. It's a great start. Miss DeBasse—" He'd have taken her hand again if he hadn't been a little leery of giving off the wrong vibrations. "You were sensational. I can't wait to start the next segment with you."

Before he'd finished thanking her, A.J. was at her side. She knew what would happen, what invariably happened. One of the crew would come up and tell Clarissa about a "funny thing that happened to him." Then there would be another asking for his palm to be read. Some would be smirking, others would be curious, but inside of ten minutes Clarissa would be surrounded.

"If you're ready, I'll drive you home," A.J. began.

"Now I thought we'd settled that." Clarissa looked idly around for her purse without any idea where she'd set it. "It's too far for you to drive all the way to Newport Beach and back again."

"Just part of the service." A.J. handed her the purse she'd been holding throughout the shoot.

"Oh, thank you, dear. I couldn't imagine what I'd done with it. I'll take a cab."

"We have a driver for you." David didn't have to look at A.J. to know she was steaming. He could all but feel the heat. "We wouldn't dream of having you take a cab all the way back."

"That's very kind."

"But it won't be necessary," A.J. put in.

"No, it won't." Smoothly Alex edged in and took Clarissa's hand. "I'm hoping Miss DeBasse will allow me to drive her home—after she has dinner with me."

"That would be lovely," Clarissa told him before A.J. could say a word. "I hope I didn't embarrass you, Mr. Marshall."

"Not at all. In fact, I was fascinated."

"How nice. Thank you for staying with me, dear." She kissed A.J.'s cheek. "It always puts me at ease. Good night, David."

"Good night, Clarissa. Alex." He stood beside A.J. as they linked arms and strolled out of the studio. "A nice-looking couple."

Before the words were out of his mouth, A.J. turned on him. If it had been possible to grow fangs, she'd have grown them. "You jerk." She was halfway to the studio doors before he stopped her.

"And what's eating you?"

If he hadn't said it with a smile on his face, she might have controlled herself. "I want to see that last fifteen minutes of tape, Brady, and if I don't like what I see, it's out."

"I don't recall anything in the contract about you having editing rights, A.J."

"There's nothing in the contract saying that Clarissa would read palms, either."

"Granted. Alex ad-libbed that, and it worked very well. What's the problem?"

"You were watching, damn it." Needing to turn her temper on something, she rammed through the studio doors.

"I was," David agreed as he took her arm to slow her down. "But obviously I didn't see what you did."

"She was covering." A.J. raked a hand through her hair. "She felt something as soon as she took his hand. When you look at the tape you'll see five, ten seconds where she just stares."

"So it adds to the mystique. It's effective."

"Damn your 'effective'!" She swung around so quickly she nearly knocked him into a wall. "I don't like to see her hit that way. I happen to care about her as a person, not just a commodity."

"All right, hold it. Hold it!" He caught up to her again as she shoved through the outside door. "There didn't seem to be a thing wrong with Clarissa when she left here."

"I don't like it." A.J. stormed down the steps toward the parking lot. "First the lousy cards. I'm sick of seeing her tested that way."

"A.J., the cards are a natural. She's done that same test, in much greater intensity, for institutes all over the country."

"I know. And it makes me furious that she has to prove herself over and over. Then that palm business. Something upset her." She began to pace on the patch of lawn bordering the sidewalk. "There was something there and I didn't even have the chance to talk to her about it before that six-foot reporter with the golden voice muscled in."

"Alex?" Though he tried, for at least five seconds, to control himself, David roared with laughter. "God, you're priceless."

Her eyes narrowed, her face paled with rage, she stopped pacing. "So you think it's funny, do you? A trusting, amazingly innocent woman goes off with a virtual stranger and you laugh. If anything happens to her—"

"Happens?" David rolled his eyes skyward. "Good God, A.J., Alex Marshall is hardly a maniac. He's a highly respected member of the news media. And Clarissa is certainly old enough to make up her own mind—and make her own dates."

"It's not a date."

"Looked that way to me."

She opened her mouth, shut it again, then whirled around toward the parking lot.

"Now wait a minute. I said wait." He took her by both arms and trapped her between himself and a parked car. "I'll be damned if I'm going to chase you all over L.A."

"Just go back inside and take a look at that take. I want to see it tomorrow."

"I don't take orders from paranoid agents or anyone else. We're going to settle this right here. I don't know what's working on you, A.J., but I can't believe you're this upset because a client's going out to dinner."

"She's not just a client," A.J. hurled back at him. "She's my mother."

Her furious announcement left them both momentarily speechless. He continued to hold her by the shoulders while she fought to even her breathing. Of course he should have seen it, David realized. The shape of the face, the eyes. Especially the eyes. "I'll be damned."

"I can only second that," she murmured, then let herself lean back against the car. "Look, that's not for publication. Understand?"

"Why?"

"Because we both prefer it that way. Our relationship is private."

"All right." He rarely argued with privacy. "Okay, that explains why you take such a personal interest, but I think you carry it a bit too far."

"I don't care what you think." Because her head was beginning to pound, she straightened. "Excuse me."

"No." Calmly David blocked her way. "Some people might say you interfere with your mother's life because you don't have enough to fill your own."

Her eyes became very dark, her skin very pale. "My life is none of your business, Brady."

"Not at the moment, but while this project's going on, Clarissa's is. Give her some room, A.J."

Because it sounded so reasonable, her hackles rose. "You don't understand."

"No, maybe you should explain it to me."

"What if Alex Marshall presses her for an interview over dinner? What if he wants to get her alone so he can hammer at her?"

"What if he simply wanted to have dinner with an interest-ing, attractive woman? You might give Clarissa more credit."

She folded her arms. "I won't have her hurt."

He could argue with her. He could even try reason. Somehow he didn't think either would work quite yet. "Let's go for a drive."

"What?"

"A drive. You and me." He smiled at her. "It happens to be my car you're leaning on."

"Oh, sorry." She straightened again. "I have to get back to the office. There's some paperwork I let hang today."

"Then it can hang until tomorrow." Drawing out his keys, he unlocked the door. "I could use a ride along the beach."

So could she. She'd overreacted—there was no question of it. She needed some air, some speed, something to clear her head. Maybe it wasn't wise to take it with him, but... "Are you going to put the top down?"

"Absolutely."

It helped—the drive, the air, the smell of the sea, the blare of the radio. He didn't chat at her or try to ease her into con-versation. A.J. did something she allowed herself to do rarely in the company of others. She relaxed.

How long had it been, she wondered, since she'd driven along the coast, no time frame, no destination? If she couldn't remember, then it had been too long. A.J. closed her eyes, emptied her mind and enjoyed.

Just who was she? David asked himself as he watched her relax, degree by degree, beside him. Was she the tough, no-nonsense agent with an eye out for ten percent of a smooth deal? Was she the fiercely protective, obviously devoted daughter—who was raking in that same ten percent of her mother's talent on one hand and raising the roof about exploi-tation the next. He couldn't figure her.

He was a good judge of people. In his business he'd be producing home movies if he weren't. Yet when he'd kissed her he hadn't found the hard-edged, self-confident woman he'd expected, but a nervous, vulnerable one. For some reason, she didn't entirely fit who she was, or what she'd chosen to be. It might be interesting to find out why.

"Hungry?"

Half dreaming, A.J. opened her eyes and looked at him. How was it he hadn't seen it before? David asked himself. The eyes, the eyes were so like Clarissa's, the shape, the color, the…depth, he decided for lack of a better word. It ran through his head that maybe she was like Clarissa in other ways. Then he dismissed it.

"I'm sorry," she murmured, "I wasn't paying attention." But she could have described his face in minute detail, from the hard cheekbones to the slight indentation in his chin. Letting out a long breath, she drew herself in. A wise woman controlled her thoughts as meticulously as her emotions.

"I asked if you were hungry."

"Yes." She stretched her shoulders. "How far have we gone?"

Not far enough. The thought ran unbidden through his mind. Not nearly far enough. "About twenty miles. Your choice." He eased over to the shoulder of the road and indicated a restaurant on one side and a hamburger stand on the other.

"I'll take the burger. If we can sit on the beach."

"Nothing I like better than a cheap date."

A.J. let herself out. "This isn't a date."

"I forgot. You can pay for your own." He'd never heard her laugh like that before. Easy, feminine, fresh. "Just for that I'll spring." But he didn't touch her as they walked up to the stand. "What'll it be?"

"The jumbo burger, large fries and the super shake. Chocolate."

"Big talk."

As they waited, they watched a few early-evening swimmers splash in the shallows. Gulls swooped around, chattering and loitering near the stand, waiting for handouts. David left them disappointed as he gathered up the paper bags. "Where to?"

"Down there. I like to watch." A.J. walked out on the beach and, ignoring her linen skirt, dropped down on the sand. "I don't get to the beach often enough." Kicking off her shoes, she slid stockinged feet in the sand so that her skirt hiked up to her thighs. David took a good long look before he settled beside her.

"Neither do I," he decided, wondering just how those legs—and the rest of her—might look in a bikini.

"I guess I made quite a scene."

"I guess you did." He pulled out her hamburger and handed it to her.

"I hate to," she said, and took a fierce bite. "I don't have a reputation as an abrasive or argumentative agent, just a tough one. I only lose objectivity with Clarissa."

He screwed the paper cups into the sand. "Objectivity is shot to hell when we love somebody."

"She's so good. I don't just mean at what she does, but inside." A.J. took the fries he offered and nibbled one. "Good people can get hurt so much easier than others, you know. And she's so willing to give of herself. If she gave everything she wanted, she'd have nothing left."

"So you're there to protect her."

"That's right." She turned, challenging.

"I'm not arguing with you." He held up a hand. "For some reason I'd like to understand."

With a little laugh she looked back out to sea. "You had to be there."

"Why don't you tell me what it was like? Growing up."

She never discussed it with anyone. Then again, she never sat on a beach eating hamburgers with associates. Maybe it was a day for firsts. "She was a wonderful mother. Is. Clarissa's so loving, so generous."

"Your father?"

"He died when I was eight. He was a salesman, so he was away a lot. He was a good salesman," she added with the ghost of a smile. "We were lucky there. There were savings and a little bit of stock. Problem was the bills didn't get paid. Not that the money wasn't there. Clarissa just forgot. You'd pick up the phone and it would be dead because she'd misplaced the bill. I guess I just started taking care of her."

"You'd have been awfully young for that."

"I didn't mind." This time the smile bloomed fully. There were, as with her mother, the faintest of dimples in her cheeks. "I was so much better at managing than she. We had a little more coming in once she started reading palms and doing charts. She really just sort of blossomed then. She has a need to help people, to give them—I don't know—reassurance. Hope. Still, it was an odd time. We lived in a nice neighborhood and people would come and go through our living room. The neighbors were fascinated, and some of them came in regularly for readings, but outside the house there was a kind of distance. It was as if they weren't quite sure of Clarissa."

"It would have been uncomfortable for you."

"Now and then. She was doing what she had to do. Some people shied away from us, from the house, but she never seemed to notice. Anyway, the word spread and she became friends with the Van Camps. I guess I was around twelve or thirteen. The first time movie stars showed up at the house I was awestruck. Within a year it became a matter of course. I've known actors to call her before they'd accept a role. She'd always tell them the same thing. They had to rely on their own feelings. The one thing Clarissa will never do is make decisions for anyone else. But they still called. Then the little Van Camp boy was kidnapped. After that the press camped on the lawn, the phone never stopped. I ended up moving her out to Newport Beach. She can keep a low profile there, even when another case comes up."

"There was the Ridehour murders."

She stood up abruptly and walked closer to the sea. Rising, David walked with her. "You've no idea how she suffered through that." Emotions trembled in her voice as she wrapped her arms around herself. "You can't imagine what a toll something like that can take on a person like Clarissa. I wanted to stop her, but I knew I couldn't."

When she closed her eyes, David put a hand on her shoulder. "Why would you want to stop her if she could help?"

"She grieved. She hurt. God, she all but lived it, even before she was called in." She opened her eyes and turned to him then. "Do you understand, even before she was called in, she was involved?"

"I'm not sure I do."

"No, you can't." She gave an impatient shake of her head for expecting it. "I suppose you have to live it. In any case, they asked for help. It doesn't take any more than that with Clarissa. Five young girls dead." She closed her eyes again. "She never speaks of it, but I know she saw each one. I know." Then she pushed the thought aside, as she knew she had to. "Clarissa thinks of her abilities as a gift…but you've no idea what a curse that can be."

"You'd like her to stop. Shut down. Is that possible?"

A.J. laughed again and drew both hands through hair the wind had tossed. "Oh, yes, but not for Clarissa. I've accepted that she needs to give. I just make damn sure the wrong person doesn't take."

"And what about you?" He would have sworn something in her froze at the casual question. "Did you become an agent to protect your mother?"

She relaxed again. "Partly. But I enjoy what I do." Her eyes were clear again. "I'm good at it."

"And what about Aurora?" He brought his hands up her arms to her shoulders.

A yearning rose up in her, just from the touch. She blocked it off. "Aurora's only there for Clarissa."

"Why?"

"Because I know how to protect myself as well as my mother."

"From what?"

"It's getting late, David."

"Yeah." One hand skimmed over to her throat. Her skin was soft there, sun kissed and soft. "I'm beginning to think the same thing. I never did finish kissing you, Aurora."

His hands were strong. She'd noticed it before, but it seemed to matter more now. "It's better that way."

"I'm beginning to think that, too. Damn if I can figure out why I want to so much."

"Give it a little time. It'll pass."

"Why don't we test it out?" He lifted a brow as he looked down at her. "We're on a public beach. The sun hasn't set. If I kiss you here, it can't go any further than that, and maybe we'll figure out why we unnerve each other." When he drew her closer, she stiffened. "Afraid?" Why would the fact that she might be, just a little, arouse him?

"No." Because she'd prepared herself she almost believed it was true. He wouldn't have the upper hand this time, she told herself. She wouldn't allow it. Deliberately she lifted her arms and twined them around his neck. When he hesitated, she pressed her lips to his.

He'd have sworn the sand shifted under his feet. He was certain the crash of the waves grew in volume until it filled the air like thunder. He'd intended to control the situation like an experiment. But intentions changed as mouth met mouth. She tasted warm—cool, sweet—pungent. He had a desperate need to find out which of his senses could be trusted. Before either of them was prepared, he plunged himself into the kiss and dragged her with him.

Too fast. Her mind whirled with the thought. Too far. But her body ignored the warning and strained against him. She wanted, and the want was clearer and sharper than any want had ever been. She needed, and the need was deeper and more intense than any other need. As the feelings drummed into her, her fingers curled into his hair. Hunger for him rose so quickly she moaned with it. It wasn't right. It couldn't be right. Yet the feeling swirled through her that it was exactly right and had always been.

A gull swooped overhead and was gone, leaving only the flicker of a shadow, the echo of a sound.

When they drew apart, A.J. stepped back. With distance came a chill, but she welcomed it after the enervating heat. She would have turned then without a word, but his hands were on her again.

"Come home with me."

She had to look at him then. Passion, barely controlled, darkened his eyes. Desire, edged with temptation, roughened his voice. And she felt…too much. If she went, she would give too much.

"No." Her voice wasn't quite steady, but it was final. "I don't want this, David."

"Neither do I." He backed off then. He hadn't meant for things to go so far. He hadn't wanted to feel so much. "I'm not sure that's going to make any difference."

"We have control over our own lives." When she looked out to sea again, the wind rushed her hair back, leaving her face unframed. "I know what I want and don't want in mine."

"Wants change." Why was he arguing? She said nothing he hadn't thought himself.

"Only if we let them."

"And if I said I wanted you?"

The pulse in her throat beat quickly, so quickly she wasn't sure she could get the words around it. "I'd say you were making a mistake. You were right, David, when you said I wasn't your type. Go with your first impulse. It's usually the best."

"In this case I think I need more data."

"Suit yourself," she said as though it made no difference. "I have to get back. I want to call Clarissa and make sure she's all right."

He took her arm one last time. "You won't always be able to use her, Aurora."

She stopped and sent him the cool, intimate look so like her mother's. "I don't use her at all," she murmured. "That's the difference between us." She turned and made her way back across the sand.

4

There was moonlight, shafts of it, glimmering. There was the scent of hyacinths—the faintest fragrance on the faintest of breezes. From somewhere came the sound of water, running, bubbling. On a wide-planked wood floor there were shadows, the shifting grace of an oak outside the window. A painting on the wall caught the eye and held it. It was no more than slashes of red and violet lines on a white, white canvas, but somehow it portrayed energy, movement, tensions with undercurrents of sex. There was a mirror, taller than most. A.J. saw herself reflected in it.

She looked indistinct, ethereal, lost. With shadows all around it seemed to her she could just step forward into the glass and be gone. The chill that went through her came not from without but from within. There was something to fear here, something as nebulous as her own reflection. Instinct told her to go, and to go quickly, before she learned what it was. But as she turned something blocked her way.

David stood between her and escape, his hands firm on her shoulders. When she looked at him she saw that his eyes were dark and impatient. Desire—his or hers—thickened the air until even breathing was an effort.

I don't want this. Did she say it? Did she simply think it? Though she couldn't be sure, she heard his response clearly enough, clipped and annoyed.

"You can't keep running, Aurora. Not from me, not from yourself."

Then she was sliding down into a dark, dark tunnel with soft edges just beginning to flame.

A.J. jerked up in bed, breathless and trembling. She didn't see moonlight, but the first early shafts of sun coming through her own bedroom windows. Her bedroom, she repeated to herself as she pushed sleep-tousled hair from her eyes. There were no hyacinths here, no shadows, no disturbing painting.

A dream, she repeated over and over. It had just been a dream. But why did it have to be so real? She could almost feel the slight pressure on her shoulders where his hands had pressed. The turbulent, churning sensation through her system hadn't faded. And why had she dreamed of David Brady?

There were several logical reasons she could comfort herself with. He'd been on her mind for the past couple of weeks. Clarissa and the documentary had been on her mind and they were all tangled together. She'd been working hard, maybe too hard, and the last true relaxation she'd had had been those few minutes with him on the beach.

Still, it was best not to think of that, of what had happened or nearly happened, of what had been said or left unsaid. It would be better, much better, to think of schedules, of work and of obligations.

There'd be no sleeping now. Though it was barely six, A.J. pushed the covers aside and rose. A couple of strong cups of black coffee and a cool shower would put her back in order. They had to. Her schedule was much too busy to allow her to waste time worrying over a dream.

Her kitchen was spacious and very organized. She allowed no clutter, even in a room she spent little time in. Counters and appliances gleamed in stark white, as much from the diligence of her housekeeper as from disuse. A.J. went down the two steps that separated the kitchen from the living area and headed for the appliance she knew best. The coffeemaker.

Turning off the automatic alarm, which would have begun the brewing at 7:05, A.J. switched it to Start. When she came out of the shower fifteen minutes later, the scent of coffee—of normalcy—was back. She drank the first cup black, for the caffeine rather than the taste. Though she was an hour ahead of schedule, A.J. stuck to routine. Nothing as foolish and insubstantial as a dream was going to throw her off. She downed a handful of vitamins, preferring them to hassling with breakfast, then took a second cup of coffee into the bedroom with her to dress. As she studied the contents of her closet, she reviewed her appointments for the day.

Brunch with a very successful, very nervous client who was being wooed for a prime-time series. It wouldn't hurt to look over the script for the pilot once more before they discussed it. A prelunch staff meeting in her own conference room was next. Then there was a late business lunch with Bob Hopewell, who'd begun casting his new feature. She had two clients she felt were tailor-made for the leads. After mentally reviewing her appointments, A.J. decided what she needed was a touch of elegance.

She went with a raw silk suit in pale peach. Sticking to routine, she was dressed and standing in front of the full-length mirrors of her closet in twenty minutes. As an afterthought, she picked up the little half-moon she sometimes wore on her lapel. As she was fastening it, the dream came back to her. She hadn't looked so confident, so—was it aloof?—in the dream. She'd been softer, hadn't she? More vulnerable.

A.J. lifted a hand to touch it to the glass. It was cool and smooth, a reflection only. Just as it had only been a dream, she reminded herself with a shake of the head. In reality she couldn't afford to be soft. Vulnerability was out of the question. An agent in this town would be eaten alive in five minutes if she allowed a soft spot to show. And a woman—a woman took terrifying chances if she let a man see that which was vulnerable. A. J. Fields wasn't taking any chances.

Tugging down the hem of her jacket, she took a last survey before grabbing her briefcase. In less than twenty minutes, she was unlocking the door to her suite of offices.

It wasn't an unusual occurrence for A.J. to open the offices herself. Ever since she'd rented her first one-room walk-up early in her career, she'd developed the habit of arriving ahead of her staff. In those days her staff had consisted of a part-time receptionist who'd dreamed of a modeling career. Now she had two receptionists, a secretary and an assistant, as well as a stable of agents. A.J. turned the switch so that light gleamed on brass pots and rose-colored walls. She'd never regretted calling in a decorator. There was class here, discreet, understated class with subtle hints of power. Left to herself, she knew she'd have settled for a couple of sturdy desks and gooseneck lamps.

A glance at her watch showed her she could get in several calls to the East Coast. She left the one light burning in the reception area and closeted herself in her own office. Within a half-hour she'd verbally agreed to have her nervous brunch appointment fly east to do a pilot for a weekly series, set out pre-negotiation feelers for a contract renewal for another client who worked on a daytime drama and lit a fire under a producer by refusing his offer on a projected mini-series.

A good morning's work, A.J. decided, reflecting back on the producer's assessment that she was a nearsighted, money-grubbing python. He would counteroffer. She leaned back in her chair and let her shoes drop to the floor. When he did, her client would get over-the-title billing and a cool quarter million. He'd work for it, A.J. thought with a long stretch. She'd read the script and understood that the part would be physically demanding and emotionally draining. She understood just how much blood and sweat a good actor put into a role. As far as she was concerned, they deserved every penny they could get, and it was up to her to squeeze it from the producer's tightfisted hand.

Satisfied, she decided to delve into paperwork before her own phone started to ring. Then she heard the footsteps.

At first she simply glanced at her watch, wondering who was in early. Then it occurred to her that though her staff was certainly dedicated enough, she couldn't think of anyone who'd come to work thirty minutes before they were due. A.J. rose, fully intending to see for herself, when the footsteps stopped. She should just call out, she thought, then found herself remembering every suspense movie she'd ever seen. The trusting heroine called out, then found herself trapped in a room with a maniac. Swallowing, she picked up a heavy metal paperweight.

The footsteps started again, coming closer. Still closer. Struggling to keep her breathing even and quiet, A.J. walked across the carpet and stood beside the door. The footsteps halted directly on the other side. With the paperweight held high, she put her hand on the knob, held her breath, then yanked it open. David managed to grab her wrist before she knocked him out cold.

"Always greet clients this way, A.J.?"

"Damn it!" She let the paperweight slip to the floor as relief flooded through her. "You scared me to death, Brady. What are you doing sneaking around here at this hour?"

"The same thing you're doing sneaking around here at this hour. I got up early."

Because her knees were shaking, she gave in to the urge to sit, heavily. "The difference is this is *my* office. I can sneak around anytime I like. What do you want?"

"I could claim I couldn't stay away from your sparkling personality."

"Cut it."

"The truth is I have to fly to New York for a location shoot. I'll be tied up for a couple of days and wanted you to pass a message on to Clarissa for me." It wasn't the truth at all, but he didn't mind lying. It was easier to swallow than the fact that he'd needed to see her again. He'd woken up that morning knowing he had to see her before he left. Admit that to a woman like A. J. Fields and she'd either run like hell or toss you out.

"Fine." She was already up and reaching for a pad. "I'll be glad to pass on a message. But next time try to remember some people shoot other people who wander into places before hours."

"The door was unlocked," he pointed out. "There was no one at reception, so I decided to see if anyone was around before I just left a note."

It sounded reasonable. Was reasonable. But it didn't suit A.J. to be scared out of her wits before 9:00 a.m. "What's the message, Brady?"

He didn't have the vaguest idea. Tucking his hands in his pockets, he glanced around her meticulously ordered, pastel-toned office. "Nice place," he commented. He noticed even the papers she'd obviously been working with on her desk were in neat piles. There wasn't so much as a paper clip out of place. "You're a tidy creature, aren't you?"

"Yes." She tapped the pencil impatiently on the pad. "The message for Clarissa?"

"How is she, by the way?"

"She's fine."

He took a moment to stroll over to study the single painting she had on the wall. A seascape, very tranquil and soothing. "I remember you were concerned about her—about her having dinner with Alex."

"She had a lovely time," A.J. mumbled. "She told me Alex Marshall was a complete gentleman with a fascinating mind."

"Does that bother you?"

"Clarissa doesn't see men. Not that way." Feeling foolish, she dropped the pad on her desk and walked to her window.

"Is something wrong with her seeing men? That way?"

"No, no, of course not. It's just…"

"Just what, Aurora?"

She shouldn't be discussing her mother, but so few people knew of their relationship, A.J. opened up before she could stop herself. "She gets sort of breathy and vague whenever she mentions him. They spent the day together on Sunday. On his boat. I don't remember Clarissa ever stepping foot on a boat."

"So she's trying something new."

"That's what I'm afraid of," she said under her breath. "Have you any idea what it's like to see your mother in the first stages of infatuation?"

"No." He thought of his own mother's comfortable relationship with his father. She cooked dinner and sewed his buttons. He took out the trash and fixed the toaster. "I can't say I have."

"Well, it's not the most comfortable feeling, I can tell you. What do I know about this man, anyway? Oh, he's smooth," she muttered. "For all I know he's been smooth with half the women in Southern California."

"Do you hear yourself?" Half-amused, David joined her at

the window. "You sound like a mother fussing over her teenage daughter. If Clarissa were an ordinary middle-aged woman there'd be little enough to worry about. Don't you think the fact that she is what she is gives her an advantage? It seems she'd be an excellent judge of character."

"You don't understand. Emotions can block things, especially when it's important."

"If that's true, maybe you should look to your own emotions." He felt her freeze. He didn't have to touch her; he didn't have to move any closer. He simply felt it. "You're letting your affection and concern for your mother cause you to over-react to a very simple thing. Maybe you should give some thought to targeting some of that emotion elsewhere."

"Clarissa's all I can afford to be emotional about."

"An odd way of phrasing things. Do you ever give any thought to your own needs? Emotional," he murmured, then ran a hand down her hair. "Physical."

"That's none of your business." She would have turned away, but he kept his hand on her hair.

"You can cut a lot of people off." He felt the first edge of her anger as she stared up at him. Oddly he enjoyed it. "I think you'd be extremely good at picking up the spear and jabbing men out of your way. But it won't work with me."

"I don't know why I thought I could talk to you."

"But you did. That should give you something to consider."

"Why are you pushing me?" she demanded. Fire came into her eyes. She remembered the dream too clearly. The dream, the desire, the fears.

"Because I want you." He stood close, close enough for her scent to twine around him. Close enough so that the doubts and distrust in her eyes were very clear. "I want to make love with you for a long, long time in a very quiet place. When we're finished I might find out why I don't seem to be able to sleep for dreaming of it."

Her throat was dry enough to ache and her hands felt like ice. "I told you once I don't sleep around."

"That's good," he murmured. "That's very good, because I don't think either of us needs a lot of comparisons." He heard the sound of the front door of the offices opening. "Sounds like you're open for business, A.J. Just one more personal note. I'm willing to negotiate terms, times and places, but the bottom line is that I'm going to spend more than one night with you. Give it some thought."

A.J. conquered the urge to pick up the paperweight and heave it at him as he walked to the door. Instead she reminded herself that she was a professional and it was business hours. "Brady."

He turned, and with a hand on the knob smiled at her. "Yeah, Fields?"

"You never gave me the message for Clarissa."

"Didn't I?" The hell with the gingerbread, he decided. "Give her my best. See you around, lady."

David didn't even know what time it was when he unlocked the door of his hotel suite. The two-day shoot had stretched into three. Now all he had to do was figure out which threads to cut and remain in budget. Per instructions, the maid hadn't touched the stacks and piles of paper on the table in the parlor. They were as he'd left them, a chaotic jumble of balance sheets, schedules and production notes.

After a twelve-hour day, he'd ordered his crew to hit the sheets. David buzzed room service and ordered a pot of coffee before he sat down and began to work. After two hours, he was satisfied enough with the figures to go back over the two and a half days of taping.

The Danjason Institute of Parapsychology itself had been impressive, and oddly stuffy, in the way of institutes. It was difficult to imagine that an organization devoted to the study of bending spoons by will and telepathy could be stuffy. The team of parapsychologists they'd worked with had been as dry and precise as any staff of scientists. So dry, in fact, David wondered whether they'd convince the audience or simply put them to sleep. He'd have to supervise the editing carefully.

The testing had been interesting enough, he decided. The fact that they used not only sensitives but people more or less off the street. The testing and conclusions were done in the strictest scientific manner. How had it been put? The application of math probability theory to massive accumulation of data. It sounded formal and supercilious. To David it was card guessing.

Still, put sophisticated equipment and intelligent, highly educated scientists together, and it was understood that psychic phenomena were being researched seriously and intensely. It was, as a science, just beginning to be recognized after decades of slow, exhaustive experimentation.

Then there had been the interview on Wall Street with the thirty-two-year-old stockbroker-psychic. David let out a stream of smoke and watched it float toward the ceiling as he let that particular segment play in his mind. The man had made no secret of the fact that he used his abilities to play the market and become many times a millionaire. It was a skill, he'd explained, much like reading, writing and calculating were skills. He'd also claimed that several top executives in some of the most powerful companies in the world had used psychic powers to get there and to stay there. He'd described ESP as a tool, as important in the business world as a computer system or a slide rule.

A science, a business and a performance.

It made David think of Clarissa. She hadn't tossed around

confusing technology or littered her speech with mathemati-
cal probabilities. She hadn't discussed market trends or the
Dow Jones Average. She'd simply talked, person to person.
Whatever powers she had…

With a shake of his head, David cut himself off. Listen to
this, he thought as he ran his hands over his face. He was beginning to buy the whole business himself, though he knew
from his own research that for every lab-contained experiment
there were dozens of card-wielding, bell-ringing charlatans
bilking a gullible audience. He drew smoke down an already
raw throat before he crushed out the cigarette. If he didn't
continue to look at the documentary objectively, he'd have a
biased mess on his hands.

But even looking objectively, he could see Clarissa as the
center of the work. She could be the hinge on which everything else hung. With his eyes half-closed, David could picture
it—the interview with the somber-eyed, white-coated parapsychologists, with their no-nonsense laboratory conditions.
Then a cut to Clarissa talking with Alex, covering more or less
the same ground in her simpler style. Then there'd be the clip
of the stockbroker in his sky-high Wall Street office, then
back to Clarissa again, seated on the homey sofa. He'd have
the tuxedoed mentalist they'd lined up in Vegas doing his
flashy, fast-paced demonstration. Then Clarissa again, calmly
identifying cards without looking at them. Contrasts, angles,
information, but everything would lead back to Clarissa
DeBasse. She was the hook—instinct, intuition or paranormal
powers, she was the hook. He could all but see the finished
product unfolding.

Still, he wanted the big pull, something with punch and
drama. This brought him right back to Clarissa. He needed that
interview with Alice Van Camp, and another with someone

who'd been directly involved in the Ridehour case. A.J. might try to block his way. He'd just have to roll over her.

How many times had he thought of her in the past three days? Too many. How often did he catch his mind drifting back to those few moments on the beach? Too often. And how much did he want to hold her like that again, close and hard? Too much.

Aurora. He knew it was dangerous to think of her as Aurora. Aurora was soft and accessible. Aurora was passionate and giving and just a little unsure of herself. He'd be smarter to remember A. J. Fields, tough, uncompromising and prickly around the edges. But it was late and his rooms were quiet. It was Aurora he thought of. It was Aurora he wanted.

On impulse, David picked up the phone. He punched buttons quickly, without giving himself a chance to think the action through. The phone rang four times before she answered.

"Fields."

"Good morning."

"David?" A.J. reached up to grab the towel before it slipped from her dripping hair.

"Yeah. How are you?"

"Wet." She switched the phone from hand to hand as she struggled into a robe. "I just stepped out of the shower. Is there a problem?"

The problem was, he mused, that he was three thousand miles away and was wondering what her skin would look like gleaming with water. He reached for another cigarette and found the pack empty. "No, should there be?"

"I don't usually get calls at this hour unless there is. When did you get back?"

"I didn't."

"You didn't? You mean you're still in New York?"

He stretched back in his chair and closed his eyes. Funny, he hadn't realized just how much he'd wanted to hear her voice. "Last time I looked."

"It's only ten your time. What are you doing up so early?"

"Haven't been to bed yet."

This time she wasn't quick enough to snatch the towel before it landed on her bare feet. A.J. ignored it as she dragged her fingers through the tangle of wet hair. "I see. The night life in Manhattan's very demanding, isn't it?"

He opened his eyes to glance at his piles of papers, overflowing ashtrays and empty coffee cups. "Yeah, it's all dancing till dawn."

"I'm sure." Scowling, she bent down to pick up her towel. "Well, you must have something important on your mind to break off the partying and call. What is it?"

"I wanted to talk to you."

"So I gathered." She began, more roughly than necessary, to rub the towel over her hair. "About what?"

"Nothing."

"Brady, have you been drinking?"

He gave a quick laugh as he settled back again. He couldn't even remember the last time he'd eaten. "No. Don't you believe in friendly conversations, A.J.?"

"Sure, but not between agents and producers long-distance at dawn."

"Try something new," he suggested. "How are you?"

Cautious, she sat on the bed. "I'm fine. How are you?"

"That's good. That's a very good start." With a yawn, he realized he could sleep in the chair without any trouble at all. "I'm a little tired, actually. We spent most of the day interviewing parapsychologists who use computers and mathematical equations. I talked to a woman who claims to have had a half a dozen out-of-body experiences. 'OOBs.'"

She couldn't prevent the smile. "Yes, I've heard the term."

"Claimed she traveled to Europe that way."

"Saves on airfare."

"I suppose."

She felt a little tug of sympathy, a small glimmer of amusement. "Having trouble separating the wheat from the chaff, Brady?"

"You could call it that. In any case, it looks like we're going to be running around on the East Coast awhile. A palmist in the mountains of western Maryland, a house in Virginia that's supposed to be haunted by a young girl and a cat. There's a hypnotist in Pennsylvania who specializes in regression."

"Fascinating. It sounds like you're having just barrels of fun."

"I don't suppose you have any business that would bring you out this way."

"No, why?"

"Let's just say I wouldn't mind seeing you."

She tried to ignore the fact that the idea pleased her. "David, when you put things like that I get weak in the knees."

"I'm not much on the poetic turn of phrase." He wasn't handling this exactly as planned, he thought with a scowl. Then again, he hadn't given himself time to plan. Always a mistake. "Look, if I said I'd been thinking about you, that I wanted to see you, you'd just say something nasty. I'd end up paying for an argument instead of a conversation."

"And you can't afford to go over budget."

"See?" Still, it amused him. "Let's try a little experiment here. I've been watching experiments for days and I think I've got it down."

A.J. lay back on the bed. The fact that she was already ten minutes behind schedule didn't occur to her. "What sort of experiment?"

"You say something nice to me. Now that'll be completely

out of character, so we'll start with that premise…. Go ahead," he prompted after fifteen seconds of blank silence.

"I'm trying to think of something."

"Don't be cute, A.J."

"All right, here. Your documentary on women in government was very informative and completely unbiased. I felt it showed a surprising lack of male, or female, chauvinism."

"That's a start, but why don't you try something a little more personal?"

"More personal," she mused, and smiled at the ceiling. When had she last lain on her bed and flirted over the phone? Had she ever? She supposed it didn't hurt, with a distance of three thousand miles, to feel sixteen and giddy. "How about this? If you ever decide you want to try the other end of the camera, I can make you a star."

"Too clichéd," David decided, but found himself grinning.

"You're very picky. How about if I said I think you might, just might, make an interesting companion. You're not difficult to look at, and your mind isn't really dull."

"Very lukewarm, A.J."

"Take it or leave it."

"Why don't we take the experiment to the next stage? Spend an evening with me and find out if your hypothesis is correct."

"I'm afraid I can't dump everything here and fly out to Pennsylvania or wherever to test a theory."

"I'll be back the middle of next week."

She hesitated, lectured herself, then went with impulse. "*Double Bluff* is opening here next week. Friday. Hastings Reed is a client. He's certain he's going to cop the Oscar."

"Back to business, A.J.?"

"I happen to have two tickets for the premiere. You buy the popcorn."

She'd surprised him. Switching the phone to his other hand, David was careful to speak casually. "A date?"

"Don't push your luck, Brady."

"I'll pick you up on Friday."

"Eight," she told him, already wondering if she was making a mistake. "Now go to bed. I have to get to work."

"Aurora."

"Yes?"

"Give me a thought now and then."

"Good night, Brady."

A.J. hung up the phone, then sat with it cradled in her lap. What had possessed her to do that? She'd intended to give the tickets away and catch the film when the buzz had died down. She didn't care for glittery premieres in the first place. And more important, she knew spending an evening with David Brady was foolish. And dangerous.

When was the last time she'd allowed herself to be charmed by a man? A million years ago, she remembered with a sigh. And where had that gotten her? Weepy and disgusted with herself. But she wasn't a child anymore, she remembered. She was a successful, self-confident woman who could handle ten David Bradys at a negotiating table. The problem was she just wasn't sure she could handle one of him anywhere else.

She let out a long lingering sigh before her gaze passed over her clock. With a muffled oath she was tumbling out of bed. Damn David Brady and her own foolishness. She was going to be late.

5

She bought a new dress. A.J. told herself that as the agent representing the lead in a major motion picture premiering in Hollywood, she was obligated to buy one. But she knew she had bought it for Aurora, not A.J.

At five minutes to eight on Friday night, she stood in front of her mirror and studied the results. No chic, professional suit this time. But perhaps she shouldn't have gone so far in the other direction.

Still, it was black. Black was practical and always in vogue. She turned to the right profile, then the left. It certainly wasn't flashy. But all in all, it might have been wiser to have chosen something more conservative than the pipeline strapless, nearly backless black silk. Straight on, it was provocative. From the side it was downright suggestive. Why hadn't she noticed in the dressing room just how tightly the material clung? Maybe she had, A.J. admitted on a long breath. Maybe she'd been giddy enough, foolish enough, to buy it because it didn't make her feel like an agent or any other sort of professional. It just made her feel like a woman. That was asking for trouble.

In any case, she could solve part of the problem with the little beaded jacket. Satisfied, she reached for a heavy silver locket clipped to thick links. Even as she was fastening it, A.J. heard the door. Taking her time, she slipped into the shoes that lay neatly at the foot of her bed, checked the contents of her purse and picked up the beaded jacket. Reminding herself to think of the entire process as an experiment, she opened the door to David.

She hadn't expected him to bring her flowers. He didn't seem the type for such time-honored romantic gestures. Because he appeared to be as off-balance as she, they just stood there a moment, staring.

She was stunning. He'd never considered her beautiful before. Attractive, yes, and sexy in the coolest, most aloof sort of way. But tonight she was breathtaking. Her dress didn't glitter, it didn't gleam, but simply flowed with the long, subtle lines of her body. It was enough. More than enough.

He took a step forward. Clearing her throat, A.J. took a step back.

"Right on time," she commented, and worked on a smile.

"I'm already regretting I didn't come early."

A.J. accepted the roses and struggled to be casual, when she wanted to bury her face in them. "Thank you. They're lovely. Would you like a drink while I put them in water?"

"No." It was enough just to look at her.

"I'll just be a minute."

As she walked away, his gaze passed down her nape over her shoulder blades and the smooth, generously exposed back to her waist, where the material of her dress again intruded. It nearly made him change his mind about the drink.

To keep his mind off tall blondes with smooth skin, he took a look around her apartment. She didn't appear to have the same taste in decorating as Clarissa.

The room was cool, as cool as its tenant, and just as streamlined. He couldn't fault the icy colors or the uncluttered lines, but he wondered just how much of herself Aurora Fields had put into the place she lived in. In the manner of her office, nothing was out of place. No frivolous mementos were set out for public viewing. The room had class and style, but none of the passion he'd found in the woman. And it told no secrets, not even in a whisper. He found himself more determined than ever to discover how many she had.

When A.J. came back she was steady. She'd arranged the roses in one of her rare extravagances, a tall, slim vase of Baccarat crystal. "Since you're prompt, we can get there a bit early and ogle the celebrities. It's different than dealing with them over a business lunch or watching a shoot."

"You look like a witch," he murmured. "White skin, black dress. You can almost smell the brimstone."

Her hands were no longer steady as she reached for her jacket. "I had an ancestor who was burned as one."

He took the jacket from her, regretting the fact that once it was on too much of her would be covered. "I guess I shouldn't be surprised."

"In Salem, during the madness." A.J. tried to ignore the way his fingers lingered as he slid the jacket over her. "Of course she was no more witch than Clarissa, but she was…special. According to the journals and documents that Clarissa gathered, she was twenty-five and very lovely. She made the mistake of warning her neighbors about a barn fire that didn't happen for two days."

"So she was tried and executed?"

"People usually have violent reactions to what they don't understand."

"We talked to a man in New York who's making a killing in the stock market by 'seeing' things before they happen."

"Times change." A.J. picked up her bag, then paused at

the door. "My ancestor died alone and penniless. Her name was Aurora." She lifted a brow when he said nothing. "Shall we go?"

David slipped his hand over hers as the door shut at their backs. "I have a feeling that having an ancestor executed as a witch is very significant for you."

After shrugging, A.J. drew her hand from his to push the button for the elevator. "Not everyone has one in his family tree."

"And?"

"And let's just say I have a good working knowledge of how different opinions can be. They range from everything from blind condemnation to blind faith. Both extremes are dangerous."

As they stepped into the elevator he said consideringly, "And you work very hard to shield Clarissa from both ends."

"Exactly."

"What about you? Are you defending yourself by keeping your relationship with Clarissa quiet?"

"I don't need defending from my mother." She'd swung through the doors before she managed to bank the quick surge of temper. "It's easier for me to work for her if we keep the family relationship out of it."

"Logical. I find you consistently logical, A.J."

She wasn't entirely sure it was a compliment. "And there is the fact that I'm very accessible. I didn't want clients rushing in to ask me to have my mother tell them where they lost their diamond ring. Is your car in the lot?"

"No, we're right out front. And I wasn't criticizing, Aurora, just asking."

She felt the temper fade as quickly as it had risen. "It's all right. I tend to be a little sensitive where Clarissa's concerned.

I don't see a car," she began, glancing idly past a gray limo before coming back to it with raised brows. "Well," she murmured. "I'm impressed."

"Good." The driver was already opening the door. "That was the idea."

A.J. snuggled in. She'd ridden in limos countless times, escorting clients, delivering or picking them up at airports. But she never took such cushy comfort for granted. As she let herself enjoy, she watched David take a bottle out of ice.

"Flowers, a limo and now champagne. I am impressed, Brady, but I'm also—"

"Going to spoil it," he finished as he eased the cork expertly out. "Remember, we're testing your theory that I'd make an interesting companion." He offered a glass. "How'm I doing?"

"Fine so far." She sipped and appreciated. If she'd had experience in anything, she reminded herself, it was in how to keep a relationship light and undemanding. "I'm afraid I'm more used to doing the pampering than being pampered."

"How's it feel to be on the other side?"

"A little too good." She slipped out of her shoes and let her feet sink into the carpet. "I could just sit and ride for hours."

"It's okay with me." He ran a finger down the side of her throat to the edge of her jacket. "Want to skip the movie?"

She felt the tremor start where his finger skimmed, then rush all the way to the pit of her stomach. It came home to her that she hadn't had experience with David Brady. "I think not." Draining her glass, she held it out for a refill. "I suppose you attend a lot of these."

"Premieres?" He tilted wine into her glass until it fizzed to the rim. "No. Too Hollywood."

"Oh." With a gleam in her eye, A.J. glanced slowly around the limo. "I see."

"Tonight seemed to be an exception." He toasted her, appreciating the way she sat with such careless elegance in the plush corner of the limo. She belonged there. Now. With him. "As a representative of some of the top names in the business, you must drop in on these things a few times a year."

"No." A.J.'s lips curved as she sipped from her glass. "I hate them."

"Are you serious?"

"Deadly."

"Then what the hell are we doing?"

"Experimenting," she reminded him, and set her glass down as the limo stopped at the curb. "Just experimenting."

There were throngs of people crowded into the roped off sections by the theater's entrance. Cameras were clicking, flashes popping. It didn't seem to matter to the crowd that the couple alighting from the limo weren't recognizable faces. It was Hollywood. It was opening night. The glitz was peaking. A.J. and David were cheered and applauded. She blinked twice as three paparazzi held cameras in her face.

"Incredible, isn't it?" he muttered as he steered her toward the entrance.

"It reminds me why I agent instead of perform." In an instinctive defense she wasn't even aware of, she turned away from the cameras. "Let's find a dark corner."

"I'm for that."

She had to laugh. "You never give up."

"A.J. A.J., *darling!*"

Before she could react, she found herself crushed against a soft, generous bosom. "Merinda, how nice to see you."

"Oh, I can't tell you how thrilled I am you're here." Merinda MacBride, Hollywood's current darling, drew her dramatically away. "A friendly face, you know. These things are such zoos."

She glittered from head to foot, from the diamonds that hung at her ears to the sequined dress that appeared to have been painted on by a very appreciative artist. She sent A.J. a smile that would have melted chocolate at ten paces. "You look divine."

"Thank you. You aren't alone?"

"Oh, no. I'm with Brad…." After a moment's hesitation, she smiled again. "Brad," she repeated, as if she'd decided last names weren't important. "He's fetching me a drink." Her gaze shifted and fastened on David. "You're not alone, either."

"Merinda MacBride, David Brady."

"A pleasure." He took her hand and, though she turned her knuckles up expectantly, didn't bring it to his lips. "I've seen your work and admired it."

"Why, thank you." She studied, measured and rated him in a matter of seconds. "Are we mutual clients of A.J.'s?"

"David's a producer." A.J. watched Merinda's baby-blue eyes sharpen. "Of documentaries," she added, amused. "You might have seen some of his work on public television."

"Of course." She beamed at him, though she'd never watched public television in her life and had no intention of starting. "I desperately admire producers. Especially attractive ones."

"I have a couple of scripts I think you'd be interested in," A.J. put in to draw her off.

"Oh?" Instantly Merinda dropped the sex-bomb act. A. J. Fields didn't recommend a script unless it had meat on it. "Have them sent over."

"First thing Monday."

"Well, I must find Brad before he forgets about me. David." She gave him her patented smoldering look. Documentaries or not, he was a producer. And a very attractive one. "I hope we run into each other again. Ta, A.J." She brushed cheeks. "Let's do lunch."

"Soon."

David barely waited for her to walk out of earshot. "You deal with that all the time?"

"Ssh!"

"I mean *all* the time," he continued, watching as Merinda's tightly covered hips swished through the crowd. "Day after day. Why aren't you crazy?"

"Merinda may be a bit overdramatic, but if you've seen any of her films, you'll know just how talented she is."

"The woman looked loaded with talent to me," he began, but stopped to grin when A.J. scowled. "As an *actress,*" he continued. "I thought she was exceptional in *Only One Day.*"

A.J. couldn't quite conquer the smile. She'd hustled for weeks to land Merinda that part. "So you have seen her films."

"I don't live in a cave. That film was the first one that didn't let's say, focus on her anatomy."

"It was the first one I represented her on."

"She's fortunate in her choice of agents."

"Thank you, but it goes both ways. Merinda's a very hot property."

"If we're going to make it through this evening, I'd better not touch that one."

They were interrupted another half a dozen times before they could get into the theater. A.J. ran into clients, acquaintances and associates, greeted, kissed and complimented while turning down invitations to after-theater parties.

"You're very good at this." David took two seats on the aisle near the back of the theater.

"Part of the job." A.J. settled back. There was nothing she enjoyed quite so much as a night at the movies.

"A bit jaded, A.J.?"

"Jaded?"

"Untouched by the glamour of it all, unaffected by the star system. You don't get any particular thrill out of exchanging kisses and hugs with some of the biggest and most distinguished names in the business."

"Business," she repeated, as if that explained it all. "That's not being jaded—it's being sensible. And the only time I saw you awestruck was when you found yourself face-to-face with three inches of cleavage on a six-foot blonde. Ssh," she muttered before he could comment. "It's started and I hate to miss the opening credits."

With the theater dark, the audience quiet, A.J. threw herself into the picture. Ever since childhood, she'd been able to transport herself with the big screen. She wouldn't have called it "escape." She didn't like the word. A.J. called it "involvement." The actor playing the lead was a client, a man she knew intimately and had comforted through two divorces. All three of his children's birthdays were noted in her book. She'd listened to him rant; she'd heard his complaints, his doubts. That was all part of the job. But the moment she saw him on film, he was, to her, the part he played and nothing else.

Within five minutes, she was no longer in a crowded theater in Los Angeles, but in a rambling house in Connecticut. And there was murder afoot. When the lights went out and thunder boomed, she grabbed David's arm and cringed in her seat. Not one to pass up an age-old opportunity, he slipped an arm around her.

When was the last time, he wondered, that he'd sat in a theater with his arm around his date? He decided it had been close to twenty years and he'd been missing a great deal. He turned his attention to the film, but was distracted by her scent. It was still light, barely discernible, but it filled his senses. He tried to concentrate on the action and drama racing across the screen. A.J. caught her breath and shifted an inch closer. The tension on the screen seemed very pedestrian compared to his own. When the lights came up he found himself regretting that there was no longer such a thing as the double feature.

"It was good, wasn't it?" Eyes brilliant with pleasure, she turned to him. "It was really very good."

"Very good," he agreed, and lifted his hand to toy with her ear. "And if the applause is any indication, your client's got himself a hit."

"Thank God." She breathed a sigh of relief before shifting away to break what was becoming a very unnerving contact. "I talked him into the part. If he'd flopped, it would have been my head."

"And now that he can expect raves?"

"It'll be because of his talent," she said easily. "And that's fair enough. Would you mind if we slipped out before it gets too crazy?"

"I'd prefer it." He rose and steered her through the pockets of people that were already forming in the aisles. They hadn't gone ten feet before A.J.'s name was called out three times.

"Where are you going? You running out?" Hastings Reed, six feet three inches of down-home sex and manhood, blocked the aisle. He was flushed with the victory of seeing himself triumph on the screen and nervous that he might have mis-judged the audience reaction. "You didn't like it?"

"It was wonderful." Understanding his need for reassurance, A.J. stood on tiptoe to brush his cheek. "You were wonderful. Never better."

He returned the compliment with a bone-crushing hug. "We have to wait for the reviews."

"Prepare to accept praise humbly, and with good grace. Hastings, this is David Brady."

"Brady?" As Hastings took David's hand, his etched in bronze face creased into a frown. "Producer?"

"That's right."

"God, I love your work." Already flying, Hastings pumped David's hand six times before finally releasing it. "I'm an honorary chairman of Rights for Abused Children. Your documentary did an incredible job of bringing the issue home and making people aware. Actually, it's what got me involved in the first place."

"It's good to hear that. We wanted to make people think."

"Made me think. I've got kids of my own. Listen, keep me in mind if you ever do a follow-up. No fee." He grinned down at A.J. "She didn't hear that."

"Hear what?"

He laughed and yanked her against him again. "This lady's incredible. I don't know what I'd have done without her. I wasn't going to take this part, but she badgered me into it."

"I never badger," A.J. said mildly.

"Nags, badgers and browbeats. Thank God." Grinning, he finally took a good look at her. "Damn if you don't look like something a man could swallow right up. I've never seen you dressed like that."

To cover a quick flush of embarrassment, she reached up to straighten his tie. "And as I recall, the last time I saw you, you were in jeans and smelled of horses."

"Guess I did. You're coming to Chasen's?"

"Actually, I—"

"You're coming. Look, I've got a couple of quick interviews, but I'll see you there in a half hour." He took two strides away and was swallowed up in the crowd.

"He's got quite an...overwhelming personality," David commented.

"To say the least." A.J. glanced at her watch. It was still early.

"I suppose I should at least put in an appearance, since he'll count on it now. I can take a cab if you'd rather skip it."

"Ever hear of the expression about leaving with the guy who brought you?"

"This isn't a country dance," A.J. pointed out as they wove through the lingering crowd.

"Same rules apply. I can handle Chasen's."

"Okay, but just for a little while."

The "little while" lasted until after three.

Cases of champagne, mountains of caviar and piles of fascinating little canapés. Even someone as practical as A.J. found it difficult to resist a full-scale celebration. The music was loud, but it didn't seem to matter. There were no quiet corners to escape to. Through her clientele and David's contacts, they knew nearly everyone in the room between them. A few minutes of conversation here, another moment there, ate up hours of time. Caught up in her client's success, A.J. didn't mind.

On the crowded dance floor, she allowed herself to relax in David's arms. "Incredible, isn't it?"

"Nothing tastes so sweet as success, especially when you mix it with champagne."

She glanced around. It was hard not to be fascinated with the faces, the names, the bodies. She was part of it, a very intricate part. But through her own choice, she wasn't an intimate part. "I usually avoid this sort of thing."

He let his fingers skim lightly up her back. "Why?"

"Oh, I don't know." Weariness, wine and pleasure combined. Her cheek rested against his. "I guess I'm more of a background sort of person. You fit in."

"And you don't?"

"Ummm." She shook her head. Why was it men smelled so

wonderful—so wonderfully different? And felt so good when you held and were held by one. "You're part of the talent. I just work with clauses and figures."

"And that's the way you want it?"

"Absolutely. Still, this is nice." When his hand ran down her back again, she stretched into it. "Very nice."

"I'd rather be alone with you," he murmured. Every time he held her like this he thought he would go crazy. "In some dim little room where the music was low."

"This is safer." But she didn't object when his lips brushed her temple.

"Who needs safe?"

"I do. I need safe and ordered and sensible."

"Anyone who chooses to be involved in this business tosses safe, ordered and sensible out the window."

"Not me." She drew back to smile at him. It felt so good to relax, to flow with the evening, to let her steps match his without any conscious thought. "I just make the deals and leave the chances up to others."

"Take ten percent and run?"

"That's right."

"I might have believed that a few weeks ago. The problem is I've seen you with Clarissa."

"That's entirely different."

"True enough. I also saw you with Hastings tonight. You get wrapped up with your clients, A.J. You might be able to convince yourself they're just signatures, but I know better. You're a marshmallow."

Her brows drew together. "Ridiculous. Marshmallows get swallowed."

"They're also resilient. I admire that in you." He touched his lips to hers before she could move. "I'm beginning to realize I admire quite a bit in you."

She would have pulled away then, but he kept her close easily enough and continued to sway. "I don't mix business and personal feelings."

"You lie."

"I might play with the truth," she said, abruptly dignified, "but I don't lie."

"You were ready to turn handsprings tonight when that movie hit."

A.J. tossed her hair out of her face. He saw too much too easily. A man wasn't supposed to. "Have you any idea how I can use that as a lever? I'll get Hastings a million-five for his next movie."

"You'll 'get Hastings,'" David repeated. "Even your phrasing gives you away."

"You're picking up things that aren't there."

"No, I think I'm finding things you've squirreled away. Have you got a problem with the fact that I've decided I like you?"

Off-balance, she missed a step and found herself pressed even closer. "I think I'd handle it better if we still got on each other nerves."

"Believe me, you get on my nerves." Until his blood was on slow boil, his muscles knotting and stretching and the need racing. "There are a hundred people in this room and my mind keeps coming back to the fact that I could have you out of what there is of that dress in thirty seconds flat."

The chill arrowed down her back. "You know that's not what I meant. You'd be smarter to keep your mind on business."

"Smarter, safer. We're looking for different things, A.J."

"We can agree on that, anyway."

"We might agree on more if we gave ourselves the chance." She didn't know exactly why she smiled. Perhaps it was because it sounded like a fantasy. She enjoyed watching them, listening to them, without really believing in them. "David." She rested her arms on his shoulders. "You're a very nice man, on some levels."

"I think I can return that compliment."

"Let me spell things out for you in the way I understand best. Number one, we're business associates at the moment. This precludes any possibility that we could be seriously involved. Number two, while this documentary is being made my first concern is, and will continue to be, Clarissa's welfare. Number three, I'm very busy and what free time I have I use to relax in my own way—which is alone. And number four, I'm not equipped for relationships. I'm selfish, critical and disinterested."

"Very well put." He kissed her forehead in a friendly fashion. "Are you ready to go?"

"Yes." A little nonplussed by his reaction, she walked off the dance floor to retrieve her jacket. They left the noise and crowd behind and stepped out into the cool early-morning air. "I forget sometimes that the glamour and glitz can be nice in small doses."

He helped her into the waiting limo. "Moderation in all things."

"Life's more stable that way." Cut off from the driver and the outside by thick smoked glass, A.J. settled back against the seat. Before she could let out the first contented sigh, David was close, his hand firm on her chin. "David—"

"Number one," he began, "I'm the producer of this project, and you're the agent for one, only one, of the talents. That means we're business associates in the broadest sense and that doesn't preclude an involvement. We're already involved."

There'd been no heat in his eyes on the dance floor, she thought quickly. Not like there was now. "David—"

"You had your say," he reminded her. "Number two, while

this documentary is being made, you can fuss over Clarissa all you want. That has nothing to do with us. Number three, we're both busy, which means we don't want to waste time with excuses and evasions that don't hold water. And number four, whether you think you're equipped for relationships or not, you're in the middle of one right now. You'd better get used to it."

Temper darkened her eyes and chilled her voice. "I don't have to get used to anything."

"The hell you don't. Put a number on this."

Frustrated desire, unrelieved passion, simmering anger. She felt them all as his mouth crushed down on hers. Her first reaction was pure self-preservation. She struggled against him, knowing if she didn't free herself quickly, she'd be lost. But he seemed to know, somehow, that her struggle was against herself, not him.

He held her closer. His mouth demanded more, until, despite fears, despite doubts, despite everything, she gave.

With a muffled moan, her arms went around him. Her fingers slid up his back to lose themselves in his hair. Passion, still unrelieved, mounted until it threatened to consume. She could feel everything, the hard line of his body against hers, the soft give of the seat at her back. There was the heat of his lips as they pressed and rubbed on hers and the cool air blown in silently through the vents.

And she could taste—the lingering punch of champagne as their tongues tangled together. She could taste a darker flavor, a deeper flavor that was his flesh. Still wilder, less recognizable, was the taste of her own passion.

His mouth left hers only to search out other delights. Over the bare, vulnerable skin of her neck and shoulders he found them. His hands weren't gentle as they moved over her. His mouth wasn't tender. Her heart began to thud in a fast, chaotic rhythm at the thought of being taken with such hunger, such fury.

Driven by her own demons she let her hands move, explore and linger. When his breath was as uneven as hers their lips met again. The contact did nothing to soothe and everything to arouse. Desperate for more, she brought her teeth down to nip, to torment. With an oath, he swung her around until they were sprawled on the long, wide seat.

Her lips parted as she looked up at him. She could see the intermittent flash of streetlights as they passed overhead. Shadow and light. Shadow and light. Hypnotic. Erotic. A.J. reached up to touch his face.

She was all cream and silk as she lay beneath him. Her hair was tousled around a face flushed with arousal. The touch of her fingers on his cheek was light as a whisper and caused the need to thunder through him.

"This is crazy," she murmured.

"I know."

"It's not supposed to happen." But it was. She knew it. She had known it from the first meeting. "It can't happen," she corrected.

"Why?"

"Don't ask me." Her voice dropped to a whisper. She couldn't resist letting her fingers play along his face even as she prepared herself to deny both of them. "I can't explain. If I could you wouldn't understand."

"If there's someone else I don't give a damn."

"No, there's no one." She closed her eyes a moment, then opened them again to stare at him. "There's no one else."

Why was he hesitating? She was here, aroused, inches away from total surrender. He had only to ignore the confused plea in her eyes and take. But even with his blood hot, the need pressing, he couldn't ignore it. "It might not be now, it might not be here, but it will be, Aurora."

It would be. Had to be. The part of her that knew it fought a frantic tug-of-war with the part that had to deny it. "Let me go, David."

Trapped by his own feelings, churning with his own needs, he pulled her up. "What kind of game are you playing?"

She was cold. Freezing. She felt each separate chill run over her skin. "It's called survival."

"Damn it, Aurora." She was so beautiful. Why did she suddenly have to be so beautiful? Why did she suddenly have to look so fragile? "What does being with me, making love with me, have to do with your survival?"

"Nothing." She nearly laughed as she felt the limo cruise to a halt. "Nothing at all if it were just that simple."

"Why complicate it? We want each other. We're both adults. People become lovers every day without doing themselves any damage."

"Some people." She let out a shuddering breath. "I'm not some people. If it were so simple, I'd make love with you right here, in the back seat of this car. I won't tell you I don't want to." She turned to look at him and the vulnerability in her eyes was haunted by regrets. "But it's not simple. Making love with you would be easy. Falling in love with you wouldn't."

Before he could move, she'd pushed open the door and was on the street.

"Aurora." He was beside her, a hand on her arm, but she shook him off. "You can't expect to just walk off after a statement like that."

"That's just what I'm doing," she corrected, and shook him off a second time.

"I'll take you up." With what willpower he had left, he held on to patience.

"No. Just go."

"We have to talk."

"No." Neither of them was prepared for the desperation in her voice. "I want you to go. It's late. I'm tired. I'm not thinking straight."

"If we don't talk this out now, we'll just have to do it later."

"Later, then." She would have promised him anything for freedom at that moment. "I want you to go now, David." When he continued to hold her, her voice quivered. "Please, I need you to go. I can't handle this now."

He could fight her anger, but he couldn't fight her fragility. "All right."

He waited until she had disappeared inside her building. Then he leaned back on the car and pulled out a cigarette. Later then, he promised himself. They'd talk. He stood where he was, waiting for his system to level. They'd talk, he assured himself again. But it was best to wait until they were both calmer and more reasonable.

Tossing away the cigarette, he climbed back into the limo. He hoped to God he could stop thinking of her long enough to sleep.

6

She wanted to pace. She wanted to walk up and down, pull at her hair and walk some more. She forced herself to sit quietly on the sofa and wait as Clarissa poured tea.

"I'm so glad you came by, dear. It's so seldom you're able to spend an afternoon with me."

"Things are under control at the office. Abe's covering for me."

"Such a nice man. How's his little grandson?"

"Spoiled rotten. Abe wants to buy him Dodger Stadium."

"Grandparents are entitled to spoil the way parents are obliged to discipline." She kept her eyes lowered, anxious not to show her own longings and apply pressure. "How's your tea?"

"It's…different." Knowing the lukewarm compliment would satisfy Clarissa saved her from an outright lie. "What is it?"

"Rose hips. I find it very soothing in the afternoons. You seem to need a little soothing, Aurora."

A.J. set down her cup and, giving in to the need for movement, rose. She'd known when she'd deliberately cleared her calendar that she would come to Clarissa. And she'd known that she would come for help, though she'd repeatedly told herself she didn't need it.

"Momma." A.J. sat on the sofa again as Clarissa sipped tea and waited patiently. "I think I'm in trouble."

"You ask too much of yourself." Clarissa reached out to touch her hand. "You always have."

"What am I going to do?"

Clarissa sat back as she studied her daughter. She'd never heard that phrase from her before, and now that she had, she wanted to be certain to give the right answers. "You're frightened."

"Terrified." She was up again, unable to sit. "It's getting away from me. I'm losing the controls."

"Aurora, it isn't always necessary to hold on to them."

"It is for me." She looked back with a half smile. "You should understand."

"I do. Of course I do." But she'd wished so often that her daughter, her only child, would be at peace with herself. "You constantly defend yourself against being hurt because you were hurt once and decided it would never happen again. Aurora, are you in love with David?"

Clarissa would know he was at the core of it. Naturally she would know without a word being said. A.J. could accept that. "I might be if I don't pull myself back now."

"Would it be so bad to love someone?"

"David isn't just someone. He's too strong, too overwhelming. Besides…" She paused long enough to steady herself. "I thought I was in love once before."

"You were young." Clarissa came as close as she ever did to true anger. She set her cup in its saucer with a little snap. "Infatuation is a different matter. It demands more and gives less back than love."

A.J. stood in the middle of the room. There was really no place to go. "Maybe this is just infatuation. Or lust."

Clarissa lifted a brow and sipped tea calmly. "You're the only one who can answer that. Somehow I don't think you'd have cleared your calendar and come to see me in the middle of a workday if you were concerned about lust."

Laughing, A.J. walked over to drop on the sofa beside her. "Oh, Momma, there's no one like you. No one."

"Things were never normal for you, were they?"

"No." A.J. dropped her head on Clarissa's shoulder. "They were better. You were better."

"Aurora, your father loved me very much. He loved, and he accepted, without actually understanding. I can't even comprehend what my life might have been like if I hadn't given up the controls and loved him back."

"He was special," A.J. murmured. "Most men aren't."

Clarissa hesitated only a moment, then cleared her throat. "Alex accepts me, too."

"Alex?" Uneasy, A.J. sat up again. There was no mistaking the blush of color in Clarissa's cheeks. "Are you and Alex…" How did one put such a question to a mother? "Are you serious about Alex?"

"He asked me to marry him."

"What?" Too stunned for reason, A.J. jerked back and gaped. "Marriage? You barely know him. You met only weeks ago. Momma, certainly you're mature enough to realize something as important as marriage takes a great deal of thought."

Clarissa beamed at her. "What an excellent mother you'll make one day. I was never able to lecture quite like that."

"I don't mean to lecture." Mumbling, A.J. picked up her tea. "I just don't want you to jump into something like this without giving it the proper thought."

"You see, that's just what I mean. I'm sure you got that from your father's side. My family's always been just the tiniest bit flighty."

"Momma—"

"Do you remember when Alex and I were discussing palm reading for the documentary?"

"Of course." The uneasiness increased, along with a sense of inevitability. "You felt something."

"It was very strong and very clear. I admit it flustered me a bit to realize a man could be attracted to me after all these years. And I wasn't aware until that moment that I could feel like that about anyone."

"But you need time. I don't doubt anything you feel, anything you see. You know that. But—"

"Darling, I'm fifty-six." Clarissa shook her head, wondering how it had happened so quickly. "I've been content to live alone. I think perhaps I was meant to live alone for a certain amount of time. Now I want to share the rest of life. You're twenty-eight and content and very capable of living alone. Still, you mustn't be afraid to share your life."

"It's different."

"No." She took A.J.'s hands again. "Love, affection, needs. They're really very much the same for everyone. If David is the right man for you, you'll know it. But after knowing, you have to accept."

"He may not accept me." Her fingers curled tightly around her mother's. "I have trouble accepting myself."

"And that's the only worry you've ever given me. Aurora, I can't tell you what to do. I can't look into tomorrow for you, as much as part of me wants to."

"I'm not asking that. I'd never ask you that."

"No, you wouldn't. Look into your heart, Aurora. Stop calculating risks and just look."

"I might see something I don't want to."

"Oh, you probably will." With a little laugh, Clarissa settled back on the sofa with an arm around A.J. "I can't tell you what to do, but I can tell you what I feel. David Brady is a very good man. He has his flaws, of course, but he is a good man. It's been a pleasure for me to be able to work with him. As a matter of fact, when he called this morning, I was delighted."

"Called?" Immediately alert, A.J. sat up straight. "David called you? Why?"

"Oh, a few ideas he'd had about the documentary." She fussed with the little lace napkin in her lap. "He's in Rolling Hills today. Well, not exactly in, but outside. Do you remember hearing about that old mansion no one ever seems able to live in for long? The one a few miles off the beach?"

"It's supposed to be haunted," A.J. muttered.

"Of course there are differing opinions on that. I think David made an excellent choice for his project, though, from what he told me about the background."

"What do you have to do with that?"

"That? Oh, nothing at all. We just chatted about the house. I suppose he thought I'd be interested."

"Oh." Mollified, A.J. began to relax. "That's all right then."

"We did set up a few other things. I'll be going into the studio—Wednesday," she decided. "Yes, I'm sure it's Wednesday of next week, to discuss spontaneous phenomena. And then, oh, sometime the following week, I'm to go to the Van Camps'. We'll tape in Alice's living room."

"The Van Camps'." She felt the heat rising. "He set all this up with you."

Clarissa folded her hands. "Yes, indeed. Did I do something wrong?"

"Not you." Fired up, she rose. "He knew better than to change things without clearing it with me first. You can't trust anyone. Especially a producer." Snatching up her purse, she strode to the door. "You don't go anywhere on Wednesday to discuss any kind of phenomena until I see just what he has up his sleeve." She caught herself and came back to give Clarissa a hug. "Don't worry, I'll straighten it out."

"I'm counting on it." Clarissa watched her daughter storm out of the house before she sat back, content. She'd done everything she could—set energy in motion. The rest was up to fate.

"Tell him we'll reschedule. Better yet, have Abe meet with him." A.J. shouted into her car phone as she came up behind a tractor-trailer.

"Abe has a three-thirty. I don't think he can squeeze Montgomery in at four."

"Damn." Impatient, A.J. zoomed around the tractor-trailer. "Who's free at four?"

"Just Barbara."

While keeping an eye peeled for her exit, A.J. turned that over in her mind. "No, they'd never jell. Reschedule, Diane. Tell Montgomery...tell him there was an emergency. A medical emergency."

"Check. There isn't, is there?"

Her smile was set and nothing to laugh about. "There might be."

"Sounds promising. How can I reach you?"

"You can't. Leave anything important on the machine. I'll call in and check."

"You got it. Hey, good luck."

"Thanks." Teeth gritted, A.J. replaced the receiver.

He wasn't going to get away with playing power games. A.J. knew all the rules to that one, and had made up plenty of her own. David Brady was in for it. A.J. reached for her map again. If she could ever find him.

When the first raindrop hit the windshield she started to swear. By the time she'd taken the wrong exit, made three wrong turns and found herself driving down a decrepit gravel road in a full-fledged spring storm, she was cursing fluently. Every one of them was aimed directly at David Brady's head.

One look at the house through driving rain and thunder-clouds proved why he'd chosen so well. Braking viciously, A.J. decided he'd arranged the storm for effect. When she swung out of the car and stepped in a puddle of mud that slopped over her ankle, it was the last straw.

He saw her through the front window. Surprise turned to annoyance quickly at the thought of another interruption on a day that had seen everything go wrong. He hadn't had a decent night's sleep in a week, his work was going to hell and he itched just looking at her. When he pulled open the front door, he was as ready as A.J. for an altercation.

"What the hell are you doing here?"

Her hair was plastered to her face; her suit was soaked. She'd just ruined half a pair of Italian shoes. "I want to talk to you, Brady."

"Fine. Call my office and set up an appointment. I'm working."

"I want to talk to you now!" Lifting a hand to his chest, she gave him a hefty shove back against the door. "Just where do you come off making arrangements with one of my clients without clearing it with me? If you want Clarissa in the studio next week, then you deal with me. Understand?"

He took her damp hand by the wrist and removed it from his shirt. "I have Clarissa under contract for the duration of filming. I don't have to clear anything with you."

"You'd better read it again, Brady. Dates and times are set up through her representative."

"Fine. I'll send you a schedule. Now if you'll excuse me—"

He pushed open the door, but she stepped in ahead of him. Two electricians inside the foyer fell silent and listened. "I'm not finished."

"I am. Get lost, Fields, before I have you tossed off the set."

"Watch your step, or my client might develop a chronic case of laryngitis."

"Don't threaten me, A.J." He gripped her lapels with both hands. "I've had about all I'm taking from you. You want to talk, fine. Your office or mine, tomorrow."

"Mr. Brady, we need you upstairs."

For a moment longer he held her. Her gaze was locked on his and the fury was fierce and very equal. He wanted, God, he wanted to drag her just a bit closer, wipe that maddening look off her face. He wanted to crush his mouth to hers until she couldn't speak, couldn't breathe, couldn't fight. He wanted, more than anything, to make her suffer the way he suffered. He released her so abruptly she took two stumbling steps back.

"Get lost," he ordered, and turned to mount the stairs.

It took her a minute to catch her breath. She hadn't known she could get this angry, hadn't allowed herself to become this angry in too many years to count. Emotions flared up inside her, blinding her to everything else. She dashed up the stairs behind him.

"Ms. Fields, nice to see you again." Alex stood on the top landing in front of a wall where the paint had peeled and cracked. He gave her an easy smile as he smoked his cigar and waited to be called back in front of the camera.

"And I want to talk to you, too," she snapped at him. Leaving him staring, she strode down the hall after David.

It was narrow and dark. There were cobwebs clinging to corners, but she didn't notice. In places there were squares of lighter paint where pictures had once hung. A.J. worked her way through technicians and walked into the room only steps behind David.

It hit her like a wall. No sooner had she drawn in the breath to shout at him again than she couldn't speak at all. She was freezing. The chill whipped through her and to the bone in the matter of a heartbeat.

The room was lit for the shoot, but she didn't see the cameras, the stands or the coils of cable. She saw wallpaper, pink roses on cream, and a four-poster draped in the same rose hue. There was a little mahogany stool beside the bed that was worn smooth in the center. She could smell the roses that stood fresh and a little damp in an exquisite crystal vase on a mahogany vanity that gleamed with beeswax and lemon. And she saw—much more. And she heard.

You betrayed me. You betrayed me with him, Jessica.

No! No, I swear it. Don't. For God's sake don't do this. I love you. I—

Lies! All lies. You won't tell any more.

There were screams. There was silence, a hundred times worse. A.J.'s purse hit the floor with a thud as she lifted her hands to her ears.

"A.J." David was shaking her, hands firm on her shoulders, as everyone else in the room stopped to stare. "What's wrong with you?"

She reached out to clutch his shirt. He could feel the iciness of her flesh right through the cotton. She looked at him, but her eyes didn't focus. "That poor girl," she murmured. "Oh, God, that poor girl."

"A.J." With an effort, he kept his voice calm. She was shuddering and pale, but the worst of it was her eyes, dark and glazed as they looked beyond him. She stared at the center of the room as if held in a trance. He took both of her hands in his. "A.J., what girl?"

"He killed her right here. There on the bed. He used his hands. She couldn't scream anymore because his hands were on her throat, squeezing. And then…"

"A.J." He took her chin and forced her to look at him. "There's no bed in here. There's nothing."

"It—" She struggled for air, then lifted both hands to her face. The nausea came, a too-familiar sensation. "I have to get out of here." Breaking away, she pushed through the technicians crowded in the doorway and ran. She stumbled out into the rain and down the porch steps before David caught her.

"Where are you going?" he demanded. A flash of lightning highlighted them both as the rain poured down.

"I've got to…" She trailed off and looked around blindly. "I'm going back to town. I have to get back."

"I'll take you."

"No." Panicked, she struggled, only to find herself held firmly. "I have my car."

"You're not driving anywhere like this." Half leading, half dragging, he pulled her to his car. "Now stay here," he ordered, and slammed the door on her.

Unable to gather the strength to do otherwise, A.J. huddled on the seat and shivered. She needed only a minute. She promised herself she needed only a minute to pull herself together. But however many it took David to come back, the shivering hadn't stopped. He tossed her purse in the back, then tucked a blanket around her. "One of the crew's taking your car back to town." After starting the engine, he headed down the bumpy, potholed gravel road. For several moments there was silence as the rain drummed and she sat hunched under the blanket.

"Why didn't you tell me?" he said at length.

She was better now. She took a steady breath to prove she had control. "Tell you what?"

"That you were like your mother."

A.J. curled into a ball on the seat, cradled her head in her arms and wept.

What the hell was he supposed to say? David cursed her, then himself, as he drove through the rain with her sobbing beside him. She'd given him the scare of his life when he'd turned around and seen her standing there, gasping for air and white as a sheet. He'd never felt anything as cold as her hands had been. Never seen anything like what she must have seen.

Whatever doubts he had, whatever criticisms he could make about laboratory tests, five-dollar psychics and executive clairvoyants, he knew A.J. had seen something, felt something, none of the rest of them had.

So what did he do about it? What did he say?

She wept. She let herself empty. There was no use berating herself, no use being angry with what had happened. She'd long ago resigned herself to the fact that every now and again, no matter how careful she was, no matter how tightly controlled, she would slip and leave herself open.

The rain stopped. There was milky sunlight now. A.J. kept the blanket close around her as she straightened in her seat. "I'm sorry."

"I don't want an apology. I want an explanation."

"I don't have one." She wiped her cheeks dry with her hand. "I'd appreciate it if you'd take me home."

"We're going to talk, and we're going to do it where you can't kick me out."

She was too weak to argue, too weak to care. A.J. rested her head against the window and didn't protest when they passed the turn for her apartment. They drove up into the hills, high above the city. The rain had left things fresh here, though a curling mist still hugged the ground.

He turned into a drive next to a house with cedar shakes and tall windows. The lawn was wide and trimmed with spring flowers bursting around the borders.

"I thought you'd have a place in town."

"I used to, then I decided I had to breathe." He took her purse and a briefcase from the back seat. A.J. pushed the blanket aside and stepped from the car. Saying nothing, they walked to the front door together.

Inside wasn't rustic. He had paintings on the walls and thick Turkish carpets on the floors. She ran her hand along a polished rail and stepped down a short flight of steps into the living room. Still silent, David went to the fireplace and set kindling to blaze. "You'll want to get out of those wet clothes," he said matter-of-factly. "There's a bath upstairs at the end of the hall. I keep a robe on the back of the door."

"Thank you." Her confidence was gone—that edge that helped her keep one step ahead. A.J. moistened her lips. "David, you don't have to—"

"I'll make coffee." He walked through a doorway and left her alone.

She stood there while the flames from the kindling began to lick at split oak. The scent was woodsy, comfortable. She'd never felt more miserable in her life. The kind of rejection she felt now, from David, was the kind she'd expected. It was the kind she'd dealt with before.

She stood there while she battled back the need to weep again. She was strong, self-reliant. She wasn't about to break her heart over David Brady, or any man. Lifting her chin, A.J. walked to the stairs and up. She'd shower, let her clothes dry, then dress and go home. A. J. Fields knew how to take care of herself.

The water helped. It soothed her puffy eyes and warmed her clammy skin. From the small bag of emergency cosmetics in her purse, she managed to repair the worst of the damage. She tried not to notice that the robe carried David's scent as she slipped it on. It was better to remember that it was warm and covered her adequately.

When she went back downstairs, the living area was still empty. Clinging to the courage she'd managed to build back up, A.J. went to look for him.

The hallway twisted and turned at angles when least expected. If the situation had been different, A.J. would have appreciated the house for its uniqueness. She didn't take much notice of polished paneling offset by stark white walls, or planked floors scattered with intricately patterned carpets. She followed the hallway into the kitchen. The scent of coffee eased the beginning of flutters in her stomach. She took a moment to brace herself, then walked into the light.

He was standing by the window. There was a cup of coffee in his hand, but he wasn't drinking. Something was simmering on the stove. Perhaps he'd forgotten it. A.J. crossed her arms over her chest and rubbed her hands over the sleeves of the robe. She didn't feel warm any longer.

"David?"

He turned the moment she said his name, but slowly. He wasn't certain what he should say to her, what he could say. She looked so frail. He couldn't have described his own feelings at the moment and hadn't a clue to hers. "The coffee's hot," he told her. "Why don't you sit down?"

"Thanks." She willed herself to behave as normally as he and took a seat on a stool at the breakfast bar.

"I thought you could use some food." He walked to the stove to pour coffee. "I heated up some soup."

Tension began to beat behind her eyes. "You didn't have to bother."

Saying nothing, he ladled out the soup, then brought both it and the coffee to her. "It's an old family recipe. My mother always says a bowl of soup cures anything."

"It looks wonderful," she managed, and wondered why she had to fight back the urge to cry again. "David…"

"Eat first." Taking no food for himself, he drew up a stool across from her and cradled his coffee. He lit a cigarette and sat, sipping his coffee and smoking, while she toyed with her soup. "You're supposed to eat it," he pointed out. "Not just re-arrange the noodles."

"Why don't you ask?" she blurted out. "I'd rather you just asked and got it over with."

So much hurt there, he realized. So much pain. He wondered where it had its roots. "I don't intend to start an interrogation, A.J."

"Why not?" When she lifted her head, her face was defiant, her eyes strong. "You want to know what happened to me in that room."

He blew out a stream of smoke before he crushed out his cigarette. "Of course I do. But I don't think you're ready to talk about what happened in that room. At least not in detail. A.J., why don't you just talk to me?"

"Not ready?" She might have laughed if her stomach wasn't tied up in knots. "You're never ready. I can tell you what she looked like—black hair, blue eyes. She was wearing a cotton gown that buttoned all the way up to her throat, and her name was Jessica. She was barely eighteen when her husband killed her in a jealous rage, strangled her with his own hands, then killed himself in grief with the pistol in the table beside the bed. That's what you want for your documentary, isn't it?"

The details, and the cool, steady way she delivered them, left him shaken. Just who was this woman who sat across from him, this woman he'd held and desired? "What happened to you has nothing to do with the project. I think it has a great deal to do with the way you're reacting now."

"I can usually control it." She shoved the soup aside so that it lapped over the edges of the bowl. "God knows I've had years of practice. If I hadn't been so angry, so out of control when I walked in there—it probably wouldn't have happened."

"You can block it."

"Usually, yes. To a large extent, anyway."

"Why do you?"

"Do you really think this is a gift?" she demanded as she pushed away from the counter. "Oh, maybe for someone like Clarissa it is. She's so unselfish, so basically good and content with herself."

"And you?"

"I hate it." Unable to remain still, she whirled away. "You've no idea what it can be like, having people stare at you, whisper. If you're different, you're a freak, and I—" She broke off, rubbing at her temple. When she spoke again, her voice was quiet. "I just wanted to be normal. When I was little, I'd have dreams." She folded her hands together and pressed them to her lips. "They were so incredibly real, but I was just a child and thought everyone dreamed like that. I'd tell one of my friends—oh, your cat's going to have kittens. Can I have the little white one? Then weeks later, the cat would have kittens and one of them would be white. Little things. Someone would lose a doll or a toy and I'd say, well, your mother put it on the top shelf in your closet. She forgot. When they looked it would be there. Kids didn't think much of it, but it made some of the parents nervous. They thought it would be best if their children stayed away from me."

"And that hurt," he murmured.

"Yes, that hurt a lot. Clarissa understood. She was comforting and really wonderful about it, but it hurt. I still had the dreams, but I stopped talking about them. Then my father died."

She stood, the heels of her hands pressed to her eyes as she struggled to rein in her emotions. "No, please." She shook her head as she heard David shift on the stool as if to rise. "Just give me a minute." On a long breath, she dropped her hands. "I knew he was dead. He was away on a selling trip, and I woke up in the middle of the night and knew. I got up and went into Clarissa. She was sitting up in bed, wide awake. I could see on her face that she was already grieving. We didn't even say anything to each other, but I got into bed with her, and we just lay there together until the phone rang."

"And you were eight," he murmured, trying to get some grip on it.

"I was eight. After that, I started to block it off. Whenever I began to feel something, I'd just pull in. It got to the point where I could go for months—at one point, two years—without something touching it off. If I get angry or upset to the point where I lose control, I open myself up for it."

He remembered the way she'd stormed into the house, strong and ready for a fight. And the way she'd run out again, pale and terrified. "And I make you angry."

She turned to look at him for the first time since she'd begun to speak. "It seems that way."

The guilt was there. David wasn't certain how to deal with it, or his own confusion. "Should I apologize?"

"You can't help being what you are any more than I can stop being what I am."

"Aurora, I think I understand your need to keep a handle on this thing, not to let it interfere with the day-to-day. I don't understand why you feel you have to lock it out of your life like a disease."

She'd gone this far, she thought as she walked back to the counter. She'd finish. "When I was twenty, scrambling around and trying to get my business rolling, I met this man. He had this little shop on the beach, renting surfboards, selling lotion, that sort of thing. It was so, well, exciting, to see someone that free-spirited, that easygoing, when I was working ten hours a day just to scrape by. In any case, I'd never been involved seriously with a man before. There hadn't been time. I fell flat on my face for this one. He was fun, not too demanding. Before I knew it we were on the point of being engaged. He bought me this little ring with the promise of diamonds and emeralds once we hit it big. I think he meant it." She gave a little laugh as she slid onto the stool again. "In any case, I felt that if we were going to be married we shouldn't have any secrets."

"You hadn't told him?"

"No." She said it defiantly, as if waiting for disapproval. When none came, she lowered her gaze and went on. "I introduced him to Clarissa, and then I told him that I—I told him," she said flatly. "He thought it was a joke, sort of dared me to prove it. Because I felt so strongly about having everything up front between us, well, I guess you could say I proved it. After—he looked at me as though..." She swallowed and struggled to keep the hurt buried.

"I'm sorry."

"I suppose I should have expected it." Though she shrugged it off, she picked up the spoon and began to run the handle through her fingers. "I didn't see him for days after that. I went to him with some grand gesture in mind, like giving him back his ring. It's almost funny, looking back on it now, the way he wouldn't look at me, the way he kept his distance. Too weird." She looked up again with a brittle smile. "I was just plain too weird."

And she was still hurting. But he didn't reach out to her. He wasn't quite sure how. "The wrong man at the wrong time."

A.J. gave an impatient shake of her head. "I was the wrong woman. Since then, I've learned that honesty isn't always the most advantageous route. Do you have any idea what it would do to me professionally if my clients knew? Those I didn't lose would ask me to tell them what role to audition for. People would start asking me to fly to Vegas with them so I could tell them what number to bet at the roulette table."

"So you and Clarissa downplay your relationship and you block the rest off."

"That's right." She picked up her cold coffee and downed it. "After today, I guess that goes to hell."

"I told Sam I'd discussed what had happened in that room with you, that we'd talked about the murder and coming up there had upset you." He rose to fetch the pot and freshen her coffee. "The crew may mumble about overimaginative women, but that's all."

She shut her eyes. She hadn't expected sensitivity from him, much less understanding. "Thanks."

"It's your secret if you feel it's necessary to keep it, A.J."

"It's very necessary. How did you feel when you realized?" she demanded. "Uncomfortable? Uneasy? Even now, you're tiptoeing around me."

"Maybe I am." He started to pull out a cigarette, then shoved it back into the pack. "Yeah, it makes me uneasy. It's not something I've ever had to deal with before. A man has to wonder if he'll have any secrets from a woman who can look inside him."

"Of course." She rose, back straight. "And a man's entitled to protect himself. I appreciate what you've done, David. I'm sure my clothes are dry now. I'll change if you'll call me a cab."

"No." He was up and blocking her way before she could walk out of the kitchen.

"Don't make this any more difficult for me, or for yourself."

"Damned if I want to," he muttered, and found he'd already reached for her. "I can't seem to help it. You make me uneasy," he repeated. "You've made me uneasy all along. I still want you, Aurora. That's all that seems to matter at the moment."

"You'll think differently later."

He drew her closer. "Reading my mind?"

"Don't joke."

"Maybe it's time someone did. If you want to look into my head now, you'll see that all I can think about is taking you upstairs, to my bed."

Her heart began to beat, in her chest, in her throat. "And tomorrow?"

"The hell with tomorrow." He brought his lips down to hers with a violence that left her shaken. "The hell with everything but the fact that you and I have a need for each other. You're not going home tonight, Aurora."

She let herself go, let herself risk. "No, I'm not."

7

There was moonlight, streaks of it, glimmering. She could smell the hyacinths, light and sweet, through the open windows. The murmur of a stream winding its way through the woods beside the house was quiet, soothing. Every muscle in A.J.'s body tensed as she stepped into David's bedroom.

The painting hung on the wall as she had known it would, vivid, sensual streaks on a white canvas. The first shudder rolled through her as she turned her head and saw her own vague reflection, not in a mirror, but in a tall glass door.

"I dreamed this." The words were barely audible as she took a step back. But was she stepping back into the dream or into reality? Were they somehow both the same? Panicked, she stood where she was. Didn't she have a choice? she asked herself. Was she just following a pattern already set, a pattern that had begun the moment David Brady had walked into her office?

"This isn't what I want," she whispered, and turned—for escape, for freedom—in denial, she couldn't have said. But he was there, blocking her way, drawing her closer, drawing her in just as she'd known he would be.

She looked up at him as she knew she had done before. His face was in shadows, as indistinct as hers had been in the glass.

But his eyes were clear, highlighted by moonlight. His words were clear, highlighted by desire.

"You can't keep running, Aurora, not from yourself, not from me."

There was impatience in his voice, impatience that became all the sharper when his mouth closed over hers. He wanted, more desperately than he had allowed himself to believe. He needed, more intensely than he could afford to admit. Her uncertainty, her hesitation, aroused some deep, primitive part of him. Demand, take, possess. The thoughts twined together into one throbbing pulsebeat of desire. He didn't feel the pleasant anticipation he had with other women, but a rage, burning, almost violent. As he tasted the first hint of surrender, he nearly went mad with it.

His mouth was so hungry, his hands were so strong. The pressure of his body against hers was insistent. He held her as though she were his to take with or without consent. Yet she knew, had always known, the choice was ultimately hers. She could give or deny. Like a stone tossed into clear water, her decision now would send ripples flowing out into her life. Where they ended, how they altered the flow, couldn't be foretold. To give, she knew, was always a risk. And risk always held its own excitement, its own fear. With each second that passed, the pleasure grew more bold and ripe, until with a moan of acceptance, she brought her hands to his face and let herself go.

It was only passion, A.J. told herself while her body strained and ached. Passion followed no patterns, kept to no course. The need that grew inside her had nothing to do with dreams or hopes or wishes. It was her passion she couldn't resist, his passion she couldn't refuse. For tonight, this one night, she'd let herself be guided by it.

He knew the instant she was his. Her body didn't weaken, but strengthened. The surrender he'd expected became a hunger as urgent as his. There would be no slow seduction for either of them, no gentle persuasion. Desire was a razor's edge that promised as much pain as pleasure. They both understood it; they both acknowledged; they both accepted. Together they fell onto the bed and let the fire blaze.

His robe tangled around her. With an impatient oath, he yanked it down from her shoulder so that the tantalizing slope was exposed. His lips raced over her face, leaving hers unfulfilled while he stoked a line of heat down her throat. She felt the rasp of his cheek and moaned in approval. He sought to torment, he sought to dominate, but she met each move with equal strength. She felt the warm trace of his tongue and shivered in anticipation. Unwilling to leave the reins in his hands, she tugged at the buttons of his shirt, unfastening, tearing, until with her own patience ended, she ripped it from his back.

His flesh was taut under her palms, the muscles a tight ridge to be explored and exploited. Male, hard, strong. His scent wound its way into her senses, promising rough demands and frantic movement. She tasted furious demands, hot intentions, then her excitement bounded upward when she felt his first tremble. Painful, urgent, desperate needs poured from him into her. It was what she wanted. As ruthless as he, she sought to drag him away from his control.

The bed was like a battlefield, full of fire and smoke and passions. The spread was soft, smooth, the air touched with spring, but it meant nothing to them. Warm flesh and sharp needs, rippling muscle and rough hands. That was their world. Her breath caught, not in fear, not in protest, but in excitement, as he pulled the robe down her body. When her arms were pinned she used her mouth as a weapon to drive him beyond reason. Her hips arched, pressing against him, tormenting, tempting, thrilling. As his hands moved over her, her strength seemed to double to race with her needs.

But here in this fuming, incendiary world there would be no winner and no loser. The fire sprinted along her skin, leaving dull, tingling aches wherever his hands or lips had touched. She wanted it, reveled in it, even while she burned for more. Not content to leave the control in his hands for long, A.J. rolled on top of him and began her own siege.

He'd never known a woman could make him shudder. He'd never known a woman could make him hurt from desire alone. She was long and limber and as ravenous as he. She was naked but not vulnerable. She was passionate but not pliant. He could see her in the moonlight, her hair pale and tumbled around her face, her skin glowing from exhilaration and needs not yet met. Her hands were soft as they raked over him, but demanding enough, bold enough, to take his breath away. The lips that followed them did nothing to soothe. She yanked his slacks down with a wild impatience that had his mind spinning and his body pounding. Then before he could react, she was sprawled across him, tasting his flesh.

It was madness. He welcomed it. It was torment. He could have begged for more. Once he'd thought he had discovered a simmering, latent passion in her, but nothing had prepared him for this. She was seduction, she was lust, she was greed. With both hands in her hair, he dragged her mouth to his so that he could taste them all.

It wasn't a dream, she thought dazedly as his mouth clung to hers and his hands again took possession. No dream had ever been so tempestuous. Reality had never been so mad. Tangled with her, he rolled her to her back. Even as she gasped for air, he plunged into her so that her body arched up, taut with the first uncontrollable climax. She reached up, too stunned to realize how badly she needed to hold on to him. Wrapped tight, their strengths fed each other as surely as their hungers did.

They lay together, weak, sated, both of them vanquished.

Gradually sanity returned. A.J. saw the moonlight again. His face was buried in her hair, but his breathing had steadied, as hers had. Her arms were still around him, her body locked tight to his. She told herself to let go, to reestablish distance, but lacked the will to obey.

It had only been passion, she reminded herself. It had only been need. Both had been satisfied. Now was the time to draw away, to move apart. But she wanted to nuzzle her cheek against his, to murmur something foolish and stay just as she was until the sun came up. With her eyes closed tight she fought the urge to soften, to give that which, once given, was lost.

No, he'd never known a woman could make him shudder. He'd never known a woman could make him weak. Yes, once he'd thought he'd discovered a simmering, latent passion in her, but he hadn't expected this. He shouldn't still feel so dazed. So involved.

He hadn't been prepared for the intensity of feeling. He hadn't planned on having the need grow and multiply even after it was satisfied. That was the reason he'd lost some part of himself to her. That was, had to be, the only reason.

But when she trembled, he drew her closer.

"Cold?"

"The air's cooled." It sounded reasonable. It sounded true. How could she explain that her body was still pumping with heat, and would be as long as he was there?

"I can shut the windows."

"No." She could hear the stream again, just smell the hyacinths. She didn't want to lose the sensations.

"Here, then." He drew away to untangle the sheets and pull them over her. It was then, in the dim light, that he noticed the pale line of smudges along her arm. Taking her elbow, he looked closer.

"Apparently I wasn't careful enough with you."

A.J. glanced down. There was regret in his voice, and a trace of a kindness she would have little defense against. If she hadn't been afraid, she would have longed to hear him speak just like that again, she would have rested her head on his shoulder. Instead, with a shrug she shifted and drew her arm away. "No permanent damage." She hoped. "I wouldn't be surprised if you found a few bruises on yourself."

He looked at her again and grinned in a way that was completely unexpected and totally charming. "It seems we both play rough."

It was too late to hold back a response to the grin. On impulse, A.J. leaned over and took a quick, none-too-gentle nip at his shoulder. "Complaining?"

She'd surprised him again. Maybe it was time for a few surprises in his life. And in hers. "I won't if you won't." Then, in a move too abrupt to evade, he rolled over her again, pinning her arms above her head with one hand.

"Look, Brady—"

"I like the idea of going one-on-one with you, A.J." He lowered his head just enough to nibble on her earlobe, until she squirmed under him.

"As long as you have the advantage." Her voice was breathy, her cheeks flushed. With his hands on her wrists he could feel the gradual acceleration of her pulse. With his body stretched full length, he could feel the dips, the curves, the fluid lines of hers. Desire began to rise again as though it had never been quenched.

"Lady, I think I might enjoy taking advantage of you on a regular basis. I know I'm going to enjoy it for the rest of the night."

She twisted one way, twisted the other, then let out a hissing breath, as he only stared down at her. Being outdone physically was nearly as bad as being outdone intellectually. "I can't stay here tonight."

"You are here," he pointed out, then took his free hand in one long stroke from her hip to her breast.

"I can't stay."

"Why?"

Because relieving pent-up passion with him and spending the night with him were two entirely different things. "Because I have to work tomorrow," she began lamely. "And—"

"I'll drop you by your apartment in the morning so you can change." The tip of her breast was already hard against his palm. He ran his thumb over it and watched passion darken her eyes.

"I have to be in the office by eight-thirty."

"We'll get up early." He lowered his head to brush kisses at either side of her mouth. "I'm not planning on getting much sleep, anyway."

Her body was a mass of nerve endings waiting to be exploited. Exploitation led to weakness, she reminded herself. And weakness to losses. "I don't spend the night with men."

"You do with this one." He brought his hand up, tracing as he went until he cupped her throat.

If she was going to lose, she'd lose with her eyes open. "Why?"

He could have given her quiet, persuasive answers. And they might have been true. Perhaps that's why he chose another way. "We haven't nearly finished with each other yet, Aurora. Not nearly."

He was right. The need was screaming through her. That she could accept. But she wouldn't accept being pressured, being cajoled or being seduced. Her terms, A.J. told herself. Then she could justify this first concession. "Let go of my hands, Brady."

Her chin was angled, her eyes direct, her voice firm. She wasn't a woman, he decided, who could be anticipated. Lifting a brow, he released her hands and waited.

With her eyes on his, she brought them to his face. Slowly her lips curved. Whether it was challenge or surrender he didn't care. "I wouldn't plan to sleep at all tonight," she warned just before she pulled his mouth to hers.

The room was still dark when A.J. roused from a light doze to draw the covers closer. There was an ache, more pleasant than annoying, in her muscles. She stretched, then shifted to glance at the luminous dial of her clock. It wasn't there. With her mind fogged with sleep, she rubbed a hand over her eyes and looked again.

Of course it wasn't there, she remembered. She wasn't there. Her clock, her apartment and her own bed were miles away. Turning again, she saw that the bed beside her was empty. Where could he have gone? she wondered as she pushed herself up. And what time was it?

She'd lost time. Hours, days, weeks, it hadn't mattered. But now she was alone, and it was time for reality again.

They'd exhausted each other, depleted each other and fed each other. She hadn't known there could be anything like the night they'd shared. Nothing real had ever been so exciting, so wild or desperate. Yet it had been very real. Her body bore the marks his hands had made while he'd been lost in passion. His taste still lingered on her tongue, his scent on her skin. It had been real, but it hadn't been reality. Reality was now, when she had to face the morning.

What she'd given, she'd given freely. She would have no regrets there. If she'd broken one of her own rules, she'd done so consciously and with deliberation. Not coolly, perhaps, but not carelessly. Neither could she be careless now. The night was over.

Because there was nothing else, A.J. picked his robe up off the floor and slipped into it. The important thing was not to be foolish, but mature. She wouldn't cuddle and cling and pretend there had been anything more between them than sex. One night of passion and mutual need.

She turned her cheek into the collar of the robe and let it linger there for a moment where his scent had permeated the cloth. Then, securing the belt, she walked out of the bedroom and down the stairs.

The living room was in shadows, but the first tongues of light filtered through the wide glass windows. David stood there, looking out, while a fire, freshly kindled, crackled beside him. A.J. felt the distance between them was like a crater, deep, wide and jagged. It took her too long to remind herself that was what she'd expected and wanted. Rather than speak, she walked the rest of the way down the stairs and waited.

"I had the place built with this window facing east so I could watch the sun rise." He lifted a cigarette and drew deep so that the tip glowed in the half-light. "No matter how many times I see it, it's different."

She wouldn't have judged him as a man drawn to sunrises. She hadn't judged him as a man who would choose a secluded house in the hills. Just how much, A.J. wondered, did she know about the man she'd spent the night with? Thrusting her hands into the pockets of the robe, her fingers brushed cardboard. A.J. curled them around the matchbook he'd stuck in there and forgotten. "I don't take much time for sunrises."

"If I happen to be right here at the right time, I usually find I can handle whatever crises the day has planned a little better."

Her fingers closed and opened, opened and closed on the matchbook. "Are you expecting any particular crisis today?"

He turned then to look at her, standing barefoot and a bit hollow-eyed in his robe. It didn't dwarf her; she was only inches shorter than he. Still, somehow it made her appear more feminine, more...accessible, he decided, than anything else he remembered. It wouldn't be possible to tell her that it had just occurred to him that he was already in the middle of a crisis. Its name was Aurora J. Fields. "You know..." He tucked his hands in the back pockets of well-broken-in jeans before he took a step closer. "We didn't spend too much time talking last night."

"No." She braced herself. "It didn't seem that conversation was what either of us wanted." Nor was it conversation she'd prepared herself to deal with. "I'm going to go up and change. I do have to be in the office early."

"Aurora." He didn't reach out to stop her this time. He only had to speak. "What did you feel that first day with me in your office?"

After letting out a long breath, she faced him again. "David, I talked about that part of my life more than I cared to last night."

He knew that was true. He'd spent some time wondering why without finding any answers. She had them. If he had to probe and prod until she gave them up, he would. "You talked about it in connection with other people, other things. This happens to involve me."

"I'm going to be late for work," she murmured, and started up the landing.

"You make a habit of running away, Aurora."

"I'm not running." She whirled back, both hands clenched

into fists in the pockets. "I simply don't see any reason to drag this all up again. It's personal. It's mine."

"And it touches me," he added calmly. "You walked into my bedroom last night and said you'd dreamed it. Had you?"

"I don't—" She wanted to deny it, but she had never been comfortable with direct lies. The fact that she couldn't use one had anger bubbling through. "Yes. Dreams aren't as easily controlled as conscious thought."

"Tell me what you dreamed."

She wouldn't give him all. A.J.'s nails dug into her palms. She'd be damned if she'd give him all. "I dreamed about your room. I could have described it for you before I'd ever gone in. Would you like to put me under a microscope now or later?"

"Self-pity isn't attractive." As her breath hissed out he stepped onto the landing with her. "You knew we were going to be lovers."

Her expression became cool, almost disinterested. "Yes."

"And you knew that day in your office when you were angry with me, frustrated with your mother, and our hands met, like this." He reached out, uncurled her fist and pressed their hands palm to palm.

Her back was against the wall, her hand caught in his. She was tired, spitting tired, of finding herself in corners. "What are you trying to prove, a theory for your documentary?"

What would she say if he told her he'd come to understand she showed her fangs only where she was most vulnerable? "You knew," he repeated, letting the venom spill off of him. "And it frightened you. Why was that?"

"I'd just had a strong, physical premonition that I was going to be the lover of a man I'd already decided was detestable. Is that reason enough?"

"For annoyance, even anger. Not for fear. You were afraid

that night in the back of the limo, and again last night when you walked into the bedroom."

She tried to jerk her arm aside. "You're exaggerating."

"Am I?" He stepped closer and touched a hand to her cheek. "You're afraid now."

"That's not true." Deliberately she unclenched her other hand. "I'm annoyed because you're pressing me. We're adults who spent the night together. That doesn't give you the right to pry into my personal life or feelings."

No, it didn't. That was his own primary rule and he was breaking it. Somehow he'd forgotten that he had no rights, could expect none. "All right, that's true. But I saw the condition you were in yesterday afternoon after walking into that room."

"That's done," she said quickly, maybe too quickly. "There's no need to get into it again."

Though he was far from convinced, he let it ride. "And I listened to you last night. I don't want to be responsible for anything like that happening to you again."

"You're not responsible—I am." Her voice was calmer now. Emotions clouded things. She'd spent years discovering that. "You don't cause anything, I do, or if you like, circumstances do. David, I'm twenty-eight, and I've managed to survive this—something extra all my life."

"I understand that. You should understand that I'm thirty-six. I haven't been personally exposed to any of this up until a few weeks ago."

"I do understand." Her voice chilled, just a little. "And I understand the natural reaction is to be wary, curious or skeptical. The same way one looks at a sideshow in the circus."

"Don't put words in my mouth." His anger came as a surprise to both of them. So much of a surprise, that when he grabbed A.J. by the shoulders, she offered no protest at all. "I can't help what reaction other people have had to you. They weren't me. Damn it, I've just spent the night making love to you and I don't even know who you are. I'm afraid to touch you, thinking I might set something off. I can't keep my hands off you. I came down here this morning because if I'd lain beside you another minute I'd have taken you again while you were half-asleep."

Before she'd had a chance to weigh her own reaction, she lifted her hands up to his. "I don't know what you want."

"Neither do I." He caught himself and relaxed his grip on her. "And that's a first. Maybe I need some time to figure it out."

Time. Distance. She reminded herself that was for the best. With a nod, she dropped her hands again. "That's reasonable."

"But what isn't is that I don't want to spend that time away from you."

Chills, anxiety or excitement, rushed up her spine. "David, I—"

"I've never had a night like the one I had with you."

The weakness came quickly, to be just as quickly fought back. "You don't have to say that."

"I know I don't." With a half laugh he rubbed his hands over the shoulders he'd just clenched. "In fact, it isn't very easy to admit it. It just happens to be true, for me. Sit down a minute." He drew her down to sit on the step beside him. "I didn't have a lot of time to think last night because I was too busy being…stunned," he decided. She didn't relax when he put his arm around her, but she didn't draw away. "I've packed a lot of thinking into the past hour. There's more to you, A.J., than there is to a lot of other women. Even without the something extra. I think what I want is to have a chance to get to know the woman I intend to spend a lot of time making love with."

She turned to look at him. His face was close, his arm more

gentle than she'd come to expect. He didn't look like a man who had any gentleness in him, only power and confidence. "You're taking a lot for granted."

"Yeah, I am."

"I don't think you should."

"Maybe not. I want you—you want me. We can start with that."

That was simpler. "No promises."

The protest sprang to his mind so quickly it stunned him. "No promises," he agreed, reminding himself that had always been rule number two.

She knew she shouldn't agree. The smart thing, the safe thing to do, was to cut things off now. One night, passion only. But she found herself relaxing against him. "Business and personal relationships completely separate."

"Absolutely."

"And when one of us becomes uncomfortable with the way things are going, we back off with no scenes or bad feelings."

"Agreed. Want it in writing?"

Her lips curved slightly as she studied him. "I should. Producers are notoriously untrustworthy."

"Agents are notoriously cynical."

"Cautious," she corrected, but lifted a hand to rub it along the stubble on his cheek. "We're paid to be the bad guys, after all. And speaking of which, we never finished discussing Clarissa."

"It isn't business hours," he reminded her, then turned her hand palm up and pressed his lips to it.

"Don't try to change the subject. We need to iron this out. Today."

"Between nine and five," he agreed.

"Fine, call my office and... Oh, my God."

"What?"

"My messages." Dragging both hands through her hair, she sprang up. "I never called in for my messages."

"Sounds like a national emergency," he murmured as he stood beside her.

"I was barely in the office two hours. As it was I had to reschedule appointments. Where's the phone?"

"Make it worth my while."

"David, I'm not joking."

"Neither am I." Smiling down at her, he slipped his hand into the opening of the robe and parted it. She felt her legs liquefy from the knees down.

"David." She turned her head to avoid his lips, then found herself in deeper trouble, as her throat was undefended. "It'll only take me a minute."

"You're wrong." He unfastened the belt. "It's going to take longer than that."

"For all I know I might have a breakfast meeting."

"For all you know you don't have an appointment until noon." Her hands were moving down his back, under his shirt. He wondered if she was aware. "What we both know is that we should make love. Right now."

"After," she began, but sighed against his lips.

"Before."

The robe fell to the floor at her feet. Negotiations ended.

$\mathcal{S}$

A.J. should have been satisfied. She should have been relaxed. In the ten days following her first night with David, their relationship had run smoothly. When her schedule and his allowed, they spent the evening together. There were simple evenings walking the beach, elegant evenings dining out and quiet evenings dining in. The passion that had pulled them together didn't fade. Rather, it built and intensified, driving them to quench it. He wanted her, as completely, as desperately, as a man could want a woman. Of the multitude of things she was uncertain of, she could be absolutely certain of that.

She should have been relaxed. She was tied up in knots.

Each day she had to rebuild a defense that had always been like a second skin. Each night David ripped it away again. She couldn't afford to leave her emotions unprotected in what was, by her own description, a casual, physical affair. They would continue seeing each other as long as both of them enjoyed it. No promises, no commitments. When he decided to pull away, she needed to be ready.

It was, she discovered, like waiting for the other shoe to drop. He would undoubtedly break things off sooner or later. Passions that flamed too hot were bound to burn themselves out, and they had little else. He read thick, socially significant novels and informative nonfiction. A.J. leaned toward slim, gory mysteries and glitzy bestsellers. He took her to a foreign film festival full of symbolism and subtitles. She'd have chosen the Gene Kelly—Judy Garland classic on late-night TV.

The more they got to know each other, the more distance A.J. saw. Passion was the magnet that drew them together, but she was very aware its power would fade. For her own survival, she intended to be prepared when it did.

On a business level she had to be just as prepared to deal with David Brady, producer. A.J. was grateful that in this particular relationship she knew every step and every angle. After listening to David's ideas for expanding Clarissa's role in the documentary, she'd agreed to the extra shoots. For a price. It hadn't been money she'd wanted to wheedle out of him, but the promise of promotion for Clarissa's next book, due out in midsummer.

It had taken two days of heated negotiations, tossing the ball back and forth, refusals, agreements and compromises. Clarissa would have her promotion directly on the program, and a review on *Book Talk*, the intellectual PBS weekly. David would have his extra studio shoots and his interview with Clarissa and Alice Van Camp. Both had walked away from the negotiating table smug that they had outdone the other.

Clarissa couldn't have cared less. She was busy with her plants, her recipes and, to A.J.'s mounting dismay, her wedding plans. She took the news of the promotions A.J. had sweated for with an absent "That's nice, dear," and wondered out loud if she should bake the wedding cake herself.

"Momma, a review on *Book Talk* isn't just nice." A.J. swung into the studio parking lot frustrated from the forty-minute drive during which she and Clarissa had talked at cross purposes.

"Oh, I'm sure it's going to be lovely. The publisher said they were sending advance copies. Aurora, do you think a garden wedding would be suitable? I'm afraid my azaleas might fade."

Brows lowered, she swung into a parking spot. "How many advance copies?"

"Oh, I'm really not sure. I probably wrote it down somewhere. And then it might rain. The weather's so unpredictable in June."

"Make sure they send at least three. One for the— June?" Her foot slipped off the clutch, so that the car bucked to a halt. "But that's next month."

"Yes, and I have dozens of things to do. Just dozens."

A.J.'s hands were very still on the wheel as she turned. "But didn't you say something about a fall wedding?"

"I suppose I did. You know my mums are at their best in October, but Alex is…" She flushed and cleared her throat. "A bit impatient. Aurora, I know I don't drive, but I think you've left your key on."

Muttering, she pulled it out. "Momma, you're talking about marrying a man you'll have known for less than two months."

"Do you really think time's so important?" she asked with a sweet smile. "It's more a matter of feelings."

"Feelings can change." She thought of David, of herself.

"There aren't any guarantees in life, darling." Clarissa reached over to cover her daughter's hand with her own. "Not even for people like you and me."

"That's what worries me." She was going to talk to Alex Marshall, A.J. promised herself as she pushed her door open. Her mother was acting like a teenager going steady with the football hero. Someone had to be sensible.

"You really don't have to worry," Clarissa told her as she stepped onto the curb. "I know what I'm doing—really, I do. But talk to Alex by all means."

"Momma." With a long sigh, A.J. linked arms. "I do have to worry. And mind reading's not allowed."

"I hardly have to when it's written all over your face. Is my hair all right?"

A.J. turned to kiss her cheek. "You look beautiful."

"Oh, I hope so." Clarissa gave a nervous laugh as they approached the studio doors. "I'm afraid I've become very vain lately. But Alex is such a handsome man, isn't he?"

"Yes," A.J. agreed cautiously. He was handsome, polished smooth and personable. She wouldn't be satisfied until she found the flaws.

"Clarissa." They'd hardly stepped inside, when Alex came striding down the hall. He looked like a man approaching a lost and valued treasure. "You look beautiful."

He had both of Clarissa's hands and looked to A.J. as though he would scoop her mother up and carry her off. "Mr. Marshall." She kept her voice cool and deliberately extended her own hand.

"Ms. Fields." With obvious reluctance, he released one of Clarissa hands to take A.J.'s. "I have to say you're more dedicated than my own agent. I was hoping to bring Clarissa down myself today."

"Oh, she likes to fuss," Clarissa put in, hoping to mollify them both. "And I'm afraid I'm so scatterbrained she has to remind me of all the little things about television interviews."

"Just relax," A.J. told her. "I'll go see if everything's set." Checking her watch as she went, she reached out to push open the thick studio doors, when David walked through.

"Good morning, Ms. Fields." The formal greeting was accompanied by the trail of his fingers over her wrist. "Sitting in again today?"

"Looking after my client, Brady. She's…" When she glanced

casually over her shoulder, the words slipped back down her throat. There in the middle of the hallway was her mother caught up in a close and very passionate embrace. Stunned, she stared while dozens of feelings she couldn't identify ran through her.

"Your client appears to be well looked after," David murmured. When she didn't reply, he pulled her into a room off the hall. "Want to sit down?"

"No. No, I should—"

"Mind your own business."

Anger replaced shock very quickly. "She happens to be my mother."

"That's right." He walked to a coffee machine and poured two plastic cups. "Not your ward."

"I'm not going to stand by while she, while she—"

"Enjoys herself?" he suggested, and handed her the coffee.

"She isn't thinking." A.J. downed half the coffee in one swallow. "She's just riding on emotion, infatuation. And she's—"

"In love."

A.J. drank the rest of the coffee, then heaved the cup in the direction of the trash. "I hate it when you interrupt me."

"I know." And he grinned at her. "Why don't we have a quiet evening tonight, at your place? We can start making love in the living room, work our way through to the bedroom and back out again."

"David, Clarissa is my mother and I'm very concerned about her. I should—"

"Be more concerned with yourself." He had his hands on her hips. "And me." They slid firm and strong up her back. "You should be very concerned with me."

"I want you to—"

"I'm becoming an expert on what you want." His mouth brushed hers, retreated, then brushed again. "Do you know your breath starts trembling whenever I do that." His voice lowered, seductive, persuading. "Then your body begins to tremble."

Weak, weaker than she should have been, she lifted both hands to his chest. "David, we have an agreement. It's business hours."

"Sue me." He kissed her again, tempting, teasing as he slipped his hands under her jacket. "What are you wearing under here, A.J.?"

"Nothing important." She caught herself swaying forward. "David, I mean it. We agreed." His tongue traced her bottom lip. "No mixing—ah—no mixing business and...oh, damn." She forgot business and agreements and responsibilities, dragging his mouth to hers.

They filled her, those wild, wanton cravings only he could bring. They tore at her, the needs, the longings, the wishes she knew could never be met. In a moment of abandon she tossed aside what should be and groped blindly for what might be.

His mouth was as hard, as ravenous, as if it were the first time. Desire hadn't faded. His hands were as strong, as possessive and demanding, as ever. Passion hadn't dimmed. It didn't matter that the room was small and smelled of old coffee and stale cigarettes. Their senses were tangled around each other. Perfume was strong and sweet; tastes were dark and exotic.

Her arms were around his neck; her fingers were raking through his hair. Her mouth was hungry and open on his.

"Oh, excuse me." Clarissa stood in the doorway, eyes lowered as she cleared her throat. It wouldn't do to look too pleased, she knew. Just as it wouldn't be wise to mention that the vibrations bouncing around in the little room might have melted lead. "I thought you'd like to know they're ready for me."

Fumbling for dignity, A.J. tugged at her jacket. "Good. I'll be right in." She waited until the door shut, then swore pungently.

"You're even," David said lightly. "You caught her—she caught you."

Her eyes, when they met his, were hot enough to sear off a layer of skin. "It's not a joke."

"Do you know one thing I've discovered about you these past few days, A.J.? You take yourself too seriously."

"Maybe I do." She scooped her purse from the sofa, then stood there nervously working the clasp. "But has it occurred to you what would have happened if a member of the crew had opened that door?"

"They'd have seen their producer kissing a very attractive woman."

"They would have seen you kissing me during a shoot. That's totally unprofessional. Before the first coffee break, everyone in the studio would be passing around the gossip."

"So?"

"So?" Exasperated, she could only stare at him. "David, that's precisely what we agreed we didn't want. We don't want your crew or our associates speculating and gossiping about our personal relationship."

Brow lifted, eyes narrowed attentively, he listened. "I don't recall discussing that in detail."

"Of course we did." She tucked her purse under her arm, then wished she still had something in her hands. "Right at the beginning."

"As I recall, the idea was to keep our personal and professional lives separate."

"That's just what I've said."

"I didn't take that to mean you wanted to keep the fact that we're lovers a secret."

"I don't want an ad in *Variety*."

He stuck his hands in his pockets. He couldn't have said why he was angry, only that he was. "You don't leave much middle ground, do you?"

She opened her mouth to spit at him, then subsided. "I guess not." On a long breath, she took a step forward. "I want to avoid the speculation, just as I want to avoid the looks of sympathy when things change."

It didn't require telepathy to understand that she'd been waiting for the change—no, he corrected, for the end—since the beginning. Knowledge brought an unexpected, and very unwelcome, twinge of pain. "I see. All right, then, we'll try it your way." He walked to the door and held it open. "Let's go punch in."

No, he couldn't have said why he was angry. In fact, he knew he shouldn't have been. A.J.'s ground rules were logical, and if anything, they made things easier for him. Or should have made things easier for him. She made absolutely no demands and accepted none. In other relationships he'd insisted on the same thing. She refused to allow emotions to interfere with her business or his. In the past he'd felt precisely the same way.

The problem was, he didn't feel that way now.

As the shoot ground to a halt because of two defective bulbs David reminded himself it was his problem. Once he accepted that, he could work on the solution. One was to go along with the terms. The other was to change them.

David watched A.J. cross the room toward Alex. Her stride was brisk, her eyes were cool. In the conservative suit she looked like precisely what she was—a successful businesswoman who knew where she was going and how to get there. He remembered the way she looked when they made love—slim, glowing and as dangerous as a neutron bomb.

David took out a cigarette then struck a match with a kind of restrained violence. He was going to have to plan out solution number two.

"Mr. Marshall." A.J. had her speech prepared and her determination at its peak. With a friendly enough smile, she interrupted Alex's conversation with one of the grips. "Could I speak with you for a minute?"

"Of course." Because he'd been expecting it, Alex took her arm in his innate old-style manner. "Looks like we'll have time for a cup of coffee."

Together they walked back to the room where A.J. had stood with David a few hours before. This time she poured the coffee and offered the cup. But before she could start the prologue for the speech she'd been rehearsing, Alex began.

"You want to talk about Clarissa." He pulled out one of his cigars, then held it out. "Do you mind?"

"No, go ahead. Actually, Mr. Marshall, I would very much like to talk to you about Clarissa."

"She told me you were uneasy about our marriage plans." He puffed comfortably on his cigar until he was satisfied it was well started. "I admit that puzzled me a bit, until she explained that besides being her agent, you happen to be her daughter. Shall we sit down?"

A.J. frowned at the sofa, then at him. It wasn't going at all according to plan. She took her place on one end, while he settled himself on the other. "I'm glad that Clarissa explained things to you. It simplifies things. You'll understand now why I'm concerned. My mother is very important to me."

"And to me." As he leaned back, A.J. studied his profile. It wasn't difficult to see why her mother was infatuated. "You of all people can understand just how easy Clarissa is to love."

"Yes." A.J. sipped at her coffee. What was it she'd planned to say? Taking a deep breath, she moved back on track. "Clarissa is a wonderfully warm and very special person. The thing is, you've known each other for such a short time."

"It only took five minutes." He said it so simply, A.J. was left fumbling for words. "Ms. Fields," he continued, then smiled at her. "A.J.," he corrected. "It doesn't seem right for me to call you 'Ms. Fields.' After all, I'm going to be your stepfather."

Stepfather? Somehow that angle had bypassed her. She sat, coffee cup halfway to her lips, and stared at him.

"I have a son your age," he began again. "And a daughter not far behind. I think I understand some of what you're feeling."

"It's, ah, it's not a matter of my feelings."

"Of course it is. You're as precious to Clarissa as my children are to me. Clarissa and I will be married, but she'd be happier if you were pleased about it."

A.J. frowned at her coffee, then set it down. "I don't know what to say. I thought I did. Mr. Marshall, Alex, you've been a journalist for over a quarter of a century. You've traveled all over the world, seen incredible things. Clarissa, for all her abilities, all her insights, is a very simple woman."

"An amazingly comfortable woman, especially for a man who's lived on the edge, perhaps too long. I had thought of retiring." He laughed then, but comfortably, as he remembered his own shock when Clarissa had held his hand and commented on it. "That wasn't something I'd discussed with anyone, not even my own children. I'd been looking for something more, something other than deadlines and breaking stories. In a matter of hours after being with Clarissa, I knew she was what I'd been looking for. I want to spend the rest of my life with her."

A.J. sat in silence, looking down at her hands. What more could a woman ask for, she wondered, than for a man to love her with such straightforward devotion? Couldn't a woman consider herself fortunate to have a man who accepted who she was, what she was, and loved her because of it, not in spite of?

Some of the tension dissolved and as she looked up at him she was able to smile. "Alex, has my mother fixed you dinner?"

"Why, yes." Though his tone was very sober, she caught, and appreciated, the gleam in his eyes. "Several times. In fact, she told me she's left a pot of spaghetti sauce simmering for tonight. I find Clarissa's cooking as—unique as she is."

With a laugh, A.J. held out her hand again. "I think Momma hit the jackpot." He took her hand, then surprised her by leaning over to kiss her cheek.

"Thank you."

"Don't hurt her," A.J. whispered. She clung to his hand a moment, then composing herself rose. "We'd better get back. She'll wonder where we are."

"Being Clarissa, I'm sure she has a pretty good idea."

"That doesn't bother you?" She stopped by the door to look up at him again. "The fact that she's a sensitive?"

"Why should it? That's part of what makes Clarissa who she is."

"Yes." She tried not to think of herself, but didn't bite back the sigh in time. "Yes, it is."

When they walked back into the studio Clarissa looked over immediately. It only took a moment before she smiled. In an old habit, A.J. kissed both her cheeks. "There is one thing I have to insist on," she began without preamble.

"What is it?"

"That I give you the wedding."

Pleasure bloomed on Clarissa's cheeks even as she protested. "Oh, darling, how sweet, but it's too much trouble."

"It certainly is for a bride. You pick out your wedding dress and your trousseau and worry about looking terrific. I'll handle the rest." She kissed her again. "Please."

"If you really want to."

"I really want to. Give me a guest list and I'll handle the details. That's what I'm best at. I think they want you." She gave Clarissa a last quick squeeze before urging her back on set. A.J. took her place in the background.

"Feeling better?" David murmured as he came up beside her.

"Some." She couldn't admit to him that she felt weepy and displaced. "As soon as the shoot's finished, I start making wedding plans."

"Tomorrow's soon enough." When she sent him a puzzled look, he only smiled. "I intend to keep you busy this evening."

He was a man of his word. A.J. had barely arrived home, shed her jacket and opened the phone book to Caterers, when the bell rang. Taking the book with her, she went to answer. "David." She hooked her finger in the page so as not to lose her place. "You told me you had some things to do."

"I did them. What time is it?"

"It's quarter to seven. I didn't think you'd be by until around eight."

"Well after business hours, then." He toyed with, then loosened the top button of her blouse.

She had to smile. "Well after."

"And if you don't answer your phone, your service will pick it up after four rings?"

"Six. But I'm not expecting any calls." She stepped closer to slide her arms up his chest. "Hungry?"

"Yeah." He tested himself, seeing how long he could hold her at arm's length. It appeared to be just over thirty seconds.

"There's nothing in the kitchen except a frozen fish dinner." She closed her eyes as his lips skimmed over her jaw.

"Then we'll have to find another way to satisfy the appetite." He unhooked her skirt and, as it fell to the floor, drew his hands down her hips.

She yanked his sweater over his head and tossed it aside. "I'm sure we'll manage."

His muscles were tight as she ran her hands over his. Taut, tense all the way from his neck to his waist. With her blouse half-open, her legs clad in sheer stockings that stopped just at her thighs, A.J. pressed against him. She wanted to make him burn with just the thought of loving her. Then she was gasping for air, her fingers digging into his back as his hands took quick and complete possession.

When her legs buckled and she went limp against him, he didn't relent. For hours and hours he'd held back, watching her sit primly in the back of the studio, looking at her make her precise notes in her book. Now he had her, alone, hot, moist and, for the first time in their lovemaking, weak.

Holding her close, he slid with her to the floor.

Unprepared, she was helpless against a riot of sensation. He took her on a desperate ride, driving her up where the air was thin, plunging her down where it was heavy and dark. She tried to cling to him but lacked the strength.

She trembled for him. That alone was enough to drive him mad. His name came helplessly through her lips. He wanted to hear it, again and again, over and over. He wanted to know she thought of nothing else. And when he pulled the remaining clothes from both of them, when he entered her with a violence neither of them could fight, he knew he thought of nothing but her.

She shuddered again and again, but he held himself back from ultimate release. Even as he drove her, his hands continued to roam, bringing unspeakable pleasures to every inch of her body. The carpet was soft at her back, but even when her fingers curled into it she could only feel the hard thrust of her lover. She heard him say her name, once, then twice, until her eyes fluttered open. His body rose above hers, taut with muscle, gleaming from passion. His breath was heaving even as hers was. She heard it, then tasted it when his mouth crushed down to devour. Then she heard nothing but her own sobbing moan as they emptied themselves.

"I like you naked." When he'd recovered enough, David propped himself on his elbow and took a long, long look. "But I have to admit, I'm fascinated by those little stockings you wear that stop right about here." To demonstrate, he ran his fingertip along her upper thigh.

Still dazed, A.J. merely moved against his touch. "They're very practical."

With a muffled laugh, he nuzzled the side of her neck. "Yes, that's what fascinates me. Your practicality."

She opened her eyes but kept them narrowed. "That's not what I meant." Because she felt too good to make an issue of it, she curled into him.

It was one of the things that charmed him most. David wondered if he told her how soft, how warm and open to affection she was after loving, if she would pull back. Instead he held her close, stroking and pleasing them both. When he caught himself half dozing, he pulled her up.

"Come on, let's have a shower before dinner."

"A shower?" She let her head rest on his shoulder. "Why don't we just go to bed?"

"Insatiable," he decided, and scooped her up.

"David, you can't carry me."

"Why not?"

"Because." She groped. "Because it's silly."

"I always feel silly carrying naked women." In the bathroom, he stood her on her feet.

"I suppose you make a habit of it," she commented dryly, and turned on the taps with a hard twist.

"I have been trying to cut down." Smiling, he pulled her into the shower with him so that the water rained over her face.

"My hair!" She reached up once, ineffectually, to block the flow, then stopped to glare at him.

"What about it?"

"Never mind." Resigned, she picked up the soap and began to rub it lazily over her body as she watched him. "You seem very cheerful tonight. I thought you were annoyed with me this morning."

"Did you?" He'd given some thought to strangling her. "Why would I be?" He took the soap from her and began to do the job himself.

"When we were talking…" The soap was warm and slick, his touch very thorough. "It doesn't matter. I'm glad you came by."

That was more than he'd come to expect from her. "Really?"

She smiled, then wrapped her arms around him and kissed him under the hot, steamy spray. "Yes, really. I like you, David. When you're not being a producer."

That, too, was more than he'd come to expect from her. And less than he was beginning to need. "I like you, Aurora. When you're not being an agent."

When she stepped out of the shower and reached for towels, she heard the bell ring again. "Damn." She gripped a towel at her breasts.

"I'll get it." David hooked a towel at his hips and strode out before A.J. could protest. She let out a huff of breath and snatched the robe from its hook on the door. If it was someone from the office, she'd have a lovely time explaining why David Brady, producer, was answering her door in a towel. She decided discretion was the better part of valor and stayed where she was.

Then she remembered the clothes. She closed her eyes on a moan as she imagined the carelessly strewn articles on her living room floor. Bracing herself, she walked down the hall back into the living room.

There was candlelight. On the ebony table she kept by the window, candles were already burning in silver holders on a white cloth. She saw the gleam of china, the sparkle of crystal, and stood where she was as David signed a paper handed to him by a man in a black suit.

"I hope everything is satisfactory, Mr. Brady."

"I'm sure it will be."

"We will, of course, be back for pickup at your convenience." With a bow to David, then another to A.J., he let himself out the door.

"David…" A.J. walked forward as if she weren't sure of her steps. "What is this?"

He lifted a silver cover from a plate. "It's coq au vin."

"But how did you—"

"I ordered it for eight o'clock." He checked his watch before he walked over to retrieve his pants. "They're very prompt." With the ease of a totally unselfconscious man, he dropped the towel and drew on his slacks.

She took another few steps toward the table. "It's lovely. Really lovely." There was a single rose in a vase. Moved, she reached out to touch it, then immediately brought her hand back to link it with her other. "I never expected anything like this."

He drew his sweater back over his head. "You said once you enjoyed being pampered." She looked stunned, he realized. Had he been so unromantic? A little uncertain, he walked to her. "Maybe I enjoy doing the pampering now and then."

She looked over, but her throat was closed and her eyes were filling. "I'll get dressed."

"No." Her back was to him now, but he took her by the shoulders. "No, you look fine."

She struggled with herself, pressing her lips together until she thought she could speak. "I'll just be a minute." But he was turning her around. His brows were already knit together before he saw her face.

"What's this?" He lifted a fingertip and touched a tear that clung to her lashes.

"It's nothing. I—I feel foolish. Just give me a minute."

He brushed another tear away with his thumb. "No, I don't think I should." He'd seen her weep before, but that had been a torrent. There was something soft in these tears, something incredibly sweet that drew him. "Do you always cry when a man offers you a quiet dinner?"

"No, of course not. It's just—I never expected you to do anything like this."

He brought her hand to his lips and smiled as he kissed her fingers. "Just because I'm a producer doesn't mean I can't have some class."

"That's not what I meant." She looked up at him, smiling down at her, her hands still close to his lips. She was losing. A.J. felt her heart weaken, her will weaken and her wishes grow. "That's not what I meant," she said again in a whisper, and tightened her fingers on his. "David, don't make me want too much."

It was what he thought he understood. If you wanted too much, you fell too hard. He'd avoided the same thing, maybe for the same reasons, until one late afternoon on a beach. "Do you really think either of us can stop now?"

She thought of how many times she'd been rejected, easily, coolly, nervously. Friendship, affection, love could be turned off by some as quickly as a faucet. He wanted her now, A.J.

reminded herself. He cared now. It had to be enough. She touched a hand to his cheek.

"Maybe tonight we won't think at all."

9

"'Item fifteen, clause B. I find the wording here too vague. As we discussed, my client feels very strongly about her rights and responsibilities as a new mother. The nanny will accompany the child to the set, at my client's expense. However, she will require regular breaks in order to feed the infant. The trailer provided by you must be equipped with a portable crib and...'" For the third time during her dictation, A.J. lost her train of thought.

"Diapers?" Diane suggested.

"What?" A.J. turned from the window to look at her secretary.

"Just trying to help. Want me to read it back to you?"

"Yes, please."

While Diane read the words back, A.J. frowned down at the contract in her hand. "'And a playpen,'" A.J. finished, and managed to smile at her secretary. "I've never seen anyone so wrapped up in motherhood."

"Doesn't fit her image, does it? She always plays the heartless sex bomb."

"This little movie of the week should change that. Okay,

finish it up with 'Once the above changes are made, the contract will be passed along to my client for signing.'"

"Do you want this out today?"

"Hmm?"

"Today, A.J.?" With a puzzled smile, Diane studied her employer. "You want the letter to go right out?"

"Oh. Yes, yes, it'd better go out." She checked her watch. "I'm sorry, Diane, it's nearly five. I hadn't realized."

"No problem." Closing her notebook, Diane rose. "You seem a little distracted today. Big plans for the holiday weekend?"

"Holiday?"

"Memorial Day weekend, A.J." With a shake of her head, Diane tucked her pencil behind her ear. "You know, three days off, the first weekend of summer. Sand, surf, sun."

"No." She began rearranging the papers on her desk. "I don't have any plans." Shaking off the mood, she looked up again. Distracted? What she was was a mess. She was bogged down in work she couldn't concentrate on, tied up in knots she couldn't loosen. With a shake of her head, she glanced at Diane again and remembered there were other people in the world beside herself. "I'm sure you do. Let the letter wait. There's no mail delivery Monday, anyway. We'll send it over by messenger Tuesday."

"As a matter of fact, I do have an interesting three days planned." Diane gave her own watch a check. "And he's picking me up in an hour."

"Go home." A.J. waved her off as she shuffled through papers. "Don't get sunburned."

"A.J.—" Diane paused at the door and grinned "—I don't plan to see the sun for three full days."

When the door shut, A.J. slipped off her glasses and rubbed at the bridge of her nose. What was wrong with her? She couldn't seem to concentrate for more than five minutes at a stretch before her attention started wandering.

Overwork? she wondered as she looked down at the papers in her hand. That was an evasion; she thrived on overwork. She wasn't sleeping well. She was sleeping alone. One had virtually nothing to do with the other, A.J. assured herself as she unstacked and restacked papers. She was too much her own person to moon around because David Brady had been out of town for a few days.

But she did miss him. She picked up a pencil to work, then ended up merely running it through her fingers. There wasn't any crime in missing him, was there? It wasn't as though she were dependent on him. She'd just gotten used to his company. Wouldn't he be smug and self-satisfied to know that she'd spent half her waking hours thinking about him? Disgusted with herself, A.J. began to work in earnest. For two minutes.

It was his fault, she thought as she tossed the pencil down again. That extravagantly romantic dinner for two, then that silly little bouquet of daisies he'd sent the day he'd left for Chicago. Though she tried not to, she reached out and stroked the petals that sat cheerful and out of place on her desk. He was trying to make a giddy, romantic fool out of her—and he was succeeding.

It just had to stop. A.J. adjusted her glasses, picked up her pencil and began to work again. She wasn't going to give David Brady another thought. When the knock sounded at her door a few moments later, she was staring into space. She blinked herself out of the daydream, swore, then called out. "Come in."

"Don't you ever quit?" Abe asked her when he stuck his head in the door.

Quit? She'd barely made a dent. "I've got a couple of loose ends. Abe, the Forrester contract comes up for renewal the first of July. I think we should start prodding. His fan mail was two to one last season, so—"

"First thing Tuesday morning I'll put the squeeze on. Right now I have to go marinate."

"I beg your pardon?"

"Big barbecue this weekend," Abe told her with a wink. "It's the only time my wife lets me cook. Want me to put a steak on for you?"

She smiled, grateful that he'd brought simpler things to her mind. Hickory smoke, freshly cut grass, burned meat. "No, thanks. The memory of the last one's a little close."

"The butcher gave me bad quality meat." He hitched up his belt and thought about spending the whole weekend in bathing trunks.

"That's what they all say. Have a good holiday, Abe. Just be prepared to squeeze hard on Tuesday."

"No problem. Want me to lock up?"

"No, I'll just be a few more minutes."

"If you change your mind about that steak, just come by."

"Thanks." Alone again, A.J. turned her concentration back to her work. She heard the sounds of her staff leaving for the day. Doors closing, scattered laughter.

David stood in the doorway and watched her. The rest of her staff was pouring out of the door as fast as they could, but she sat, calm and efficient, behind her desk. The fatigue that had had him half dozing on the plane washed away. Her hair was tidy, her suit jacket trim and smooth over her shoulders. She held the pencil in long, ringless fingers and wrote in quick, static bursts. The daisies he'd sent her days before sat in a squat vase on her desk. It was the first, the only unbusinesslike accent he'd ever seen in her office. Seeing them made him smile. Seeing her made him want.

He could see himself taking her there in her prim, organized office. He could peel that tailored, successful suit from her and find something soft and lacy beneath. With the door locked and traffic rushing by far below, he could make love with her until all the needs, all the fantasies, that had built in the days he'd been away were satisfied.

A.J. continued to write, forcing her concentration back each time it threatened to ebb. It wasn't right, she told herself, that her system would start to churn this way for no reason. The dry facts and figures she was reading shouldn't leave room for hot imagination. She rubbed the back of her neck, annoyed that tension was building there out of nothing. She would have sworn she could feel passion in the air. But that was ridiculous.

Then she knew. As surely as if he'd spoken, as surely as if he'd already touched her. Slowly, her hand damp on the pencil, she looked up.

There was no surprise in her eyes. It should have made him uneasy that she'd sensed him there when he'd made no sound, no movement. The fact that it didn't was something he would think of later. Now he could only think of how cool and proper she looked behind the desk. Of how wild and wanton she was in his arms.

She wanted to laugh, to spring up from the desk and rush across the room. She wanted to be held close and swung in dizzying circles while the pleasure of just seeing him again soared through her. Of course she couldn't. That would be foolish. Instead she lifted a brow and set her pencil on her blotter. "So you're back."

"Yeah. I had a feeling I'd find you here." He wanted to drag her up from her chair and hold her. Just hold her. He dipped his hands into his pockets and leaned against the jamb.

"A feeling?" This time she smiled. "Precognition or telepathy?"

"Logic." He smiled, too, then walked toward the desk. "You look good, Fields. Real good."

Leaning back in her chair, she gave herself the pleasure of a thorough study. "You look a little tired. Rough trip?"

"Long." He plucked a daisy from the vase and spun it by the stem. "But it should be the last one before we wrap." Watching her, he came around the desk, then, resting a hip on it, leaned over and tucked the daisy behind her ear. "Got any plans for tonight?"

If she'd had any, she would have tossed them out the window and forgotten them. With her tongue caught in her teeth, A.J. made a business out of checking her desk calender. "No."

"Tomorrow?"

She flipped the page over. "Doesn't look like it."

"Sunday?"

"Even agents need a day of rest."

"Monday?"

She flipped the next page and shrugged. "Offices are closed. I thought I'd spend the day reading over some scripts and doing my nails."

"Uh-huh. In case you hadn't noticed, office hours are over."

Her heart was drumming. Already. Her blood was warming. So soon. "I'd noticed."

In silence he held out his hand. After only a slight hesitation, A.J. put hers into it and let him draw her up. "Come home with me."

He'd asked her before, and she'd refused. Looking at him now, she knew the days of refusal were long past. Reaching down, she gathered her purse and her briefcase.

"Not tonight," David told her, and took the briefcase to set it back down.

"I want to—"

"Not tonight, Aurora." Taking her hand again, he brought it to his lips. "Please."

With a nod, she left the briefcase and the office behind.

They kept their hands linked as they walked down the hall. They kept them linked still as they rode down in the elevator. It didn't seem foolish, A.J. realized, but sweet. He hadn't kissed her, hadn't held her, and yet the tension that had built so quickly was gone again, just through a touch.

She was content to leave her car in the lot, thinking that sometime the next day, they'd drive back into town and arrange things. Pleased just to be with him again, she stopped at his car while he unlocked the doors.

"Haven't you been home yet?" she asked, noticing a suitcase in the back seat.

"No."

She started to smile, delighted that he'd wanted to see her first, but she glanced over her shoulder again as she stepped into the car. "I have a case just like that."

David settled in the seat, then turned on the ignition. "That is your case."

"Mine?" Baffled, she turned around and looked closer. "But—I don't remember you borrowing one of my suitcases."

"I didn't. Mine are in the trunk." He eased out of the lot and merged with clogged L.A. weekend traffic.

"Well, if you didn't borrow it, what's it doing in your car?"

"I stopped by your place on the way. Your housekeeper packed for you."

"Packed…" She stared at the case. When she turned to him, her eyes were narrowed. "You've got a lot of nerve, Brady. Just where do you come off packing my clothes and assuming—"

"The housekeeper packed them. Nice lady. I thought you'd be more comfortable over the weekend with some of your own things. I had thought about keeping you naked, but that's a little tricky when you take walks in the woods."

Because her jaw was beginning to ache, she relaxed it. "You thought? *You* didn't think at all. You drop by the office and calmly assume that I'll drop everything and run off with you. What if I'd had plans?

"Then that would've been too bad." He swung easily off the ramp toward the hills.

"Too bad for whom?"

"For the plans." He punched in the car lighter and sent her a mild smile. "I have no intention of letting you out of my sight for the next three days."

"You have no intention?" The fire was rising as she shifted in her seat toward him. "What about my intention? Maybe you think it's very male and macho to just—just bundle a woman off for a weekend without asking, without any discussion, but I happen to prefer being consulted. Stop the car."

"Not a chance." David had expected this reaction. Even looked forward to it. He touched the lighter to the tip of his cigarette. He hadn't enjoyed himself this much for days. Since the last time he'd been with her.

Her breath came out in a long, slow hiss. "I don't find abductions appealing."

"Didn't think I did, either." He blew out a lazy stream of smoke. "Guess I was wrong."

She flopped back against her seat, arms folded. "You're going to be sorry."

"I'm only sorry I didn't think of it before." With his elbow resting lightly on the open window, he drove higher into the hills, with A.J. fuming beside him. The minute he stopped the car in his drive, A.J. pushed open her door, snatched her purse up and began to walk. When he grabbed her arm, she spun around, holding the pastel-dyed leather like a weapon.

"Want to fight?"

"I wouldn't give you the satisfaction." She yanked her arm out of his hold. "I'm walking back."

"Oh?" He look a quick look at the slim skirt, thin hose and fragile heels. "You wouldn't make it the first mile in those shoes."

"That's my problem."

He considered a minute, then sighed. "I guess we'll just carry through with the same theme." Before she realized his intention, he wrapped an arm around her waist and hauled her over his shoulder.

Too stunned to struggle, she blew hair out of her eyes. "Put me down."

"In a few minutes," he promised as he walked toward the house.

"Now." She whacked him smartly on the back with her purse. "This isn't funny."

"Are you kidding?" When he stuck his key in the lock, she began to struggle. "Easy, A.J., you'll end up dropping on your head."

"I'm not going to tolerate this." She tried to kick out and found her legs pinned behind the knee. "David, this is degrading. I don't know what's gotten into you, but if you get hold of yourself now, I'll forget the whole thing."

"No deal." He started up the steps.

"I'll give you a deal," she said between her teeth as she made a futile grab for the railing. "If you put me down now, I won't kill you."

"Now?"

"Right now."

"Okay." With a quick twist of his body, he had her falling backward. Even as her eyes widened in shock, he was tumbling with her onto the bed.

"What the hell's gotten into you?" she demanded as she struggled to sit up.

"You," he said, so simply she stopped in the act of shoving him away. "You," he repeated, cupping the back of her neck. "I thought about you the whole time I was gone. I wanted you in Chicago. I wanted you in the airport, and thirty thousand feet up I still wanted you."

"You're—this is crazy."

"Maybe. Maybe it is. But when I was on that plane flying back to L.A. I realized that I wanted you here, right here, alone with me for days."

His fingers were stroking up and down her neck, soothing. Her nerves were stretching tighter and tighter. "If you'd asked," she began.

"You'd have had an excuse. You might have spent the night." His fingers inched up into her hair. "But you'd have found a reason you couldn't stay longer."

"That's not true."

"Isn't it? Why haven't you spent a weekend with me before?"

Her fingers linked and twisted. "There've been reasons."

"Yeah." He put his hand over hers. "And the main one is you're afraid to spend more than a few hours at a time with me." When she opened her mouth, he shook his head to cut her off. "Afraid if you do, I might just get too close."

"I'm not afraid of you. That's ridiculous."

"No, I don't think you are. I think you're afraid of us." He drew her closer. "So am I."

"David." The word was shaky. The world was suddenly shaky. Just passion, she reminded herself again. That's what made her head swim, her heart pound. Desire. Her arms slid up his back. It was only desire. "Let's not think at all for a while." She touched her lips to his and felt resistance as well as need.

"Sooner or later we're going to have to."

"No." She kissed him again, let her tongue trace lightly over his lips. "There's no sooner, no later." Her breath was warm, tempting, as it fluttered over him. "There's only now. Make love with me now, in the light." Her hands slipped under his shirt to tease and invite.

Her eyes were open and on his, her lips working slowly, steadily, to drive him to the edge. He swore, then pulled her to him and let the madness come.

"It's good for you."

"So's calves' liver," A.J. said breathlessly, and paused to lean against a tree. "I avoid that, too."

They'd taken the path behind his house, crossed the stream and continued up. By David's calculations they'd gone about three-quarters of a mile. He walked back to stand beside her. "Look." He spread his arm wide. "It's terrific, isn't it?"

The trees were thick and green. Birds rustled the leaves and sang for the simple pleasure of sound. Wildflowers she'd never seen before and couldn't name pushed their way through the underbrush and battled for the patches of sunlight. It was, even to a passionately avowed city girl, a lovely sight.

"Yes, it's terrific. You tend to forget there's anything like this when you're down in L.A."

"That's why I moved up here." He put an arm around her shoulder and absently rubbed his hand up and down. "I was beginning to forget there was any place other than the fast lane."

"Work, parties, meetings, parties, brunch, lunch and cocktails."

"Yeah, something like that. Anyway, coming up here after a day in the factory keeps things in perspective. If a project bombs in the ratings, the sun's still going to set."

She thought about it, leaning into him a bit as he stroked her arm. "If I blow a deal, I go home, lock the doors, put on my headset and drown my brain in Rachmaninoff."

"Same thing."

"But usually I kick something first."

He laughed and kissed the top of her head. "Whatever works. Wait till you see the view from the top."

A.J. leaned down to massage her calf. "I'll meet you back at the house. You can draw me a picture."

"You need the air. Do you realize we've barely been out of bed for thirty-six hours?"

"And we've probably logged about ten hours' sleep." Straightening a bit, she stretched protesting muscles. "I think I've had enough health and nature for the day."

He looked down at her. She wasn't A. J. Fields now, in T-shirt and jeans and scuffed boots. But he still knew how to play her. "I guess I'm in better shape than you are."

"Like hell." She pushed away from the tree.

Determined to keep up, she strode along beside him, up the winding dirt path, until sweat trickled down her back. Her leg muscles whimpered, reminding her she'd neglected her weekly tennis games for over a month. At last, aching and exhausted, she dropped down on a rock.

"That's it. I give up."

"Another hundred yards and we start circling back."

"Nope."

"A.J., it's shorter to go around this way than to turn around."

Shorter? She shut her eyes and asked herself what had possessed her to let him drag her through the woods. "I'll just stay here tonight. You can bring me back a pillow and a sandwich."

"I could always carry you."

She folded her arms. "No."

"How about a bribe?"

Her bottom lip poked out as she considered. "I'm always open to negotiations."

"I've got a bottle of cabernet sauvignon I've been saving for the right moment."

She rubbed at a streak of dirt on her knee. "What year?"

"Seventy-nine."

"A good start. That might get me the next hundred yards or so."

"Then there's that steak I took out of the freezer this morning, the one I'm going to grill over mesquite."

"I'd forgotten about that." She brought her tongue over her top lip and thought she could almost taste it. "That should get me halfway back down."

"You drive a hard bargain."

"Thank you."

"Flowers. Dozens of them."

She lifted a brow. "By the time we get back, the florist'll be closed."

"City-oriented," he said with a sigh. "Look around you."

"You're going to pick me flowers?" Surprised, and foolishly pleased, she lifted her arms to twine them around his neck. "That should definitely get me through the front door."

Smiling, she leaned back as he stepped off the path to gather blossoms. "I like the blue ones," she called out, and laughed as he muttered at her.

She hadn't expected the weekend to be so relaxed, so easy. She hadn't known she could enjoy being with one person for so long. There were no schedules, no appointments, no pressing deals. There were simply mornings and afternoons and evenings.

It seemed absurd that something as mundane as fixing break-fast could be fun. She'd discovered that spending the time to eat it instead of rushing into the morning had a certain appeal. When you weren't alone. She didn't have a script or a business letter to deal with. And she had to admit, she hadn't missed them. She'd done nothing more mind-teasing in two days than a crossword puzzle. And even that, she remembered happily, had been interrupted.

Now he was picking her flowers. Small, colorful wildflowers. She'd put them in a vase by the window where they'd be cozy and bright. And deadly.

For an instant, her heart stopped. The birds were silent and the air was still as glass. She saw David as though she were looking through a long lens. As she watched, the light went gray. There was pain, sharp and sudden, as her knuckles scraped over the rock.

"No!" She thought she shouted, but the word came out in a whisper. She nearly slipped off the rock before she caught herself and stumbled toward him. She gasped for his name twice before it finally ripped out of her. "David! No, stop."

He straightened, but only had time to take a step toward her before she threw herself into his arms. He'd seen that blank terror in her eyes before, once before, when she'd stood in an old empty room watching something no one else could see.

"Aurora, what is it?" He held her close while she shuddered, though he had no idea how to soothe. "What's wrong?"

"Don't pick any more. David, don't." Her fingers dug hard into his back.

"All right, I won't." Hands firm, he drew her away to study her face. "Why?"

"Something's wrong with them." The fear hadn't passed. She pressed the heel of her hand against her chest as if to push it out. "Something's wrong with them," she repeated.

"They're just flowers." He showed her what he held in his hands.

"Not them. Over there. You were going to pick those over there."

He followed the direction of her gaze to a large sunny rock with flowers around the perimeter. He remembered he'd just been turning in their direction when her shouts had stopped him. "Yes, I was. Let's have a look."

"No." She grabbed him again. "Don't touch them."

"Calm down," he said quietly enough, though his own nerves were starting to jangle. Bending, he picked up a stick. Letting the flowers he'd already picked fall, he took A.J.'s hand in his and dragged the end of the stick along the edge of the rock through a thick clump of bluebells. He heard the hissing rattle, felt the jolt of the stick he held as the snake reared up and struck. A.J.'s hand went limp in his. David held on to the stick as he pulled her back to the path. He wore boots, thick and sturdy enough to protect against the snakes scattered through the hills. But he'd been picking flowers, and there had been nothing to protect the vulnerable flesh of his hands and wrists.

"I want to go back," she said flatly.

She was grateful he didn't question, didn't probe or even try to soothe. If he had, she wasn't sure what idiotic answers she'd have given him. A.J. had discovered more in that one timeless moment than David's immediate danger. She'd discovered she was in love with him. All her rules, her warnings, her precautions hadn't mattered. He could hurt her now, and she might never recover.

So she didn't speak. Because he was silent, as well, she felt the first pang of rejection. They entered through the kitchen door. David took a bottle of brandy and two water glasses out of a cupboard. He poured, handed one to A.J., then emptied half the contents of his own glass in one swallow.

She sipped, then sipped again, and felt a little steadier. "Would you like to take me home now?"

He picked up the bottle and added a dollop to his glass. "What are you talking about?"

A.J. wrapped both hands around her glass and made herself speak calmly. "Most people are uncomfortable after—after an episode. They either want to distance themselves from the source or dissect it." When he said nothing, only stared at her, she set her glass down. "It won't take me long to pack."

"You take another step," he said in a voice that was deadly calm, "and I don't know what the hell I'll do. Sit down, Aurora."

"David, I don't want an interrogation."

He hurled his glass into the sink, making her jolt at the sudden violence. "Don't we know each other any better than that by now?" He was shouting. She couldn't know it wasn't at her, but himself. "Can't we have any sort of discussion, any sort of contact, that isn't sex or negotiations?"

"We agreed—"

He said something so uncharacteristically vulgar about agreements that she stopped dead. "You very possibly saved my life." He stared down at his hand, well able to imagine what might have happened. "What am I supposed to say to you? Thanks?"

When she found herself stuttering, A.J. swallowed and pulled herself back. "I'd really rather you didn't say anything."

He walked to her but didn't touch. "I can't. Look, I'm a little shaky about this myself. That doesn't mean I've suddenly decided you're a freak." He saw the emotion come and go in her eyes before he reached out to touch her face. "I'm grateful. I just don't quite know how to handle it."

"It's all right." She was losing ground. She could feel it. "I don't expect—"

"Do." He brought his other hand to her face. "Do expect. Tell me what you want. Tell me what you need right now."

She tried not to. She'd lose one more foothold if she did. But his hands were gentle, when they never were, and his eyes offered. "Hold me." She closed her eyes as she said it. "Just hold me a minute."

He put his arms around her, drew her against him. There was no passion, no fire, just comfort. He felt her hands knead at his back until both of them relaxed. "Do you want to talk about it?"

"It was just a flash. I was sitting there, thinking about how nice it had been to do nothing. I was thinking about the flowers. I had a picture of them in the window. All at once they were black and ugly and the petals were like razors. I saw you bending over that clump of bluebells, and it all went gray."

"I hadn't bent over them yet."

"You would have."

"Yeah." He held her closer a moment. "I would have. Looks like I reneged on the last part of the deal. I don't have any flowers for you."

"It doesn't matter." She pressed her lips against his neck.

"I'll have to make it up to you." Drawing back, he took both of her hands. "Aurora…" He started to lift one, then saw the caked blood on her knuckles. "What the hell have you done to yourself?"

Blankly she looked down. "I don't know. It hurts," she said as she flexed her hand.

"Come on." He led her to the sink and began to clean off dried blood with cool water.

"Ow!" She would have jerked her hand away if he hadn't held it still.

"I've never had a very gentle touch," he muttered.

She leaned a hip against the sink. "So I've noticed."

Annoyed at seeing the rough wound on her hand, he began to dab it with a towel. "Let's go upstairs. I've got some Merthiolate."

"That stings."

"Don't be a baby."

"I'm not." But he had to tug her along. "It's only a scrape."

"And scrapes get infected."

"Look, you've already rubbed it raw. There can't be a germ left."

He nudged her into the bathroom. "We'll make sure."

Before she could stop him, he took out a bottle and dumped medicine over her knuckles. What had been a dull sting turned to fire. "Damn it!"

"Here." He grabbed her hand again and began to blow on the wound. "Just give it a minute."

"A lot of good that does," she muttered, but the pain cooled.

"We'll fix dinner. That'll take your mind off it."

"You're supposed to fix dinner," she reminded him.

"Right." He kissed her forehead. "I've got to run out for a minute. I'll start the grill when I get back."

"That doesn't mean I'm going to be chopping vegetables while you're gone. I'm going to take a bath."

"Fine. If the water's still hot when I get back, I'll join you."

She didn't ask where he was going. She wanted to, but there were rules. Instead A.J. walked into the bedroom and watched from the window as he pulled out of the drive. Weary, she sat on the bed and pulled off her boots. The afternoon had taken its toll, physically, emotionally. She didn't want to think. She didn't want to feel.

Giving in, she stretched out across the bed. She'd rest for a minute, she told herself. Only for a minute.

David came home with a handful of asters he'd begged from a neighbor's garden. He thought the idea of dropping them on A.J. while she soaked in the tub might bring the laughter back to her eyes. He'd never heard her laugh so much or so easily as she had over the weekend. It wasn't something he wanted to lose. Just as he was discovering she wasn't something he wanted to lose.

He went up the stairs quietly, then paused at the bedroom door when he saw her. She'd taken off only her boots. A pillow was crumpled under her arm as she lay diagonally across the bed. It occurred to him as he stepped into the room that he'd never watched her sleep before. They'd never given each other the chance.

Her face looked so soft, so fragile. Her hair was pale and tumbled onto her cheek, her lips unpainted and just parted. How was it he'd never noticed how delicate her features were, how slender and frail her wrists were, how elegantly feminine the curve of her neck was?

Maybe he hadn't looked, David admitted as he crossed to the bed. But he was looking now.

She was fire and thunder in bed, sharp and tough out of it. She had a gift, a curse and ability she fought against every waking moment, one that he was just beginning to understand. He was just beginning to see that it made her defensive and defenseless.

Only rarely did the vulnerabilities emerge, and then with such reluctance from her he'd tended to gloss over them. But now, just now, when she was asleep and unaware of him, she looked like something a man should protect, cherish.

The first stirrings weren't of passion and desire, but of a quiet affection he hadn't realized he felt for her. He hadn't realized it was possible to feel anything quiet for Aurora. Unable to resist, he reached down to brush the hair from her cheek and feel the warm, smooth skin beneath.

She stirred. He'd wanted her to. Heavy and sleep-glazed, her eyes opened. "David?" Even her voice was soft, feminine.

"I brought you a present." He sat on the bed beside her and dropped the flowers by her hand.

"Oh." He'd seen that before, too, he realized. That quick surprise and momentary confusion when he'd done something foolish or romantic. "You didn't have to."

"I think I did," he murmured, half to himself. Almost as an experiment, he lowered his mouth to hers and kissed her softly, gently, with the tenderness she'd made him feel as she slept. He felt the ache move through him, sweet as a dream.

"David?" She said his name again, but this time her eyes were dark and dazed.

"Ssh." His hands didn't drag through her hair now with trembles of passion, but stroked, exploring the texture. He could watch the light strike individual strands. "Lovely." He brought his gaze back to hers. "Have I ever told you how lovely you are?"

She started to reach for him, for the passion that she could understand. "It isn't necessary."

His lips met hers again, but they didn't devour and demand. This mood was foreign and made her heart pound as much with uncertainty as need. "Make love with me," she murmured as she tried to draw him down.

"I am." His mouth lingered over hers. "Maybe for the first time."

"I don't understand," she began, but he shifted so that he could cradle her in his arms.

"Neither do I."

So he began, slowly, gently, testing them both. Her mouth offered darker promises, but he waited, coaxing. His lips were patient as they moved over hers, light and soothing as they kissed her eyes closed. He didn't touch her, not yet, though he wondered what it would be like to stroke her while the light was softening, to caress as though it were all new, all fresh. Gradually he felt the tension in her body give way, he felt what he'd never felt from her before. Pliancy, surrender, warmth.

Her body seemed weightless, gloriously light and free. She felt the pleasure move through her, but sweetly, fluidly, like wine. Then he was the wine, heady and potent, drugging her with the intoxicating taste of his mouth. The hands that had clutched him in demand went lax. There was so much to absorb—the flavor of his lips as they lingered on hers; the texture of his skin as his cheek brushed hers; the scent that clung to him, part man, part woods; the dark, curious look in his eyes as he watched her.

She looked as she had when she'd slept, he thought. Fragile, so arousingly fragile. And she felt… At last he touched, fingertips only, along skin already warm. He heard her sigh his name in a way she'd never said it before. Keeping her cradled in his arms, he began to take her deeper, take himself deeper, with tenderness.

She had no strength to demand, no will to take control. For the first time her body was totally his, just as for the first time her emotions were. He touched, and she yielded. He tasted, and she gave. When he shifted her, she felt as though she could float. Perhaps she was. Clouds of pleasure, mists of soft, soft delight. When he began to undress her, she opened her eyes, needing to see him again.

The light had gone to rose with sunset. It made her skin glow as he slowly drew off her shirt. He couldn't take his eyes off her, couldn't stop his hands from touching, though he had no desire to be quick. When she reached up, he helped her pull off his own shirt, then took her injured hand to his lips. He kissed her fingers, then her palm, then her wrist, until he felt her begin to tremble. Bending, he brushed her lips with his again, wanting to hear her sigh his name. Then, watching her, waiting until she looked at him, he continued to undress her.

Slowly. Achingly slowly, he drew the jeans down her legs,

pausing now and then to taste newly exposed skin. Pulses beat at the back of her knees. He felt them, lingered there, exploited them. Her ankles were slim, fragile like her wrists. He traced them with his tongue until she moaned. Then he waited, letting her settle again as he stripped off his own jeans. He came to her, flesh against flesh.

Nothing had been like this. Nothing could be like this. The thoughts whirled in her brain as he began another deliciously slow assault. Her body was to be enjoyed and pleasured, not worshiped. But he did so now, and enticed her to do the same with his.

So strong. She'd known his strength before, but this was different. His fingers didn't grip; his hands didn't press. They skimmed, they traced, they weakened. So intense. They'd shared intensity before, but never so quietly.

She heard him say her name. Aurora. It was like a dream, one she'd never dared to have. He murmured promises in her ear and she believed them. Whatever tomorrow might bring, she believed them now. She could smell the flowers strewn over the bed and taste the excitement that built in a way it had never done before.

He slipped into her as though their bodies had never been apart. The rhythm was easy, patient, giving.

Holding himself back, he watched her climb higher. That was what he wanted, he realized, to give her everything there was to give. When she arched and shuddered, the force whipped through him. Power, he recognized it, but was driven to leash it. His mouth found hers and drew on the sweetness. How could he have known sweetness could be so arousing?

The blood was pounding in his head, roaring in his ears, yet his body continued to move slowly with hers. Balanced on the edge, David said her name a last time.

"Aurora, look at me." When her eyes opened, they were dark and aware. "I want to see where I take you."

Even when control slipped away, echoes of tenderness remained.

10

Alice Robbins had exploded onto the screen in the sixties, a young, raw talent. She had, like so many girls before her and after her, fled to Hollywood to escape the limitations of small-town life. She'd come with dreams, with hopes and ambitions. An astrologer might have said Alice's stars were in the right quadrant. When she hit, she hit big.

She had had an early, turbulent marriage that had ended in an early, turbulent divorce. Scenes in and out of the courtroom had been as splashy as anything she'd portrayed on the screen. With her marriage over and her career climbing, she'd enjoyed all the benefits of being a beautiful woman in a town that demanded, then courted, beauty. Reports of her love affairs sizzled on the pages of glossies. Glowing reviews and critical praise heaped higher with each role. But in her late twenties, when her career was reaching its peak, she found something that fulfilled her in a way success and reviews never had. Alice Robbins met Peter Van Camp.

He'd been nearly twenty years her senior, a hard-bitten, well-to-do business magnate. They'd married after a whirlwind two-week courtship that had kept the gossip columns salivating. Was it for money? Was it for power? Was it for prestige? It had been, very simply, for love.

In an unprecedented move, Alice had taken her husband's name professionally as well as privately. Hardly more than a year later, she'd given birth to a son and had, without a backward glance, put her career on hold. For nearly a decade, she'd devoted herself to her family with the same kind of single-minded drive she'd put into her acting.

When word leaked that Alice Van Camp had been lured back into films, the hype had been extravagant. Rumors of a multimillion-dollar deal flew and promises of the movie of the century were lavish.

Four weeks before the release of the film, her son, Matthew, had been kidnapped.

David knew the background. Alice Van Camp's triumphs and trials were public fodder. Her name was legend. Though she rarely consented to grace the screen, her popularity remained constant. As to the abduction and recovery of her son, details were sketchy. Perhaps because of the circumstances, the police had never been fully open and Clarissa DeBasse had been quietly evasive. Neither Alice nor Peter Van Camp had ever, until now, granted an interview on the subject. Even with their agreement and apparent cooperation, David knew he would have to tread carefully.

He was using the minimum crew, and a well-seasoned one. "Star" might be an overused term, but David was aware they would be dealing with a woman who fully deserved the title and the mystique that went with it.

Her Beverly Hills home was guarded by electric gates and a wall twice as tall as a man. Just inside the gates was a uniformed guard who verified their identification. Even after they had been passed through, they drove another half a mile to the house.

It was white, flowing out with balconies, rising up with Doric columns, softened by tall, tall trellises of roses in full bloom. Legend had it that her husband had had it built for her in honor of the last role she'd played before the birth of their son. David had seen the movie countless times and remembered her as an antebellum tease who made Scarlett O'Hara look like a nun.

There were Japanese cherry trees dripping down to sweep the lawn in long skirts. Their scent and the citrus fragrance of orange and lemon stung the air. As he pulled his car to a halt behind the equipment van, he spotted a peacock strutting across the lawn.

I wish A.J. could see this.

The thought came automatically before he had time to check it, just as thoughts of her had come automatically for days. Because he wasn't yet sure just how he felt about it, David simply let it happen.

And how did he feel about her? That was something else he wasn't quite sure of. Desire. He desired her more, even more now after he'd saturated himself with her. Friendship. In some odd, cautious way he felt they were almost as much friends as they were lovers. Understanding. It was more difficult to be as definite about that. A.J. had an uncanny ability to throw up mirrors that reflected back your own thoughts rather than hers. Still, he had come to understand that beneath the confidence and drive was a warm, vulnerable woman.

She was passionate. She was reserved. She was competent. She was fragile. And she was, David had discovered, a tantalizing mystery to be solved, one layer at a time.

Perhaps that was why he'd found himself so caught up in her. Most of the women he knew were precisely what they seemed. Sophisticated. Ambitious. Well-bred. His own taste had invariably drawn him to a certain type of woman. A.J. fit. Aurora didn't. If he understood anything about her, he understood she was both.

As an agent, he knew, she was pleased with the deal she'd made for her client, including the Van Camp segment. As a daughter, he sensed, she was uneasy about the repercussions.

But the deal had been made, David reminded himself as he walked up the wide circular steps to the Van Camp estate. As a producer, he was satisfied with the progress of his project. But as a man, he wished he knew of a way to put A.J.'s mind at rest. She excited him; she intrigued him. And as no woman had ever done before, she concerned him. He'd wondered, more often than once, if that peculiar combination equaled love. And if it did, what in hell he was going to do about it.

"Second thoughts?" Alex asked as David hesitated at the door.

Annoyed with himself, David shrugged his shoulders, then pushed the bell. "Should there be?"

"Clarissa's comfortable with this."

David found himself shifting restlessly. "That's enough for you?"

"It's enough," Alex answered. "Clarissa knows her own mind."

The phrasing had him frowning, had him searching. "Alex—"

Though he wasn't certain what he had been about to say, the door opened and the moment was lost. A formally dressed, French-accented maid took their names before leading them into a room off the main hall. The crew, not easily impressed, spoke in murmurs.

It was unapologetically Hollywood. The furnishings were big and bold, the colors flashy. On a baby grand in the center of the room was a silver candelabra dripping with crystal prisms. David recognized it as a prop from *Music at Midnight*.

"Not one for understatement," Alex commented.

"No." David took another sweep of the room. There were brocades and silks in jewel colors. Furniture gleamed like mirrors. "But Alice Van Camp might be one of the few in the business who deserves to bang her own drum."

"Thank you."

Regal, amused and as stunning as she had been in her screen debut, Alice Van Camp paused in the doorway. She was a woman who knew how to pose, and who did so without a second thought. Like others who had known her only through her movies, David's first thought was how small she was. Then she stepped forward and her presence alone whisked the image away.

"Mr. Marshall." Hand extended, Alice walked to him. Her hair was a deep sable spiked around a face as pale and smooth as a child's. If he hadn't known better, David would have said she'd yet to see thirty. "It's a pleasure to meet you. I'm a great admirer of journalists—when they don't misquote me."

"Mrs. Van Camp." He covered her small hand with both of his. "Shall I say the obvious?"

"That depends."

"You're just as beautiful face-to-face as you are on the screen."

She laughed, the smoky, sultry murmur that had made men itch for more than two decades. "I appreciate the obvious. And you're David Brady." Her gaze shifted to him and he felt the unapologetic summing up, strictly woman to man. "I've seen several of your productions. My husband prefers documentaries and biographies to films. I can't think why he married me."

"I can." David accepted her hand. "I'm an avid fan."

"As long as you don't tell me you've enjoyed my movies since you were a child." Amusement glimmered in her eyes again before she glanced around. "Now if you'll introduce me to our crew, we can get started."

David had admired her for years. After ten minutes in her

company, his admiration grew. She spoke to each member of the crew, from the director down to the assistant lighting technician. When she'd finished, she turned herself over to Sam for instructions.

At her suggestion, they moved to the terrace. Patient, she waited while technicians set up reflectors and umbrellas to exploit the best effect from available light. Her maid set a table of cold drinks and snacks out of camera range. Though she didn't touch a thing, she indicated to the crew that they should enjoy. She sat easily through sound tests and blocking. When Sam was satisfied, she turned to Alex and began.

"Mrs. Van Camp, for twenty years you've been known as one of the most talented and best-loved actresses in the country."

"Thank you, Alex. My career has always been one of the most important parts of my life."

"One of the most. We're here now to discuss another part of your life. Your family, most specifically your son. A decade ago, you nearly faced tragedy."

"Yes, I did." She folded her hands. Though the sun shone down in her face, she never blinked. "A tragedy that I sincerely doubt I would have recovered from."

"This is the first interview you've given on this subject. Can I ask you why you agreed now?"

She smiled a little, leaning back in her weathered rattan chair. "Timing, in life and in business, is crucial. For several years after my son's abduction I simply couldn't speak of it. After a time, it seemed unnecessary to bring it up again. Now, if I watch the news or look in a store window and see posters of missing children, I ache for the parents."

"Do you consider that this interview might help those parents?"

"Help them find their children, no." Emotion flickered in

her eyes, very real and very brief. "But perhaps it can ease some of the misery. I'd never considered sharing my feelings about my own experience. And I doubt very much if I would have agreed if it hadn't been for Clarissa DeBasse."

"Clarissa DeBasse asked you to give this interview?"

After a soft laugh, Alice shook her head. "Clarissa never asks anything. But when I spoke with her and I realized she had faith in this project, I agreed."

"You have a great deal of faith in her."

"She gave me back my son."

She said it with such simplicity, with such utter sincerity, that Alex let the sentence hang. From somewhere in the garden at her back, a bird began to trill.

"That's what we'd like to talk about here. Will you tell us how you came to know Clarissa DeBasse?"

Behind the cameras, behind the crew, David stood with his hands in his pockets and listened to the story. He remembered how A.J. had once told him of her mother's gradual association with celebrities. Alice Van Camp had come to her with a friend on a whim. After an hour, she'd gone away impressed with Clarissa's gentle style and straightforward manner. On impulse, she'd commissioned Clarissa to do her husband's chart as a gift for their anniversary. When it was done, even the pragmatic and business-oriented Peter Van Camp had been intrigued.

"She told me things about myself," Alice went on. "Not about tomorrow, you understand, but about my feelings, things about my background that had influenced me, or still worried me. I can't say I always liked what she had to say. There are things about ourselves we don't like to admit. But I kept going back because she was so intriguing, and gradually we became friends."

"You believed in clairvoyance?"

Alice's brows drew together as she considered. "I would say I first began to see her because it was fun, it was different. I'd chosen to lead a secluded life after the birth of my son, but that didn't mean I wouldn't appreciate, even need, little touches of flash. Of the unique." The frown smoothed as she smiled. "Clarissa was undoubtedly unique."

"So you went to her for entertainment."

"Oh, yes, that was definitely the motivation in the beginning. You see, at first I thought she was simply very clever. Then, as I began to know her, I discovered she was not simply clever, she was special. That certainly doesn't mean I endorse every palmist on Sunset Boulevard. I certainly can't claim to understand the testing and research that's done on the subject. I do believe, however, that there are some of us who are more sensitive, or whose senses are more finely tuned."

"Will you tell us what happened when your son was abducted?"

"June 22. Almost ten years ago." Alice closed her eyes a moment. "To me it's yesterday. You have children, Mr. Marshall?"

"Yes, I do."

"And you love them."

"Very much."

"Then you have some small glimmer of what it would be like to lose them, even for a short time. There's terror and there's guilt. The guilt is nearly as painful as the fear. You see, I hadn't been with him when he'd been taken. Jenny was Matthew's nanny. She'd been with us over five years and was very devoted to my son. She was young, but dependable and fiercely protective. When I made the decision to go back into films, we leaned on Jenny heavily. Neither my husband nor myself wanted Matthew to suffer because I was working again."

"Your son was nearly ten when you agreed to do another movie."

"Yes, he was quite independent already. Both Peter and I wanted that for him. Very often during the filming, Jenny would bring him to the studio. Even after the shooting was complete, she continued in her habit of walking to the park with him in the afternoon. If I had realized then how certain habits can be dangerous, I would have stopped it. Both my husband and myself had been careful to keep Matthew out of the limelight, not because we were afraid for him physically, but because we felt it was best that his upbringing be as normal and natural as possible. Of course he was recognized, and now and then some enterprising photographer would get a shot in."

"Did that sort of thing bother you?"

"No." When she smiled, the sultry glamour came through. "I suppose I was accustomed to such things. Peter and I didn't want to be fanatics about our privacy. And I wonder, and always have, if we'd been stricter would it have made any difference? I doubt it." There was a little sigh, as though it were a point she'd yet to resolve. "We learned later that Matthew's visits to the park were being watched."

"For a time the police suspected Jennifer Waite, your son's nanny, of working with the kidnappers."

"That was, of course, absurd. I never for a minute doubted Jenny's loyalty and devotion to Matthew. Once it was over, she was completely cleared." A trace of stubbornness came through. "She's still in my employ."

"The investigators found her story disjointed."

"The afternoon he was abducted, Jenny came home hysterical. We were the closest thing to family she had, and she blamed herself. Matthew had been playing ball with several other children while she watched. A young woman had come up to her asking for directions. She'd spun a story about missing her bus and being new in town. She'd distracted Jenny only a few moments, and that's all it took. When she looked back, Jenny saw Matthew being hustled into a car at the edge of the park. She ran after him, but he was gone. Ten minutes after she came home alone the first ransom call came in."

She lifted her hands to her lips a moment, and they trembled lightly. "I'm sorry. Could we stop here a moment?"

"Cut. Five minutes," Sam ordered the crew.

David was beside her chair before Sam had finished speaking. "Would you like something, Mrs. Van Camp? A drink?"

"No." She shook her head and looked beyond him. "It isn't as easy as I thought it would be. Ten years, and it still isn't easy."

"I could send for your husband."

"I told Peter to stay away today because he's always so uncomfortable around cameras. I wish I hadn't."

"We can wrap for today."

"Oh, no." She took a deep breath and composed herself. "I believe in finishing what I start. Matthew's a sophomore in college." She smiled up at David. "Do you like happy endings?"

He held her hand. For the moment she was only a woman. "I'm a sucker for them."

"He's bright, handsome and in love. I just needed to remember that. It could have been…" She linked her hands again and the ruby on her finger shone like blood. "It could have been much different. You know Clarissa's daughter, don't you?"

A bit off-balance at the change of subject, David shifted. "Yes."

She admired the caution. "I meant it when I said Clarissa and I are friends. Mothers worry about their children. Do you have a cigarette?"

In silence he took one out and lit it for her.

Alice blew out smoke and let some of the tension fade.

"She's a hell of an agent. Do you know, I wanted to sign with her and she wouldn't have me?"

David forgot his own cigarette in simple astonishment. "I beg your pardon?"

Alice laughed again and relaxed. She'd needed a moment to remember life went on. "It was a few months after the kidnapping. A.J. figured I'd come to her out of gratitude to Clarissa. And maybe I had. In any case, she turned me down flat, even though she was scrambling around trying to rent decent office space. I admired her integrity. So much so that a few years ago I approached her again." Alice smiled at him, enjoying the fact that he listened very carefully. Apparently, she mused, Clarissa was right on target, as always. "She was established, respected. And she turned me down again."

What agent in her right mind would turn down a top name, a name that had earned through sheer talent the label of "megastar"? "A.J. never quite does what you expect," he murmured.

"Clarissa's daughter is a woman who insists on being accepted for herself, but can't always tell when she is." She crushed out the cigarette after a second quick puff. "Thanks. I'd like to continue now."

Within moments, Alice was deep into her own story. Though the camera continued to roll, she forgot about it. Sitting in the sunlight with the scent of roses strong and sweet, she talked about her hours of terror.

"We would have paid anything. Anything. Peter and I fought bitterly about calling in the police. The kidnappers had been very specific. We weren't to contact anyone. But Peter felt, and rightly so, that we needed help. The ransom calls came every few hours. We agreed to pay, but they kept changing the terms. Testing us. It was the worst kind of cruelty. While we waited, the police began searching for the car Jenny had seen and the woman she'd spoken with in the park. It was as if they'd vanished into thin air. At the end of forty-eight hours, we were no closer to finding Matthew."

"So you decided to call in Clarissa DeBasse?"

"I don't know when the idea of asking Clarissa to help came to me. I know I hadn't slept or eaten. I just kept waiting for the phone to ring. It's such a helpless feeling. I remembered, God knows why, that Clarissa had once told me where to find a diamond brooch I'd misplaced. It wasn't just a piece of jewelry to me, but something Peter had given me when Matthew was born. A child isn't a brooch, but I began to think, maybe, just maybe. I needed some hope.

"The police didn't like the idea. I don't believe Peter did, either, but he knew I needed something. I called Clarissa and I told her that Matthew had been taken." Her eyes filled. She didn't bother to blink the tears away. "I asked her if she could help me and she told me she'd try.

"I broke down when she arrived. She sat with me awhile, friend to friend, mother to mother. She spoke to Jenny, though there was no calming the poor girl down even at that point. The police were very terse with Clarissa, but she seemed to accept that. She told them they were looking in the wrong place." Unselfconsciously she brushed at the tears on her cheek. "I can tell you that didn't sit too well with the men who'd been working around the clock. She told them Matthew hadn't been taken out of the city, he hadn't gone north as they'd thought. She asked for something of Matthew's, something he would have worn. I brought her the pajamas he'd worn to bed the night before. They were blue with little cars across the top. She just sat there, running them through her hands. I remember wanting to scream at her, plead with her, to give me something. Then she started to speak very quietly.

"Matthew was only miles away, she said. He hadn't been taken to San Francisco, though the police had traced one of the ransom calls there. She said he was still in Los Angeles. She described the street, then the house. A white house with blue shutters on a corner lot. I'll never forget the way she described the room in which he was being held. It was dark, you see, and Matthew, though he always tried to be brave, was still afraid of the dark. She said there were only two people in the house, one man and the woman who had spoken to Jenny in the park. She thought there was a car in the drive, gray or green, she said. And she told me he wasn't hurt. He was afraid—" her voice shuddered, then strengthened "—but he wasn't hurt."

"And the police pursued the lead?"

"They didn't have much faith in it, naturally enough, but they sent out cars to look for the house she'd described. I don't know who was more stunned when they found it, Peter and myself or the police. They got Matthew out without a struggle because the two kidnappers with him weren't expecting any trouble. The third accomplice was in San Fransico, making all the calls. The police also found the car he'd been abducted in there.

"Clarissa stayed until Matthew was home, until he was safe. Later he told me about the room he'd been held in. It was exactly as she'd described it."

"Mrs. Van Camp, a lot of people claimed that the abduction and the dramatic rescue of your son was a publicity stunt to hype the release of your first movie since his birth."

"That didn't matter to me." With only her voice, with only her eyes, she showed her complete contempt. "They could say and believe whatever they wanted. I had my son back."

"And you believe Clarissa DeBasse is responsible for that?"

"I know she is."

"Cut," Sam mumbled to his cameraman before he walked

to Alice. "Mrs. Van Camp, if we can get a few reaction shots and over-the-shoulder angles, we'll be done."

He could go now. David knew there was no real reason for him to remain during the angle changes. The shoot was essentially finished, and had been everything he could have asked for. Alice Van Camp was a consummate actress, but no one watching this segment would consider that she'd played a part. She'd been a mother, reliving an experience every mother fears. And she had, by the telling, brought the core of his project right back to Clarissa.

He thought perhaps he understood a little better why A.J. had had mixed feelings about the interview. Alice Van Camp had suffered in the telling. If his instincts were right, Clarissa would have suffered, too. It seemed to him that empathy was an intimate part of her gift.

Nevertheless he stayed behind the camera and restlessly waited until the shoot was complete. Though he detected a trace of weariness in her eyes, Alice escorted the crew to the door herself.

"A remarkable woman," Alex commented as they walked down the circular steps toward the drive.

"And then some. But you've got one yourself."

"I certainly do." Alex pulled out the cigar he'd been patiently waiting for for more than three hours. "I might be a little biased, but I believe you have one, as well."

Frowning, David paused by his car. "I haven't got A.J." It occurred to him that it was the first time he had thought of it in precisely those terms.

"Clarissa seems to think you do."

He turned back and leaned against his car. "And approves?"

"Shouldn't she?"

He pulled out a cigarette. The restlessness was growing. "I don't know."

"You were going to ask me something earlier, before we went in. Do you want to ask me now?"

It had been nagging at him. David wondered if by stating it aloud it would ease. "Clarissa isn't an ordinary woman. Does it bother you?"

Alex took a contented puff on his cigar. "It certainly intrigues me, and I'd be lying if I didn't admit I've had one or two uneasy moments. What I feel for her cancels out the fact that I have five senses and she has what we might call six. You're having uneasy moments." He smiled a little when David said nothing. "Clarissa doesn't believe in keeping secrets. We've talked about her daughter."

"I'm not sure A.J. would be comfortable with that."

"No, maybe not. It's more to the point what you're comfortable with. You know the trouble with a man your age, David? You consider yourself too old to go take foolish risks and too young to trust impulse. I thank God I'm not thirty." With a smile, he walked over to hitch a ride back to town with Sam.

He was too old to take foolish risks, David thought as he pulled his door open. And a man who trusted impulse usually landed flat on his face. But he wanted to see her. He wanted to see her now.

A.J.'s briefcase weighed heavily as she pulled it from the front seat. Late rush–hour traffic streamed by the front of her building. If she'd been able to accomplish more during office hours, she reminded herself as she lugged up her case, she wouldn't have to plow through papers tonight. She would have accomplished more if she hadn't been uneasy, thinking of the Van Camp interview.

It was over now, she told herself as she turned the key to lock both car doors. The filming of the documentary was all but over. She had other clients, other projects, other contracts.

It was time she put her mind on them. Shifting her briefcase to her free hand, she turned and collided with David.

"I like running into you," he murmured as he slid his hands up her hips.

She'd had the wind knocked out of her. That's what she told herself as she struggled for breath and leaned into him. After a man and a woman had been intimate, after they'd been lovers, they didn't feel breathless and giddy when they saw each other. But she found herself wanting to wrap her arms around him and laugh.

"You might have cracked a rib," she told him, and contented herself with smiling up at him. "I certainly didn't expect to see you around this evening."

"Problem?"

"No." She let herself brush a hand through his hair. "I think I can work you in. How did the shoot go?"

He heard it, the barest trace of nerves. Not tonight, he told himself. There would be no nerves tonight. "It's done. You know, I like the way you smell up close." He lowered his mouth to brush it over her throat. "Up very close."

"David, we're standing in the parking lot."

"Mmm-hmm." He shifted his mouth to her ear and sent the thrill tumbling to her toes.

"David." She turned her head to ward him off and found her mouth captured by his in a long, lingering kiss.

"I can't stop thinking about you," he murmured, then kissed her again, hard, until the breath was trembling from her mouth into his. "I can't get you out of my mind. Sometimes I wonder if you've put a spell on me. Mind over matter."

"Don't talk. Come inside with me."

"We don't talk enough." He put his hand under her chin and drew her away before he gave in and buried himself in her again. "Sooner or later we're going to have to."

That's what she was afraid of. When they talked, really talked, she was sure it would be about the end. "Later, then. Please." She rested her cheek against his. "For now let's just enjoy each other."

He felt the edge of frustration compete with the first flares of desire. "That's all you want?"

No, no, she wanted more, everything, anything. If she opened her mouth to speak of one wish, she would speak of dozens. "It's enough," she said almost desperately. "Why did you come here tonight?"

"Because I wanted you. Because I damn well can't keep away from you."

"And that's all I need." Was she trying to convince him or herself? Neither of them had the answer. "Come inside, I'll show you."

Because he needed, because he wasn't yet sure of the nature of his own needs, he took her hand in his and went with her.

11

"Are you sure you want to do this?" A.J. felt it was only fair to give David one last chance before he committed himself.

"I'm sure."

"It's going to take the better part of your evening."

"Want to get rid of me?"

"No." She smiled but still hesitated. "Ever done anything like this before?"

He took the collar of her blouse between his thumb and forefinger and rubbed. The practical A.J. had a weakness for silk. "You're my first."

"Then you'll have to do what you're told."

He skimmed his finger down her throat. "Don't you trust me?"

She cocked her head and gave him a long look. "I haven't decided. But under the circumstances, I'll take a chance. Pull up a chair." She indicated the table behind her. There were stacks of paper, neatly arranged. A.J. picked up a pencil, freshly sharpened, and handed it to him. "The first thing you can do is mark off the names I give you. Those are the people who've sent an acceptance. I'll give you the name and the number of people under that name. I need an amount for the caterer by the end of the week."

"Sounds easy enough."

"Just shows you've never dealt with a caterer," A.J. mumbled, and took her own chair.

"What's this?" As he reached for another pile of papers, she waved his hand away.

"People who've already sent gifts, and don't mess with the system. When we finish with this, we have to deal with the guests coming in from out of town. I'm hoping to book a block of rooms tomorrow."

He studied the tidy but extensive arrangement of papers spread between them. "I thought this was supposed to be a small, simple wedding."

She sent him a mild look. "There's no such thing as a small, simple wedding. I've spent two full mornings haggling with florists and over a week off and on struggling with caterers."

"Learn anything?"

"Elopement is the wisest course. Now here—"

"Would you?"

"Would I what?"

"Elope."

With a laugh, A.J. picked up her first stack of papers. "If I ever lost a grip on myself and decided on marriage, I think I'd fly to Vegas, swing through one of those drive-in chapels and have it over with."

His eyes narrowed as he listened to her, as if he were trying to see beyond the words. "Not very romantic."

"Neither am I."

"Aren't you?" He put a hand over hers, surprising her. There was something proprietary in the gesture, and something completely natural.

"No." But her fingers linked with his. "There's not a lot of room for romance in business."

"And otherwise?"

"Otherwise romance tends to lead you to see things that aren't really there. I like illusions on the stage and screen, not in my life."

"What do you want in your life, Aurora? You've never told me."

Why was she nervous? It was foolish, but he was looking at her so closely. He was asking questions he'd never asked. And the answers weren't as simple as she'd once thought. "Success," she told him. Hadn't it always been true?

He nodded, but his thumb moved gently up and down the side of her hand. "You run a successful agency already. What else?" He was waiting, for one word, one sign. Did she need him? For the first time in his life he wanted to be needed.

"I…" She was fumbling for words. He seemed to be the only one who could make her fumble. What did he want? What answer would satisfy him? "I suppose I want to know I've earned my own way."

"Is that why you turned down Alice Van Camp as a client?"

"She told you that?" They hadn't discussed the Van Camp interview. A.J. had purposely talked around it for days.

"She mentioned it." She'd pulled her hand from his. David wondered why every time they talked, really talked, she seemed to draw further away from him.

"It was kind of her to come to me when I was just getting started and things were…rough." She shrugged her shoulders, then began to slide her pencil through her fingers. "But it was out of gratitude to my mother. I couldn't sign my first big client out of gratitude."

"Then later you turned her down again."

"It was too personal." She fought the urge to stand up, walk away from the table, and from him.

"No mixing business with personal relationships."

"Exactly. Do you want some coffee before we get started?"

"You mixed a business and personal relationship with me."

Her fingers tightened on the pencil. He watched them. "Yes, I did."

"Why?"

Though it cost her, she kept her eyes on his. He could strip her bare, she knew. If she told him she had fallen in love with him, had started the tumble almost from the first, she would have no defense left. He would have complete and total control. And she would have reneged on the most important agreement in her life. If she couldn't give him the truth, she could give him the answer he'd understand. The answer that mirrored his feelings for her.

"Because I wanted you," she said, and kept her voice cool. "I was attracted to you, and wisely or not, I gave in to the attraction."

He felt the twinge, a need unfulfilled. "That's enough for you?"

Hadn't she said he could hurt her? He was hurting her now with every word. "Why shouldn't it be?" She gave him an easy smile and waited for the ache to pass.

"Why shouldn't it be?" he murmured, and tried to accept the answer for what it was. He pulled out a cigarette, then began carefully. "I think you should know we're shooting a segment on the Ridehour case." Though his eyes stayed on hers, he saw her tense. "Clarissa agreed to discuss it."

"She told me. That should wrap the taping?"

"It should." She was holding back. Though no more than a table separated them, it might have been a canyon. "You don't like it."

"No, I don't, but I'm trying to learn that Clarissa has to make her own decisions."

"A.J., she seems very easy about it."

"You don't understand."

"Then let me."

"Before I convinced her to move, to keep her residence strictly confidential, she had closets full of letters." She took her glasses off to rub at a tiny ache in her temple. "People asking for her to help them. Some of them involved no more than asking her to locate a ring, and others were full of problems so heartbreaking they gave you nightmares."

"She couldn't help everyone."

"That's what I kept telling her. When she moved down to Newport Beach, things eased up. Until she got the call from San Francisco."

"The Ridehour murders."

"Yes." The ache grew. "There was never a question of her listening to me on that one. I don't believe she heard one argument I made. She just packed. When I saw there was no stopping her from going, I went with her." She kept her breathing even with great effort. Her hands were steady only because she locked them so tightly together. "It was one of the most painful experiences of her life. She saw." A.J. closed her eyes and spoke to him what she'd never spoken to anyone. "I saw."

When he covered her hand with his, he found it cold. He didn't have to see her eyes to know the baffled fear would be there. Comfort, understanding. How did he show them? "Why didn't you tell me before?"

She opened her eyes. The control was there, but teetering. "It isn't something I like to remember. I've never before or since had anything come so clear, so hideously clear."

"We'll cut it."

She gave him a blank, puzzled look. "What?"

"We'll cut the segment."

"Why?"

Slowly he drew her hands apart and into his. He wanted to explain, to tell her so that she'd understand. He wished he had the words. "Because it upsets you. That's enough."

She looked down at their hands. His looked so strong, so dependable, over hers. No one except her mother had ever offered to do anything for her without an angle. Yet it seemed he was. "I don't know what to say to you."

"Don't say anything."

"No." She gave herself a moment. For reasons she couldn't understand, she was relaxed again. Tension was there, hovering, but the knots in her stomach had eased. "Clarissa agreed to this segment, so she must feel as though it should be done."

"We're not talking about Clarissa now, but you. Aurora, I said once I never wanted to be responsible for your going through something like this. I mean it."

"I think you do." It made all the difference. "The fact that you'd cut the segment because of me makes me feel very special."

"Maybe I should have told you that you are before now."

Longings rose up. She let herself feel them for only a moment. "You don't have to tell me anything. I realize that if you cut this part because of me I'd hate myself. It was a long time ago, David. Maybe it's time I learned to deal with reality a little better."

"Maybe you deal with it too well."

"Maybe." She smiled again. "In any case I think you should do the segment. Just do a good job of it."

"I intend to. Do you want to sit in on it?"

"No." She glanced down at the stacks of papers. "Alex will be there for her."

He heard it in her voice, not doubt but resignation. "He's crazy about her."

"I know." In a lightning change of mood, she picked up her pencil again. "I'm going to give them one hell of a wedding."

He grinned at her. Resiliency was only one of the things that attracted him to her. "We'd better get started."

They worked side by side for nearly two hours. It took half that time for the tension to begin to fade. They read off lists and compiled new ones. They analyzed and calculated how many cases of champagne would be adequate and argued over whether to serve salmon mousse or iced shrimp.

She hadn't expected him to become personally involved with planning her mother's wedding. Before they'd finished, she'd come to accept it to the point where she delegated him to help seat guests at the ceremony.

"Working with you's an experience, A.J."

"Hmm?" She counted the out-of-town guests one last time.

"If I needed an agent, you'd head the list."

She glanced up, but was too cautious to smile. "Is that a compliment?"

"Not exactly."

Now she smiled. When she took off her glasses, her face was abruptly vulnerable. "I didn't think so. Well, once I give these figures to the caterer, that should be it. Everyone who attends will have me to thank that they aren't eating Clarissa's Swedish meatballs. And you." She set the lists aside. "I appreciate all the help."

"I'm fond of Clarissa."

"I know. I appreciate that, too. Now I think you deserve a reward." She leaned closer and caught her tongue in her teeth. "Anything in mind?"

He had plenty in mind every time he looked at her. "We can start with that coffee."

"Coming right up." She rose, and out of habit glanced at her watch. "Oh, God."

He reached for a cigarette. "Problem?"

"*Empire*'s on."

"A definite problem."

"No, I have to watch it."

As she dashed over to the television, he shook his head. "All this time, and I had no idea you were an addict. A.J., there are places you can go that can help you deal with these things."

"Ssh." She settled on the sofa, relieved she'd missed no more than the opening credits. "I have a client—"

"It figures."

"She has a lot of potential," A.J. continued. "But this is the first real break we've gotten. She's only signed for four episodes, but if she does well, they could bring her back through next season."

Resigned, he joined her on the sofa. "Aren't these repeats, anyway?"

"Not this one. It's a teaser for a spin-off that's going to run through the summer."

"A spin-off?" He propped his feet on an issue of *Variety* on the coffee table. "Isn't there enough sex and misery in one hour a week?"

"Melodrama. It's important to the average person to see that the filthy rich have their problems. See him?" Reaching over, she dug into a bowl of candied almonds. "That's Dereck, the patriarch. He made his money in shipping—and smuggling. He's determined that his children carry on his business, by his rules. That's Angelica."

"In the hot tub."

"Yes, she's his second wife. She married him for his money and power and enjoys every minute of them. But she hates his kids."

"And they hate her right back."

"That's the idea." Pleased with him, A.J. patted his leg.

"Now the setup is that Angelica's illegitimate daughter from a long-ago relationship is going to show up. That's my client."

"Like mother like daughter?"

"Oh, yes, she gets to play the perfect bitch. Her name's Lavender."

"Of course it is."

"You see, Angelica never told Dereck she had a daughter, so when Lavender shows up, she's going to cause all sorts of problems. Now Beau—that's Dereck's eldest son—"

"No more names." With a sigh, he swung his arm over the back of the sofa. "I'll just watch all the skin and diamonds."

"Just because you'd rather watch pelicans migrate— Here she is."

A.J. bit her lip. She tensed, agonizing with her client over each line, each move, each expression. And she would, David thought with a smile, fluff him off if he mentioned she had a personal involvement. Just business? Not by a long shot. She was pulling for her ingenue and ten percent didn't enter into it.

"Oh, she's good," A.J. breathed at the commercial break. "She's really very good. A season—maybe two—of this, and we'll be sifting through offers for feature films."

"Her timing's excellent." He might consider the show itself a glitzy waste of time, but he appreciated talent. "Where did she study?"

"She didn't." Smug, A.J. sat back. "She took a bus from Kansas City and ended up in my reception area with a homemade portfolio and a handful of high school plays to her credit."

He gave in and tried the candied almonds himself. "You usually sign on clients that way?"

"I usually have Abe or one of the more maternal members of my staff give them a lecture and a pat on the head."

"Sensible. But?"

"She was different. When she wouldn't budge out of the office for the second day running, I decided to see her myself. As soon as I saw her I knew. Not that way," she answered, understanding his unspoken question. "I make it a policy not to sign a client no matter what feelings might come through. She had looks and a wonderful voice. But more, she had the drive. I don't know how many auditions I sent her on in the first few weeks. But I figured if she survived that, we were going to roll." She watched the next glittery set of *Empire* appear on the screen. "And we're rolling."

"It took guts to camp out in one of the top agencies in Hollywood."

"If you don't have guts in this town, you'll be flattened in six months."

"Is that what keeps you on top, A.J.?"

"It's part of it." She found the curve of his shoulder an easy place to rest her head. "You can't tell me you think you're where you are today because you got lucky."

"No. You start off thinking hard work's enough, then you realize you have to take risks and shed a little blood. Then just when everything comes together and a project's finished and successful, you have to start another and prove yourself all over again."

"It's a lousy business." A.J. cuddled against him.

"Yep."

"Why do you do it?" Forgetting the series, forgetting her client, A.J. turned her head to look at him.

"Masochism."

"No, really."

"Because every time I watch something I did on that little screen, it's like Christmas. And I get every present I ever wanted."

"I know." Nothing he could have said could have hit more directly home. "I attended the Oscars a couple of years ago and two of my clients won. Two of them." She let her eyes close as she leaned against him. "I sat in the audience watching, and it was the biggest thrill of my life. I know some people would say you're not asking for enough when you get your thrills vicariously, but it's enough, more than enough, to know you've had a part in something like that. Maybe your name isn't a household word, but you were the catalyst."

"Not everyone wants his name to be a household word."

"Yours could be." She shifted again to look at him. "I'm not just saying that because—" *Because I love you.* The phrase was nearly out before she checked it. When he lifted his brow at her sudden silence, she continued quickly. "Because of our relationship. With the right material, the right crew, you could be one of the top ten producers in the business."

"I appreciate that." Her eyes were so earnest, so intense. He wished he knew why. "I don't think you throw around compliments without thinking about them first."

"No, I don't. I've seen your work, and I've seen the way you work. And I've been around long enough to know."

"I don't have any desire, not at this point, anyway, to tie myself up with any of the major studios. The big screen's for fantasies." He touched her cheek. It was real; it was soft. "I prefer dealing in reality."

"So produce something real." It was a challenge—she knew it. By the look in his eyes, he knew it, as well.

"Such as?"

"I have a script."

"A.J.—"

"No, hear me out. David." She said his name in frustration when he rolled her under him on the sofa. "Just listen a minute."

"I'd rather bite your ear."

"Bite it all you want. After you listen."

"Negotiations again?" He drew himself up just to look down at her. Her eyes were lit with enthusiasm, her cheeks flushed with anticipation of excitement to come. "What script?" he asked, and watched her lips curve.

"I've done some business with George Steiger. You know him?"

"We've met. He's an excellent writer."

"He's written a screenplay. His first. It just happened to come across my desk."

"Just happened?"

She'd done him a few favors. He was asking for another. Doing favors without personal gain at the end didn't fit the image she'd worked hard on developing. "We don't need to get into that. It's wonderful, David, really wonderful. It deals with the Cherokees and what they called the Trail of Tears, when they were driven from Georgia to reservations in Oklahoma. Most of the point of view is through a small child. You sense the bewilderment, the betrayal, but there's this strong thread of hope. It's not your 'ride off into the sunset' Western, and it's not a pretty story. It's real. You could make it important."

She was selling, and doing a damn good job of it. It occurred to him she'd probably never pitched a deal while curled up on the sofa before. "A.J., what makes you think that if I were interested, Steiger would be interested in me?"

"I happened to mention that I knew you."

"Happened to again?"

"Yes." She smiled and ran her hands down to his hips. "He's seen your work and knows your reputation. David, he needs a producer, the right producer."

"And so?"

As if disinterested, she skimmed her fingertips up his back. "He asked if I'd mention it to you, all very informally."

"This is definitely informal," he murmured as he fit his body against hers. "Are you playing agent, A.J.?"

"No." Her eyes were abruptly serious as she took his face in her hands. "I'm being your friend."

She touched him, more deeply, more sweetly, than any of their loving, any of their passion. For a moment he could find nothing to say. "Every time I think I've got a track on you, you switch lanes."

"Will you read it?"

He kissed one cheek, then the other, in a gesture he'd seen her use with her mother. It meant affection, devotion. He wondered if she understood. "I guess that means you can get me a copy."

"I just happened to have brought one home with me." With a laugh, she threw her arms around him. "David, you're going to love it."

"I'd rather love you."

She stiffened, but only for a heartbeat. Their loving was physical, she reminded herself. Deeply satisfying but only physical. When he spoke of love, it didn't mean the emotions, but the body. It was all she could expect from him, and all he wanted from her.

"Then love me now," she murmured, and found his mouth with hers. "Love me now."

She drew him to her, tempting him to take everything at once, quickly, heatedly. But he learned that pleasure taken slowly, given gently, could be so much more gratifying. Because it was still so new, she responded to tenderness with hesitation. Her stomach fluttered when he skimmed her lips with his, offering, promising. She heard her own sigh escape, a soft, giving sound that whispered across his lips. Then he murmured her name, quietly, as if it were the only sound he needed to hear.

No rush. His needs seemed to meld with her own. No hurry. Content, she let herself enjoy easy kisses that aroused the soul before they tempted the body. Relaxed, she allowed herself to thrill to the light caresses that made her strong enough to accept being weak.

She wanted to feel him against her without boundaries. With a murmur of approval, she pulled his shirt over his head, then took her hands on a long stroke down his back. There was the strength she'd understood from the beginning. A strength she respected, perhaps even more now that his hands were gentle.

When had she looked for gentleness? Her mind was already too clouded to know if she ever had. But now that she'd found it, she never wanted to lose it. Or him.

"I want you, David." She whispered the words along his cheek as she drew him closer.

Hearing her say it made his heart pound. He'd heard the words before, but rarely from her and never with such quiet acceptance. He lifted his head to look down at her. "Tell me again." As he took her chin in his hand, his voice was low and husky with emotion. "Tell me again, when I'm looking at you."

"I want you."

His mouth crushed down on hers, smothering any more words, any more thoughts. He seemed to need more; she thought she could feel it, though she didn't know what to give. She offered her mouth, that his might hungrily meet it. She offered her body, that his could greedily take it. But she held back her heart, afraid he would take that, as well, and damage it.

Clothes were peeled off as patience grew thin. He wanted to feel her against him, all the long length of her. He trembled when he touched her, but he was nearly used to trembling for her now. He ached, as he always ached. Light and subtle along her skin was the path of scent. He could follow it from her throat, to the hollow of her breasts, to the pulse at the inside of her elbows.

She shuddered against him. Her body seemed to pulse, then sigh, with each touch, each stroke. He knew where the brush of a fingertip would arouse, or the nip of his teeth would inflame. And she knew his body just as intimately. Her lips would find each point of pleasure; her palms would stroke each flame higher.

He grew to need. Each time he loved her, he came to need not only what she would give, but what she could. Each time he was more desperate to draw more from her, knowing that if he didn't find the key, he'd beg. She could, simply because she asked for nothing, bring him to his knees.

"Tell me what you want," he demanded as she clung to him.

"You. I want you."

She was hovering above the clouds that shook with lightning and thunder. The air was thick and heavy, the heat swirling. Her body was his; she gave it willingly. But the heart she struggled so hard to defend lost itself to him.

"David." All the love, all the emotion she felt, shimmered in his name as she pressed herself against him. "Don't let me go."

They dozed, still wrapped together, still drowsily content. Though most of his weight was on her, she felt light, free. Each time they made love, the sense of her own freedom came stronger. She was bound to him, but more liberated than she had ever been in her life. So she lay quietly as his heart beat slowly and steadily against hers.

"TV's still on," David murmured.

"Uh-huh." The late-night movie whisked by, sirens blaring, guns blasting. She didn't care.

She linked her hands behind his waist. "Doesn't matter."

"A few more minutes like this and we'll end up sleeping here tonight."

"That doesn't matter, either."

With a laugh, he turned his face to kiss her neck where the skin was still heated from excitement. Reluctantly he shifted his weight. "You know, with a few minor changes, we could be a great deal more comfortable."

"In the bed," she murmured in agreement, but merely snuggled into him.

"For a start. I'm thinking more of the long term."

It was difficult to think at all when he was warm and firm against her. "Which long term?"

"Both of us tend to do a lot of running around and over-night packing in order to spend the evening together."

"Mmmm. I don't mind."

He did. The more content he became with her, the more discontent he became with their arrangement. *I love you.* The words seemed so simple. But he'd never spoken them to a woman before. If he said them to her, how quickly would she pull away and disappear from his life? Some risks he wasn't ready to take. Cautious, he approached in the practical manner he thought she'd understand.

"Still, I think we could come up with a more logical arrange-ment."

She opened her eyes and shifted a bit. He could see there was already a line between her brows. "What sort of arrangement?"

He wasn't approaching this exactly as he'd planned. But then he'd learned that his usual meticulous plotting didn't work when he was dealing with A.J. "Your apartment's con-venient to the city, where we both happen to be working at the moment."

"Yes." Her eyes had lost that dreamy softness they always had after loving. He wasn't certain whether to curse himself or her.

"We only work five days a week. My house, on the other hand, is convenient for getting away and relaxing. It seems a logical arrangement might be for us to live here during the week and spend weekends at my place."

She was silent for five seconds, then ten, while dozens of thoughts and twice as many warnings rushed through her mind. "A logical arrangement," he called it. Not a commitment, an "arrangement." Or more accurately, an amendment to the arrangement they'd already agreed on. "You want to live together."

He'd expected more from her, anything more. A flicker of pleasure, a gleam of emotion. But her voice was cool and cautious. "We're essentially doing that now, aren't we?"

"No." She wanted to distance herself, but his body kept hers trapped. "We're sleeping together."

And that was all she wanted. His hands itched to shake her, to shake her until she looked, really looked, at him and saw what he felt and what he needed. Instead he sat up and, in the unselfconscious way she always admired, began to dress. Feeling naked and defenseless, she reached for her blouse.

"You're angry."

"Let's just say I didn't think we'd have to go to the negotiating table with this."

"David, you haven't even given me five minutes to think it through."

He turned to her then, and the heat in his eyes had her bracing. "If you need to," he said with perfect calm, "maybe we should just drop it."

"You're not being fair."

"No, I'm not." He rose then, knowing he had to get out,

get away from her, before he said too much. "Maybe I'm tired of being fair with you."

"Damn it, David." Half-dressed, she sprang up to face him. "You casually suggest that we should combine our living arrangements, then blow up because I need a few minutes to sort it through. You're being ridiculous."

"It's a habit I picked up when I starting seeing you." He should have left. He knew he should have already walked out the door. Because he hadn't, he grabbed her arms and pulled her closer. "I want more than sex and breakfast. I want more than a quick roll in the sheets when our schedules make it convenient."

Furious, she swung away from him. "You make me sound like a—"

"No. I make us both sound like it." He didn't reach for her again. He wouldn't crawl. "I make us both sound like precisely what we are. And I don't care for it."

She'd known it would end. She'd told herself she'd be prepared when it did. But she wanted to shout and scream. Clinging to what pride she had left, she stood straight. "I don't know what you want."

He stared at her until she nearly lost the battle with the tears that threatened. "No," he said quietly. "You don't. That's the biggest problem, isn't it?"

He left her because he wanted to beg. She let him go because she was ready to.

12

Nervous as a cat, A.J. supervised as folding chairs were set in rows in her mother's garden. She counted them—again—before she walked over to fuss with the umbrella-covered tables set in the side yard. The caterers were busy in the kitchen; the florist and two assistants were putting the finishing touches on the arrangements. Pots of lilies and tubs of roses were placed strategically around the terrace so that their scents wafted and melded with the flowers of Clarissa's garden. It smelled like a fairy tale.

Everything was going perfectly. With her hands in her pockets, she stood in the midmorning sunlight and wished for a crisis she could dig her teeth into.

Her mother was about to marry the man she loved, the weather was a blessing and all of A.J.'s preplanning was paying off. She couldn't remember ever being more miserable. She wanted to be home, in her own apartment, with the door locked and the curtains drawn, with her head buried under the covers. Hadn't it been David who'd once told her that self-pity wasn't attractive?

Well, David was out of her life now, A.J. reminded herself. And had been for nearly two weeks. That was for the best. Without having him around, confusing her emotions, she could get on with business. The agency was so busy she was seriously considering increasing her staff. Because of the increased work load, she was on the verge of canceling her own two-week vacation in Saint Croix. She was personally negotiating two multimillion-dollar contracts and one wrong move could send them toppling.

She wondered if he'd come.

A.J. cursed herself for even thinking of him. He'd walked out of her apartment and her life. He'd walked out when she'd kept herself in a state of turmoil, struggling to keep strictly to the terms of their agreement. He'd been angry and unreasonable. He hadn't bothered to call and she certainly wasn't going to call him.

Maybe she had once, she thought with a sigh. But he hadn't been home. It wasn't likely that David Brady was mooning and moping around. A. J. Fields was too independent, and certainly too busy, to do any moping herself.

But she'd dreamed of him. In the middle of the night she'd pull herself out of dreams because he was there. She knew, better than most, that dreams could hurt.

That part of her life was over, she told herself again. It had been only an…episode, she decided. Episodes didn't always end with flowers and sunlight and pretty words. She glanced over to see one of the hired help knock over a line of chairs. Grateful for the distraction, A.J. went over to help set things to rights.

When she went back into the house, the caterers were busily fussing over quiche and Clarissa was sitting contentedly in her robe, noting down the recipe.

"Momma, shouldn't you be getting ready?"

Clarissa glanced up with a vague smile and petted the cat that curled in her lap. "Oh, there's plenty of time, isn't there?"

"A woman never has enough time to get ready on her wedding day."

"It's a beautiful day, isn't it? I know it's foolish to take it as a sign, but I'd like to."

"You can take anything you want as a sign." A.J. started to move to the stove for coffee, then changed her mind. On impulse, she opened the refrigerator and pulled out one of the bottles of champagne that were chilling. The caterers muttered together and she ignored them. It wasn't every day a daughter watched her mother marry. "Come on. I'll help you." A.J. swung through the dining room and scooped up two fluted glasses.

"I wonder if I should drink before. I shouldn't be fuzzy-headed."

"You should absolutely be fuzzy-headed," A.J. corrected. Walking into her mother's room, she plopped down on the bed as she had as a child. "We should both be fuzzy-headed. It's better than being nervous."

Clarissa smiled beautifully. "I'm not nervous."

A.J. sent the cork cannoning to the ceiling. "Brides have to be nervous. I'm nervous and all I have to do is watch."

"Aurora." Clarissa took the glass she offered, then sat on the bed beside her. "You should stop worrying about me."

"I can't." A.J. leaned over to kiss one cheek, then the other. "I love you."

Clarissa took her hand and held it tightly. "You've always been a pleasure to me. Not once, not once in your entire life, have you brought me anything but happiness."

"That's all I want for you."

"I know. And it's all I want for you." She loosened her grip on A.J.'s hand but continued to hold it. "Talk to me."

A.J. didn't need specifics to understand her mother meant David. She set down her untouched champagne and started to rise. "We don't have time. You need to—"

"You've had an argument. You hurt."

With a long, hopeless sigh, A.J. sank back down on the bed. "I knew I would from the beginning. I had my eyes open."

"Did you?" With a shake of her head, Clarissa set her glass beside A.J.'s so she could take both her hands. "Why is it you have such a difficult time accepting affection from anyone but me? Am I responsible for that?"

"No. No, it's just the way things are. In any case, David and I... We simply had a very intense physical affair that burned itself out."

Clarissa thought of what she had seen, what she had felt, and nearly sighed. "But you're in love with him."

With anyone else, she could have denied. With anyone else, she could have lied and perhaps have been believed. "That's my problem, isn't it? And I'm dealing with it," she added quickly, before she was tempted into self-pity again. "Today of all days we shouldn't be talking about anything but lovely things."

"Today of all days I want to see my daughter happy. How do you think he feels about you?"

It never paid to forget how quietly stubborn Clarissa could be. "He was attracted. I think he was a little intrigued because I wasn't immediately compliant, and in business we stood toe-to-toe."

Clarissa hadn't forgotten how successfully evasive her daughter could be. "I asked you how you think he feels."

"I don't know." A.J. dragged a hand through her hair and rose. "He wants me—or wanted me. We match very well in bed. And then I'm not sure. He seemed to want more—to get inside my head."

"And you don't care for that."

"I don't like being examined."

Clarissa watched her daughter pace back and forth in her quick, nervous gait. So much emotion bottled up, she thought.

Why couldn't she understand she'd only truly feel it when she let it go? "Are you so sure that's what he was doing?"

"I'm not sure of anything, but I know that David is a very logical sort of man. The kind who does meticulous research into any subject that interests him."

"Did you ever consider that it was you who interested him, not your psychic abilities?"

"I think he might have been interested in one and uneasy about the other." She wished, even now, that she could be sure. "In any case, it's done now. We both understood commitment was out of the question."

"Why?"

"Because it wasn't what he—what we," she corrected herself quickly, "were looking for. We set the rules at the start."

"What did you argue about?"

"He suggested we live together."

"Oh." Clarissa paused a moment. She was old-fashioned enough to be anxious and wise enough to accept. "To some, a step like that is a form of commitment."

"No, it was more a matter of convenience." Was that what hurt? she wondered. She hadn't wanted to analyze it. "Anyway, I wanted to think it over and he got angry. Really angry."

"He's hurt." When A.J. glanced over, surprised protest on the tip of her tongue, Clarissa shook her head. "I know. You've managed to hurt each other deeply, with nothing more than pride."

That changed things. A.J. told herself it shouldn't, but found herself weakening. "I didn't want to hurt David. I only wanted—"

"To protect yourself," Clarissa finished. "Sometimes doing one can only lead to the other. When you love someone, really love them, you have to take some risks."

"You think I should go to him."

"I think you should do what's in your heart."

Her heart. Her heart was broken open. She wondered why everyone couldn't see what was in it. "It sounds so easy."

"And it's the most frightening thing in the world. We can test, analyze and research psychic phenomena. We can set up labs in some of the greatest universities and institutions in the world, but no one but a poet understands the terror of love."

"You've always been a poet, Momma." A.J. sat down beside her again, resting her head on her mother's shoulder. "Oh, God, what if he doesn't want me?"

"Then you'll hurt and you'll cry. After you do, you'll pick up the pieces of your life and go on. I have a strong daughter."

"And I have a wise and beautiful mother." A.J. leaned over to pick up both glasses of wine. After handing one to Clarissa, she raised hers in a toast. "What shall we drink to first?"

"Hope." Clarissa clinked glasses. "That's really all there is."

A.J. changed in the bedroom her mother always kept prepared for her. It hadn't mattered that she'd spent only a handful of nights in it over nearly ten years; Clarissa had labeled it hers, and hers it remained. Perhaps she would stay there tonight, after the wedding was over, the guests gone and the newlyweds off on their honeymoon. She might think better there, and tomorrow find the courage to listen to her mother's advice and follow her heart.

What if he didn't want her? What if he'd already forgotten her? A.J. faced the mirror but closed her eyes. There were too many "what ifs" to consider and only one thing she could be certain of. She loved him. If that meant taking risks, she didn't have a choice.

Straightening her shoulders, she opened her eyes and studied herself. The dress was romantic because her mother preferred it. She hadn't worn anything so blatantly feminine and flowing in years. Lace covered her bodice and caressed her throat, while the soft blue silk peeked out of the eyelets. The skirt swept to a bell at her ankles.

Not her usual style, A.J. thought again, but there was something appealing about the old-fashioned cut and the charm of lace. She picked up the nosegay of white roses that trailed with ribbon and felt foolishly like a bride herself. What would it be like to be preparing to bond yourself with another person, someone who loved and wanted you? There would be flutters in your stomach. She felt them in her own. Your throat would be dry. She lifted a hand to it. You would feel giddy with a combination of excitement and anxiety. She put her hand on the dresser to steady herself.

A premonition? Shaking it off, she stepped back from the mirror. It was her mother who would soon promise to love, honor and cherish. She glanced at her watch, then caught her breath. How had she managed to lose so much time? If she didn't put herself in gear, the guests would be arriving with no one to greet them.

Alex's children were the first to arrive. She'd only met them once, the evening before at dinner, and they were still a bit awkward and formal with one another. But when her future sister offered to help, A.J. decided to take her at her word. Within moments, cars began pulling up out front and she needed all the help she could get.

"A.J." Alex found her in the garden, escorting guests to chairs. "You look lovely."

He looked a little pale under his tan. The sign of nerves had her softening toward him. "Wait until you see your bride."

"I wish I could." He pulled at the knot in his tie. "I have to admit I'd feel easier if she were here to hold on to. You know, I talk to millions of people every night, but this…" He glanced around the garden. "This is a whole different ball game."

"I predict very high ratings." She brushed his cheek. "Why don't you slip inside and have a little shot of bourbon?"

"I think I might." He gave her shoulder a squeeze. "I think I just might."

A.J. watched him make his way to the back door before she turned back to her duties. And there was David. He stood at the edge of the garden, where the breeze just ruffled the ends of his hair. She wondered, as her heart began to thud, that she hadn't sensed him. She wondered, as the pleasure poured through her, if she'd wished him there.

He didn't approach her. A.J.'s fingers tightened on the wrapped stems of her flowers. She knew she had to take the first step.

She was so lovely. He thought she looked like something that had stepped out of a dream. The breeze that tinted the air with the scents of the garden teased the lace at her throat. As she walked to him, he thought of every empty hour he'd spent away from her.

"I'm glad you came."

He'd told himself he wouldn't, then he'd been dressed and driving south. She'd pulled him there, through her thoughts or through his own emotions, it didn't matter. "You seem to have it all under control."

She had nothing under control. She wanted to reach out to him, to tell him, but he seemed so cool and distant. "Yes, we're nearly ready to start. As soon as I get the rest of these people seated, I can go in for Clarissa."

"I'll take care of them."

"You don't have to. I—"

"I told you I would."

His clipped response cut her off. A.J. swallowed her longings and nodded. "Thanks. If you'll excuse me, then." She walked away, into the house, into her own room, where she could compose herself before she faced her mother.

Damn it! He swung away, cursing her, cursing himself, cursing everything. Just seeing her again had made him want to crawl. He wasn't a man who could live on his knees. She'd looked so cool, so fresh and lovely, and for a moment, just a moment, he'd thought he'd seen the emotions he needed in her eyes. Then she'd smiled at him as though he were just another guest at her mother's wedding.

He wasn't going to go on this way. David forced himself to make polite comments and usher well-wishers to their seats. Today, before it was over, he and A. J. Fields were going to come to terms. His terms. He'd planned it that way, hadn't he? It was about time one of his plans concerning her worked.

The orchestra A.J. had hired after auditioning at least a half-dozen played quietly on a wooden platform on the lawn. A trellis of sweet peas stood a few feet in front of the chairs. Composed and clear-eyed, A.J. walked through the garden to take her place. She glanced at Alex and gave him one quick smile of encouragement. Then Clarissa, dressed in dusky rose silk, stepped out of the house.

She looks like a queen, A.J. thought as her heart swelled. The guests rose as she walked through, but she had eyes only for Alex. And he, A.J. noted, looked as though no one else in the world existed but Clarissa.

They joined hands, and they promised.

The ceremony was short and traditional. A.J. watched her mother pledge herself, and fought back a sense of loss that vied with happiness. The words were simple, and ultimately so complex. The vows were timeless, and somehow completely new.

With her vision misted, her throat aching, she took her mother in her arms. "Oh, be happy, Momma."

"I am. I will be." She drew away just a little. "So will you."

Before A.J. could speak, Clarissa turned away and was swept up in an embrace by her new stepchildren.

There were guests to feed and glasses to fill. A.J. found keeping busy helped put her emotions on hold. In a few hours she'd be alone. Then she'd let them come. Now she laughed, brushed cheeks, toasted and felt utterly numb.

"Clarissa." David had purposely waited until she'd had a chance to breathe before he approached her. "You're beautiful."

"Thank you, David. I'm so glad you're here. She needs you."

He stiffened and only inclined his head. "Does she?"

With a sigh, Clarissa took both of his hands. When he felt the intensity, he nearly drew away. "Plans aren't necessary," she said quietly. "Feelings are."

David forced himself to relax. "You don't play fair."

"She's my daughter. In more ways than one."

"I understand that."

It took her only a moment, then she smiled. "Yes, you do. You might let her know. Aurora's an expert at blocking feelings, but she deals well with words. Talk to her?"

"Oh, I intend to."

"Good." Satisfied, Clarissa patted his hand. "Now I think you should try the quiche. I wheedled the recipe out of the caterer. It's fascinating."

"So are you." David leaned down to kiss her cheek.

A.J. all but exhausted herself. She moved from group to group, sipping champagne and barely tasting anything from the impressive display of food. The cake with its iced swans and hearts was cut and devoured. Wine flowed and music played. Couples danced on the lawn.

"I thought you'd like to know I read Steiger's script." After stepping beside her, David kept his eyes on the dancers. "It's extraordinary."

Business, she thought. It was best to keep their conversation on business. "Are you considering producing it?"

"Considering. That's a long way from doing it. I have a meeting with Steiger Monday."

"That's wonderful." She couldn't stop the surge of pleasure for him. She couldn't help showing it. "You'll be sensational."

"And if the script ever makes it to the screen, you'll have been the catalyst."

"I like to think so."

"I haven't waltzed since I was thirteen." David slipped a hand to her elbow and felt the jolt. "My mother made me dance with my cousin, and at the time I felt girls were a lower form of life. I've changed my mind since." His arm slid around her waist. "You're tense."

She concentrated on the count, on matching her steps to his, on anything but the feel of having him hold her again. "I want everything to be perfect for her."

"I don't think you need to worry about that anymore."

Her mother danced with Alex as though they were alone in the garden. "No." She sighed before she could prevent it. "I don't."

"You're allowed to feel a little sad." Her scent was there as he remembered, quietly tempting.

"No, it's selfish."

"It's normal," he corrected. "You're too hard on yourself."

"I feel as though I've lost her." She was going to cry. A.J. steeled herself against it.

"You haven't." He brushed his lips along her temple. "And the feeling will pass."

When he was kind, she was lost. When he was gentle, she was defenseless. "David." Her fingers tightened on his shoulder. "I missed you."

It cost her to say it. The first layer of pride that covered all the rest dissolved with the words. She felt his hand tense, then gentle on her waist.

"Aurora."

"Please, don't say anything now." The control she depended on wouldn't protect her now. "I just wanted you to know."

"We need to talk."

Even as she started to agree, the announcement blared over the mike. "All unmarried ladies, line up now for the bouquet toss."

"Come on, A.J." Her new stepsister, laughing and eager, grabbed her arm and hustled her along. "We have to see who's going to be next."

She wasn't interested in bouquets or giddy young women. Her life was on the line. Distracted, A.J. glanced around for David. She looked back in time to throw up her hands defensively before her mother's bouquet landed in her face. Embarrassed, A.J. accepted the congratulations and well-meaning teasing.

"Another sign?" Clarissa commented as she pecked her daughter's cheek.

"A sign that my mother has eyes in the back of her head and excellent aim." A.J. indulged herself with burying her face in the bouquet. It was sweet, and promising. "You should keep this."

"Oh, no. That would be bad luck and I don't intend to have any."

"I'm going to miss you, Momma."

She understood—she always had—but she smiled and gave A.J. another kiss. "I'll be back in two weeks."

She barely had time for another fierce embrace before her mother and Alex dashed off in a hail of rice and cheers.

Some guests left, others lingered. When the first streaks of sunset deepened the sky she watched the orchestra pack up their instruments.

"Long day."

She turned to David and reached out a hand before she could help it. "I thought you'd gone."

"Just got out of the way for a while. You did a good job."

"I can't believe it's done." She looked over as the last of the chairs were folded and carted away.

"I could use some coffee."

She smiled, trying to convince herself to be light. "Do we have any left?"

"I put some on before I came back out." He walked with her to the house. "Where were they going on their honeymoon?"

The house was so empty. Strange, she'd never noticed just how completely Clarissa had filled it. "Sailing." She laughed a little, then found herself looking helplessly around the kitchen. "I have a hard time picturing Clarissa hoisting sails."

"Here." He pulled a handkerchief out of his pocket. "Sit down and have a good cry. You're entitled."

"I'm happy for her." But the tears began to fall. "Alex is a wonderful man and I know he loves her."

"But she doesn't need you to take care of her anymore." He handed her a mug of coffee. "Drink."

Nodding, she sipped. "She's always needed me."

"She still does." He took the handkerchief and dried her cheeks himself. "Just in a different way."

"I feel like a fool."

"The trouble with you is you can't accept that you're supposed to feel like a fool now and again."

She blew her nose, unladylike and indignant. "I don't like it."

"Not supposed to. Have you finished crying?"

She sulked a moment, sniffled, then sipped more coffee. "Yes."

"Tell me again that you missed me."

"It was a moment of weakness," she murmured into the mug, but he took it away from her.

"No more evasions, Aurora. You're going to tell me what you want, what you feel."

"I want you back." She swallowed and wished he would say something instead of just staring at her.

"Go on."

"David, you're making this difficult."

"Yeah, I know." He didn't touch her, not yet. He needed more than that. "For both of us."

"All right." She steadied herself with a deep breath. "When you suggested we live together, I wasn't expecting it. I wanted to think it through, but you got angry. Well, since you've been away, I've had a chance to think it through. I don't see why we can't live together under those terms."

Always negotiating, he thought as he rubbed a hand over his chin. She still wasn't going to take that last step. "I've had a chance to think it through, too. And I've changed my mind."

He could have slapped her and not have knocked the wind from her so successfully. Rejection, when it came, was always painful, but it had never been like this. "I see." She turned away to pick up her coffee, but her hands weren't nearly steady enough.

"You did a great job on this wedding, A.J."

Closing her eyes, she wondered why she felt like laughing. "Thanks. Thanks a lot."

"Seems to me like you could plan another standing on your head."

"Oh, sure." She pressed her fingers to her eyes. "I might go into the business."

"No, I was thinking about just one more. Ours."

The tears weren't going to fall. She wouldn't let them. It helped to concentrate on that. "Our what?"

"Wedding. Aren't you paying attention?"

She turned slowly to see him watching her with what appeared to be mild amusement. "What are you talking about?"

"I noticed you caught the bouquet. I'm superstitious."

"This isn't funny." Before she could stalk from the room he had caught her close.

"Damn right it's not. It's not funny that I've spent eleven days and twelve nights thinking of little but you. It's not funny that every time I took a step closer, you took one back. Every time I'd plan something out, the whole thing would be blown to hell after five minutes with you."

"It's not going to solve anything to shout at me."

"It's not going to solve anything until you start listening and stop anticipating. Look, I didn't want this any more than you did. I liked my life just the way it was."

"That's fine, then. I liked my life, too."

"Then we both have a problem, because nothing's going to be quite the same again."

Why couldn't she breathe? Temper never made her breathless. "Why not?"

"Guess." He kissed her then, hard, angry, as if he wanted to kick out at both of them. But it only took an instant, a heartbeat. His lips softened, his hold gentled and she was molded to him. "Why don't you read my mind? Just this once, Aurora, open yourself up."

She started to shake her head, but his mouth was on hers again. The house was quiet. Outside, the birds serenaded the lowering sun. The light was dimming and there was nothing but that one room and that one moment. Feelings poured into her, feelings that once would have brought fear. Now they offered, requested and gave her everything she'd been afraid to hope for.

"David." Her arms tightened around him. "I need you to tell me. I couldn't bear to be wrong."

Hadn't he needed words? Hadn't he tried time and again to pry them out of her? Maybe it was time to give them to her. "The first time I met your mother, she said something to me about needing to understand or discover my own tenderness. That first weekend you stayed with me, I came home and found you sleeping on the bed. I looked at you, the woman who'd been my lover, and fell in love. The problem was I didn't know how to make you fall in love with me."

"I already had. I didn't think you—"

"The problem was you did think. Too much." He drew her away, only to look at her. "So did I. Be civilized. Be careful. Wasn't that the way we arranged things?"

"It seemed like the right way." She swallowed and moved closer. "It didn't work for me. When I fell in love with you, all I could think was that I'd ruin everything by wanting too much."

"And I thought if I asked, you'd be gone before the words were out." He brushed his lips over her brow. "We wasted time thinking when we should have been feeling."

She should be cautious, but there was such ease, such quiet satisfaction, in just holding him. "I was afraid you'd never be able to accept what I am."

"So was I." He kissed one cheek, then the other. "We were both wrong."

"I need you to be sure. I need to know that it doesn't matter."

"Aurora. I love you, who you are, what you are, how you are. I don't know how else to tell you."

She closed her eyes. Clarissa and she had been right to drink to hope. That was all there was. "You just found the best way."

"There's more." He held her, waiting until she looked at him again. And he saw, as he'd needed to, her heart in her eyes. "I want to spend my life with you. Have children with you. There's never been another woman who's made me want those things."

She took his face in her hands and lifted her mouth to his. "I'm going to see to it there's never another."

"Tell me how you feel."

"I love you."

He held her close, content. "Tell me what you want."

"A lifetime. Two, if we can manage it."

★ ★ ★ ★ ★

Discover the power of love with two classic tales from
#1 *New York Times* and *USA TODAY* bestselling author

NORA ROBERTS

Duets

featuring "The Name of the Game"
and "Once More with Feeling."

Available now wherever trade paperbacks are sold!

Silhouette®

Where love comes alive™